Stephen Lloyd Jones's debut novel, *The String Diaries*, was a BBC Radio 2 Book Club selection, a Kindle Editor's Pick, and was translated into nine languages. *The Disciple* is his third novel, and his previous books have both been optioned for television. Aside from his family, Stephen's passions are strong coffee, telling stories and spending time in the mountains. He lives with his wife and three young sons.

Praise for Stephen Lloyd Jones:

'So gripping you'll want to read late into the night; so terrifying you shouldn't' Simon Mayo, Radio 2 Book Club

'Original, richly imagined and powerfully told' *Guardian*

'Will keep you awake late into the night' *SFX*

'Few living writers of supernatural thrillers equal Jones' powers of imagination and overall vision' *Kirkus Reviews*

'*The String Diaries* is edge-of-your-seat-turn-on-all-the-lights-lock-the-doors-and-cancel-all-appointments brilliant' *Bookbag*

'Terrifying, and deliciously so . . . A sophisticated horror story that induces elemental terror' *New York Daily News*

'Jones doles out his narrative revelations with patience, turning over his cards deliberately like a well-trained casino dealer' *Entertainment Weekly*

'A rich story that has the detail and precision of a scholastic study thrust upon the suspense and visual grandeur of a cinematic t'

By Stephen Lloyd Jones

The String Diaries
Written in the Blood
The Disciple

THE
DISCIPLE
STEPHEN LLOYD JONES

headline

First published in paperback in 2016 by
HEADLINE PUBLISHING GROUP

1

Cataloguing in Publication Data is available from the British Library

ISBN 978 1 4722 2890 1

Typeset in Bembo by Avon DataSet Ltd, Bidford-on-Avon, Warwickshire

Printed and bound by CPI Group (UK) Ltd, Croydon, CR0 4YY

Headline's policy is to use papers that are natural, renewable and recyclable
products and made from wood grown in well-managed forests and other
controlled sources. The logging and manufacturing processes are expected to
conform to the environmental regulations of the country of origin.

HEADLINE PUBLISHING GROUP
An Hachette UK Company
Carmelite House
50 Victoria Embankment
London EC4Y 0DZ

www.headline.co.uk
www.hachette.co.uk

Dedicated to the memory of Alan Lloyd Jones.
Thanks, Dad.

PART I

CHAPTER 1

Near Devil's Kitchen, Snowdonia National Park

By the time Edward Schwinn discovered the crash site around one-thirty a.m., an easterly wind crossing the Glyderau range had emptied the skies of cloud. A poacher's moon hung sentinel, companion to a cold scattering of stars.

He'd been driving these mountain roads for an hour, maybe more. Moisture misted the inside of the Defender's windscreen, defying the heater's attempts to disperse it. On a tarp in the back, Argus dozed, a damp coil of doggy fur and rabbit breath.

Lulled into a trance by the 4x4's diesel engine, Edward noticed the first wreckage almost too late. The road, which until now had knifed along the rim of a coal-dark slope, kinked right and plunged through a conifer grove. The trunks of Sitka spruce and Scots pine flashed past, bark bleached white by the headlights. On the road surface, a skin of frost glimmered. And there, lying to the left of the dividing line, a smoking wheel rim, shreds of rubber hanging from it like blackened flesh.

Jaw clenching, Edward hauled the Defender over to the oncoming lane. The vehicle seesawed on its suspension, slinging around the obstacle with inches to spare. The moment it righted itself he stood on the brakes and the nose dived. He heard Argus slide across the tarp and thump into the back of his seat. They were on the wrong side of the road now, twenty yards from a blind bend. But no lights grew from that direction. No indication of approaching traffic. He knew these mountains; at this time of night the chance of an encounter was slim.

Rolling to a stop, he glanced up at the rear-view mirror. In the back, Argus scrambled onto all fours. The dog shot him a doleful look. Edward tilted the mirror. Examined the reflection of road behind him. The smoking wheel was a stark black shape in the darkness, tinged red by the Defender's brake lights.

Ahead, wind-tattered streamers of smoke blew across the road from a source out of sight around the bend. Watching them, Edward felt his stomach tighten in anticipation.

Argus wormed through the gap between the front seats and rested both paws on the dash. His tongue lolled and he panted. This close, the dog's breath was monstrous – a hot blast of masticated flesh and blood.

'What's out there?'

Argus licked his lips. Whined.

Static, like soft rain, hissed from the Defender's radio. Edward switched it off. From the door cavity he retrieved a chamois hardened into a limpet-like sculpture. A few swabs of the damp windscreen softened it, until he was polishing a perfect porthole of unobscured glass. He peered through it. To his right, the land climbed at a steep angle towards the Carneddau; to his left it fell away to the valley floor. Tossing the chamois onto the dash, he steered off the road and killed the engine.

The mountain stillness dropped like a sackcloth; but its silence did not reign unchallenged. Argus panted metronomically, breath fogging the circle of glass Edward had wiped clean. Outside, a grazing wind stirred the needles of nearby trees. And, from somewhere further away, a ripping, or a fizzing, like the sound of poured champagne.

He could smell the smoke now, could taste it in his throat. When he switched off the Defender's headlights an inky darkness raced up to the windows. His eyes took a few moments to adjust; then the landscape coalesced. Above the Glyderau rose an indigo sky salted with stars. Directly ahead, the frost riming the road flickered scarlet. Edward unclipped his seat belt and put a hand to the door.

Hesitated.

He didn't need to do this. Five miles away, cupped in a forested elbow of land, waited his cabin, but he didn't have to follow this road to reach it. He could double back, take the Defender on a detour across the scree fields until he found the old ranger's track. The ground was hard-packed and dry; yet to freeze. He'd made the trip in worse conditions.

But what if someone needed his help around that bend? What if someone lay injured? Trapped? Even if that were unlikely, could he really leave the wheel rim blocking the road behind him? Although visibility was good right now, it could deteriorate quickly out here, especially this close to winter. A wind change might drag down a mist from the western peaks. Clouds sailing in from the Atlantic could glove the moon's light in an instant. In either scenario, a following motorist might not see the hazard. A collision at speed, so close to these trees, would likely be fatal.

How long since you cared about things like that?

He frowned at the thought. Shook his head free of it.

Beside him, Argus chuffed. Yawned.

Edward recoiled. 'Jesus, buddy.'

Mystified, now, at his earlier hesitation, he cranked open his door and jumped down onto gravel. The bitter night air slapped his face, drew instant tears. His breath spooled away, unravelling in gossamer threads. For the first time, he noticed that the dog's flanks were trembling. 'You coming?'

Argus glanced over. Again, his jaw hinged wide and his tongue lolled. He returned his attention to the view through the windscreen.

'Suit yourself.' Reaching inside, Edward retrieved his torch and flicked on the vehicle's hazards. Their amber pulses washed away all traces of reflected firelight. Somehow they felt comforting; a statement of intent. 'I'll leave the door open, rabbit-breath. 'Case you change your mind.'

Turning from the dog, he trudged around the front of the vehicle and stepped onto the road. Strange, but for a moment he thought he felt it hum beneath him, vibrating like a plucked guitar string. He glanced over his shoulder. Inside the Defender, Argus was a still black shape. Further down the road, the broken wheel rim threw off a few dying coughs of smoke. Beyond that, absolute dark, as if the land there had folded into a trench. He saw no headlights from following traffic, no illumination from nearby houses or farms. Overhead, the outer spirals of the Milky Way rotated, their scattered lights a distant congregation.

He turned back around. Ahead lay twenty yards of empty tarmac before the road curved out of sight. He saw no slicks of rubber interrupting its jacket of frost. No evidence of a crash. The trees on either side were unmarked, their lower branches intact.

Somewhere in the darkness, a night animal shrieked. The cry, high-pitched and stark, pierced his skin. Polecat probably, announcing a kill. Out here it was a mournful sound, laced with despair. Grimacing, Edward tugged his coat zipper up to his throat.

At the bend's apex the trees grew thick and tall, their boughs screening the moon's light. The road there was clotted with shadow. As Edward approached, instinct told him to keep his torch extinguished.

The stink of burning was stronger now. He could hear fire crackling, the pop of shattering glass. Moments later the road washed an angry red. Through the trees he saw a fireball erupt, heard the *whump* of combusting gasses. A hot wind rolled over him.

He stopped, close to the centre line. Again he felt the road thrum beneath his feet, as if he stood upon a fault line, or over some vast machine buried in the earth. Crouching, he touched his hand to its surface. Sharp frost and cold tarmac; nothing unusual in that. And yet through it he detected a susurration, like a low surge of electricity passing through his fingertips.

For three years, ever since the tragedy that had brought him here, Edward Schwinn had lived alone among these peaks. Only once in all that time had he ever seen something he might have been wise to fear. Now, out here on this lonely stretch of road at the foot of the Glyderau, he felt his heart begin to quicken. When the breeze blew, he sensed sweat prickling on his forehead.

Defiant, he rose to his feet. Eyes fixed on the centre line, shoulders squared, he walked around the corner to confront what waited there.

What Edward Schwinn saw next changed everything.

CHAPTER 2

Near Devil's Kitchen, Snowdonia National Park

Only minutes earlier he'd been contemplating a detour, driving his Defender south across the scree fields. Had he chosen that option he would have avoided this sight altogether. Now he would never forget it.

Strewn along the road, in a haphazard procession, lay the pulverised wrecks of five motor vehicles. Their chassis were crumpled and twisted, as if crushed by the hands of giants. The vehicle furthest from him, an unrecognisable 4x4 heavily modified for off-road use, lay on its roof. Bright snakes of flame leaped from its windows, twisting up into the night.

Hanging upside down in the front seats, the remains of its two occupants burned like candles. Flaming gobs of rubber, or upholstery foam, or human fat, dripped onto the roadway and burned in liquid pools.

Edward squinted. Even from here he could feel the heat. Something exploded in the back of the 4x4 and its windows vented white devils of fire. As the flames intensified, their light brightened the entire scene.

The nearest vehicle, Edward saw, was a 4x4 just like the one on fire. Had he not spotted the Mitsubishi logo on its tailgate he would have been unable to identify it. Anyone who remained inside could not have survived; the vehicle's metal shell had been wrung like a dishcloth. Dismissing it, he focused his attention on the three cars at the convoy's centre, all identical MPVs. None bore registration plates. Where windows remained intact, the glass was tinted black.

Out of the three, the centremost vehicle seemed to have suffered the least damage. It rested on naked wheel rims even so, skewed at a right angle with all four tyres blown. Both its front doors had come off, exposing an empty driver's compartment and—

Edward frowned. Looked again. Those doors hadn't peeled off naturally during a collision. They'd been intentionally ripped loose, excised with brutal yet surgical precision. One of them lay at the base of a nearby tree, bent out of shape.

Now he noticed something else: none of the cars looked as if they had collided with each other. The damage, in every case, had been inflicted side-on. They'd clearly been driving as a group, in a single direction. And yet . . . that didn't make any sense.

In the grass to the left of the road he spotted a crumpled form. It lay too far away for the flames to illuminate it clearly but Edward knew, in his gut, that it must be a casualty from the vehicle at the convoy's heart. Whatever had burst the MPV's front doors loose had plucked and tossed its occupants as if they'd been no more substantial than rice grains.

Edward closed his eyes. Shielded from the sight of the devastation, he heard the flames crackle as if with greater urgency. He felt the wind change direction, heard the tree boughs creak as it pressed them.

When something brushed his leg he flinched, eyes snapping open, but it was only Argus. The dog shivered at his side, attention fixed on the MPV missing its front doors.

The fire, Edward knew, might burn all night without others discovering it; the road was unlikely to carry further traffic until the sun rose in around five hours. He had no means of calling for assistance – had owned no mobile phone since relocating to this area of Wales three years earlier. He wanted to retreat to his Defender and get the hell out of here. But while that was an attractive thought, he could not abandon any victims who might have survived, even if instinct told him they were all either dead or beyond his help.

Why not? You've done it before.

He scowled at that, felt his fingers tighten into fists. To the dog, he muttered, 'All right. Let's get it done.'

Edging towards the broken shape slumped at the roadside, Edward clicked on his torch. Its beam cut a white finger through the smoke sloughing off the nearby wreck. He knew what awaited him would be grim, but even so the discovery was a shock.

The man had landed in such a way that both the back of his head and his kneecaps were pressed into the soil. No body could survive such a violent reshaping. His spine must have twisted in his torso like a screw until it shattered. Even if by some miracle he had endured that torment, his head injury would have finished him. From right eyebrow to hairline his skull had been flattened. What remained was a dark mush, wet with blood. One eye stared heavenward. The other had loosened in its socket, a slippery white oyster canted towards Edward.

Staring at it, Edward couldn't shake the feeling that the man's head, just like the vehicles on the road, had been clutched, or squeezed; the word he really wanted to use was *popped*.

Despite the gruesome nature of his discovery, he stepped closer. He'd seen corpses before. This one couldn't harm him, and he needed to search it for a phone. The sooner he found one, the sooner he could summon help and deal with the fall-out. Ahead lay conversations with people he didn't know. Questions. Hard looks. The mere thought of all that human interaction threw him into a panic, but what choice did he have? If he wanted to get back to his cabin with the remains of his dignity intact, he needed to get this done.

Kneeling in the grass, Edward felt icy mud soak through his jeans. He ignored it, resting his torch in his lap. Beside him, Argus whined. The dog's eyes were orange pools, iridescent with reflected firelight. 'Yeah, well. Would've been quick, at least.'

Reaching out, he patted the stranger's hips, recoiling a little from the warmth they still radiated. Something awful, he thought, about a warm corpse. Still, the trapped heat would dissipate fast under this cloudless sky. He could smell blood leaking into the soil.

Frowning, he pulled his hands away, picked up the torch and angled it. The beam confirmed what his fingers had surmised. Secured to the dead man's thigh with a double leg strap was a tactical holster containing a semi-automatic pistol. As Edward played his beam back and forth, he saw that the firearm was not the only equipment the stranger carried. Around the man's belt, nylon pouches held spare magazines, handcuffs, an unmarked aerosol. His twisted torso was encased in body armour constructed from heavy ceramic plates. Underneath he wore a flight suit, its soft khaki dark with spreading blood.

Edward glanced up. Gazed along the road. At Anglesey, thirty miles north-west, was RAF Valley, a fighter base and pilot training school. Further military sites were scattered throughout the region, yet instinct told him the dead man had no such affiliation. The flight suit and the armour lacked any insignia that might suggest otherwise.

Leaning forward, he examined the stranger's face close-up. He found cheeks sooted with stubble, dark collar-length hair. A clear acoustic tube coiled from one ear to a push-to-talk clipped to the armour vest.

Gingerly, Edward plucked the earpiece loose. A brown slug of wax clogged the teat. Wiping it clean on the man's flight suit, he lifted it close to his own ear and heard faint, electronic music, a high-pitched stream of shifting oscillations. While the sounds had no discernible rhythm they suggested a vaguely mathematical progression. It was like nothing he had previously heard. Captivated, he lifted the earpiece closer, sensing suddenly that between the fluctuating tones of that strange music was a—

He blinked. Lurched back.

The tube's coils stretched taut and the socket popped loose from the push-to-talk. The music vanished. Edward hurled the device into the trees.

What the hell? You were about to screw that thing into your ear!

Climbing to his feet, wiping his hands clean, he thought he heard movement in the undergrowth to his left. He swabbed the nearby trees with his torch beam. Inside the grove, giraffe shadows swung away from him. He glimpsed a rotting pine on a quilt of needles. A pale crop of death cap mushrooms.

By his leg, Argus whined once more.

'Me too,' he muttered, touching the dog's head. 'We'll do this and then we're gone.'

The convoy's second vehicle, although not on fire, was just as badly damaged as the first. Its doors had buckled inwards, windows bursting from the pressure. The roof had been forced down into the passenger compartment. Edward only needed to aim his torch for a moment to see that his help was not needed inside. Its two occupants wore the same body armour as the corpse beside the road. It hadn't saved them, either. The roof had compressed their heads into their torsos. The resultant trauma was both horrific and irreversible. If the remaining wrecks offered Edward no better option he would search the bodies, but not otherwise.

Turning away, he stared across the tarmac towards the MPV at the convoy's heart. Inexplicable, he thought, that it had suffered so little damage compared to the others. Its tyres had blown out and its front doors had ripped free, but other than that it looked unmarked. No dents or scratches marred its bodywork. Its black paint was pristine, its windows intact.

The vehicle sat patiently, as if awaiting his inspection. Studying it, he noticed something else that had escaped him until now: the engine was still running, steadily chugging vapours into the night.

As Edward drew closer, the MPV's hazards pulsed once. He stopped dead, knocked off kilter. From where he stood he had direct line of sight through the front door cavities. No one remained behind the wheel to operate those lights.

Again, as he watched, its hazards pulsed. After everything he had witnessed, the spectacle should have disturbed him more than it did. Instead, the lights had a strangely hypnotic effect. He felt his legs working beneath him even before he made the decision to move, found himself walking, as if in sleep, towards the car. His pace accelerated until he stood right beside it, shining his torch through the opening revealed by the missing driver's door.

Inside, the grey upholstery was spotless, unblemished by blood. The rear passenger compartment, he saw, was cordoned by a privacy wall partitioned at the top by a slab of black security glass. A single crack zigzagged through it. Edward tapped it with the metal rim of his torch. Despite the damage, it seemed sound.

On the dashboard, the sat nav screen glowed blue. As he watched, it concertinaed into a press of jagged lines before returning to the same uninterrupted hue.

Edward leaned in and switched off the engine. As an afterthought, he pulled the key from the ignition and examined it. Nothing hung from its metal loop – no personal items that might offer him clues of ownership.

He moved to the nearside sliding door. When he tried to peer through the window, the tint on its glass defeated him. He tested the door handle: locked. Somehow he'd known it would be. Turning from the MPV, he scanned the landscape. Still no lights anywhere on the surrounding hills.

'OK, time to go.'

He'd done what he could, had tried to offer assistance. His conscience – in that, at least – was clear. Something violent and inexplicable had occurred along this stretch of mountain road. He wanted no further part of it. Seven miles back east was a payphone. He could call in the accident from there, return to the safety of his cabin.

Decision made, he started walking. He'd taken perhaps three steps when he sensed the return of that strange vibration through his feet. He slowed and glanced down, almost expecting to see blue zips of electricity sparking from his boots. Behind him the MPV's central locking disengaged with a clunk.

Edward stiffened at the sound. He still held the ignition key. Had he depressed it? He didn't think so. He'd threaded his finger through its metal hoop, but the key itself hung loose. Turning back, he stared at the vehicle, feeling a bizarre compulsion to return.

Its hazard lights flashed twice.

Edward swallowed. He looked up and down the road. Over the pop and hiss of the burning wreck he could hear the sighing of the wind. He closed his eyes, tried to clear his thoughts. It felt as if he were caught in a dream here, that he might swab the air and watch it distort like an image glimpsed through water.

For the first time in three years, he felt like he had surrendered control, hostage to whatever strangeness had befallen him. By the time he opened his eyes, he discovered he had already returned to the MPV's sliding door. When he tested it a second time, it rolled back without complaint. Edward shone his torch inside.

In the back, slumped across the rear seats, lay a motionless human form. Its head was covered by a loose black hood. Its hands were cuffed with a single plastic tie. Looking at the tips of those fingers, he noticed something else: nail polish. The passenger the dead men had been transporting was a woman.

He leaned into the car, took hold of the hood and lifted it free.

For the first time in three years, Edward Schwinn found himself staring into his dead wife's face.

CHAPTER 3

Near Devil's Kitchen, Snowdonia National Park

For a moment the sight paralysed him. Then he felt terror soaking into his bones like meltwater, wicking away his body heat. His fingers loosened on the torch and it fell from his hand, weaving marionette shadows as it twisted through the air. It bounced once on the carpet and rolled under the seat.

The darkness leaped at him, and it was infinitely worse. He heard himself moan, utter a denial. Felt his hand, as if controlled by another, snake beneath the seat and grope for the torch's metal shaft. It took him a few seconds at most, but in the moment before his fingers closed around it and he swung the beam back to her face, he wondered if this time he might illuminate a rotten cadaver, a worm-riddled husk stitched together from past nightmares. He knew that wasn't possible – couldn't be – because he'd stood outside the crematorium in Chamonix three years earlier while her body was offered to the flames, had even heard the hymns they'd sung to send her on her way. And yet *this* wasn't possible either, because when the torchlight touched her a second time there she was again: whole, unblemished, serene.

Her eyes were closed, skin so cold it looked blue. He had forgotten how, while she'd been alive, his gaze had always been drawn to her lips; how their fullness had stolen his attention through three years of marriage. Perhaps that slow fade of memory had been a mercy, because now the sight of her mouth raised a sluice gate in him, and through it crashed a torrent: love; guilt; regret. All the armour he'd constructed during the last three years — all the rules he'd built to frame this destitute existence — were like matchsticks against that tide. He felt all his defences go crashing away, and in their loss he was cast adrift; a floundering soul, helpless.

Her dark hair, *exactly* the same style and length he'd last seen it, had parted above her left eye, revealing a swelling on her forehead bisected by a two-inch cut; possibly an injury sustained during whatever incident had brought this convoy to a halt, possibly not. Over her ears she wore a set of closed-cup wireless headphones.

When at last he looked away from her face to study the rest of her, he discovered the cruelty that this dream, or nightmare, had saved for its climax. Thrusting out from beneath swollen breasts, his wife's belly was huge, almost spherical with late-stage pregnancy.

The sight was too much.

Edward sensed his world tilting, felt himself sit down hard on the roadway. The impact through his spine was enough to shock him halfway back to his senses. Close by, he heard Argus's high-pitched keening. When he glanced sideways, he saw that the dog's attention was on the tree line yards from where the car had come to rest.

In the back seat, his dead wife's chest swelled with a sound like inflating bellows. Her back arched.

'Laura?' His voice, hollow and distant, came as if through a tunnel.

Her eyelids flickered. When, finally, they prised open, he saw two white jewels of reflected moonlight. Her pupils moved left and right. They took in the vehicle's interior, the open door. Edward.

She moaned, then, and even though the sound was wordless,

it opened in him a tranche of memories, threw him into turmoil all over again. Fighting his emotions, he hauled himself to his feet and leaned into the car.

'*Laura?*'

The sight of the plastic loop cutting into her wrists choked him with rage. He grabbed the hunting knife strapped to his belt. Tugging it loose, he used its blade to sever the tie.

Laura's hands fell either side of her. She lifted them to her belly and her fingers spread wide, as if seeking reassurance that life grew there still. 'I'm alive?' she whispered.

Edward opened his mouth. Closed it. So many possible answers. He had no clue which one to choose. He pulled off her headphones, tossed them onto the seat. 'You're OK,' he told her. 'You're safe now.'

Laura shook her head. 'No.'

'Yes, nothing's going to—'

'*No.*' She lurched upright, eyes wide. 'We have to go. Now.'

He nodded, sensing her panic, feeling it too. 'Give me your hand.'

With his help she clambered out. He slung his arm around her, careful not to crush the—

Don't. Don't think it. This is a dream, nothing more. A chance to spend a little time with Laura. Don't screw it up.

Even as he thought it, he knew it wasn't true. Argus was barking wildly now, forelegs jumping back and forth on the tarmac. Edward steered Laura towards the bend in the road where his Defender waited. When she leaned into him, he felt the heat pouring off her, and for a moment his fear was smothered by unadulterated joy.

This was no moon-resurrected corpse he guided. No bewitchment or night trickery. It was Laura, with hot blood flowing through her veins and warming his skin. He could feel her breath against his neck, could smell her hair, her perfume. And while it didn't make sense, any of it, he could no longer question it, could focus only on preserving it.

At his side, Argus ceased barking. The dog stood tall, tail erect, the whites of his eyes gleaming. Mouth closed, his lips skinned back from his teeth. The sound that now issued from his throat was half growl, half whine. His flanks shivered.

'Hurry,' Laura urged. 'They're coming.'

No need for further words. The Defender was in sight. Dropping the torch, Edward scooped Laura up in his arms. He braced his back and carried her the last ten yards to the car. Balancing her against it, he yanked open the passenger door and lowered her onto the seat. The moment she swung her legs around he shut her inside.

Still he saw no lights on the slopes. It seemed *too* dark out there now, as if all of humanity's evidence had been scoured away. He scrambled towards his own door, shoulders bunched against the night.

It was still open. Argus bolted past him and leaped through the gap. Edward dived after the dog, dragging the door shut. His fingers found the keys in the ignition, twisted. The engine fired.

Reaching out, Laura hit the button for the hazards, killing their orange pulses. Edward took her cue, keeping the headlights extinguished. He crunched into reverse and slipped the clutch. Wheels shredding topsoil, the Defender lurched backwards onto the tarmac. He whipped the wheel to the left and held on while the nose swung around.

The rear-view mirror blushed red as the brake lights lit up the road behind. Edward wrestled the gearbox, found first. Another lurch, a shocked bleat of rubber, and they were accelerating as hard as the old engine would allow. He changed up a gear, stomach flopping like an eel.

Hurry. They're coming.

Without lights on this exposed mountain road, anything faster than a sprinter's pace would be suicidal. To their right, a low dry-stone wall offered the only protection from a sixty-foot drop onto jagged slate. To their left stretched an unbroken escarpment of stone.

Edward glanced across at his wife, saw her eyes scanning the landscape. 'Laura—'

'Don't.'

He tore his eyes away. Studied the road. Steered the Defender around a shallow bend. Forced a little more speed.

'I don't know you,' she said.

He risked another glance. Tears, kissed by moonlight, shone on her cheeks.

'You don't?'

She shook her head. 'I'm not who you think.'

He had no answer for that; no question to follow it.

The road kinked, straightened. Edward glanced up at the rear-view mirror and touched the brakes, just to see what their lights might illuminate. But the road behind was a black void, empty of any pursuers. He pressed the accelerator pedal further to the floor.

'Laura, can you—'

'Please. Don't call me that. Don't let your eyes deceive you.' She raised her arm and pointed through the windscreen, at a procession of headlights winding up towards them from the valley floor. 'Look.'

Altogether he counted three vehicles, steadily climbing. 'I thought we might be the only ones left out here.'

'Tell me your name.'

'Edward,' he replied, feeling, as he told her, that he must be suspended in a dream. 'Although you always called me Eddie.'

'Eddie, listen to me. Forget everything else and just listen.' Her finger stabbed towards the approaching convoy. 'We have to get off the road. Now, Eddie. We have to do it *right now*.'

He frowned. Looked again at that collection of twinkling lights. Something in her voice convinced him. He'd come this far; pointless to question the sanity of it now. He was a visitor in this new reality. He sensed Laura might be his only guide.

On his right, the sheer drop disappeared, replaced by a steep slope. Ahead, Edward saw a break in the stone wall. It was risky, he knew, but he felt he had little choice. He slowed the Defender, steered off the road and, taking a breath and holding it, plunged down the mountainside into the waiting darkness.

CHAPTER 4

Near Devil's Kitchen, Snowdonia National Park

Four times, as they crashed down through the blackness, Edward thought they would roll, or strike one of the many house-sized boulders that loomed, like wandering icebergs, out of the dark. The noise was brutal, the Defender's chassis creaking and lurching beneath them, Edward's gear clattering around in the back.

Beside him, Laura – or Not-Laura – braced herself with one hand clutching her belly and the other gripping the handle above the door. She held on grimly, mouth set. Once or twice, as he avoided an obstacle by mere inches, or stamped the Defender's paintwork against another, she cried out.

In his hands the steering wheel bucked and spun. The dashboard cavity ejected its clutter across Laura's knees: maps, beer cans, fishing reels, screwdrivers. He waited for a tyre to shred, or an axle to snap, or the exhaust to rip loose from beneath them. Yet somehow, the worst never happened, and that singular impact never came. Soon the land began to level out, the moon providing enough light to steer an unobstructed path. Behind, a rocky fold of the Glyderau's cape hid them from the main road. Those travelling lights, silent and ominous, disappeared from view.

Edward was still a few miles from his usual detour. But he knew, merely by glancing at the stars, which direction to take. He lifted his eyes from the scree-strewn landscape to consider his passenger, and dared to ask himself a few of the questions he had avoided until now.

It made his head ache to look at Laura for long. On her finger glimmered the wedding ring he'd bought six years earlier, and three years later had cast into the depths of Llyn Cau. Another sight that defied all explanation.

For the first time, he noticed what she was wearing: a simple black maternity dress that fit snugly across her stomach and trailed to her knees; over it, a frayed angora cardigan the colour of hill fog. He recognised the garment; he had packed it, along with the rest of her clothes, into charity bags before leaving their old home.

'Looks like you hit your head,' he said. 'Do you remem—'

'Where are we going?'

Edward flinched, jolted by her urgency. 'The cabin,' he told her. 'Place I've lived . . . since.'

Odd, but as he considered his existence *since*, the very paucity of it, he felt his throat constricting. Felt something else, too, an emotion that was all too familiar: shame.

Could he really take Laura back there? Show her what he'd become?

'How far?' she asked.

'Five miles. Maybe a little more if we keep off all the roads in between.'

'Not far enough.'

He tapped the glass housing of the Defender's fuel gauge. 'Want to find a petrol station instead?'

'Not right now.'

'Then we'd better get to the cabin. It's safe. Hidden away. There's a full drum of diesel there.' He snatched a look at Laura. 'Weapons, too.'

She nodded at that. Settled down in her seat.

Reaching behind him, Edward found an old blanket and hauled it over her.

'Smells of dog,' she murmured, eyes closing.

'Everything does,' he replied. And found, when he blinked, that the night dissolved into sharp wet blades.

By the time Edward nudged the Defender down into the wooded bowl of land near his cabin, Laura was asleep. Screened by the surrounding trees, he felt comfortable enough at last to switch on the headlights. Their beams woke a sparkling carpet of frost on the mud track. Soon he spotted the old sheep trailer marking the boundary to his land. A rack of red deer antlers hung from its rusting metal supports. They glowed bone-pale in lonely greeting.

A final turn and there it was up ahead: his home. Calling it a cabin was, he knew, an exercise in crass deception; it was little more than an ancient twin-axle caravan that someone had towed here to die. Its tyres were flat, its chassis supported by breeze blocks that had sunk into the earth. Its roof, stained by years of falling tree sap, bird shit and sunlight, had darkened to the colour of rotten teeth. Cobwebs felted the windows, strung heavy with insect husks and leaf litter. A water butt captured rainwater from a tarpaulin thrown across the branches of a dead tree. Close by stood a ramshackle network of chicken coops nailed together from scavenged timber and mesh. Ten yards from the caravan's front door was a blackened fire circle six feet in diameter, a few charred stumps of wood at its heart.

Beside him, Laura stirred. She sat up in her seat, staring through the windscreen in undisguised dismay. 'This is home?'

He opened his mouth. Nodded.

'Some bachelor pad.'

The comment stung, for reasons he could not fathom. He didn't want Laura to see his pain so he climbed out of the Defender. 'Let's get inside.'

She shook her head. 'Uh-uh.'

Edward slammed his door, then went to open hers. 'There's nowhere else.'

'You said it was safe.'

'It is.'

'One kick and that thing'll fall apart.'

'Then don't kick it.' He waited until her eyes met his. 'Need me to lift you?'

'I think . . .' She glanced away. 'Yeah.'

Impossible not to dwell on their closeness as he carried her to the caravan – that inch or so of distance between her mouth and his neck. He climbed the steps and hooked the door with a finger. Inside, to the left of the kitchenette, stood a narrow galley table. Two bench seats, dotted with greasy orange cushions, lined the walls on either side. Gently, he deposited her on one of them. Once Argus had bounded up the steps, Edward locked the door. At the stove he found matches and lit a paraffin lantern, placing it on the table. Then he pulled the curtains, little more than rags hung over plastic-coated wire.

Edward followed Laura's eyes as she took in her surroundings, and saw the place himself, as if for the first time. Such a wretched, squalid hole. Whatever colour the carpet had been, it had long ago turned black, half-buried beneath a layer of wood shavings and sawdust. A saucepan on the floor collected drips from a leak in the roof. In one corner a stack of books mouldered. Plates and bowls slumped in piles, their surfaces dull with dried food. Empty whisky bottles cluttered the drainer.

Beside the lantern on the galley table, Edward's wood-carving tools lay heaped: fishtails and slicks, veiners and gouges; chisels, hammers, knives. On every remaining surface crowded the results of his labours. By the door, a family of oak-carved foxes lazed. A knot of toads in polished walnut crouched near the base of the stove. The shelf opposite bowed beneath the weight of its woodland menagerie: ebony stags with limewood antlers; hares carved from mahogany; badgers, dormice, hedgehogs and squirrels. Above the door, two peregrine falcons guarded a tiny driftwood barn owl.

Edward found a bin liner and swept into it the whisky bottles from the drainer. He stacked the discarded crockery in the sink. Into the back bedroom, partitioned by a broken concertina door, he tossed clothes and books.

As fast as he tidied away the clutter, he saw Laura's eyes lighting on the areas he hadn't touched or couldn't – the pale mark on the wall where a crucifix had once hung; the newspaper clippings he'd taped up as penance . . . as if he'd ever needed reminding; the broken picture frames, the broken radio, the smashed TV.

Eventually, she seemed to tire of it and her eyes settled on him instead. Edward ignored her, discovered that within these walls he wasn't ready for her, wasn't ready for whatever her return might imply. She had told him she wasn't who he thought. Well, neither was he. Not any more. He had ceased to be the man she'd married a long time ago.

When, finally, Edward ran out of things to shove into cupboards or drawers, he lit one of the rings on the stove, filled a kettle and placed it down on top. Palms spread, he leaned against the counter and closed his eyes.

Outside, a breeze stirred. The caravan creaked. The tarpaulin in the dead tree flapped like an injured bird.

'This is a sad place,' Laura said.

Edward opened his eyes, blinked. On the sill above the sink stood a half-empty bottle of Canadian Club. His fingers itched to hold it. Instead, he forced himself to face Laura. They stared at each other for long seconds, until he said, 'I need to know what's happening here.'

She nodded. 'Come sit down.'

Reluctantly he complied, sliding onto the bench seat opposite. Argus clambered up, resting his head on Edward's lap.

'Who's Laura?' she asked.

He cupped his hands around his mouth and nose, heard his breath, amplified. 'You are.'

Laura licked her lips. Searched his eyes. 'Who's Laura to you?'

'You're my wife,' he said. Paused. 'Were my wife. This . . . what *is* this? How can—'

'Were?'

'You don't remember?'

'Tell me, Eddie. Please.'

'You . . . you died.' The word spilled out. He felt his shoulders tremble.

She reached across the table and seized his hands, her features creasing in sympathy. 'I'm sorry.' Slowly, she shook her head. 'But this Laura, this woman I resemble – your wife, Eddie. I'm so sorry, but if Laura died, then she's gone. I know it must seem like the most unspeakable cruelty, but I'm not the same person. I don't know what your eyes are showing you but this –' she gestured at herself – 'is a deceit, an illusion. I'm no monster, but it's a kind of witchcraft you're caught up in, all the same. I swear it's not designed to hurt you, just protect me. A defence mechanism, in a way. I don't really understand it. But this . . .' She opened her fingers, breaking their contact. 'It was never meant to do *this*.'

The bottle of Canadian Club was exerting a gravity all of its own. Edward knew that even if he capitulated, its contents would never be enough to dull the shocks of the last hour. All the whisky in the world would not be enough to steer him safely through the impossibilities this night had so far delivered.

'Maybe you're wrong,' he said.

She looked at his hands, as if considering whether to reach for them again. Finally, she shook her head. 'I don't know why I'm here, and I don't know who I am. But I know I'm not Laura.'

'A witch, then, or a faerie. Is that what you want me to believe? That you're some kind of . . .' He groped for words and laughed, hollow, when he found them: 'Forest sprite?'

'Is that any more difficult to accept than the idea that I'm your dead wife, resurrected? But no, I'm none of those things. I told you, I don't—'

Wincing, she sucked in a breath and dropped a hand to her bump.

Edward was about to crab around the table when he heard a low rumbling from outside. It sounded like distant thunder but deeper, more physical; and coming from beneath rather than above. The caravan shifted, as if it had cut loose from its breeze-block moorings. The bottle of Canadian Club fell off the sill and smashed apart in the sink, its contents gurgling away. On a shelf by the door, two red stag carvings toppled over.

Edward planted his feet and braced his hand against the wall. But already the reverberations were diminishing, grumbling echoes chasing out into the night. With their departure Laura's pain seemed to ease. She leaned back against the cushions and sighed.

He stared at her, awe-struck. Her earlier gasp of pain, and the arrival of the thunder, had occurred too closely to be unconnected. 'What *is* this?' he whispered.

Laura swallowed. 'I don't remember much. Not really. But a few things are coming back. Memories, or thoughts. Snatches.' She curled her fingers around her belly. 'I know one thing. This is what's important. This baby, Eddie. Given a chance, I think it's going to change the world. Don't ask me how I know that, but I do. And something out there, something very powerful and very ruthless, really doesn't want that to happen.'

The kettle began to whistle. Edward stood and switched off the gas. He listened to the rolling water begin to calm.

As the sounds inside the caravan faded, Laura – or the woman who looked so much like her – tilted her head towards the window. A moment later, gripping the table with whitening fingers, she sat up straight.

On the seat opposite, Argus lifted his head. The dog's eyes were huge.

CHAPTER 5

Aberffraw Hall, Snowdonia National Park

Aiden Urchardan walked the blood-soaked carpets of Aberffraw Hall in near-darkness, his way lit by the tiny Maglite he carried with his keys. The torch batteries were dying, the murky yellow light produced by its beam insufficient to illuminate all of the carnage, all of the dead. Urchardan could have returned to his car and retrieved a larger flashlight, but he had no wish to see slaughter on this scale in greater detail than he must.

He had encountered the first bodies, not in the main residence itself, but half a mile away, just beyond the gatehouse of the private road that served it. The estate's huge front entrance – arched ironwork gates in a split-portcullis style – hung open in silent invitation, but the spotlights that usually lit the surrounding stonework were dark.

With his vehicle's headlamps extinguished, Urchardan kept his speed low. Despite the frozen temperatures, and the dangers he knew might lurk outside, he rolled down his windows and peered into the darkness either side of the car.

Behind him, the estate's perimeter wall ran east to west, bordering the main road in an unbroken line. No trees had been allowed to grow near it; what vegetation remained was closely cropped, a low-lying mulch of grass and blown leaves.

Twenty yards further in, the manmade land-moat reverted first to well-tended rhododendrons and then to trees stripped bare by Atlantic winds. At the base of one, Urchardan spotted two slumped forms and felt his heart, so often a sluggish prisoner inside his chest, begin to thump at a greater pace.

He had known neither the identity of the woman who had phoned him, nor how she had known whom to call. Her instructions had been calm and precise. Urchardan had dismissed her as a fantasist at first, certain that if he made the trip to Aberffraw Hall he would find nothing amiss. But the woman had got one thing right: this was the only evening in eight peaceful years when such an event *could* happen. That solitary fact had dragged him out here in the middle of the night, when all he wanted was his bed.

As Urchardan steered the car closer to those two black humps, he realised that his anonymous caller had been right about something else, too: appalling events had unfolded here at Aberffraw Hall; might still *be* unfolding.

The men at the base of the tree were in their mid-thirties. Dressed for winter weather, they wore hats, gloves, black body armour. Each had a sub-machine gun slung across his chest.

Urchardan climbed out of the car and hurried to the tree. He played his Maglite beam over the men for only a moment, but he saw enough to establish that there was nothing he could do. The first had been shot through the forehead. The second had been killed from behind; a sizeable chunk of skull was missing where the bullet had punched out.

They looked professional types, hard-faced and competent. Unlikely that they had died in such close proximity – which meant they had probably been dragged here, out of sight of the main road.

Clicking off the torch, Urchardan raised his head and listened to the night. He could hear the wind crackling in the branches of a nearby silver birch, the cry of some night animal off to the north. But other than those small lonely sounds, the overarching silence spoke of a disastrous absence of life up at Aberffraw Hall, a purge of intelligent minds and beating hearts.

Would this be the sound of the world if *she* were allowed to return? Urchardan could feel every one of his many years tonight, but the contemplation of *that* was enough to sluice the fatigue from his limbs.

Not wishing to re-examine the corpses, but knowing that he must, he screwed up his face and switched the torch back on. This time he noticed something that had escaped him before: both men wore closed-cup headphones. His lungs deflated. He could think of only one reason for such cumbersome equipment, and it confirmed his fear that the anonymous caller had been genuine. Might the headphones explain how the men had been so effortlessly ambushed? What terrible irony if so.

Urchardan crouched and laid his fingers against the closest man's neck. Icy to the touch, like meat hanging in a freezer. When he pulled the headphones free, he heard faint music issuing from their cups: eerie, randomised notes.

For a moment he remained beside the corpse, considering whether to relieve it of its weapon. But if death waited for him inside the main residence, he knew he would not avoid it by use of arms. Nor would he, after all these years of service, seek to delay it.

Back inside the car he cleaned his fingers with a chamois, restarted the engine and followed the road as it began to rise. He closed the front windows and turned on the heater, but the circulating air failed to warm him.

Ahead, emerging from the night, he saw the coal-black outline of Aberffraw Hall. Even in silhouette it was a marvel of Baroque architecture. Out of its central façade rose an enormous triangular pediment. Wings branched east and west, stretching the length of two football pitches. No lights shone in any of its windows. To Urchardan it looked as desolate as a grave.

The road bowed out, curving around the perimeter of a lawn crowned by an elaborate hedge maze. Directly outside the building's front entrance, at the centre of a gravelled courtyard, stood a fountain resplendent with green-tinged statuary. Its splash pool was dark and still. Urchardan saw a corpse floating head-down on the surface.

He stopped the car and climbed out, and it took every ounce of his will to climb the portico steps and walk through the gaping front doors. He arrived in a hall so vast, and of such splendour, that it could have swallowed an entire parish church. Urchardan's heels echoed off its marble floor and bounced away from him. He cringed at the sound, but there was no remedy for it. He was too old for stealth; let his footsteps precede him if they must.

So tall were the columns rising up around him that his torch could reveal nothing of the ceiling they supported. He perceived a capacious dome of glass somewhere far above; through it he could see the tattered edges of storm clouds racing east. Three arched entranceways gave him a choice of destinations. Beneath one, leading to the west wing, a dark pool of blood decided him. He passed under the arch and into another colossal chamber. Here, marble floor surrendered to polished wood. Tall mullioned windows stretched the length of the south wall, receding into darkness. A row of enormous oil paintings hung opposite. Urchardan's torch did not illuminate their subjects, and he did not want to see. He kept his eyes pointed at the floor, following a trail of irregular blood splashes. His heart thumped harder. No denying it, now: the woman had spoken true.

Through open doorways he entered a succession of morning rooms decorated in differing and distinctive styles. All were deserted. Except for the blood trail – heavier as it progressed, as if something inside the victim had ruptured – none bore signs of violence. Finally Urchardan arrived in a grand banqueting hall, and it was there that he saw the first indications of brutality.

A mahogany table, with chairs enough for sixty guests, dominated the room. At the far end, a single place setting had been laid with silverware. Nobody sat there now, but the one whose blood he had been trailing had collapsed nearby. Urchardan didn't examine the corpse, but he muttered a curse at the stranger's folly as he passed. The next door opened into a library. There the echoes from his heels died, polished parquet floor yielding to carpet.

Its fibres had soaked up blood like sawdust. Strewn among the room's bookcases, reading tables and chairs lay a montage of twisted human shapes.

CHAPTER 6

Near Devil's Kitchen, Snowdonia National Park

What frightened Edward most, as he stood in the caravan's grimy kitchenette, deep inside this forgotten bowl of woodland, was his complete inability to sense what was coming. Because something *was* coming, he was sure of it. He could read it in the expression on Laura's face, and in the behaviour of his dog.

Argus slipped off the seat and stood rigid, tail curled beneath him, head angled towards the door, as if he wanted to look away, but couldn't.

'They followed us,' Laura whispered. She climbed to her feet, edged out from the table. 'It's too early. Too soon.' When she met his eyes he saw how pale her face had grown.

From somewhere, out in the night, Edward thought he heard something: a directionless vibration, growing and fading. He lifted the rag curtains, bent to the window. 'Who's out there?'

'No one you'd want to meet.'

Laura joined him beside the glass, eyes searching the sky, and Edward realised that the sound he had caught was the rhythmic chop of helicopter blades. An image came to him, from earlier: the lead convoy vehicle on its roof in the road, its occupants bright with flames.

He went to the bedroom's concertina door and dragged it

open. Swinging up the bed frame, he retrieved his hunting crossbow, followed by his rifle and a satchel of ammunition. Back in the living area, he placed his foot in the crossbow's stirrup and rope-cocked it.

'Eddie?'

'This place has one road out. We're leaving on it.'

Laura pressed a hand against his chest. Shook her head. 'It's too late to run.'

'There's time. If—'

'*No*. If we try to go now, they'll find us. Kill us.'

From the far side of the hill that shielded these woods from the road came the distant sound of engines: powerful 4x4s, travelling fast.

Laura leaned over the table and blew out the paraffin lantern, plunging the caravan into darkness. A moment later the moonlight leaking through the curtains raised silhouettes from the shadows.

Edward could no longer see his wife's eyes, but he could hear her breathing, shallow and fast. She stepped so close that he felt that strange heat pouring off her. Her voice trembled when she spoke. 'We have one chance to live. Please, trust me.'

'What do we do?'

'Hide. Before they get here.' Laura's head snapped back towards the window. 'Oh Jesus, Eddie, your *car* – it's still hot. You've got to move it. They'll have infrared. Other stuff, too.'

That vibration in the air was louder now: an insistent throbbing, rolling towards them. From the road he heard a shriek of brakes. Car doors slamming.

We have one chance to live. Please, trust me.

So many emotions those words had stirred in him. So many old ghosts.

Leaning the crossbow beside the oven, handing Laura the rifle, he threw open the caravan door. A star-etched dome of indigo hung above him, framed by a perimeter of black treetops.

Edward bounded down the caravan's steps and sprinted to

the dead tree. Crouching, he ripped out the metal pegs that secured its rainwater tarp, breath fleeing from his lips in ragged white bursts. After pulling the last peg, he dragged the tarp from the tree, cursing when it snagged in the branches.

Low on the northern horizon he could see the helicopter's anti-collision light, a flashing red beacon. A white beam extended from the cockpit, sweeping the land beneath.

Freeing the tarpaulin, bunching it in his arms, Edward sprinted back to the caravan. How long did he have? A minute? Less than that? His skin itched in anticipation of its searchlight falling on him.

He used nylon ties to secure one side of the tarp to the caravan roof. Paying out the rest of it, he backed into the woods. He had erected similar shelters countless times before; rope-ends dedicated to the task still hung from neighbouring trees. He threaded them through the tarp's eyelets, hoisting it to form a taut screen. As soon as it was secure he drove his Defender into cover. All the while, Laura watched his progress from the caravan's front step, her face sallow with fear.

Edward jumped from the 4x4 and slammed the door. While the tarp would fool an infrared device hovering directly overhead, a more oblique angle would betray the vehicle's areas of latent heat. Working as fast as he could, he stacked old packing crates and pieces of wood around the Defender's wheels and exhaust, plugging the gaps with armfuls of wet leaves. At his water butt, he broke through a layer of surface ice and sunk a jerrycan into its depths.

Abruptly the helicopter banked, angling directly towards the clearing.

'*Get inside, Eddie!*' Laura hissed. '*Now!*'

Instinct told him to risk it. Lugging the jerrycan across the fire pit, he popped the Defender's bonnet release and tipped the contents over the engine block. It steamed for a few seconds as it cooled. Slamming down the lid, he shook the last dregs of water over the top. Then he piled on more leaves.

'*Eddie!*'

He could feel the helicopter at his back, knew that at any moment its white searchlight could lance down and pin him. The pulsing of its blades and the shrill whistle of its turbine bounced off the surrounding hills.

With the Defender as disguised as he could make it, Edward raced back to the caravan's entrance and dived inside. Laura slammed the door behind him.

'Walls,' she shouted. 'What are they made of?'

'Aluminium skin.'

'Roof?'

'Same thing.'

'We've got to cover the windows, skylight too. Something metal. Quickly.'

Infected by her urgency, by her apparent conviction that their lives depended on it, Edward ripped open the door of a wall cabinet. He rummaged around inside, dislodging a half-bottle of tequila that toppled and smashed at his feet. His fingers closed on a battered roll of kitchen foil. He stripped away its cardboard liner, tore off a long sheet.

'Let me help,' she said.

He nodded, heart a hummingbird in his chest. While he began to line the front-facing window with foil, Laura concentrated on the two above the bench seats. The aluminium adhered easily to the damp glass, but the skylight casing was less obliging. Edward used its ventilation hatch to fix the foil in place.

Moving to the bedroom – working, now, in near-darkness – he used the last of the roll to shield the remaining window. He returned to find Laura on her knees beside the oven, rooting around inside.

She pulled out a grime-caked baking tray and handed it to him. 'Door panel.'

Behind him, a viewing window in the caravan's entrance door admitted the last traces of moonlight. Edward yanked down its roller blind and pressed the baking tray over the top. Just before he sealed the caravan in darkness he glimpsed the ground outside, and wondered whether he was hallucinating: the hard-packed earth seemed to be moving, *writhing*, as if a deluge of rain had forced every earthworm and burrowing creature to the surface.

Mind stumbling over the image he had caught, Edward said: 'Duct tape, in the drawer on your left. Grab it.' He heard Laura fumbling. Seconds later she passed him the tape. Together they fixed the tray in place.

'Get a duvet,' she told him. 'Blankets too.'

Above, the helicopter began to circle. The sound of its turbine scratched claws into the back of Edward's neck. He leaned into the bedroom and grabbed as many bedclothes as he could, no longer questioning Laura's demands. Obeying her – and closing his mind to everything else – felt like his only option.

She tugged him down to the floor, onto an accumulation of wood shavings, dirt and foul-smelling carpet. Into his ear, she whispered, '*Cover us.*'

Edward threw the duvet and blankets over them. Perfect dark. He wondered whether, outside, a searchlight now pinned them.

Overhead, the helicopter began to descend, its rotor blades stripping the clearing of leaves.

Laura's hand found Edward's. Squeezed.

CHAPTER 7

Aberffraw Hall,
Snowdonia National Park

Aiden Urchardan sagged, made older than his years by the sight of such barbarity.

The dead were of differing ages; men and women alike. In the library's eastern wall the doors had been barricaded with a heavy oak desk piled with antique furniture. It hadn't saved the room's occupants. The attack had come through the five windows looking onto the puzzle maze. Broken glass lay heaped beneath them. A cold wind twined through, stirring the pages of books littering the floor.

In two grand fireplaces bright flames still danced. The sight jolted Urchardan, made him realise just how recent this had been. He glanced around at the thousands of volumes arranged in their racks and shook his head. All this knowledge, all this learning, and *still* they had attempted such a wicked, wicked thing. What chance for humanity if *this* was the kind of choice it made?

That was an unworthy thought, and he knew it. The people who had died here – fools though they may have been – were no representation of society as a whole. And while they had been misguided, naïve beyond belief, he did not doubt that they had believed in the fundamental rightness of what they had attempted. He saw no depravity in their faces, no evidence of immorality or sin. These had been good people, twisted by a subversive ideology.

And that, you old fossil, might be the most dangerous — and asinine — thought you've had yet.

He moved around the room, bending beside each corpse and closing its eyes. Some remained shut, others sprang open in defiance. He cringed away from those that did, feeling the accusation in their sightless stares. When his task was done he went to the east wall and dismantled the barricade, removing the stacked furniture and dragging the desk away.

The doors opened into a lavish chamber, this one utterly dark. Heavy drapes concealed the south-facing windows. The fabric hung still, indicating that the glass behind it remained intact. His faltering torch beam picked out a candelabra on a nearby table. From his pocket, Urchardan pulled out a book of matches. He lit several of the candles, and stood back as their glow began to warm the room.

Details emerged from darkness. Colours bloomed from shadow. Again, his heart beat heavily at what the light revealed.

They had died in a circle; eight of them in total. While the cause of their deaths was unclear, he saw they had given their lives attempting to defend the one they had loved. Because in the centre of that protective ring lay a final body, this one covered by a black silk sheet. Urchardan drew a stunned breath, letting it trickle from his lungs like drifting smoke. He did not need to peel back the coverlet to know who lay beneath; he could feel a power radiating from her corpse even now.

While, in truth, he should have considered the dead woman an adversary, he would not desecrate her resting place any more than he must. Enemy she may have been, rival to the cause he served, but such a gulf existed between them that he could not help but feel awe at her proximity, and a grief, utterly inexplicable, at her passing.

Careful with that thought. On any other night it might be your last.

He glanced at his watch, anxious. The golden digits did not mark time in the traditional sense. Instead they showed him a countdown. The accuracy was questionable by a few minutes either way, but he saw that he had not long left in isolation. Usually that was a comforting thought. Tonight, less so.

After bowing his head and muttering a few words of farewell, Urchardan walked through an arch in the chamber's north wall, knocking the Maglite against his leg to wake what remained of its batteries. He arrived in an antechamber devoid of windows. Gilded chairs lined one wall, along with two sofas plumped with cushions. In a nod to modernity, a pod-style coffee machine sat on a lacquered bureau. In the far wall, hanging off broken hinges, he saw a smashed door. Urchardan stepped through it. In the room beyond he discovered what he had been searching for, and had hoped never to find.

To his left, a metal wall panel contained a bank of switches. He flicked them on, not expecting any reaction. To his surprise a row of fluorescents above his head began to blink, until all six cast their ice-white light down upon him. The floor was coated with pale-blue rubber. Where it met the walls it curved up six inches without forming a break or seam. Wheeled trolleys stood in the corners. Stainless-steel cabinets hung from the walls. He saw hand sanitisers, tanks of Entonox, a medical sink with elbow-action taps. Extending from one wall loomed a surgical lighting rig like a multi-faceted eye on a retractable stalk.

In the very centre of the room stood a single hospital bed covered with a white cotton sheet. Urchardan stared at it, shocked into paralysis. For a moment he did not know how he should feel: rage at what, in their ignorance, they had attempted to bring about, or despair at what they had suffered as a result.

At the foot of the bed he saw a clear plastic incubator unit lined with paper. On the shelves beneath it lay folded blankets, hygiene rolls and wipes. Someone had placed a tiny stuffed elephant among them. Contemplating it, Urchardan felt his heart ache with grief. What madness this had been; what stupidity.

It did not take a trained eye to see that the room had not been used. Considering that the information he'd been passed had been reliable so far, he saw no reason to suspect that the rest was a fabrication. None of the dead women Urchardan had encountered showed signs of pregnancy; neither did he think he would find any in the rooms waiting to be searched.

It meant that this attack, for all its brutality, had failed in its ultimate task.

Out there, somewhere in the night, walked a living time-bomb. If the child she carried were allowed to survive, the consequences would be unimaginable.

Abruptly, Urchardan's head snapped up. He strode from the delivery suite and back into the lushly appointed chamber where so many had fallen. Going to a window, he drew back its drapes and peered out at the night.

In the far distance he saw the silhouette peaks of the Glyderau: Glyder Fach, Tryfan, Y Garn, Foel Goch. From somewhere beyond that range of mountains he felt himself being called. It was a soft string of thought at first; a tentative exploration, like groping fingers inside his head.

Is that you? he asked. *Please tell me it is. I'm out of my depth in this. Alone.*

Those fingers, their strength suddenly surging, latched on. And now, in a rush, here it came: The Bliss.

It coursed through him, raced through his blood like electricity. At once it renewed him, enlivened him, made his nerves sing and his pulse quicken. His mouth dropped open and he sighed.

HERE.

Not a voice, exactly, but a presence nonetheless, an aware-ness; and one to which he had pledged himself for longer than he could remember. Urchardan felt its love envelop him and he smiled. Then, with a twinge, he remembered the devastation he had seen.

They defied you. Brought her back.

YES.

She's out there, right now. Hiding. Biding her time.

The moment he thought it, Urchardan sensed that awareness change, its temperament shift. His mind opened, and he felt his memories sifted. He had nothing to fear from such close scrutiny. Or did he? Unbidden, an earlier thought returned and he tried, in his shame, to banish it.

FORGIVEN.

Urchardan felt his shoulders relax at that. Felt his guilt evaporate into euphoria. He raised his head to the night beyond the window, and listened intently as The Bliss began to talk.

CHAPTER 8

Near Devil's Kitchen, Snowdonia National Park

Huddled on his right side, Edward felt the tequila from the smashed bottle soaking into his jeans. The broken glass must have sliced him when Laura tugged him to the floor, because his hip was a sharp blaze of pain – through the wound, alcohol stung open flesh.

Caught in the helicopter's downdraught, the caravan shuddered and rocked. Edward felt pulses of pressure in his throat.

Beside him lay his rifle. By his boot he felt the satchel of ammunition. If he snagged the strap and lifted his leg, he might be able to drag it within reach. Until he managed it, the weapon was useless.

Laura seemed to sense his thoughts. She snaked her arm over his torso and leaned in tight, her hard round belly pressing against him. For a fleeting moment he thought he felt the life growing inside her shift and stir.

Lips close against his ear, she whispered, '*Don't move.*' Then, her voice almost lost to the shriek of the helicopter's turbine, she added: '*Not an inch.*'

Not for the first time this night Edward felt only partially in control of his actions – as if at any moment his body or his mind might betray him, operating in opposition to his will. He recalled the discordant music issuing from the dead man's earpiece, his disturbing compulsion to plug himself into it. He remembered how he had returned to the rear door of the MPV almost without thinking, intent on freeing whoever remained trapped inside.

Something touched his leg. He nearly kicked out. But it was only Argus, tunnelling under the duvet to find him. He felt the dog rest its head on his stomach, seeking warmth.

The helicopter seemed so close overhead that Edward would not have been surprised to feel its landing skids nudge the caravan roof. He visualised his patch of land as viewed from above: the blackened fire pit, the abandoned chicken coops, the stained and rotten dwelling sinking into the damp earth. His only hope was that the place appeared too decrepit to be habitable.

He thought of the vehicles he had heard on the main road. If the searchers in the sky spotted something, how quickly would the ground-based team appear? Too late, now, to attempt an escape. Even without aerial observation, he could not hike out of these woods with Laura so immobile. And the road, by now, was sure to be blocked.

Impossible, this.

Three years he had lived in sombre purgatory, shackled by the millstone of his wife's death. And now here she was beside him, belly swollen with life. He did not know what any of it meant, had no clue what part he'd been asked to play. He'd failed at so many things; the very notion that he could prevail, here, was laughable.

Abruptly, the helicopter began to ascend. Moments later it turned and flew south, its turbine diminishing to a distant whine. Edward would have allowed himself to relax a little had he not heard shouts from the other side of the hill. The voices came not from the main road, but closer, inside the woods. He wondered if the hunters had dogs with them.

Moving his foot in a slow arc, he dragged the satchel up

towards his waist and groped around inside. His fingers touched the cold brass of rifle rounds. With Laura tensing at his side, Edward retrieved his hunting rifle.

He was certain, now, that the weapon would be near useless against whatever forces opposed them. But it felt such a basic response, such an instinctive, necessary act – to load his gun, to arm himself against the unknown and protect his wife, even if he'd failed to protect her before – that he found himself a slave to the motions.

The rounds clicked as he loaded them. They were tiny sounds, inconsequential, and they raised no objections from Laura. That the weapon was loaded gave him some comfort, but his heart still galloped in his chest. He clutched the rifle like a talisman, finger curled inside the trigger guard.

For the next hour the searchers lingered, their shouts swelling and fading. Sometimes they seemed to come from right inside the clearing itself. But Edward knew how easily these woods played tricks. And he could hear in the tone of those voices – if not in their words – that their hopes were dying. From the other side of the hill, diesel engines revved. Tyres shrieked against wet road. The voices in the woods stilled.

'They're leaving,' he muttered, turning to face Laura.

Edward heard the breath go out of her.

'He's weak right now,' she replied. 'It's the only explanation.'

'He?'

She quieted at that. Took a slow breath.

'Who were they, Laura?'

'Did you see?'

He shook his head.

'Nor me.'

Despite the frigid conditions outside, it was growing hot beneath the duvet. 'You know something, though,' he said. 'Laura—'

'I told you. That's not my name.'

The comment startled him, made him flinch. He had all but

forgotten her earlier protestations that she was not his wife. And yet *forgotten* wasn't quite right. It felt more as if the part of his brain that stored that knowledge had simply gone dark; as if a tumour had flared there, destroying what memories lingered. It chilled him to consider it.

'I have a photo. Somewhere,' he said. 'Just one. It might help you to remember.' He lifted his arm away from her, began to rise.

'No.' She grabbed him. Held on tight. 'It's not safe, Eddie. Not yet.'

'All right,' he told her. 'Whatever you want. We'll stay here, just like this. And while we're here, you can tell me everything. As much of it as you know. Once you've done that, we can start to fill in the gaps. Work this out.'

She was silent for a while, until finally her grip on him loosened. Incredibly, he heard her yawn.

'When was the last time you slept?' he asked.

'I don't know. Too long.'

'Those men from earlier. The ones you were travelling with . . .'

She tensed. 'Are they all right? Did they get away?' When Edward didn't reply immediately, she added, in a smaller voice: 'No. They're dead. All of them.'

Until now, he had assumed that Laura had been a prisoner of the strangers operating the convoy. Her distress at their loss suggested otherwise. He had so many questions, such a need for answers, but he knew that to pressure her so soon after her ordeal would be irresponsible. She was exhausted, close to collapse, and he was deeply concerned at the amount of heat her body was generating.

Earlier he had imagined that the night had weaved him a ghost. While he believed that no longer, he could think of no rational explanation for Laura's return. And the one that she'd offered him . . . Edward frowned. He could hardly even remember it.

He pressed his nose to her hair. 'Sleep,' he murmured.

'If they come back—'

'I'll stay awake. I promise.'

'So tired.' She tucked her head into his chest. Within moments, her breathing softened and slowed.

Edward lay there silent in the dark. The pain in his hip where the glass had cut him was beginning to fade. He felt Laura press herself against him as she slept, an intimacy so incongruous, and yet so natural, that his mind reeled at its contemplation.

Despite the return of his wife, despite the intoxicating heat trapped beneath the bedclothes – perhaps, even, because of it – Edward felt his eyes growing heavy, felt himself, just like Laura, falling inexorably towards sleep.

He had promised her that he would stay awake. Like so many other vows he had broken during his life, he broke that one, too.

The wind crackling in the dead tree's branches was the last thing he heard.

CHAPTER 9

Chamonix, France

He opened his eyes and found that he was standing in the cramped kitchenette of their old apartment, as it once was. Morning sunlight sloped through the window with an intensity that made him squint. Outside, the sky held a uniquely Alpine sharpness: lucent and pure, the promise of something good. He saw that the snow had refrozen overnight, forming a stiff crust.

No, he pleaded. *Please don't show me this. Not again.*

But either the dream wasn't listening, or it was in no mood to concede, because just then Edward's nose tingled in recognition of the vanilla-caramel notes of Laura's favourite perfume, and when he turned she was there in the doorway, grinning at him; and all his awareness that this was just a dream faded like cobwebs spun from smoke.

She wore a pair of his old climbing socks and a cotton dressing gown wrapped around her five-month bump. Her hair was piled up in a loose knot. 'Morning,' she said. Her eyes sparkled like mountain spring water. 'I have a cunning plan.'

'Oh yeah?' he replied. 'Which is?'

'Tell you after breakfast. Did you make coffee?'

'Made it and drank it.'

Laura pouted playfully. 'Such a gentleman.'

'You were asleep. In fact,' he pointed out, 'you were snoring. Like a walrus.'

'A *walrus*?'

'Or maybe a gorilla.'

Laura raised an eyebrow. 'You married a gorilla? Jeez, Eddie. That was smart.'

'Smartest thing I ever did.'

She grinned at that, came towards him and slipped her arms around his waist. Her bump pressed against his stomach. 'I've a feeling *this* was the smartest thing you ever did. Make another pot, will you? Not too strong. Do we have croissants?'

'Fresh from Florentin's. In the bag by the toaster.'

'Why, you *are* a gentleman.'

'Sometimes the disguise slips.'

'Lucky for me.'

Edward leaned forward and kissed her. He tasted the sleepy sourness of Laura's mouth and felt his heart kick pleasurably in his chest. Placing his hands on her shoulders, he eased her away from him. 'One weak coffee coming up. And two fat croissants.'

'And jam,' she said, disappearing through the arch to their breakfast nook. 'Emergency quantities of jam. Has to be blackcurrant today.'

'What happened to raspberry?'

'Raspberry is out on his ear. He's homeless now, just like his old friends blueberry and apricot. They're crowding round an oil drum fire, wearing fingerless gloves and drinking meths.'

Laughing, Edward spooned a half-scoop of coffee into the machine.

They ate breakfast sitting on fold-out chairs in the breakfast nook, knees bumping together beneath the tiny table. Laura licked pastry crumbs from her fingers and glanced through the window. 'Looks frozen out there today.'

'Nothing to get concerned about.'

'What time are you leaving?'

'Christophe says they're arriving at eleven. Three Americans in their fifties. All pretty fit, from what I hear. We'll ease them into it today – teach them a little rope work, dummy a few crevasse escapes.'

'When are you taking them up?'

'Probably Thursday, if the weather holds.'

'How long are they here?'

'They fly out Sunday. Doing some kind of European tour, apparently.'

'And then you'll have a few days off.'

'More like a week, I expect.'

She nodded, patting her bump. 'Good. Because we're going on a climb of our own when you get back. Just the two of us. One last time before Little Schwinny arrives.'

'Sure,' Edward said. He loved being outside with Laura; she made him look differently at the world, revealing the beauty that would otherwise have remained obscured. 'What've you got in mind?'

'The big one.'

He jerked backwards in his chair, began to laugh. 'Uh-uh. Something else, maybe, but not that.'

She frowned. '*Yes*, that. Yes, *exactly* that.'

Sobering, Edward realised his error. The one thing Laura hated was being told there was something she couldn't do. 'What about something with better views?' he asked, switching tack. 'Le Prarion, perhaps, or—'

Laura snorted. 'I don't want to *look* at the top, I want to *be* at the top.'

'It's a nice idea. I just—'

She raised her eyebrows.

'Oh, come *on*. I'm hardly a Neanderthal for pointing it out. Climbing Mont Blanc when you're five months pregnant is crazy.'

'It's been done. I know someone who did it at six months.'

'Yeah, an extreme case, as you well know. You don't have anything to prove. Why risk it?'

'Childbirth is a risk.'

'That's different.'

'Is it? How?'

'It's completely different.'

Laura watched him, but her eyes were somewhere else. 'I need this,' she told him, and for a moment her face grew solemn, until her customary grin returned, pulling at the corners of her mouth. 'What risk is there, anyway? I'll have the world's greatest guide right beside me.'

Edward shook his head. 'Cheap flattery will get you nowhere.'

'It got me pregnant.'

'Oh, piss off.'

Laura punched his shoulder. When a car horn sounded outside she glanced through the window. 'There's your lift. You'd better go and teach those Americans how to tie knots. We can talk later.'

'Le Prarion.'

'Screw Le Prarion.'

'Le Prarion, or maybe Aiguillette des Posettes.'

Rolling her eyes, Laura shooed him out of the apartment.

Christophe was waiting behind the wheel in the lane outside. As always, he seemed oblivious to the fug of Gauloises Blondes cigarette smoke that filled his tiny Honda. Edward rolled down the window and sucked gratefully on unadulterated Chamonix air.

'The woman is insane,' the Frenchman announced five minutes later, flicking ash towards the tray in what was, at best, a token gesture. 'But that is why you love her, I suppose. Are you going to say yes?'

'Of course not.'

'Man, I think you should.'

Edward turned in his seat. 'Say again?'

'She's a fit lady. Tough. You deny her this, it might bite you. Right on the ass.'

'Chris, she's going to have a baby.'

'So? Laura's a climber, just like you.' He shrugged. 'If she'd married me—'

'Which she didn't.'

'A tragedy, that. For her as well as me.' The man crushed out his cigarette in the graveyard jutting from the Honda's dash. 'But if she *had* married me, I would not deny her in this.'

The Americans turned out to be three dentists from Florida. All three were as fit as they had promised, but they were new to the demands of Alpine climbing. Edward liked their confidence and enthusiasm, and he fell into an easy banter with them. After a light lunch in Chamonix, he drove ten minutes out of town to a place where he taught them snow anchors and axe work. He observed them walking in their crampons, pleased at what he saw. Over the next two days he would take them on a series of acclimatising practice climbs, one of which would include an evening descent into Chamonix. As long as the group made it through without any major problems, he would lead them up to one of the high-altitude mountain huts on Mont Blanc's flanks. There they would stay the night, in preparation for a summit attempt early the next morning.

After dropping the Americans at their hotel, Edward returned home before sunset. The apartment was empty when he arrived. Laura's battered Renault was absent from its usual space. She had left him a note, propped up by the toaster:

Oops, we've run out of jam. Gone for reinforcements.
Please start dinner! Xxo

He switched on the radio, took out a wok and began to cook a pad thai with tofu and prawns, one of her favourite dishes. Laura appeared twenty minutes later. They ate dinner on the living-room sofa with a blanket spread across them, watching fat white flakes fall from a black sky.

'How did they get on?' she asked.

'Fast learners. Competent.'

'Your new rucksack arrived.'

'About time.'

'You ordered the exact same one as last time. Even down to the colour.'

'It's a good brand.'

'They don't make different colours?'

He shrugged. 'I guess they might. It's just a rucksack, really. You can't see the colour when you're wearing it.'

'Then next time I'm ordering you one in hot pink.'

'That'll go down well with Chris.'

She grinned. 'You'll have to fight him off.'

They finished their meal. Afterwards, Laura snuggled up to him. 'I can't wait to get up there.'

'We talked about that.'

'We'll take the Three Monts route, I think. Cable car to the Aiguille du Midi, then—'

'*No*, Laura.'

'It's prettier than Goûter.'

'And more dangerous.'

Laura's hand snaked beneath the blanket. 'I'm a lot fitter than those dentists you're guiding.'

'I don't like it,' he replied.

Her fingers found his belt, began to loosen it. 'A lot more adventurous, too.'

'I still don't like it,' Edward murmured, but his voice was quieter now, huskier. Soon his thoughts were elsewhere.

Outside, the falling snow delivered a tomblike silence.

Eight days later, after putting three contented Americans onto a train bound for Geneva, Edward found himself in a cable car with Laura, heading up to the Aiguille du Midi. From there they strapped on packs and crampons and dropped down to the surface of the Vallée Blanche glacier. While the descent was relatively untaxing, it was perilous even so. The first section led them down a razor-like snow ridge only a few feet in width. It felt like walking along the edge of a cuttlebone; a slip over either side would result in a plummet of hundreds of feet. All around them, peaks rose like black teeth out of snowy white gums.

Edward roped himself to Laura and made her walk in front. He watched his wife carefully as they crossed the glacier but it was a simple traverse, and she completed it with no sign of fatigue.

It took them an hour to reach the Refuge des Cosmiques. Supported by a scaffold of steel braces and fluted wooden beams, it perched improbably on a ridge like a shoebox balanced on the blade of a knife. That afternoon they stood on its balcony and gazed down upon the southern Alps, a world of rock towers purified by snow and ice, and Edward – even with all his misgivings about this trip – thought he had never been happier.

He recalled the words of his old hero, Chamonix guide Gaston Rébuffat: *What an extraordinary creation this is, wrought by earth and time!*

Edward could think of no more appropriate words. Below, clouds seeped like liquid smoke among the peaks but up here the sky was clear, made tangerine by melting sun. He put his arm around Laura, and when she leaned her head on his shoulder he felt such a powerful feeling of love for her that a tightness formed in his throat. She looked up and laughed, and neither of them had to say a thing.

Back inside the hut, they retired to its rough-hewn dining room. There they ate a simple dinner of chicken and potatoes prepared by Édouard, the refuge guardian, a stick-thin man from Annecy. Afterwards they escaped to their bunks, donned their earplugs and tried to catch a few hours' sleep.

Edward woke Laura at two a.m., as planned. By timing their arrival at the summit to coincide with sunrise he hoped to minimise their risk, during the descent, of encountering an avalanche or a late afternoon storm. Within five minutes they were packed and ready to go. In the dining room, Laura lingered longer over her tea than Edward would have liked but he said nothing, not wishing to spoil her anticipation. As she drank, she scrolled through a weather app on her phone. 'Forecast still looks OK.'

'You checked your gear?'

She nodded.

'Feeling good?'

'Yep.'

Edward screwed up his face. 'Still want to do this?'

'Double yep.'

'How's bump?'

'Awake. Determined.'

At the hut entrance, Edward tested Laura's harness and activated her avalanche transceiver. The temperature outside had dropped to minus ten, but a steady wind blowing from the east made it feel twice as cold. The summit, he knew, would be brutal by comparison; they would not be able to tarry long.

Overhead, the sky was a diamond mine of twinkling stars. A carved shard of moon fell slowly towards the western horizon; what little light it shed would soon be gone. All around them the snow was a mauve shadow on the rocks. When Edward switched on his head torch, his world shrank to a narrow cone of light. He saw Laura's torch wink on.

'All set?' he asked, his words muffled inside his balaclava. She nodded. Edward performed one last check of his equipment: ice axe, rope, harness, pack. Everything secure. '*Allez!*' he called, surprised by the eagerness in his voice. How long since the two of them had climbed together? Not this year, certainly. Despite his excitement, he could not entirely cage his misgivings about this expedition. The thought of Laura plummeting into a crevasse made him cringe. Even if he arrested her fall, the trauma caused by her sudden deceleration might be significant. And for all their dangers, glacial crevasses represented just one hazard on a long list. The weather could change quickly up here: fresh snow could trigger avalanches; sudden rain could trigger rock falls. A strong wind on the summit might produce a wind chill of thirty-five below. Nothing survived those kinds of conditions for long.

Despite the dangers, Edward knew that the moment Laura had set her mind to this task, she would not have been turned back. If he had refused to accompany her, she would have found another way. She would have done it not to spite him, but because failure was unthinkable, unbearable; hers was a kind of selfishness he could understand and forgive, not least because he harboured a sliver of it himself. It meant, too, that the moment Laura made her decision, he was bound to it. Whom, after all, could he better trust with her safety than himself?

They walked through the darkness in companionable silence. Edward listened to the rhythms of his body; his heart beating steady and slow; his lungs expanding and contracting, drawing air through teeth clenched against the cold. Laura walked with a methodical precision, axe held ready by her side. He watched her movements with fierce pride. In the far distance he could see the pinprick spotlights of another climbing party, but soon they winked out, hidden by a rising needle of rock. After that they were alone, just the two of them.

Edward smiled, corrected himself: the *three* of them.

Their ascent up Mont Blanc du Tacul, first of the summits along their route, was hard going. Laura paused regularly, finding excuses to fiddle with her harness or readjust her pack. She breathed hard, condensation blasting from her lungs in ever-increasing gouts. Edward was just about to call a break when she vanished from view.

The support rope went taut, dragging him off his feet. He swung his arm high in a practised movement and buried the head of his axe into compacted snow. But he was no longer being pulled. There was a slackness to the rope; an absence of weight. He heard Laura cry out.

It was not a trailing scream. It contained no trace of horror or fear, merely exasperation. When he rolled onto his side he saw that Laura had not plummeted from a severed safety line into a crevasse. She had simply lost her balance, tumbling forward so that her head-torch had sunk into snow. When Edward hauled her to her feet she flashed him an abashed grin. He smiled in return, even though in his ribcage his heart was a bird beating broken wings. After that, they progressed even more cautiously. The ascent was steeper now; vertical faces, serrated *aiguilles*, blades of rock and ice. Two hours after leaving the hut, and still in perfect darkness, they reached the shoulder of Mont Blanc du Tacul. From there, alert for the sound of serac fall, they crossed the Col du Mont Maudit. They climbed that peak's northern face by front pointing, arriving at its summit as dawn began to chase the darkness from the sky.

Laura was blowing harder now, and her eyes were bright with pain. Her pace had slowed dramatically: one breath; one step; one breath. The cold sang in Edward's teeth and throat and lungs. What skin he'd left exposed felt flayed. When he rubbed his nose he felt the crunch of ice crystals inside it. Despite his layers of clothing and protective gear, a numbness was beginning to seep into his joints, a worrying brittleness in his hands and feet. Looking at his watch, he considered calling a retreat. But it was only a short time now until sun-up. The conditions were still favourable; he would give it a while longer.

Again they found themselves descending instead of climbing, this time along the Col de la Brenva. Southwards Edward could see Italy rolled out before him. The views were astonishing. They might not be on top of the world, but they were approaching the top of Western Europe; only Mount Elbrus in Russia's Caucasus, a peak Edward had climbed twice, reached higher.

He was so cold now that he could hardly leash his thoughts.

Never in all his previous ascents had he encountered temperatures as biting as these. In front of him Laura sank to her knees. Ten seconds passed before she pushed herself back to her feet. He tugged gently on the rope but she ignored him, lifting her right foot and placing it stubbornly before her. The summit waited a few hundred yards ahead, up a gentle slope of compacted crust.

Laura raised her left foot, planted it. Edward followed, teeth clenched. Every one of his senses was screaming: *Get her off the mountain! Get her down to the hut, right now!*

If Laura had been one of his clients, he would have turned back long ago. Why, then, was he allowing her to continue?

Because that was the deal you struck when you married her.

That word – *allow* – had not been part of their vocabulary. Edward did as he pleased, and Laura did likewise; and by happy stroke of fortune what pleased one tended to please the other.

So caught up was he by those thoughts, and by his dogged endurance of Mont Blanc's final test, that he arrived at the summit almost without realising it. One moment his legs – muscles burnt and frozen in equal measure – were working in tortuous rhythm. The next there was no more mountain left to climb. Laura turned to face him and he saw that her eyes, behind her ski goggles, gleamed with triumph. She laughed, flung her arms around his waist, pressed her head against him.

A moment later she disentangled herself and gestured at the Mont Blanc Massif beneath them. The dawning sun had steeped the sky in layers of orange peel and lavender. 'I love you, Edward Schwinn!' she cried, and he grinned through his weariness.

'You're a bloody headcase,' he shouted. 'Now let's get down before my balls freeze and everything else besides.'

She kissed him, long and deep.

Had he known it would be their last kiss, Edward would have enjoyed it far less than he did.

CHAPTER 10

Near Devil's Kitchen, Snowdonia National Park

Argus woke him. The dog was scratching at the door, begging to be let out. Edward shrugged off a flap of duvet and sat up, disorientated. A strip of aluminium had peeled away from one of the windows, revealing a sky the colour of wet ashes.

Screwing up his eyes, he gazed around the caravan. When he saw the kitchen foil lining every remaining window and skylight, and his loaded weapons lying within easy reach, the events of the previous evening came flooding back.

Gasping, Edward scrambled out of the makeshift bed. He snatched up his rifle and joined Argus at the door. There he paused, listening for sounds in the clearing outside; but he heard nothing but the pounding of his heart.

Argus blinked, licked his chops. The dog had been a reliable barometer of danger so far, and now he seemed uninterested, calm.

Removing the duct-taped baking tray from the door's viewing hatch, Edward raised the blind and peered through the window. Outside, the light was already dying. Clouds, pregnant with rain, dragged their underbellies across the valley floor, wetting everything they touched. The clearing, ringed by dripping trees, had lost its skin of frost. Around the fire pit, the earth – in fact everywhere he looked – appeared churned, as if a plough had circled the site, dredging damp black soil to the surface. Other than that, the clearing and its surrounds seemed utterly devoid of life. His internal clock told him it was late afternoon, which meant that they had slept through most of the day.

They.

Edward glanced behind him to the duvet on the caravan's floor, and the soft shape that gently rose and fell beneath it. He wasn't ready to process that yet, wasn't ready to contemplate it all afresh.

He blinked, climbed to his feet. Felt a nip of pain from his hip and saw a curve of broken glass protruding from his side. Around the wound, his clothes were brown with dried blood. Grimacing, he eased the shard out of his flesh and tossed it into the sink. He cinched his jeans tighter and checked the view through the window once more. Finally, he opened the door.

Argus nosed past him. The dog bounded down the steps, trotted to a nearby tree and began to relieve itself. Urine steamed on the air, and it woke a need in Edward too. He tramped outside and took up position by a neighbouring tree. 'Some night,' he said. His voice sounded scratchy; unlike his own.

Argus glanced over, panted his agreement.

The tarpaulin that stretched from the caravan roof still concealed the Defender, but it sagged considerably. One corner hung loose; legacy, perhaps, of the helicopter's downdraught.

Returning inside, Edward lit a ring on the stove and set the kettle to boil. He found two mugs and swilled them under the tap. He didn't trust himself to look again at the shape beneath the duvet. Instead he searched around for his coffee jar and spooned its contents into the mugs.

From the duvet under the galley table came a moan. Edward dropped the jar onto the drainer with a crash. He turned just as Laura pushed herself to a sitting position, and then he cried out, leaping away and cracking his head against a cupboard. He shrugged the rifle from his shoulder, disengaged the safety. Aiming the weapon with shaking hands, he backed into the doorway of his bedroom, clenching his teeth. 'Where is she?'

The woman sitting on the floor, two hands pressed to her belly, wasn't anyone he had seen before. She certainly wasn't Laura. Her face had a lean, malnourished look: scooped-out cheeks, tight lips, watery blue eyes; the kind of hungry, dried-up expression he'd always associated with drug addicts. Her hair hung in greasy ropes around her ears. Her forehead was red with an unsightly rash. When she swallowed, he noticed a poorly inked tattoo bobbing around her throat: barbed wire, faded and indistinct.

She stared at him, uncomprehending. Then the skin around her eyes creased. 'Oh,' she said. Not his wife's voice. This one had no music to it, no warmth.

Edward realised that he was hunched over in the doorframe, bracing himself with shoulder and boot. He straightened, raised the barrel of his rifle. Lined up the sights between her eyes. 'I'll ask you again, but no more than that. Where is she?'

The woman scratched her forehead. 'If that's coffee you're making, count me in. Whatever mouldy crap you've been breeding on this carpet's broken me out in hives, I reckon. Plus, I got cramps like you wouldn't believe. Which is kind of bad news, considering.'

Her accent was east coast Irish, but it barely softened her voice. To Edward it was a nettle dragged across his flesh.

She raised her hand, gestured at the rifle. 'All right, look. I'm pretty sure I told you this already, but it was a weird night – maybe I forgot. Eddie, that it? Eddie, I'm sorry, very sorry, but your wife – she was never here. Just me, the whole time, like I was trying to tell you.'

She took a breath that dissolved into a bout of coughing. 'Looking at your face, I reckon I'm not the most appealin'' prospect to wake up to, but you best put the gun down. I hope you wouldn't use it on a pregnant woman, Eddie, but it's dangerous even so. You've not had much sleep and you're not thinking too straight. You could make a mistake, harm the baby.'

One corner of her mouth lifted, as if she sought to elicit from him a companionable smile. But as Edward watched her the meaning of her words began to penetrate. A hopelessness, like slow-spreading poison, seeped into him and headed at once for his heart.

It hadn't been his wife he'd discovered in the smashed convoy; hadn't been his wife he'd brought back to the caravan with him. Nor had it been his wife he'd stretched out beside on this filth-strewn floor and hugged to his side as he slept.

He hadn't been given a second chance. Far from it.

Laura was never here. All of this, just a trick.

Only now, as he stared at the gaunt stranger opposite, did he begin to understand just how deeply he had wanted that fantasy to be real. Its sudden unravelling was too much to bear. The strength fled from his limbs and he sat down hard. His eyelids flickered. For a moment he thought he might be sick, or perhaps just faint away.

'Hey, Eddie.' The woman crawled over to him and put a hand on his shoulder. 'I'm sorry. I mean it. That's a tough thing to happen.'

A thought reached him, shocking in its simplicity, that he could kill this wounded creature, kill them both and end this.

Fearful to contemplate the possibility longer, lest he convince himself of its merit, Edward pushed himself up and staggered outside. His feet splashed through mud. Water-filled potholes sucked at his boots. Finally his shoulder slammed a tree and he pirouetted to the earth, rifle tumbling from his fingers. Down on his knees, he vomited onto the soil; once, twice. Stomach purged, throat burning with bile, he wiped his mouth with the back of his hand.

Of course she was never here, you dumb shit. Laura's dead and gone, and there was only ever one person to blame for that. You're alone in these woods. With nothing but booze-addled hallucinations to sustain you.

He sucked in a breath. Spat on the ground.

Except the woman inside his caravan *wasn't* a hallucination. He knew that much, if nothing else. He spat again. Retrieved his rifle from the soil. Stood.

Legs moving without conscious thought, he crossed the churned soil of the clearing back to the caravan. He placed a foot on its front step, took a breath. For a second or two he wondered if some dark part of him had decided to kill her after all, distracting his conscience while he closed the distance between them.

He found the woman in the same position that he'd left her, slumped on the floor with the duvet arranged around her waist. She glanced up when he reappeared, and she looked miserable.

'You goin' to shoot me?'

'No.'

'I never meant to hurt you.'

He didn't like her voice. Didn't like anything about her. As he watched, she rolled up a sleeve of her cardigan and scratched at her wrist. Her arm, as scrawny as a birch twig, was a smorgasbord of scars: needle marks, cigarette burns, length-ways slashes.

'Are you going to tell me what's happening?' he asked, the words slow and distinct. 'Because I really fucking think that you should.'

She barked a laugh. It morphed into a hiss of pain. Clutching her belly with both hands, she dropped her head and moaned.

Despite whatever trickery was at work here, Edward knew genuine pain when he heard it. However little he liked his guest, he had never been able to ignore suffering when he witnessed it. He leaned his rifle in a corner and dropped to the woman's side. 'How many weeks?'

'Wish I could remember.' She clenched her teeth, let out a breath.

'How?' he whispered. 'How did you do that?'

Edward raised his head and saw that she was watching him closely. Pain had dilated her pupils, but her eyes seemed filled with empathy nonetheless.

'It were a gift she gave me.'

'She?'

'They. Kind of a defence mechanism, I think. I don't control it. I reckon you could say it's a little bit of telepathy mixed up with somethin' cleverer . . . if you believe in that stuff.'

'I don't.'

'Well.' She shrugged. 'I was in trouble out there. You came along. Somehow I reached into your head and planted a picture of someone you'd want to protect. For a while your eyes and ears played tricks – showed you your wife instead of me. Saved my life, but gave me a bitch of a headache. Messed you up some, too.' She grinned, and he noticed that one of her teeth was missing. 'Would you have rescued me otherwise?'

'I'd have done what I could.'

'You reckon?'

He tried to ignore that. Found himself dwelling on it, even so.

'I could really do with that coffee,' she said.

He nodded. 'I want to take a look at you first.'

With that, Edward lifted back the duvet. 'Ah, goddamn,' he whispered.

CHAPTER 11

Near Devil's Kitchen, Snowdonia National Park

Below her waist, the black maternity dress was sodden. On the floor beneath her thighs, the wood shavings and sawdust were stained a dark amber with fluid.

'Your waters have broken.'

She stared down at herself. 'Is that bad?'

Edward shook his head. And then the strangeness of her question jolted him. 'You don't know what that means?'

'Not really.' She saw the surprise in his face, and looked away as if ashamed.

'Well,' he replied, 'it means your baby is coming. Nothing more.'

'I thought I was dying. That maybe—'

'You're not. Least not as far as I can tell. Are you having contractions?'

She glanced up. Averted her eyes a second time when she saw him watching. 'Do they hurt? Like, really hurt?'

He nodded.

'Then yeah . . . I reckon I must be.'

'How far apart?'

'Haven't been keeping track.'

'Just let me know when the next one hits.'

'Reckon you'll notice.' The hard lines of her face softened.

'But sure, if that's what you need.'

He had no watch on his wrist, no phone with which to measure time. An idea struck him. He opened a cupboard and rooted around inside.

Behind him the woman hissed in pain. 'Here it comes,' she said. 'Ah, shit.'

Edward found what he was looking for – a glass egg-timer imprisoned inside a scarred wooden frame. He placed it on the table. 'When the pain stops, let me know. Are you comfortable? You want to sit up here instead?'

She raised a hand, palm outwards. Teeth clenched, she waited for the contraction to pass. 'Done,' she said, exhaling in a rush. Edward upended the egg-timer. Then he helped her onto one of the alcove seats. 'You never told me your name.'

'Gráinne.'

He inclined his head.

'Problem with that?' she snapped.

'No.'

'Thought you were making coffee.'

It was a relief, in a way, to turn his back and busy himself. He wasn't used to company, certainly wasn't used to conversation – if that was what you could call these exchanges.

It made no sense. *She* made no sense: this woman who could fool him into seeing his dead wife, and whose knowledge about the basic facts of pregnancy seemed woefully incomplete. She had roused in him such a whirlwind of emotion he hardly knew how to think. He was furious at what she'd done. And yet her vulnerability compelled him. She was a wounded creature; dependent. Utterly alone.

He poured boiling water into the mugs, added sugar and stirred. There was no milk. When he turned back to the table, Gráinne's face creased.

'It's back,' she hissed. 'Ah crap, this is a bad one.'

Edward glanced at the egg-timer. A third of the sand had yet to fall. 'Two minutes apart,' he told her.

She nodded, gripped the table. The cords of her neck thickened, bowing the barbed-wire tattoo. 'Means what?'

'It means your baby's nearly here.'

At his words, her eyes grew large and scared. 'Now?'

'Soon.'

'You know what to do, Eddie? You know how to help me?'

He gazed around the caravan: at the filthy carpet, the dirty crockery, the mildew-stained walls. 'You can't have it here.'

'Why?'

'Look at this place. You need somewhere clean. Hygienic.'

'They'll be looking for me.'

'Who will?'

Gráinne's face tightened in agony. Her hands sharpened into fists. 'Sweet *fuck*, that hurts.' She panted through clenched teeth. 'Please, Eddie. You gotta have some pain killers around.'

''Fraid not.'

'How about whisky?'

For the next few hours, as the light outside died, Edward tended her. He dampened rags and mopped her brow. He helped her onto his bed and made her hot drinks that she invariably declined. He coaxed her into eating a little dry food, all the while treating her the way he would an injured bird, offering calm encouragement, soothing sounds.

He measured Gráinne's contractions, worried himself about how their frequency never seemed to increase. Once, during a lull, he went outside to the Defender and checked the time on the dashboard clock: eight twenty p.m.

Gráinne, by now, had lapsed into a state of near delirium. When the contractions came, she thrashed and clawed at the bed sheets, mumbling in a language that Edward could not understand. The phrases she spoke during those episodes seemed twisted and dark to his ear – guttural – and they frightened him very badly indeed. He paced up and down the tiny floorspace, debating with himself what he should do. The closest accident and emergency department was at Ysbyty Gwynedd, in Bangor. But she had been adamant in her plea to avoid hospitals, and after all that had happened, Edward was loath to ignore her wishes.

Half an hour later, with Gráinne screaming and writhing on the bed, her maternity dress hitched up to reveal bleached-white thighs slick with blood, he changed his mind.

On the mattress, Gráinne arched her back. '*An Toiseach*,' she moaned. '*An Toiseach. Balla-dìon!*'

She gripped the sheets and howled her agony. The sound sent a shudder through him. In tandem with Gráinne's cry, a mutter of thunder seemed to rise up from the earth. The caravan began to rock. Gently at first, and then with increasing violence. One of Edward's wood-carved animals toppled from the shelf. A cupboard door flew open. Mugs and plates slid out, smashing to pieces on the floor.

As the shaking intensified, he put out a hand to anchor himself. Outside, he could see the clods of soil churned up the previous evening begin to vibrate and break apart. His Defender shivered on its suspension. The vehicle moved in a slow arc as the ground beneath it shifted.

Gráinne slumped back on the mattress, the muscles in her jaw releasing. Immediately the shaking subsided, and the thunder rolled out into the night. Edward picked up his rifle and stepped closer to the window. Yesterday evening that same thunder had heralded the arrival of the hunters. Suddenly he knew, without any doubt, that he had to take Gráinne and Argus and get out of these woods right now.

He slipped a hand into his pocket. Fished for his keys.

There's no diesel in the tank.

Edward ground his teeth in frustration. Kicking open the caravan door, he hurried down the steps into the waiting darkness. A gust of wind slammed the door shut behind him. He reached the Defender, opened its tailgate and grabbed an empty jerrycan. As he carried it to the fuel drum he heard

Gráinne shriek with pain. An instant later something lifted him up and carried him back ten feet, slamming him against the ground and crushing the air from his lungs.

Edward tried to raise his head but a brutal wind gusted over him, pressing him flat. He heard the branches of nearby trees splintering, the gunshot cracks of severed saplings. The pressure in his ears was huge. He lay prone, eyes closed and fingers dug into the wet soil.

Then, as abruptly as the wind had arrived, it eddied out of the clearing and vanished. Rolling onto his side, spitting blood and dirt, Edward realised that his only assailant had *been* the wind, springing up from nowhere to complement Gráinne's cries. All around him lay evidence of the destruction it had wreaked: broken branches, uprooted saplings, blown needles – all spiralling outwards with the caravan at its epicentre.

Edward got up and retrieved his jerrycan from where it had landed in a patch of holly. He made five trips back and forth across the clearing, ferrying fuel to the Defender's tank. Tossing the empty can, he went back inside and lifted Grainne from the bed. She turned her face into his chest and he heard her chanting: '*For the world . . . for the world . . . get it out of me. An Toiseach! Get it out!*'

She felt cold to his touch. Like ice.

He staggered outside and picked his way across the churned earth, careful not to take a wrong step and turn an ankle. Opening the Defender's passenger door, he lifted Gráinne onto the seat.

'Argus!'

The dog did not need calling twice. It leaped into the vehicle and Edward climbed behind the wheel.

Last night the moon had offered him a guiding light. Now it sailed the heavens sheathed in cloud. Up there, the sky was a swathe of black velvet draped across the surrounding hills.

The Defender's engine woke with a roar. Edward slipped the clutch. The wheels chewed through damp soil and sodden roots, seeking purchase. At last they bit. The 4x4 lurched backwards and slewed around in a tight arc.

As Edward accelerated out of the glade he glanced into the rear-view mirror. The caravan – a sad, decaying wreck in a lonely clearing – seemed a foreign country already, certainly not the place he had called home these last three years. A moment later, as the Defender slithered around the final turn, it disappeared from sight.

CHAPTER 12

Near Devil's Kitchen, Snowdonia National Park

The Lleuad Valley Mountain Rescue Centre was a dour single-storey grey-brick building that squatted on the lower slopes of the Carneddau to the west of Capel Curig, its entrance shielded from the elements by a stout wooden porch.

The slate-tiled roof rose at a shallow angle, culminating in a chimney stack bristling with aerials and dishes. A twin garage and workshop housed its two rescue vehicles. The door of the nearest bay was rolled up halfway, the lights on inside. In the small car park Edward counted two more vehicles: a mud-splattered Mitsubishi Shogun and a pristine Mercedes C-Class.

Although he had lived as a recluse these last three years, economic necessity had forced him, on occasion, to mix with a few of the locals. Surviving on hunted meat alone had proved impossible – there was diesel to buy, propane, whisky – and while most of the time Edward preferred to sequester himself far from the world's attention, he found he still needed to look into the eyes of another human being every now and again, and hear his name spoken aloud.

Over in Betws-Y-Coed he sold wood carvings to the gift shops. He traded chickens, and the bounty from his foraging, with other smallholders: mushrooms, berries, chestnuts, whatever he could find. As a result, he knew that the Mitsubishi belonged to Terfel Williams, an LVMRA stalwart. Gruffydd Vaughn, the rescue centre's chairman, owned the Mercedes.

Edward pulled up outside and flung open the Defender's door. Immediately the wind, which had wound itself up to gale-force during the journey here, tried to slam it shut. Battling against it, he forced his way outside. Sheets of rain strafed the car park, whipped into a frenzy by the storm. He opened the passenger door and lifted Gráinne from the seat. Argus jumped down onto the tarmac.

By the time Edward reached the centre's front entrance and ducked into the porch, the deluge had soaked all three of them. Rainwater drizzled down his spine in a cold torrent; it ran into his eyes, dripped from his hair and beard. Gráinne's dress clung to her skin. She clutched him fiercely, the storm's ferocity shocking her awake, and blinked away rainwater as she stared up at him. With Argus following close behind, Edward elbowed open the door and carried her inside.

The reception hall was a functional vinyl-floored space lit by two ceiling-mounted fluorescent strips. A relief map of Snowdonia dominated one wall; hard plastic chairs lined the other. A cupboard, missing both its doors, swelled with jackets, climbing helmets and boots.

As Edward stepped inside he saw Gruffydd Vaughn appear through a doorway at the far end, holding a mug of coffee. The man – barrel-chested, with a bald head fringed by a last defence of white stubble – wore a chunky cable-knit, sleeves pushed up to reveal forearms matted with hair. A thick gold chain hung around his throat. Rings adorned most of his fingers. On his nose sat a pair of half-moon spectacles.

He slopped coffee onto the floor when he saw Edward, the woman and the dog. 'Drowned rats!' he announced. When he focused more closely on Gráinne, he added, 'Bloody 'ell, Ed. You best bring her in, quick-like. Watch your step. Floor's just been mopped.'

He shepherded Edward into the building's kitchen and living space. Inside, the air was heavy with the aroma of garlic and basil. At a refectory table in one corner sat a man and woman eating steaming bowls of Bolognese. A Pyrex dish between them contained enough leftovers to feed a starting fifteen.

Terfel Williams sat at the head of the table, upper lip hidden beneath a dispirited moustache. When he saw the newcomers, the man frowned and laid down his fork. Beside Terfel, apron still tied over her clothes, his wife, Beth, turned to face them. Her double chin bobbed, mouth forming a surprised circle. She stood quickly, shifting her weight onto thick nylon-stuffed ankles.

'Put her down here, Ed,' Gruffydd said. He tapped a throw-covered sofa with blunt-tipped fingers.

Edward complied, lowering Gráinne onto it. Her eyes, bright with pain, darted around the room. 'It's OK,' he told her. 'You're safe.'

'I said no hospitals,' she moaned. When he let go of her she tried to stand, but her strength failed her and she slumped backwards.

Beth Williams hurried over. She perched on the edge of the sofa and took Gráinne's hand. 'Oh, you poor soul,' she said. To her husband, she added: 'Don't just sit there, love. These two are soaked to their bones. Get them some towels.'

Spurred into action by his wife's words, Terfel rose and disappeared through a side door. He returned with an armful of towels, which he placed down at her side.

'OK, *bach*,' Beth said. 'I might look a little long in the tooth, but I'm a qualified nurse. I'm going to look after you.'

'I shouldn't be here,' Gráinne whispered. 'Get out, all of you. You have to leave me.'

Beth studied Gráinne's pupils. She draped a towel around the woman's shoulders, and then turned to Edward. 'What's her name?'

'Gráinne.'

'When did it start?'

'Maybe last night,' he said. 'A while, now.'

If Beth was surprised by his uncertainty, she covered it well. 'Gráinne, my love,' she said. 'I'm going to reach under your dress and take off your underwear. Is that all right with you? I need to have a quick nosy at what we're dealing with.'

Outside, tines of ice-white lightning speared the mountain. Such were the strikes' intensity that everyone except Gráinne flinched away from the window. The slopes clattered with thunder, as if a cavalcade of boulders rolled down them, intent on smashing the rescue centre to rubble.

Gráinne put her hands over her ears. She closed her eyes and wailed.

Knees popping, Beth slipped off the sofa and onto the floor. She eased her hands under Gráinne's dress and tugged down the woman's underwear.

'You'd better fill us in,' Terfel said to Edward. 'Looks like you've been busier in those woods than any of us had imagined.'

Edward didn't like the narrow-eyed look the man gave him. 'It's not mine,' he muttered.

'What isn't?'

'The baby.'

'Course it's not.'

'It isn't.'

'Why'd you bring her here, anyway?' Terfel pressed. 'Surely the obvious place would have been Bangor.'

Edward saw three sets of eyes appraising him now, and felt his cheeks colouring beneath their scrutiny. He stared at the floor, chest growing tight. He had known that coming here would lead to questions – judgements, too – but it didn't make the attention any easier to bear. As if sensing his distress, Argus padded over. The dog licked his wrist.

Gruffydd Vaughn broke the impasse, clapping a hand on Edward's back. 'Give the lad a chance, Terf. Have you seen that weather? God only knows how long the drive would have taken him. This amount of rain, roads'll be treacherous.'

Terfel sucked in a breath and blew it out. 'Well, there's no chance of the Sea King flying for her, not now. And I haven't reached Valley all night. No signal, nothing. Even the wired Internet's down.'

Beth had rolled up the hem of Gráinne's dress, and now she parted the woman's knees. 'No time anyway, Gruff, even if you notified them. This baby's not hanging around. Fetch the wheelchair, will you? She'll not give birth on your rotten old couch. We've a bed in the recovery room. Let's take her there. I'll want that Entonox tank that Tom dropped off, as well.'

To Gráinne she said, 'OK, love, I've delivered sixteen babies in my time. One of those halfway up Glyder Fawr, if you'll believe that. All healthy souls, and their mothers up and dancing within days. You're in safe hands, I promise you.'

'No,' Gráinne said. 'You don't understand. *No.*' She doubled over, clutched her belly. Screamed.

Edward winced. He wanted to go to her but here, beneath these reproachful eyes, he felt impotent. He saw Gruffydd return with a wheelchair and waited as the others helped Gráinne into it. All the while he felt like he watched the scene from afar; a witness now rather than an active participant.

No signal, nothing. Even the wired Internet's down.

Those words had loosened his insides and he couldn't forget them. Yet in this tiny space, so full of people and voices and accusations, his feet felt anchored to the floor.

They wheeled Gráinne through the comms office, unlocked the recovery room and switched on the lights. Inside, after lifting her onto an examination table, they supported her with pillows. Beth prepped the Entonox tank and handed Gráinne a mask. 'Breathe deep, love. Whenever you need it.'

Gruffydd Vaughn slipped his hand around Edward's arm and pulled him back to the doorway. 'Spill the beans then, Ed. Who's your friend?'

Edward shrugged his arm free. 'She's just been staying with me, is all.'

'No place for a pregnant woman, that,' Terfel said. 'No place for anyone with half a brain in their head.'

'Terf,' Gruffydd warned. 'Not the time.'

Gráinne clutched at the examination table's paper cover, fingers puncturing it. She ground her teeth. From between her lips came a thin squeal. 'Eddie,' she gasped. '*Eddie.*'

Grim-faced, he went to her. Strange, but the nearer he got, the less uncomfortable he felt. 'I'm here,' he said. 'I'm not going anywhere.'

She was panting now, the mask misting with her expelled breath. 'All dead . . . all . . . *dead* . . .' Clutching his hand, she whispered: 'Get them out, Eddie. You, too. Otherwise—'

Another jagged fork of lightning splintered the sky. Edward waited for its thunder to gallop rough-shod across the building's roof before he said, 'I'm not leaving you.'

'All dead, unless you get them out. *Please*, Eddie. They won't sur—'

Gráinne clenched her teeth, arching her back as another contraction hit. Every tendon in her neck tightened. '*Oh, God help me, it's*—'

Her scream, when it came, was equal parts agony and despair.

'There's no rush,' Beth said, rubbing Gráinne's legs. 'You've plenty of time, plenty of it. You don't need to . . .' She hesitated, eyes widening, and her tone suddenly changed. 'OK, forget what I said – here we go, that's good, that's great. My word, the head's already crowned. That's it, *bach*. One more push is all we need.'

Strangely, at the moment of delivery, at the very height of her pain, Gráinne fell silent. Her eyes glazed over and her body went slack; her head dropped onto the pillows and her fingers loosened their grip on Edward's hand. The only sound was the soft sucking release of her baby as it slid into Beth Williams's hands.

Outside, the wind stilled.

The rain eased. Then it stopped completely.

'Hurry, Terf,' the nurse whispered. 'Pass me a towel.'

Her husband blinked, as if coming awake from a dream. Slowly he passed his wife one from the pile.

Beth worked quickly and calmly. She cut the newborn's cord with a sterilised blade and wiped its face clean of fluids.

'A girl,' she announced softly, swaddling it tightly. 'Just adorable.' Eyes shining, she placed the bundle into Gráinne's arms and stepped away.

Edward watched mother and baby together, feeling a rawness in his throat that he hadn't expected. Gráinne hugged her daughter into the crook of her arm and gazed down into dark eyes that appeared almost indigo in hue, unworldly in their beauty.

Tears rolled down the woman's hollow cheeks. She wiped them away, her mouth moving wordlessly. Edward saw such tenderness in her expression that it seemed as if some great weight had been pressed against his chest, then lifted.

'Piper,' Gráinne murmured, and kissed the girl's head. 'We'll call you Piper.' She glanced up, studying each of the room's occupants. At last, her eyes fell on Edward. When she spoke, her voice was hoarse. 'It's all come back,' she told him. 'I remember.'

He stepped closer to the bed, angling his head to get a better look at the baby. Piper's eyes, as deep and mysterious as moon-touched lotus pools, tracked her mother's in mutual wonder. 'You remember what?' he asked.

'You shouldn't have brought me, but you weren't to know,' Gráinne said. She swallowed. A tear spilled down her cheek. 'I can't save you all. And I'm sorry about that, Eddie. Sorry about your friends. But we're almost out of time. If you go now – if you take Piper and run – I might just keep you alive long enough to get away.'

CHAPTER 13

Near Devil's Kitchen, Snowdonia National Park

Inside the recovery room, nobody moved. Everyone stared at Gráinne, digesting the woman's words.

Finally, Beth Williams opened her mouth. It was a moment before she spoke. 'Terf, perhaps you should go and put the kettle on. Make this girl some tea.'

Her husband nodded, eyes fixed on Gráinne's face. 'Yeah,' he said. 'Been a strange old night. Think we could all use a brew, not least of all me.' On his way out he gave Edward a long, measured look.

Gruffydd moved to the window. 'I should check the radio mast. Sound of that thunder, wouldn't be surprised if we took a direct hit.'

Gráinne shook her head. 'Don't go outside.'

'Why not?'

'You'll die.'

The man glanced over at Beth, and his eyebrows raised. 'OK,' he said, the word elongating on his lips.

'I'm serious.'

'Ed, where *did* you find this lass?' Gruffydd asked. But his face showed no scorn, merely curiosity.

Ignoring the man for now, Edward focused his attention on Gráinne. 'Tell me,' he said.

She swung a blood-slicked leg off the mattress, clenching her teeth at the pain it caused her.

'Oh no you don't, young lady,' Beth said. 'You're staying right where you are. In case you forgot, you just gave birth. We haven't even delivered your placenta, yet. Back you go.'

'There's no *time*.'

The nurse had been hovering on the edge of the bed, but now she pushed herself to her feet, ankles cracking. 'Nonsense and bluster, girl. I'm not having you—'

Face twisted in panic, Gráinne flung up her free hand. 'Get *back*!' she screamed.

Edward could not explain what happened next. Although he saw no contact between the two women, Beth Williams's stockinged feet flew up from beneath her and she shot backwards across the room as if launched from a catapult. Her shoulders slammed into the wall beside the window and her skull hit the plaster with the force of a hammer strike. She rebounded, eyes loose in her head, and collided with a shelving unit, toppling boxes of supplies, notebooks, files. Knees buckling, she collapsed to the floor, leaving a bright bloodstain on the wall behind her.

'What have you done?' Gruffydd cried, dropping to Beth's side. He reached out to her, then snatched back his hands as if afraid to make contact.

Gráinne swung her other leg off the examination table. She held Piper out to Edward. 'You have to take her.'

Ignoring that, he grabbed the vacant wheelchair and dragged it around. 'Get in.'

Frantic, she shook her head. 'Eddie, you have to take Piper. I can't—'

'Get *in*.'

As if sensing that he would not be dissuaded, that any argument would result in pointless delays, she lowered herself into the chair.

Outside, as if a switch had been flicked, the black night pressing against the window turned a deep and angry red.

Edward twisted towards the glass, the skin shrinking on his scalp. He could see no obvious source for the unnatural light. But its effect, inside the room, was immediate; the faces of Beth Williams and Gruffydd Vaughn shone as if with blood.

Gráinne's eyes grew large, terrified. 'Get out!' she screamed. 'Eddie, get us out!'

Edward saw Gruffydd tilt his head, as if the man were listening to something only he could hear. On the floor, Beth's jaw hinged wide and she sucked air into her lungs. The sound was like a shriek of rubber in her throat.

Until now, something about that red light had locked Edward in place, but when Gráinne cried his name a second time his paralysis disintegrated. He shoved the wheelchair out of the recovery room. Argus bounded after him.

'Lock the door!' Gráinne shrieked.

'But they—'

'*Lock* it!'

Edward wheeled around. He saw Gruffydd Vaughn still crouched on the floor beside Beth. The man wore an expression of childlike wonder, as if a revelation had struck him of profound significance. He lifted his hand towards Gráinne, but before he could speak Edward slammed the door and locked it.

When he turned back to the wheelchair he discovered that Gráinne had already climbed out.

She came at him, pressing into his hands the tiny bundle containing Piper, and he was so surprised that he took the child without protest.

'Go, both of you,' she begged him. 'Now.'

Edward tried to hand the newborn back but Gráinne retreated to one of the comms room's desks. Ripping open a drawer, she began to search through it.

From inside the recovery room came sounds of frenzied movement. Fists began to pound against the door.

Whatever Gráinne was looking for, she didn't find it. She searched the second drawer without success, dumping its contents onto the floor. Spying on the desk's surface a glass paperweight the size of a grapefruit, she snatched it up. She faced him, furious, tears cascading down her face. 'What don't you *understand*, Eddie? Take her and go! Now! Get *out* of here!'

Behind her was the doorway that led to the main reception. Through it came Terfel Williams. He wore a look of calm detachment, as if the red light seeping through the rescue centre's windows bothered him not at all. In his right hand he carried a carving knife, and as Gráinne turned towards him he plunged it into her belly up to the hilt.

She grunted, deep in her throat. When she took a step backwards the blade slid out of her with a wet sigh.

Somehow, Gráinne managed to straighten. She raised the paperweight above her head. 'Don't go home,' she hissed through gritted teeth, and it took Edward a moment to realise that her words were meant for him.

Terfel Williams, wearing a dreamy half-smile, walked forwards and stabbed Gráinne a second time. In reaction she brought the paperweight down onto his skull, using every ounce of her strength.

The blow would have felled an ordinary man, but right now Terfel seemed far from that. The paperweight opened his flesh from hairline to nose. Blood sheeted down his face like dark syrup, obscuring his features.

'Don't go to a hot*uhhhh* . . .'

As the blade sank into her again, Gráinne's words dissolved into a gasp. Terfel raised an arm and mopped blood from his face. He stared past her, and when he saw the baby in Edward's arms his eyes glittered. He pulled his knife free of the newborn's mother.

'Don't go near *anyone*,' Gráinne whispered. She swung the paperweight with savage force. It caught Terfel below the cheek, shattering bone. He staggered back, his jaw hanging loose, his mouth a mulch of broken teeth and bloodied flesh.

His fingers opened and he dropped the knife. It bounced on the floor and skittered away.

Relieved of his weapon, Terfel reached out and seized Gráinne's throat. She leaned into him, sinking her thumbs into his eyes. Locked together, they moved in an awkward circle, shoes squeaking on blood-slicked lino.

Somehow, even half-strangled, Gráinne found the energy to speak. '*Go*,' she urged Edward. '*Now.*'

He had promised himself that he would not abandon her, and now that seemed exactly what he was about to do. While he had no explanation for the horror unfolding around him, he suddenly understood one thing with dreadful clarity: those who lingered at the rescue centre, by choice or by fate, would perish. Gráinne, it seemed, had resigned herself to that, choosing to trade her life for that of her child.

If her words hadn't convinced him, the naked plea in her eyes did. Edward turned Piper's face towards his chest. The newborn could not know what was happening, but he wished to shield her from the sight of her mother's slaughter.

Gráinne's knees sagged. She collapsed to the floor, pulling Terfel down on top of her. They rolled in blood and somehow she landed on top. Her thumbs sank deeper. Terfel's jaw flapped like a broken bird.

Edward backed away. He heard the beating of fists against the recovery room door intensify. Behind him was the door to the garage. He kicked it open. Inside, lights blazed. Cradling Piper's head, he stepped through, Argus close behind. The last image Edward had of Gráinne was her face, spattered with Terfel's blood, and her eyes, blazing with determination. Then the door, fitted with an automatic closer, banged shut.

The sudden silence was shocking. Edward glanced left and right, checking the garage for movement. In each of the bays stood a white Land Rover bristling with emergency lights and equipment. When he had arrived at the rescue centre, one of the bay doors had been rolled up halfway. As he eased along the space between the vehicles, he saw that it remained open to the night.

Except that it wasn't night any more.

That unrelenting red light poured through the gap from outside, staining everything it touched. Although Edward could not see its source, some strange instinct told him that it came not from above the ground but below, leaching out of the earth itself.

He edged towards the half-closed door. On the threshold, he hesitated. For three years he'd known fear only in his dreams. In the space of a single day and night those dreams, too corrosive to be contained, had seeped into the world around him.

Piper – no more than a few minutes old, a tiny scrap of life bundled inside a woollen emergency blanket – struggled against Edward's chest. He rocked her back and forth, heard himself whisper soothing sounds.

He wasn't ready for this, wasn't suitable for it. He couldn't protect a child; he'd already proved that.

With Piper tucked into the crook of his arm, Edward raised the door fully.

A dome of blood-red light, perhaps a few hundred yards in height, soaked the slopes of the surrounding Carneddau. Beyond its hemisphere, darkness pressed. The sight woke something in him, as if, deep within the unexplored parts of his mind where ancestral memories lurked, an awareness stirred. He felt himself groping towards a revelation that was perhaps too frightening to confront.

Edward focused on his Defender, still parked outside the front porch. Twenty yards of red tarmac separated him. Behind, he had the choice of two rescue vehicles far better equipped and maintained. But he had seen their keys on a pegboard inside the comms room. There was no way he was going back there.

Argus nudged his leg. The dog stared out at the crimson night, tail curled low.

Edward searched the surrounding landscape for movement.

He saw none, neither on the mountainside itself nor in the clotted shadows sloping from the building's walls. To the dog – or perhaps to the newborn he cradled to his chest – he whispered, 'I don't know where I'm going.'

His words evaporated on a white mist of breath, twining out through the garage entrance and up into the night. Again, he searched the slopes for movement. While he knew that no chance of survival lay behind him, his prospects, out in that blood-drenched light, seemed almost as bleak.

Gráinne had begged him to leave, to take her baby and escape. Should he do as she asked, placing his faith in a woman he knew almost nothing about?

What choice do you have?

Edward had never held any great love for Terfel Williams, but the man was no murderer. Whatever compulsion had driven him to attack Gráinne had not originated inside his own head.

'I don't know where I'm going,' he said again. He looked down at Piper. She stared back at him with dark, unknowable eyes.

Taking a breath, hugging her close, Edward Schwinn crossed the threshold into the waiting night.

CHAPTER 14

Aberffraw Hall, Snowdonia National Park

They called him Eber. He sat in the back seat of the Bentley Mulsanne, a blanket of Clan Donnachaidh tartan spread across his lap. Through the security partition that separated him from the driver he saw the tail-lights of the lead car, a dark Mercedes with tinted windows. Behind them an identical vehicle followed.

His son Cameron had organised the transport. The Bentley had appeared outside Eber's rough-hewn Argyll cabin earlier that day, driving across rain-sodden peatland to collect him. Already it felt like a hundred years had passed. How little he cared for the claustrophobia of this new world. Give him glens and lochs and the simple pleasures of a warm hearth. As for travelling in such luxury – well, he would have made this journey by horseback had his old bones allowed it.

So far he had managed to conceal his involvement in the events playing out, directing the actions of those he could trust while depending on their ability to remain hidden. But although there was a need for secrecy – and what true clansman could, after all, resist the lure of that? – there were times, such as now, when one must show one's face and express solidarity.

In front, the Mercedes slowed and turned. Its headlamps swabbed the pale stonework of Aberffraw Hall's gatehouse.

Eber reached inside his coat and took out a hip flask. He unscrewed the cap, observing with displeasure how his fingers jittered and knocked. Raising the neck to his lips, he took a sip: Old Pulteney, aged for forty years. Usually he could taste every note of its heritage. Not tonight. The whisky rolled sour on his tongue and he swallowed, grimacing.

'The lights are out,' he said.

His driver raised eyes to the rear-view mirror. 'Sir?'

They passed beneath the gatehouse arch and Eber looked around him. 'She aye has this place lit up like a Christmas tree.' In a harder voice, he added: 'Someone should turn them back on.'

Although the gatehouse had been dark, lights blazed in the main residence. Behind the building's central pediment, a glass dome glowed white, an unblinking eye staring up at the heavens. Eber followed its trajectory. Overhead, the sky was robed in cloud. He could see none of the constellations that usually gave him peace. Nor, in truth, the ones that troubled him.

They passed Ériu's puzzle maze and the road swept around. Directly outside Aberffraw Hall he saw the fountain Ériu had built years earlier, along with its pale green statuary. The four enormous bronzes – a stag, a bear, a wolf, a fox – had been her idea of a joke back when they were young; one sculpt for each of the *Triallaichean*: Ériu, Eber, Orla and Drustan. Privately he had always considered them somewhat crass. Now, after his long absence, he looked upon them more kindly. His own beast was the stag. Ériu, naturally, had been the wolf.

Parked around the perimeter of the fountain's splash pool were three dark 4x4s. A few clansmen milled around them, their expressions grim. Nearby, Eber spotted his son.

Cameron Kinraid leaned against one of the building's Corinthian columns. Six foot four in height, the man was two hundred and fifty pounds of prime Argyll brawn zipped into skin that was beef-fat pale. Eber's heart swelled; in earlier times his son could have stood companion to Wallace or Bruce without shame.

As the Bentley rolled to a halt, Cameron opened the rear door and climbed in beside his father.

'Is it true?' Eber asked. 'Is she dead?'

Cameron pursed his lips, eyes red-rimmed. He opened his mouth to speak. Then he nodded.

Eber felt a tremor pass through him. 'I havenae words.'

'There *are* no words.'

With some effort, he replaced the cap on his flask. 'The one night in eight years when this shouldnae happen, and happen it does.'

'Someone betrayed her. Betrayed us all.'

'Aye, but who?' Eber raised a hand, laid it on his son's arm. 'Ye cannae answer that, so dinnae try. I want to see her.'

'Are you sure? It's . . . graphic.'

'She wouldhae fought like a wildcat, I'm sure. But I'll pay my respects. Was she successful? In what she attempted?'

'We found a room that would have served the purpose. But it looks unused.'

'Her volunteer is dead as well, I suppose.'

'If she is, we can't find her.'

Eber lurched forwards at that, heard something pop in his spine. For a moment, jaw working silently, he failed to find his voice.

'We haven't finished the search,' his son confessed. 'But if the woman's still here, she's hiding. Of the dead, none were pregnant.'

'Ye *must* find her. The consequences otherwise . . .'

Cameron nodded, but his eyes did not contain much hope.

They walked together through Aberffraw's staterooms, Eber leaning on a dog-head cane. A wandering blood slick trailed ahead of them, terminating in the banqueting hall where two of Cameron's clansmen were loading a corpse into a plastic sheet.

They continued to Ériu's library. Eber had fond memories of it. Whole evenings he had spent here in younger days, reading and arguing with Ériu, and using her telescope to monitor the heavens.

All across the floor the dead were strewn, limbs stiffening, faces grotesque. He could taste their suffering like a mould on the tongue. How must it have felt, he wondered, to experience such undoing on the brink of such triumph?

Beside a door in the east wall stood the remains of a makeshift barricade, now dismantled: a slanted desk, a collection of overturned chairs. Passing it, they entered the most private of Ériu's chambers.

Above their heads a chandelier blazed with light. Eber paused when he saw the circle of dead beneath it. His jaw clenched. 'Has anything been touched?'

'Not a thing.'

He crossed the room and stepped inside the ring of corpses. There, a black silk sheet covered a final body. Eber knelt beside it. Delicately, he lifted it away.

A minute passed. 'Help me put her on her back,' he said. With infinite care, the two men eased Ériu over until she lay with her shoulder blades pressed into the blood-sodden carpet.

For all the violence wreaked on her body, the woman's face remained mercifully untouched. In death, she seemed to Eber as fierce as she had been in life. Her eyes were open. Her expression retained a terrible intensity. With her coal-black hair and alabaster skin, she looked like a young woman in her physical prime, untroubled by time or gravity.

He wondered what would happen to her remaining followers. He had no doubt that the few who had avoided tonight's massacre would enact their revenge as soon as they knew where to focus it. But afterwards, would they melt away? Or would this tragedy bind them to Ériu's memory forever?

Eber grunted. If what she had unleashed survived the night, such questions were academic. 'To the end she was the strongest of us,' he said, placing his palm on Ériu's forehead. 'She cared nothing for her own survival. Only what she thought was right.'

'For all your bickering, you loved her very much.'

Eber's chin began to tremble. He forced it to still. 'Help me up.'

Cameron guided his father to his feet. Then he cocked his head. 'We've company.'

It was a full ten seconds before Eber heard the chop of rotor blades. 'Outside,' he said. 'I should be there tae meet her.'

By the time they emerged onto Aberffraw Hall's front steps, the helicopter was sweeping in from the mountains, a bright star trailing a flashing beacon. As it closed on the estate its light grew stronger, the sound of its blades more insistent. Cameron's team had marked out a landing grid on the lawn with smoking red flares. The helicopter, its turbine whistling, landed with a thump. A door in its black bubble flew open.

Orla emerged first. Tall and lithe, she strode across the lawn, coat flowing out behind her. Watching her, Eber thought of the fountain's statuary; thought too, of how, over the years, their paths had branched. Orla's eyes locked onto his with unblinking intensity and he straightened, feeling a familiar stirring of his blood. She climbed the steps and came to a halt in front of him, two of her retinue flanking her.

One of them, Eber saw, was Nora Kinraid, Cameron's wife; the woman kept her eyes from straying to her husband. Her face was pale, troubled. Was there something to be gleaned from that?

Probably not.

'Is it true?' Orla demanded. Her gaze flickered to the cavernous hall behind him.

Eber nodded. 'Aye.'

For a moment she stood motionless. He saw a vein flicker in her throat. Then she stepped forward and embraced him. 'Who, and how?'

'I'm still piecing that together.'

'Did she succeed? Before she died?'

'I don't know.'

'How can you not?'

Eber scowled at that, felt his anger rising. 'Because everyone is *dead*, Orla.' He paused, forced himself to breathe. When he spoke next, it was with a calmer voice. 'You'll understand better when ye go inside. The suite hadnae been used, we know that much. And none of those that died couldhae been the volunteer.'

'Then the woman might yet survive.'

'Unlikely.'

'But possible.'

He conceded that with a nod.

'If she lives long enough to give birth—'

'Then the killing wullnae end here, will it?'

Orla stared. Then she turned to Cameron. 'Show me,' she said. 'Show me everything.'

An hour later, after Orla had surveyed the carnage and kept watch for a time with Ériu, she spent thirty minutes in closed conference with her advisers – something Eber did not like at all. Afterwards, he walked with her through the residence that stood, now, as a mausoleum to their fallen sister. On the front steps, they gazed down at the fountain and its statuary. 'I'll never know why she cast ye as a fox,' he said.

'Hardly a compliment.'

'Maybe, maybe not.' Eber raised a hand to their surroundings. 'What'll happen to the place?'

'We'll have it cleared in an hour.'

'And then?'

'Ériu's story will have been impeccable. She was always a stickler for that. No doubt it'll pass into the hands of lawyers and the money will disperse into the ether. A few years from now there'll be a National Trust sign out front, families picnicking on the lawn.'

'And the truth'll be buried.'

'A lot depends on the next twenty-four hours.'

'What has she started, Orla?'

Sourly, the woman laughed. 'The beginning or the end. One of the two, perhaps both. Will you stay a while? It's been long since we talked.'

'I cannae. I need tae be home, where I can think.'

'You'll die of boredom up there if you're not careful.'

He smiled. 'A comforting thought.'

'Oh, enough with this helpless old man routine,' she snapped. 'It's as much an affectation as any other.'

'This is who I am, now.'

'No, this is who you *want* to be, for reasons I can't begin to fathom.'

Her jaw tensed momentarily. 'I don't mean to be harsh. It's just . . . seeing her like that. How can she possibly be gone?'

'Ériu knew the risks.'

'She never imagined them to come from within. We need to find that traitor, Eber.'

'Aye,' he said, eyeing her carefully. 'We do.'

While Orla went back inside to deal with the clear-up, Eber sought out his son. 'Keep me informed.'

'You're leaving?'

'Ye have things in hand.'

'I'd prefer it if you stayed.'

'Exactly why I should go.' They embraced. Into Cameron's ear, Eber whispered, 'Rest an eye on her.'

'Orla?'

'If ye notice anything, anything at all, let me know.'

'You don't think—'

Eber kissed his son's cheek. 'Of course not. But nothing's ever what it seems.'

Closing the door to Ériu's private chamber, ensuring that she had total privacy, Orla knelt at the dead woman's side. 'We're alone now,' she said. 'Just the two of us. So you can tell me. Where did you hide them?'

Ériu's sightless eyes gazed at the ceiling. In death, her face had lost a little of its warmth. Her expression was disdainful, cold.

'Secretive to the last,' Orla muttered. 'I suppose I don't blame you. But they're here, somewhere. You're the one Drustan chose.'

Inside the chamber, the only sound came from a ticking ormolu clock on the mantelpiece. Orla closed her eyes, breathed. A few moments later she blinked. 'I should have guessed. You always liked your little jokes.'

She leaned forward and placed a hand on Ériu's forehead. The woman's skin was cool, its texture like candle wax. 'I'm sorry,' she whispered, and rose to her feet.

Nora Kinraid was waiting for her in the banqueting hall. 'I've briefed the pilot,' the woman said. 'We're ready to resume the search.'

Orla nodded. 'Don't wait for me. You can co-ordinate from the air.'

'You're not coming?'

'I have things to do here.'

Nora opened her mouth to protest, then seemed to think better of it. 'We have three more helicopters in-bound. If you need me to divert one—'

'What I *need* is for you to be my eyes. Up there. Now go, Nora – please. We don't have much time.'

Alone once more, Orla opened a side door in the north wall. It revealed a narrow windowless passage, used to transport food from Aberffraw's kitchens to its banqueting table. She toggled a light switch, but either the ceiling bulbs had blown or the power to this part of the mains circuit had been cut.

From a pocket she removed a penlight torch. Activating its beam, she followed the passage for twenty yards until she arrived at another closed door. This one opened into a modern industrial kitchen. Stainless-steel worktops glimmered in the torchlight. She saw walk-in freezers, sinks and ovens, spotless fryers and griddle tops.

Orla aimed her beam and found the archway she sought, passing through it to a final door. She half expected to find this one locked, but it swung open when she tested it, revealing a flight of stairs.

She descended cautiously, eyes straining to see more than the greyish shapes her torch illuminated. Here the walls were stone, cold to the touch. Cobwebs looped from oak beams like dirty rags.

The stairs led her down to a barrel-arched chamber furnished with a table and sixteen chairs. An empty wine bottle, its label faded and brittle, stood on the table's surface. Beside it, a single glass. A spot of wine had dried inside. To Orla it looked like crusted blood.

Shivering, she passing through the chamber and into the cellar beyond. Wooden wine racks receded in straight lines past the limitations of her torch. The further she progressed through Ériu's collection, the more she felt as if she were journeying back through time. The dust lay thick; she could taste it in her throat. 'Close,' she whispered. 'I know they are. Come on, Ériu. Give me a hint.'

The cellar's far wall was in sight now, a barrier of white-washed brick. Orla frowned, placing her hand against it. Could it be false? No. That wasn't Ériu's style. Far truer to her character to hide things in plain sight.

She turned around and aimed her light back along the stacks. Somewhere, a breeze wafted.

Hidden in plain sight.

Of course.

Orla flicked off the torch. Perfect darkness rushed in. It took her eyes a full minute to adjust. Finally, she saw it. Twenty yards back down the tunnel, something glowed with a soft amber light. Pocketing the torch, she retraced her steps. She moved cautiously, stealthily, alert for any sign that she might not be alone. The silence down here had become a pressure in her ears, almost like a heartbeat.

She stopped in front of a rack, smiled. Lesser eyes than hers would have missed it. 'Clever, Ériu.'

In one of the rack's columns, four wine bottles glowed with lambent light. She gripped one by the neck. Breath catching in her throat, she pulled. The bottle popped free of its resting place with far less resistance than she had expected. The light grew immediately brighter, and she saw that the bottle she held had been cut neatly in half. Putting it aside, she reached into the cavity and felt the hard edge of a cylinder. Carefully, she removed it.

It looked a little like a mason jar, although the material was not glass. A warm energy pulsed within.

Placing the first container on the floor, she reached into the cavity and retrieved a second. Behind that she found a third and a fourth. From the racks below, she recovered many more.

Orla glanced over her shoulder.

She did not have long.

CHAPTER 15

Near Devil's Kitchen, Snowdonia National Park

Once Edward made up his mind to move, he wasted no time. Eyes scanning the deserted car park, Piper cradled to his chest, he sprinted across the tarmac towards his Defender.

The instant the red light touched his skin he felt every hair on his body stand erect, as if he raced across the surface of an immense Van de Graaff generator buried in the earth. When he made a grab for the 4x4's passenger door a blue spark jumped from his finger to the metal.

Balancing Piper with one arm, he yanked the door open, ducked his head inside and flicked on the interior light. He considered placing Piper on the passenger seat but he could see no way of securing her. Instead he scooped out an armload of rubbish from the footwell and laid her on the floor as carefully as he could.

You're abandoning the others. Gruffydd; Terfel; Beth. You made them a part of this and now you're leaving them to die.

Edward slammed the door and ran to the driver's side. Once Argus had jumped into the back, he climbed behind the wheel. He twisted the keys in the ignition, grunting with relief when the engine fired. From the footwell came a snuffling cry. Behind him, the dog whined.

Edward flicked on the Defender's full beams. They cut a

white path through the haze. He slammed the stick into reverse and blipped the accelerator as hard as he dared. The 4x4 lurched backwards, slewing around in a wide circle. He crunched into first gear, floored the pedal. The Defender barrelled out of the car park and bounced onto the road. Edward hauled at the wheel. He found second gear. Third.

Ahead lay the threshold where the red dome's perimeter met the night. Its defining edge seemed a deeper shade than the surrounding air, dense and plasma-rich. The Defender charged towards it. He wondered what would happen when they met. Would the Land Rover crumple like a paper plane? Would it – and its passengers – burst into flames?

He thought of the throttled metal carcasses from the convoy he'd discovered. Shook himself free of the thought. Accelerated.

That blood-red wall filled the windscreen. Immutable.

Edward gripped the steering wheel. Screwed up his face.

Without a whisper of resistance, the Defender punched through. Suddenly the view in front was of black mountains and crystalline sky. He filled his lungs and yelled his defiance.

The air seemed colder out here, brittle, as if he'd plunged into currents far deeper than those he'd left behind. He could think of no explanation for the rapid transition from storm to starlit calm, but he welcomed it.

In the footwell, Piper mewled. Edward shook his head. Wondered what he was going to do.

He thought of Gráinne, then; that odd, wrung-out creature who'd played tricks on his mind, wormed her way past his defences. He should hate her, despise her. And yet, incredibly, he didn't. Instead he mourned her, and that was crazy, because he hardly even knew her.

The thought returned: What *was* he going to do? He had to get Piper to a doctor, he knew that. But questions would no doubt be asked of him. Around people and their talk his thoughts grew sluggish, his behaviour suspect. He would not be able to provide the answers they would need. And what would happen once the carnage at the rescue centre was discovered? What would happen when his connection was exposed? What little effort would be made to understand the testimony of an oddball loner who carved animal figurines in exchange for whisky? Although getting Piper the care she required was his primary task, he had to be careful how he approached it. For three years now he had cared little for preserving what life remained to him, but he had no wish to add incarceration to his list of miseries.

Such concerns, of course, might be academic. After the events at his caravan and those just now at the rescue centre, the chances of surviving the night looked increasingly slim. Planning for contingencies more than a few hours ahead seemed redundant.

Edward blinked away his fatigue.

Down in the footwell, Piper kicked her legs.

They drove.

How he ended up on the shore of Llyn Tywyll, or quite why he chose the lake as a refuge, Edward would never remember. Gráinne had begged him, even as Terfel attacked her, to stay away from population centres; but as desperate as the dying woman's words had been, he hadn't stopped here merely to honour them. He had needed to pause a while, retreat from the road, bleed off a little adrenalin. Out here, with the huge bowl of sky offering a silent auditorium for his thoughts, he could function a little better, think a little clearer.

The road ran past Llyn Tywyll's southern tip, separated by a thin line of trees. Edward pulled off it, following a dirt track that wound around the lake's northern edge. The Defender's tyres lurched over boulders, bounced through ditches. He switched off the headlights and an inky darkness smothered the land, until his eyes began to adjust. Ahead he saw a clearing beside the water. Nearby, a rotting wooden rowing boat lay canted over on its side. He pulled up next to it and killed the engine.

Silence flooded in, punctuated by quiet rustles from the footwell.

Edward glanced at the rear-view mirror, but it was too dark to see Argus's reflection. He reached out, felt the dog lick his hand. 'Don't ask,' he said. 'Because I don't know.'

He climbed out, and it was only as he walked around to the tailgate that he considered his sudden calm. Whoever had been hunting Gráinne would doubtless be seeking him now, and yet a peacefulness had settled on him, a tranquillity he had not experienced for longer than he could remember.

He swung open the tailgate and the dog bounded out. Argus, too, seemed to have lost his earlier anxiety. He snuffled around in the weeds, oblivious of Edward's scrutiny.

Turning back to the Defender, Edward stripped away the tarp that covered the gear he kept stowed inside. He found his tent and pitched it close to the water's edge. He carried in blankets and sleeping bags. He set up a propane stove, filled a kettle from a plastic water bottle and set it to boil.

Piper would need milk, warmth, shelter. He could provide only two of the three. But if he boiled some water and allowed it to cool, he could at least give her that. The method of delivery he would need to figure out.

His stomach growled. He realised that neither he nor Argus had eaten in at least twenty-four hours. Rummaging through his supplies, he located a can of corned beef and keyed it open, squeezing the contents onto the grass. While the dog chomped greedily, he opened the passenger door.

Piper stared at him from the footwell, and when Edward met her eyes, a tremor of unease rolled through him. Swallowing his apprehension, he lifted her out. She turned her head towards the lake, where the moon spilled across the surface in a row of bobbing smiles.

He crouched down and slipped inside the tent, fashioning

Piper a nest from the blankets and sleeping bags. After rubbing his hands on his jeans he touched a finger to her cheek. Hot, just like her mother's skin had been.

Edward made a second trip to the Defender, retrieving his rifle and ammunition. Back inside the tent, he sat down beside Piper and hugged his knees to his chest, waiting for the kettle to whistle.

Outside, he heard a crunch of stones, and then a voice:

'Thank you, Eddie.'

CHAPTER 16

Mont Blanc, France

He had decided, far in advance of setting off from Chamonix, that if they made it to the summit they would descend via the Goûter route rather than retrace their steps. Laura had acquiesced happily enough. Her goal was to stand on top of Mont Blanc, the roof of Western Europe; she cared little for how they made their escape.

Now, *escape* felt exactly what they were attempting. The tiger stripes of dawn's first light had faded. Although the sky was as clear as leaded glass overhead, off to the north a pack of angry clouds was racing in. Edward viewed them with growing alarm. He had seen nothing in the forecast to suggest a storm.

With Laura leading the way, they trudged down Bosses Ridge, carefully placing their feet. No rock remained exposed here. They descended along a spine of hard-packed snow. The wind whipped and snatched, gleeful to harry them on such precarious ground. Climbers fell and died here all the time. In a good year the mountain might claim thirty lives, in a bad year twice that.

Already the storm-front was closing, chewing up the lower-lying clouds that strayed into its path. The landscape to the east, where the Matterhorn raised its single tooth heavenward, looked sullen and dark.

Every one of Edward's senses shrieked: *Hurry! Hurry! Hurry!*

But he did not want to rush Laura, did not want to infect

her with his fear. She seemed aware enough of the danger, regularly studying the approaching cloud mass.

Five minutes later, she fell. Nothing dramatic. She simply stopped walking and sank down on her knees. Edward forced his tired legs through the snow, nearly tripping over the rope that connected him to his wife. Over the roaring wind he shouted, 'What is it?'

Laura glanced up at him. Blood seeped from her nose. A frozen crust of it had accumulated on her upper lip. Her eyes moved independently of each other. 'Are we there?' she asked.

Edward felt his stomach shrinking away. 'I'm going to get you down,' he told her. 'I'm going to get you down right now.'

Laura nodded.

'Can you stand?'

'Yes.' She shook her head. 'No.'

Bending, he slipped his hands under her armpits, hauled her up. 'It's the altitude,' he told her. 'I'll get you down and you'll feel better. Does your head hurt?'

'Some.'

'Can you see?'

She blinked. 'The baby . . .'

'Is going to be fine. Come on. You go first. Slow and steady.'

Laura looked at him uncertainly. Finally she began to move – one short step followed with another, marked by a breath in between. 'That's it,' he said. 'That's great.'

It was anything *but* great. He needed to get her off this mountain; quickly, too. But he could not risk a traverse of the Grand Couloir in these conditions, and they would need to drop far lower than the Goûter hut before the effects of altitude sickness diminished. Edward knew well the graduated symptoms of the climber's curse. A nose bleed was one thing; Laura's apparent confusion was worse.

★ ★ ★

They walked. Laura raised her crampons, planted them. She hunched forward at the waist, as if her pack were stuffed with rocks. He saw bright splashes of blood in the snow.

The weather front was closing with ruthless speed. Edward knew, now, that they wouldn't even reach Goûter before it hit. That left the Refuge Vallot, the unmanned emergency bivouac station at the base of Bosses Ridge. At an altitude of over fourteen thousand feet, it was still far too high to offer Laura much relief. But he could phone in an emergency from there. While a helicopter rescue was unlikely in the face of the approaching weather, at least their plight would be known. If Laura's condition worsened, getting her down to the Nid d'Aigle single-handed might prove impossible. Edward had notified the Goûter hut of their planned descent. He knew that the guardian, Nicolas, would raise the alarm when they did not appear. Christophe, too, knew of their plans, and would grow worried if they failed to return to Chamonix on time.

Ahead, Laura tripped. She sprawled forward and began to slide. Edward locked his feet and raised his ice axe, ready to make an anchor if she tugged him off balance. When the rope snapped taut his crampons saved him, arresting Laura's slide.

She rolled over. Coughed up a pink froth.

'Oh, Jesus.' Sliding off his rucksack, he rooted through it for his phone. They could no longer afford to wait until Vallot.

Three bars of reception. A full battery.

Edward eased off his outer glove, shocked at how quickly his fingers began to numb. He started to dial Chamonix's *Peleton de Gendarmerie de Haute Montagne*. Then he changed his mind and called Christophe instead. His friend knew many of the rescue team socially, had even served for a year as one of their number. While the group would do its best regardless, a personal connection might just offer additional motivation for a helicopter deployment.

Christophe answered on the third ring. 'Tell me you didn't take her up.'

Edward closed his eyes. 'We're in trouble. It's bad.'

'Where are you now?'

'Bosses Ridge.'

'Laura?'

'Altitude's got her. Don't think I can get her down alone.'

'You called Chamonix?'

'About to.'

'OK. I will, too. Then I'm on my way up. Get her to the Vallot.'

'I'll try.'

'Don't try, Eddie. Do it. You'll freeze up there otherwise. Have you seen what's coming?'

'I'm staring down its throat. Will they get the chopper up?'

'Can't say. This one took everyone by surprise.'

Edward considered the man's words. 'Do what you can.'

'Get her to Vallot,' Christophe repeated.

It took him five attempts to dial Chamonix; he could no longer feel his fingers on the phone's screen. He described his location and Laura's condition, then shoved the phone into a pocket. With some effort, he pulled on his outer glove.

Tell me you didn't take her up.

He shook his head, trying to clear it. Laid a hand on his wife's shoulder. 'Laura.'

She sat up. Stared at him. There was something not quite right about her expression. He raised her goggles and felt his world begin to unravel. Her left eye was dark with a retinal haemorrhage. 'I'm going to get you down, OK? I'm going to get you down.'

'Can't walk.'

'Doesn't matter. I'm going to get you down.'

'Scared.'

'We're leaving.'

Edward stripped off Laura's pack, cast it aside along with his own. He paid out some slack from the rope that connected

them and picked up her ice axe. Climbing to his feet, he began
to tow her through the snow.

He made it ten yards before Laura sank into a deep drift,
her body an anchor on the rope. Edward turned back and
dug her out. She tried to stand, collapsed onto her front. He
rolled her over so that her face was clear of the snow. Then
he pressed on, the teeth of his crampons biting deep. He
descended another five yards before Laura snagged again. This
time, when he went back for her, her eyes were closed.

'Hey!' he shouted, slapping her face.

Laura flinched, fluttered blood-darkened eyes. 'Burning,'
she told him. 'Burning up.' Before he could stop her she
stripped off her gloves and tossed them into the snow. She
began to fumble with her jacket zip.

Edward fought her. He seized her wrists, pinned them with
one hand. With the other he tried to reach her discarded
gloves. 'Don't do this.'

'Get off me.'

'You're hypothermic.'

'No.'

'*Listen*,' he pleaded. 'Please, Laura. I love you too much for
this. You're hypothermic and you have altitude sickness, too.
We need to keep you warm, get you down off this mountain. I
can do it, I think, but not if you fight me. Fight me and we die,
Laura. All three of us.'

Her hands moved reflexively to her stomach. Her eyes grew
large. 'Home.'

'Yeah. That's what we'll do. We'll go home.'

'Can't move.'

'Just keep your head out of the snow. Stay awake.'

She nodded.

Edward pushed himself to his feet. He wanted to lift her
over his shoulder, but this part of the ridge was precarious; he
couldn't afford a misstep. Instead he began to tow her again. He
made it twenty yards before he needed a break. When he

looked behind him she was lying on her front with her head buried.

Edward trudged back up the slope and rolled her over. Laura's eyes were closed. This time, whatever he tried, he could not rouse her. He checked her airways, positioned her on her side. There was a danger, now, that hypothermia might kill her before the effects of altitude did.

Climbers attempting a summit of Mont Blanc rarely packed tents, but Edward always carried an emergency bivvy bag. He reached for the straps of his rucksack, ready to peel it off, and remembered he had discarded it further up the slope. He screamed into the wind.

As if to mock him, the first snowflakes began to spiral from the sky. Below, the ridgeline had faded to a white haze. Legs leaden with fatigue, Edward retraced his steps to the place where he'd abandoned the rucksacks. The cold burned in his cheeks, his teeth, his throat. He fell once, and would have slipped over the edge if not for an ice axe anchor that barely found purchase. He found the bivvy bag stowed in a side pocket of his rucksack. It took him a minute to climb back down to Laura.

On hands and knees he unrolled the bag and manhandled Laura into it. He climbed in beside her and zipped it over their heads.

The relief was immediate. While the wind still ripped and clawed, it no longer stripped their skin of heat. Edward switched on his head torch and pulled Laura close.

She wasn't breathing.

His mobile phone started ringing.

For a moment he lay rigid, too stunned to react. His phone continued to trill, amplified by the bag's foil lining. Laura's face lay inches from his own. Her lips were blue. Purple capillaries traced contour lines across her face.

Edward exploded into movement. He couldn't operate freely inside the bag so he burrowed back out. He lifted his wife's neck, opened her airways. Stripping off his gloves he pushed a finger into her mouth and checked the position of her tongue. Then he bent over her and started CPR.

Two quick breaths to inflate Laura's lungs. Thirty compressions of her chest. Repeat.

'Going home,' he muttered, and found he couldn't stop. 'Going home. Going home.' He chanted in time with his compressions, wondering if he should unzip his wife's jacket and press his hands directly over her heart.

Two breaths. Thirty depressions.

The skies darkened. Snowflakes lashed his cheeks. Far off he thought he heard the sound of helicopter rotors. For a while they seemed to grow close. Then they receded.

Two breaths. Thirty depressions.

She had such a magnificent heart. How could it possibly fail? He had seen first-hand how strong she was, how unbreakable. When his eyes wandered to her belly something flickered, lizard-quick, inside his head.

Two breaths. Thirty depressions.

His phone rang again. Hard metallic sounds. Had he left it in the bivvy bag? He couldn't see it.

Laura coughed. Gasped.

Edward was too exhausted to do anything except crouch over her, but he forced himself to act, manoeuvring her back inside the bag. 'Stay awake, now,' he told her.

She closed her eyes. 'Are we home?'

'Soon.'

'I dreamed. I dreamed you were all alone. All alone, standing on a mountain road.'

'Just a dream. Nothing more.'

'You looked lonely. So much older. Oh, Eddie, I'm sorry.'

'No need for that.'

She sobbed. 'Yes. All my fault.'

He laughed, a hard clacking in his throat. 'What a thing to say. If this is anyone's fault it's mine. But we don't need to think like that. We're going to get through this.'

She nodded. Closed her eyes. 'Keep talking.'

So he did. With his arms holding her close, with the snow cushioning them both, he took her back to the time they first met.

It was summer in Chamonix. He was down at Denny's bar with Christophe on a rare night out. The business was in its infancy and money, as always, was tight. Queuing for drinks, Edward noticed a party of women in one of the booths. Straws in their mouths, they were working on a large, ice-filled margarita bowl in the centre of the table. One of the girls raised her eyes to him.

Denny's was heaving, a regular Friday night, and it took him a while to get served. So long, in fact, that soon the girl from the booth was standing beside him. She cast a glance back at her friends. 'Not a good look, I'll admit.'

'What's the occasion?'

'See the girl in the red dress? She's getting married next month. Decided to bankrupt us all first.'

'Hen party.'

'Ugh,' she said. 'I hate that phrase.'

His drinks came, then. The worst possible timing. The girl gave him a lopsided grin and turned away.

That should have been that. But fate chose to intervene. Edward had been supplementing his income with shifts at Pierre's Mountain Outfitters in town. The girl came in the next day, looking for boots.

'I'm not stalking you,' she told him.

He nodded his head towards the stacks. 'See anything you like?'

'Not sure, yet.'

'You shouldn't go climbing in brand-new boots.'

'Wow,' she replied. 'That's some sales patter you've developed.'

'New boots'll take a while to wear in, that's all I meant.' He gazed at the floor, too uncomfortable to look elsewhere. And that was when he noticed. 'What's wrong with the boots you're wearing?'

The girl glanced down. 'These?' Two spots of colour appeared on her cheeks. She wrinkled her nose. 'Busted.'

'I'm Edward,' he said.

'Laura. Know a funny thing?'

'What's that?'

'This might just work.'

And it had. She flew back to London and three weeks later reappeared outside his door with a rucksack, fifty euros and an expression halfway between fear and euphoria. 'Will you sell me a pair of boots?' she asked.

'For fifty euros?'

'I know it's not much.'

'We'll figure something out.'

'That's what I was hoping.'

Back in London, Laura had been training as a nurse. She completed her course in France and started work in Chamonix. Within a few months, they married. They bought a tiny apartment, filled it with second-hand furniture and wondered if life could get any better. When Laura fell pregnant two years later they discovered that yes, in fact, it could.

Christophe was the first of the rescuers to reach them. He had talked his way onto the helicopter that lifted off from Chamonix. The wind had been too strong to allow a winch rescue so the pilot had been forced to retreat, dropping the team just above Goûter. The first Edward knew of it was when his bivvy bag unzipped and a racing wind inflated it.

'*Oy veh,*' muttered a voice, and Edward recognised it instantly. He blinked, and saw the Frenchman staring down at him. Frost rimed Christophe's beard, and ice crystals clung to the hairs inside his nostrils. This close, Edward could smell the stale musk of Gauloises-Blondes cigarette smoke. He tried to speak, tried to communicate his gratitude and his shame, but the words would not come.

Christophe reached past him, raised one of Laura's eyelids and nodded to himself.

'Is she?' Edward managed to ask.

'She's fine. We're going to get you back down. Put a hot cup of tea inside you both.'

He began to cry. For a while the world went dark. It took the rescue team two hours to bring them down to a sheltered spot from which the helicopter could complete their evacuation.

They told him the truth of what had happened an hour later, after he drifted back to consciousness in Chamonix Hospital. He had suffered frostbite in his right hand and in both feet, none severe enough to require amputation. Laura had not been so lucky. She lay on a gurney in another part of the hospital. To where, in death, her spirit had fled, no one could say.

CHAPTER 17

Near Devil's Kitchen, Snowdonia National Park

The rifle was already loaded, so Edward only needed to snatch it up and thumb off the safety. Inside the tent he was at a disadvantage so he scrambled through the flaps, swinging the gun left and right.

Although the voice had been Gráinne's, he had seen the injuries she had sustained: no one could have survived that. Even if survival *had* been possible, it would have required prolonged medical intervention.

Yet what was one more impossibility in a night filled with them? When Gráinne stepped out from behind the Defender, barefoot, he trained the rifle on her in a half-hearted way at best.

In the moonlight her face was paper-white, her lips blue-tinged. Edward had never seen someone look so weary, so sad. The front of her dress glistened with blood, sliced to tatters where Terfel Williams's knife had done its work.

'I saw,' he murmured, only half aware of his words. 'I saw what he did.'

Haltingly, as if she waded through mud, Gráinne closed the distance between them. 'I told you no hospitals. Guess I should have told you no people.'

'You can't be here.'

She stopped in front of him. 'Yet here I am.'

'How?'

'Walked.'

'That's not what I meant.' Edward pointed his rifle at her belly. 'Show me.'

Gráinne raised her eyebrows. 'Little forward, don't you think?' Her lips spread tight but he saw what effort it cost her. He wondered whether the humour was for his sake or hers. After a moment's hesitation, her hands moved to the belt of her maternity dress and untied it. The garment slithered off her shoulders, pooling at her feet.

The moon daubed her nakedness with its ivory light, and Edward gasped at what it revealed. Around her torso, and each of her limbs, coiled tattooed vines in lush and verdant shades. The effect was extraordinary – both hypnotic and strangely beautiful, making it appear that she had stood with her feet planted in the soil for so long that nature had begun to reclaim her.

Yet however exotic the mural, underneath it Gráinne's body looked wasted. Her muscles and tendons were like taut ropes stretched across bone. What reserves of fat she retained from her pregnancy sagged around her belly in a distended apron.

Terfel's knife had brutalised her. While the moonlight wasn't sufficient to illuminate the damage clearly, Edward could see the uneven edges of her wounds, and the dark glimmer of organs beneath. An oozing blackness seeped down the inside of one leg.

This time, when Gráinne tried to smile, she only managed a grimace. 'Kind of a rough day for me.'

Edward shook his head, as if by that simple movement he could rid himself of his confusion. 'You died,' he said. 'Back there, you died.'

'Yeah. Guess I did. Had to keep going, though – put a little more juice in the tank, just for a while. Needed to talk to you.'

'Keep going how?'

'Wasn't that hard. Not now I've remembered everything. Hurts like hell, though, which is why I need to get this over with quick. You got something to drink? I don't mean coffee.'

Edward stared, as bewildered at his acceptance of her as he was by her arrival. He slung the rifle over his shoulder and dropped to his knees. Averting his eyes from her nakedness, he scooped up the dress and wrapped her in it, retying the belt as loosely as he could. Then he opened the Defender's passenger door and helped her onto the seat. He had expected her flesh to be cold, but it wasn't. She radiated a feverish heat.

From the door cavity he took out a hip flask and passed it to her. Gráinne took a long swallow, wiping her mouth on her sleeve. Moments later he smelled whisky – and something far sourer – rising from her lap. He tried to close his mind to that.

Gráinne stared out across the water, eyes tracing the moon-touched mountains beyond. 'It's a beautiful world, isn't it, Eddie?'

'You're asking the wrong guy.'

His reply seemed to surprise her. She turned from the view, studied him. For a while neither of them spoke. Then she added, 'Seems kind of cruel, don't you think? To only notice it now, I mean. At the end.'

'Cruel's a better word for this world than beautiful.'

'You don't believe that.'

'Yeah. I do.'

She took another swig from the flask, settled back in the seat. 'Will you fetch her for me? I'd like to feed her if I can. Just this once.'

Edward took a breath, nodded. Retreating to the tent, he fetched Piper from her nest of blankets and lowered her into her mother's arms as gently as he could. When Gráinne smiled, Edward felt a pressure in his throat that surprised him. He watched as she pulled open her dress and guided Piper to her breast. The child needed no encouragement to latch on.

Gráinne closed her eyes, laid back her head. 'I don't have

long, so listen as carefully as you can. After we're finished here, you're going to have a dead body on your hands. I know it's an imposition, Eddie, but you'll have to deal with that, get rid of it. I don't want to come back again. Next time . . . it wouldn't be me.'

His jaw tightened. Pointless to consider the insanity of her words. 'What do you want me to do?'

'Had my heart set on a horse-drawn cortege.' Gráinne laughed, and her eyes opened. 'Sorry. I'm not making this easy.' She stared down at her daughter and her chest heaved, and Edward thought he knew why she joked, even now; especially now. 'She's no ordinary girl, Eddie. But she's going to need protection, and it has to be you. I know you've probably been sat here trying to figure out a way to give her up, but you can't do that. For the sake of everyone you've ever loved, you have to keep her safe.'

'Everyone I've ever loved is dead.'

'Well,' Gráinne replied, 'I'm afraid that's just tough shit.'

'I can't just—'

'You've no fucking *choice*.' She arched her spine, hissed. A few seconds later she slumped back in the seat. In a quieter voice, but one that was no less determined, she added, 'There's too much at stake here for you to just opt out. She chose *you*, Eddie. Or at least someone did. You'd better get used to it.'

Shamed by the pain he had caused her, Edward raised his hands. The irony was, he already knew his destiny lay with the child's, however implausible that might appear. Voicing an objection that he did not feel seemed like a betrayal, a dereliction of duty.

'I don't know what happened to you,' Gráinne said. 'I'm guessing it was something pretty bad. But that's done. This is what you have now. You need to listen.'

'I am.'

'Good. Because if you fail at this, Piper dies. And if *she* dies, *everyone* dies, do you understand me? Everyone on this beautiful, fucked-up planet of ours is toast. I can't make it any plainer. Those are the stakes.' She stared at him, eyes so focused that they could have burned holes through his skull. 'You're going to have to get moving, and *keep* moving, starting from the moment I stop talking. No more than a year in the same place, six months if you can manage it. And I don't mean same house or same town. Put an ocean behind you. Same goes for your names, your identities – don't carry them with you. You'll have to get pretty smart about that, too.

'Watch her closely. The moment you see her do something odd – or unexplained – get out of wherever you are straight away. Until she's learned how to control it she'll be vulnerable. You both will. But if she *doesn't* learn to control it, if bad stuff starts—'

'Control what? What are you talking about?'

Gráinne ignored him. She began to talk even faster. Her words slurred, merged. 'If she figures things out, she'll tell you what she needs. Listen to her, OK? What else, what else? People will be drawn to her. They'll likely just show up. Some will be genuine, there to offer help, but not everyone. Keep your guard up, at all times.'

Edward reached out and touched Piper's head, felt the delicate warmth of her skin through his fingertips. Thought he felt something else, too; something that made his insides slippery with foreboding. 'Who is she?' he asked. 'Why's she so important?'

'She's the one, Eddie.' Gráinne's pupils had dilated so far that her eyes, as she stared at him, looked like pools of black ink. 'She's going to redeem us.' Her face contorted. She sobbed, a harrowing sound. 'Ah shit, I'm losing it. I can't even see you.'

Edward gripped her hand. 'I'm right here.'

'I thought I'd have longer,' Gráinne said, tears sliding down her face. 'I wanted to tell you some stuff about me, things you could share when she's older. Now there's no time.'

'Plenty of time.'

She shook her head. 'No, this is it. I can tell.' The tendons in her neck thickened. Her fingers tightened around his hand. 'Never thought I'd be this frightened.'

'Don't be.'

Gráinne panted through gritted teeth. 'Says you.'

'I'm going to look after your daughter.'

She nodded. Swallowed. 'Better take her, then. I can't die with her in my lap. Wouldn't be right.' Her chin trembled as he lifted her baby away. 'Let me kiss her.'

Edward held Piper out, watching as Gráinne pressed her lips to the child's cheek.

'Eddie?'

'I'm still here.'

'Will you kiss me?'

Earlier that day, the thought would have repulsed him. No longer. He bent and kissed Gráinne's mouth. Her lips were hot, her breath musty and dark.

'I'm not a good man,' he said, and wondered why he sought to tell her such a thing now.

'You can change,' she murmured. The breath went out of her. It spiralled from her mouth, twisting up towards the heavens like a ghost. She didn't take another.

Edward cradled Piper against his chest. He gazed down at her: less than an hour old, with the only drops of mother's milk she'd receive in this life warming her belly. Piper's eyes captured the night and reflected it back at him.

She's the one, Eddie.

She's going to redeem us.

Could he do this? The very idea seemed ludicrous. For three years he had lived a subsistence existence, barely able to support his own basic needs. What little money he had earned he had poured straight down his throat.

It took him less than five minutes to pack up the tent and stove. He remade the nest of blankets in the Defender's footwell and laid Piper amongst them. It wasn't ideal. But until he could organise something more permanent it would have to do. Argus padded over and nuzzled his leg. Edward scratched the dog behind its ears. Around them the night was cathedral-quiet.

With utmost care, he lifted Gráinne from the passenger seat. He carried her to the abandoned rowing boat and lowered her into it. The vessel was holed and rotten. Out on the water it wouldn't last long.

With his knife he cut off a scrap of Piper's blanket and tucked it into Gráinne's hand. He brushed the hair away from her face.

Her eyes were open. He closed them. 'Peace,' he said. 'Wherever you've gone.'

From the Defender's jerrycan, he shook over her what fuel remained.

I don't want to come back again. Next time . . . it wouldn't be me.

He thought of Terfel Williams – the way the man had smiled as he plunged the knife into her. He recalled the sound of Gruffydd Vaughn raining frenzied blows upon the recovery room's locked door

From his pocket, Edward removed a box of windproof matches. Placing a boot against the boat's transom, he shoved it out into the water. He struck a match and tossed it in.

Fire bloomed. The lake glittered with rubies. Gráinne sailed out into its midst, her silhouetted face angled towards the stars.

Edward turned his back. He climbed into the Defender, started the engine and drove back along the track to the main road.

It was the 1st of November. A date he would need to remember.

Piper's birthday.

PART II

Seven years later

CHAPTER 18

Stallockmore, County Mayo, Ireland

The grandfather clock in Old Man McAllister's hall showed half past two in the morning but to Edward, eyes scratchy from exhaustion, it could have been any time of day or night.

On a console table near the front door, where the farmer kept his keys and his mail, stood an Easter card intricately coloured by Piper. Around here, Easter meant lambing, with all the sleep deprivation that it entailed.

In the sheds outside, Stallockmore Farm's twelve hundred Suffolk ewes were pregnant with nearly double that number of lambs. McAllister had sought his bed around midnight, leaving Edward to manage alone until dawn.

In truth it was work enough for four, but McAllister could stretch a teabag to five cups; prising enough coins from the old miser's fists to cover additional labour had been an impossible task. While the man provided lodgings for Edward and Piper in the farmhouse itself, the building's poor heating and insulation meant it was scant comfort.

In the kitchen, Edward shrugged on a waxed jacket and grabbed a torch. He stepped into his boots and let himself out through the back door. Immediately a salt wind whipped his hair flat against his head. McAllister's land rolled right up to the edge of the sea cliffs that faced north into the Atlantic. The weather, even this side of winter, was harsh and unrelenting; during the fiercest gales the spray lifted high over those towering defences to lash the skin.

Tonight the sky was cloudless, the moon a bitten crescent. Except for a platinum rash of stars, the only light came from the nearest lambing shed. Edward pulled up his collar and trudged across the mud-streaked courtyard to reach it.

Inside, the Suffolks seemed subdued, milling around beneath the strip lights in relative quiet. The sound of the wind was muted within these stone walls but it tugged insistently at the corrugated iron roof.

Edward slipped over the bars of the main enclosure. He went to the lambing pens first, checking on the new mothers and their offspring. He saw nothing there to concern him, no signs of hunger, hypothermia or illness. Wading back through the ewes, he hunted for any that had separated themselves or were lying down. The air was thick with the stench of livestock but it didn't bother him; he found its richness calming. At the back of the shed he discovered what he'd been looking for, and had hoped not to find.

The ewe was in labour, and quite obviously distressed. She lay on her side, head canted back, her bleats thin and high-pitched. The straw near her hind legs was thick with blood and mucus. A newborn lamb lay there, unmoving. Edward crouched and saw immediately that the creature was dead. Its head was grossly malformed, a knobbly excrescence of bone far too large for its frail body. How much damage that head had caused its mother remained to be seen.

Offering soothing sounds, he pulled back the ewe's lips and counted her teeth: a yearling, still growing. When he knelt at her side and pressed his hands to her flank, he thought he felt two more lambs inside. She was exhausted already, and he knew he would have to assist her if the remaining offspring stood any chance of being delivered alive. From a shelf he grabbed a pair of veterinarian's sleeves and slipped them on, lubing them with the contents of a squeeze bottle.

A closer inspection showed that the ewe's condition was worse than he had thought. Edward made a wedge of his fingers and pressed his hand inside her. Immediately he touched a lamb's nose. Moving his fingers, he found one foreleg, then two. When they kicked against him he breathed a sigh of relief. Two hours had passed since he'd last been out to the sheds – this could have been going on for some time. His priority now was a quick delivery, as free of trauma as possible.

He tried to drag the lamb out but its head was as large as its dead sibling's; he felt it lodge tight inside the birth canal. The ewe's legs scissored and she squealed in agony. Edward braced his knee against her hind leg and tried again, pulling with all his strength. This time the lamb's head burst free. The body followed, slipping out in a dark torrent of blood.

Shuddering, the ewe vomited onto the straw, too weak even to lift her head. The newborn struggled up on its forelegs and shook its head, dripping birth fluids and blood. Edward knew he needed to towel it dry as quickly as possible, but first he needed to assist the last lamb.

The mother was barely conscious now, making little effort to expel. He was fairly sure he was going to lose her. When he pushed his hand back inside he felt a ropey mass of intestines pressing through a rupture in her uterus. Gritting his teeth, he groped around until he found one of the lamb's bony forelegs, then the other. He couldn't locate its head.

Edward felt as carefully as he could, mindful of the blood that flowed passed his wrist every time he moved. When at last he found what he was searching for his heart quickened in dismay. The lamb's skull was huge: a grotesquely swollen eruption of bone. He could foresee no way of delivering the animal naturally; its head and legs would not emerge without ripping the ewe apart.

Checking for life-signs, he pinched the creature's toes; he placed a finger in its mouth, testing for a suckle reflex; he applied pressure to its eye. Nothing. All his instincts told him that the lamb was dead. His priority, now, was to ease the ewe's suffering. A Caesarean birth would require a vet; and the shock of the procedure after such a difficult labour would likely kill her anyway. He'd known farmers to saw the heads off stillborn lambs to help the mother deliver the carcass, but he couldn't even work the head free of her womb to enable a decapitation.

The ewe, perhaps mercifully, decided her own fate a few moments later. As Edward debated whether to raise McAllister from his bed, she sucked in a last lungful of air before her chest deflated and stilled.

Sighing, Edward stripped off his gloves. Every farm expected to lose animals during the birthing season, but this particular loss had been graphic, visceral, distressing to witness. He patted the dead ewe's flank, muttered an apology.

Behind her, the surviving newborn was wandering aimlessly. Fearing that it would stumble into the flock and get trampled, Edward picked it up and cradled it to his chest. It shivered against him, cold to the touch.

'They died.'

Flinching, he wheeled around. Piper stood behind him, her hair sleep-tousled, her face pale. She wore a grimy quilted jacket over her pyjamas, and pink wellies on her feet.

'Damn it, Pie, what're you doing?'

'I heard her crying. It woke me up.'

Edward stared. No way she could have heard any such thing from the farmhouse. No way, either, that she should be out here in the middle of night. He noticed the haunted look she wore, the wet tracks of tears on her cheeks. 'How long have you been standing there?'

'The mother's dead. Isn't she?'

He hesitated. Nodded.

'There's one still inside her.'

Edward nodded again.

'It's dead too.'

He blew air out through his cheeks. Conversations with Piper often took unexpected turns. The surviving lamb squirmed against him. 'But this one made it,' he said. 'Against the odds, too.'

'Can I help you with him?'

'It's late.'

'Please, Dad.'

Edward scrunched up his eyes, tried to fight the growing throb of a headache. He felt too exhausted to argue. Instead he fetched a blanket and handed it to the girl. They sat together on a hay bale while Piper wiped the newborn down. Edward studied the lamb as she worked: oversized head like its siblings, wasted body, few reserves of fat. With the mother dead, its chances were bleak. On the subject of orphans, McAllister was characteristically ruthless. Powdered milk was expensive and bottle-feeding was time-inefficient. Economically, it made no sense to persevere with a struggling lamb.

But to hell with McAllister right now. While the old man slept on in oblivion, Piper was here in the lambing shed, pale from the trauma of what she had witnessed.

Knowing that he stored up trouble, doing it anyway, Edward hurried across the courtyard to the farmhouse. In the kitchen he made up a syringe of warm colostrum from the tub of formula McAllister kept there – a sample from a visiting vet. He returned to the shed and knelt at Piper's side. The lamb looked too weak to suckle, so he pushed a feeding tube through its mouth and down into its stomach. Attaching the syringe, he handed it to his daughter. 'Slowly, now. Nice and easy.'

Tongue caught between her teeth, Piper depressed the plunger, gradually filling the newborn's belly. The colostrum would help, but the vet's sample tub would not last long.

More trouble. Still, Piper was smiling now, at least.

She wiped her face clean of tears. 'Disney.'

'What?'

'Disney. That's going to be his name.'

Edward frowned, shook his head. 'You know that's not a good idea.'

'Just this once.'

'Pie,' he said gently. 'He might not even live till morning.'

'He will,' she replied. Her smile widened. 'I know it.'

It was an hour before Edward could coax his daughter back into bed. He left Disney in an empty pen while he attended to her. When he returned to the shed ten minutes later, the orphan was still alive. First test passed.

Edward picked him up and carried him to another pen, this one occupied by a ewe and her lamb delivered earlier that day. He lowered Disney into the stall and rubbed him against the other newborn's fleece. It was a half-chance at best, and whatever gods were watching seemed unimpressed. Every time Disney approached the ewe, she turned and butted him away. Edward tried to intervene, without success. Finally accepting defeat, he lifted Disney out and checked his wristwatch: four a.m. He made up a second syringe of colostrum and used the feeding tube to supply it.

At six a.m., as he was administering a third dose, McAllister clumped into the shed. The farmer looked dishevelled, sour from lack of sleep. His mood didn't improve when he saw Edward with the lamb. His eyebrows knitted together, a single scrambled hedgerow, and he spat on the ground. 'What's gone on?'

Edward explained.

'You deal with the dead 'uns?' the old man asked.

'Not yet.'

Standard disposal for deadstock on McAllister's farm involved hurling the carcasses from the cliffs into the waiting sea. The farmer fetched a wheelbarrow, wrestled the dead ewe into it and tossed her stillborn lamb on top. Grunting with effort, he steered out of the shed. Five minutes later he returned with an empty barrow. He stared at Disney, then thrust his chin towards the lambing pens. 'You tried pairing it?'

'Thought I'd give him this first,' Edward lied.

'Can't afford formula.' Again, McAllister spat on the ground. 'And it's not worth the effort.'

'I know that.'

'So let me have it.'

Edward lifted his head. 'This should see him through for a few hours. I'll grab some sleep, come back, try him with one of the ewes. Let's hold off till then.'

The farmer regarded him, his eyes lizard-cold. 'You do it on your own time, not mine. This in't a petting zoo.'

Edward glanced at the blood-streaked barrow. 'No shit.'

'You say?'

'I said deal.'

McAllister nodded. 'Two hours. And that powder comes out of your pay.'

Mrs Dougherty would arrive at eight o'clock to home-school Piper, which gave Edward perhaps an hour's rest before he had to make the girl's breakfast. He looked in on her before finding his bed. Her eyes flickered behind their lids, her brow creased in sleep.

I heard them crying, she had told him in the lambing shed. Edward went to her window and eased aside the curtain. Piper's room looked over an ill-kept vegetable garden at the back of the house. From here he could not even see the lambing sheds, let alone hear the sheep. But the girl had been adamant.

He woke her an hour later. Downstairs, he cooked breakfast while he waited for her to get dressed, and stoked the kitchen fire with logs. McAllister would likely notice the woodsmoke, but Edward had no time for the old man's temper this morning. After weeks of tending the ewes at all hours of day and night, his tolerance was starting to thin.

He stirred a pan of porridge on the stove, removing it from

the heat when Piper trudged through the door. He spooned the cooked oats into a bowl and put it down in front of her. 'Eat up.'

She eased the lid off a tin of Lyle's syrup and dipped her spoon inside. 'How's Disney?'

'I told you not to call it that,' he snapped.

'*Him*, Dad. Disney's a boy.'

Edward stared, trying to sustain an irritation he did not really feel. 'I'll give him another feed after breakfast,' he said. 'Then we'll see.'

Piper grinned. Edward sighed and shook his head.

Twenty minutes later he was back in the sheds with McAllister. During his absence, one of the ewes had given birth to a pair of healthy lambs. Already the farmer had put them in their own pen. Disney stood alone in the furthest stall, and he didn't look good. His eyes were fixed on the ground. He shivered relentlessly.

Feeling the old man's stare, Edward made up a bottle of formula using water as hot as he dared. He eschewed the feeding tube this time. Instead, he picked up the orphan, tucked him inside his coat and proffered the teat. Hungrily, Disney latched on.

'That's it, boy,' Edward whispered. 'That's it.'

Once the bottle was empty he tried to introduce another surrogate, again without success. After that he worked with McAllister until noon. Just before he left to relieve Mrs Dougherty he gave Disney another bottle. The lamb seemed fractionally stronger this time, and was no longer shivering.

Back in the farmhouse Edward made Piper lunch, then dragged himself upstairs to catch another hour's sleep.

He woke twenty minutes later to screams.

CHAPTER 19

Stallockmore, County Mayo, Ireland

The cries, Edward knew instantly, were Piper's. They came from outside. He rolled out of bed, dragged on his jeans and thundered down the stairs. At the back door he pulled on boots and ran outside.

In the distance he saw McAllister limping down the grass slope towards the lambing sheds. A gust of wind, twisting over the sea cliffs, caught the old man and spun him.

Edward sprinted across the courtyard, his stomach plummeting as Piper screamed again. It gave him a location, at least – behind the nearest shed, where he had spent most of the previous evening. He skidded around the corner and saw the girl on her knees in the mud. Tears streamed from her eyes.

Edward raced up behind her, slowing to a stop when he realised she was unhurt. 'Ah, goddamn him.'

Disney lay stretched out on the cobbles. The lamb was dead, killed by a blow to the top of its skull that had left a depression the diameter and depth of a wine cork. Close by Edward spotted a bloodied hammer, McAllister's weapon of choice when it came to the efficient dispatch of orphans.

'He would have *lived*!' Piper screamed.

Edward crouched beside her, placed his hand on her back. She shrugged him off. When she faced him her eyes were dark, her expression so rage-filled that he drew back from her.

Above their heads the sky was a grey torrent. A savage wind tore down the slope from the sea cliffs, blasting them with spray and flattening the surrounding grass.

'Pie,' he cautioned.

Her focus changed and her nostrils flared. Edward turned to see McAllister standing behind them, and rose to his feet.

For all his bloodlessness, the old man had always thawed a little around the girl. Now, though, McAllister's face hardened, defiant. His raisin eyes moved from Piper to the carcass. He spat into the wind. 'This is a farm. Livestock die.'

Piper's chest rose and fell. She pushed herself to her feet. 'You *killed* him. For*ever*!'

McAllister stared. 'Better this way. That's a lesson your da should've taught you by now.' Without another word he clomped off towards the sheds.

The wind became a living thing then, corkscrewing down through Edward's clothes. It snatched at Piper's hair, obscuring her face. He saw her bend to the ground. When she stood, she was clutching the hammer.

'Pie,' he warned again, louder this time.

She angled the tool in front of her. Its blunt head gleamed with blood. Eyes creased against the wind, Piper studied the departing farmer. For a moment Edward thought she was going to hurl the hammer at his back. Instead, she turned towards the sea and launched it high into the air. It tumbled end over end, but her throw lacked the energy to carry it far. It landed in the grass well short of the cliff-edge.

She cried out her fury, and the wind shrieked its allegiance. A cannonade of hailstones struck the wall of the lambing shed, ricocheting into the mud around her feet. Seconds later a larger gust delivered a white curtain of the tiny missiles. A handful hit Edward's face, and they hit Piper too. She yelped in pain. Sinking to her knees, worming her fingers beneath Disney, she lifted him. The dead lamb's head lolled over her forearm. Blood dripped from its fractured skull, whipped to a dark spray by the wind's intensity.

Piper raised her head. Her eyes were bloodshot. Two channels of mucus ran from her nose. 'There was no need!'

'I'm sorry,' Edward told her. 'Sometimes . . .'

He shrugged. How could he explain? He had killed enough animals in his time; he certainly couldn't claim moral superiority over McAllister. 'It might not make sense to you. But this . . .' Again he paused, berating himself for his inability to elucidate. 'Sometimes it's necessary.'

Beyond the sea cliffs he could see the surging steel of the Atlantic. Its surface looked angry, ferocious, as if it wanted to drag the land and everything upon it down into its throat.

Piper clenched her teeth. 'He would have *lived*,' she hissed. Turning away, she began to walk; not north, towards the sea, but to the far side of the lambing shed, and the hay barn beyond.

'Pie,' he said, starting after her. But the girl ignored him, and he knew enough not to intervene. He trusted her not to go near the cliffs.

Edward stared at the gritty specks of ice melting in the mud. Already, the wind seemed to be abating. He was wet, cold, and so tired that he could have lain down right here in the mud and closed his eyes. Instead, he hunched his shoulders and trudged towards the lambing shed after his employer.

By dinnertime they had delivered another twenty lambs between them, one of those stillborn. They worked together in virtual silence. McAllister avoided mention of the incident with Piper, and so did Edward.

Mrs Dougherty returned during the afternoon, but Piper didn't appear for her lessons. Edward tried to pay the woman for her trouble but she refused. 'You look like you're going to fall over,' she told him. 'That old bastard should be ashamed, pushing you this hard.'

'It's not for much longer.'

She stared at him for a long moment, hands on hips, and then she shooed him upstairs. 'I'll find the scrap, cook her some dinner,' she said. 'I'll see her to bed, too. Just this once.'

Edward was too tired to argue, and so grateful that he could have kissed her. He dragged himself upstairs and lay down on his bed fully clothed, falling asleep within seconds.

Piper woke him. He blinked hard in the darkness, wincing at a crashing pain behind his eyes. How long had he slept? He grappled for the bedside lamp, switched it on. The light seared him. He shielded his face with his hand. 'Time is it?'

'Come on.'

'What's up?'

She didn't reply, and for a moment he felt himself drifting back towards sleep. Instead he pulled himself upright. Squinted open one eye.

The alarm clock showed nine p.m. He had slept for four hours, but it felt like four minutes. Worse, he was expected back in the sheds at midnight.

Piper hovered by the edge of his bed. Over her clothes she wore the quilted jacket he'd bought from a charity shop in Ballina. Like most of her things it was too small, too grimy, too frayed. Just seeing her in it made his throat grow tight.

Then he noticed something else: her hair was soaked through, jeans too. 'What the hell?'

'Please, Dad. You need to come. Quick.'

Cursing, he climbed out of bed, felt every muscle shriek in protest.

Piper's chin trembled and a sob spilled out of her. 'I'm sorry. I didn't mean to. I didn't.'

He frowned, disturbed by her sudden display of emotion. 'What's happened?'

She took his hand and led him from the room. He followed her across the landing and down the stairs. A light was on in the living room. Inside he could hear McAllister's TV set blaring.

They passed the door without speaking. In the kitchen, at Piper's instruction, he slung on jacket and boots. She found his torch, switching it on the moment they stepped outside.

It was raining now, a miserable deluge that gurgled in the gutters and spattered off the courtyard stones. He grimaced as it trickled into his collar. Piper passed the lambing sheds without slowing. She led him inside the hay barn and rolled the door closed behind them.

'Let me get the lights,' he said.

Piper shook her head. 'McAllister might see us. Might see this.'

'See what?'

'I . . .'

'Show me.'

She nodded, eyes downcast. Using the torch to light their way, she led him through the barn to where a simple drop pen stood. It hadn't been here yesterday. His daughter's handiwork, he was sure of it.

Something was moving inside the pen. Edward couldn't see it clearly so he took the torch from her and aimed it.

He recoiled. Shadows leaped.

'I'm sorry, Dad.'

Edward sucked in a breath. When he angled the torch back towards the pen, its beam shook. 'What happened here?'

'I don't know.'

He hesitated, forced himself to ask a question he did not want answered. 'Did you do this?'

Piper glanced up at him. Her expression was hollow. 'Maybe.'

'Is that him?'

'Yes. No.' She sobbed, clutched her arms. 'I don't know.'

Inside the pen, Disney stood on four twitching legs. One side of the lamb's face was matted with blood from the hammer wound in its skull. Edward could see tooth-like shards of bone, greyish brain matter.

The newborn moved forward shakily, as if powered by clock-work springs. Watching it, Edward felt his heart knock in his chest. He dropped to a crouch so that he could get a better view.

The lamb's eyes were black globes. Edward waved his hand in front of its head but it ignored him. Another three steps brought it to the side of the pen where it butted gently against the bars. With painful slowness, it turned around. Finally, it set off in the opposite direction.

'That's all he does,' Piper moaned. 'Back and forth, back and forth.'

Edward snaked an arm through the bars. He touched Disney's flank and then snatched his hand away, wiping his fingers on the straw. The lamb's flesh was cold.

He turned to Piper. 'You brought him back.'

'I think so.'

'How?'

'I don't know.'

'That wasn't a good thing to do. Wasn't right.'

She shivered, hugged herself. 'I took him in here, out of the rain. I only wanted to stroke him for a little while, say goodbye. He didn't have much of a life, did he? Didn't even have a mother that he knew. I was thinking about how unfair it was, how I wished I could have done something, given him another chance, and then . . . and then . . .'

She stopped, chewed her lip, glanced at the monstrosity crossing the pen with jerky, scissor-like steps. 'What are we going to do?'

Edward kept his eyes on the girl. 'What do you *think* we should do?'

Piper swallowed. 'I think we should kill it. Properly kill it. I tried, Dad, but . . . I couldn't.'

'You don't have to explain.'

Her eyes filled with tears. 'You'll do it?'

He glanced back at the creature inside the pen, felt revulsion for what he saw. 'Yeah.'

Relieved, the girl came forward for a hug. Edward slipped his arms around her, and found himself thinking, even as he kissed her cheek: *Who are you? What are you?*

'I'm your daughter,' she whispered. 'That's all that matters.'

He nodded, smoothed her hair.

She knew the truth, of course; knew that she was no such thing – Edward had told her the story of her birth, had not wanted to hold anything back. But sometimes, like now, she preferred the fiction they had created. Sometimes, they both did.

'Time we moved on, I think,' she said.

'Soon as I get paid.'

'We have to wait?'

'Lambing won't last forever.'

'We can't go now?'

'Not without money, we can't.' He pulled back from her, gave her arms a rub. 'If we skip out now, McAllister won't give me a penny.'

Piper nodded, miserable. She glanced over at the pen. 'How will you do it?'

'You don't need to know that. Can you make it back to the house on your own?'

'I guess.'

'Go on, then. I'll join you once it's done.'

He watched her leave, a fragile scrap of a girl huddled in a coat two sizes too small; and then he turned back to the lamb. For a few minutes he didn't move, watching in silence as it butted up against the far side of the pen and turned back, unblinking.

Death had been a mercy compared to this. Whatever gift Piper had tapped, she needed to control it. He found himself thinking of Gráinne, all those years ago, returning to visit him beside the moonlit waters of Llyn Tywyll; of the nurse, Beth Williams, flung against the wall in the Lleuad Valley Mountain Rescue Centre, her head leaving a vivid scarlet print; of the blood-red light that had soaked the slopes of the Carneddau; and of the turned soil all around his old caravan, as if every creature that made its home beneath the earth had burrowed in protest to the surface.

Edward recalled all that, and then he wrapped it up and buried it somewhere deep.

In one corner of the hay barn he found an axe. He would need to do this quickly, before he lost his nerve. Grabbing a metal bucket, he returned to the pen and stepped over the rail.

Edward kicked the lamb's legs from under it and pressed his boot against its ribs. He hefted the axe and swung. It took seven strokes to fully sever the head. He grabbed it by a blood-soaked ear and tossed it into the bucket. Even then its legs continued to jerk back and forth. Edward counted to fifty before the movement ceased. He picked up the torso and dropped it on top of the head. Outside, rain stinging his eyes, he walked to the cliff-edge and flung the bucket into the darkness. He thought he heard it splash into the sea, but he couldn't be sure.

I'm your daughter. That's all that matters.

On his way back to the farmhouse he tried to ignore the dark thoughts that had begun to envelop him.

CHAPTER 20

*Stallockmore,
County Mayo, Ireland*

Back inside the farmhouse kitchen, Edward hung up his jacket and kicked off his boots. His headache had sharpened now: his brain felt as if it were being flambéed. The pain came in waves, nausea chasing hard on its heels. At the sink by the window, he stood with palms braced to support himself and stared at his reflection in the glass.

He looked dreadful: pouched eyes and ashen skin, a decade older than he should. For the first time in months, he ached for a drink, for the anaesthetising effects of a whisky bottle. If McAllister had kept a drop of the stuff on the property, Edward would have rampaged through the house to find it, but he had known the farmer long enough to understand that they caged the same demons. Stallockmore, in its mercy, was as dry as a dead man's throat.

Instead Edward went to a cupboard, found a box of aspirin and popped three pills, crunching them like breath mints. Bitterness flooded his mouth. Turning on the cold tap, he dropped his head and sucked up water until he rid himself of the taste. Then he locked the back door and switched off the kitchen light.

Upstairs he found Piper lying on her bed in darkness. Her coat lay discarded on the floor. He picked it up and draped it over her chair. 'Pie?'

He had expected to find her awake – had intended to question her, to walk her through what had happened as gently as he could. Moving to the bed, he saw that she was asleep. The girl's eyes flickered behind their lids. She moaned, fighting whatever dream had claimed her.

'Pie.'

Her mouth fell open and she sighed, and the sound was so pitiful, so lamentable, that Edward felt as if boulders had been piled upon his chest. He dropped to his knees and smoothed Piper's hair from her brow. For a moment he thought about waking her. But even in sleep her eyes were ringed with shadow. Better to let her rest while she could.

'*Ìobairt,*' she whispered, the word thick on her lips. '*Beò-Ìobairt.*'

Chilled, Edward removed his hand. He hadn't heard such language spoken in seven years, and never from the girl lying before him, only from her mother.

'*I don't.*' Piper's lips twisted into a grimace. '*I can't.*'

Edward bent forward and kissed her head. Her skin was cool, damp against his lips. He retreated to the door, easing it closed on his way out.

His own room waited opposite. He slipped inside, gritting his teeth as another wave of nausea rolled over him. When he sat on the bed, its creaking springs were like daggers in his ears. He didn't want to turn on the lamp but he forced himself. Its brightness speared him, until he found an old shirt and threw it over the shade.

Beneath the bed, among the few of his belongings that wouldn't fit inside the room's single wardrobe, he found what he sought: a small spiral-bound notebook. Its cloth covers were water-stained, streaked with dirt.

Edward opened it up, flicking through pages of shivery longhand. The first part of the notebook detailed his memories of the night he had discovered the convoy on the road towards the Glyderau, followed by his recollection of the events surrounding Piper's birth.

Later pages recorded milestones in the girl's development. They were pitifully sparse. He had intended to give her a history, but now he saw how badly he had failed. His notes were little more than a record of weights and heights, injuries and illnesses, dates of lost teeth.

Towards the back of the book he found his research on the words Gráinne had spoken in his caravan as she thrashed around in the early stages of labour. He had scrawled them phonetically at first, adjusting them as his understanding grew.

An Toiseach was the first phrase he deciphered. For over a year the meaning eluded him; he had little idea how to spell it and few people to ask. But once he worked out that it was Gaelic, and Scottish Gaelic at that, he discovered its literal translation: *The First.*

One of the three Goidelic languages, Scottish Gaelic had evolved from Middle Irish, which in turn had arisen from Old Irish. In ancient times, *An Toiseach* had been used to describe the vanguard of an army. The word *Toiseach* had likely developed from the Irish *Taoiseach*, a term still used to denote that country's head of government.

Before Edward and Piper had travelled to County Mayo, they had lived for a time in squalid accommodation on the Isle of Man. He had found casual work on one of the island's dairy farms. While there, he happened across a tattered old book of Manx folklore. It contained a few references to *An Toiseach*.

The details were vague, and further reading hadn't enlightened him a great deal. But slowly he began to piece together references to an obscure creation myth, now lost. *An Toiseach*, or *The First*, was used in the context of an original race, a first people. Frequently the term appeared alongside references to *The False Mother* and *The Warrior*.

Balla-dìon, the second word Gráinne had uttered all those years ago, had eluded Edward for just as long. He finally translated it, again from Scottish Gaelic, as *barrier wall*. Unlike

An Toiseach, he had been unable to derive any further meaning, mythological or otherwise.

Had Gráinne been part of some cult, he wondered? As part of his attempt to give Piper a broader history, he had researched her mother's name. It was thought to derive from the Irish word for *grain*, and was commonly associated with *gráidh*, or love. Numerous Irish queens and princesses, both historic and folkloric, had taken the name in the past.

Whether Piper's mother had belonged to a cult or not, none of Edward's findings explained the bizarre and disturbing phenomena he had witnessed during those two short days he had spent in her company. He had known Gráinne for such a short period, and for such a long time distant, that the clarity of his memories had faded. But he still remembered her instructions as she breastfed Piper on the shore of Llyn Tywyll.

Watch her closely. The moment you see her do something odd, something unexplained, get out of wherever you are straight away. Until she's learned how to control it, she'll be vulnerable. You both will.

He remembered, too, that although he had softened towards Gráinne before her death, she had entered his life through deception and trickery.

The pain behind his eyes was receding now, as the aspirin began to work its cure. Edward reached under the bed for his rucksack. From it he retrieved the Scottish Gaelic dictionary he had bought years earlier. Within a minute he found the entry for *Ìobairt*, and its translation: *Sacrifice.*

Next he found the entry for *Beò*. His skin raised into goosebumps when he read the translation: *Living.*

Beò-Ìobairt.

Living Sacrifice.

He thought of the dead lamb walking across the hay barn, its eyes like globes of volcanic glass. He recalled the coldness of its flesh. An image came to him: the creature's severed head sinking beneath the waves to the Atlantic sea floor. He felt the skin along his spine prickle, as if insects marched beneath his clothes.

Edward had always assumed that *The First* somehow referred to Piper. But if that were the case, who, or what, was the *Sacrifice?*

I'm your daughter. That's all that matters.

Finding a pen, he scribbled down *Beò-Ìobairt* in his note-book, along with its translation. Beneath that he wrote the date, and a summary of the day's events.

Scant moments after Edward closed the book, the first shockwave hit the house. The force of it knocked him to the floor. All around him the wooden floorboards began to jostle and bounce, like tongues caught in mirthless laughter.

CHAPTER 21

Ballina, County Mayo, Ireland

When Jenna Black's eyes snapped open a few minutes before midnight, the first thing she saw, in the shadows of the hotel suite, was Vivian's wide shape. The woman was crouched near a wardrobe, hurriedly tossing clothes into a case. Blinking, Jenna sat up in the mahogany-carved four-poster and threw aside the covers. She switched on a lamp.

They had arrived at Belleek Castle three days earlier, in time for a week-long conference on Gaelic phonology. The building stood on the banks of the Moy river surrounded by a thousand acres of woodland. The views were stunning, and Jenna had been delighted to discover that the solitude nourished her as effectively as good food or prayer.

Vivian turned. 'You felt it, then.'

Except for a single streak of purple that fell across her brow, the woman had secured her hair in a severe grey bun. Her usually ruddy cheeks were pale. She wore her signature clothes: long black skirt, embroidered and tasselled; shapeless black blouse. Around her throat, over a collection of necklaces, hung a delicate silk scarf. From her ears dangled tiny silver bells.

'I was dreaming,' Jenna said. 'And then . . .'

Vivian shook her head. 'No dream.'

Swinging her legs off the bed, Jenna sank her feet into the suite's deep carpet. 'You really think it's her?'

Vivian stared. Then, grimly, she nodded.

Jenna felt a coldness spread out from her spine. She retrieved her jeans from the back of a chair and slipped them on, then scooped up her boots. 'What do we do?'

'We'll figure that out once we're moving.'

'We're going after her?'

'Soon as you're dressed.'

Jenna's heart thumped, heavy in her chest, and began to accelerate. 'Have you spoken to the others?'

'Tristan, before you woke. He's checking to see who else is nearby.' The older woman looked away and Jenna thought: *You think we're the only ones.*

It took a minute to throw her scattered belongings into a bag. She shrugged on her coat and felt inside her pocket for the hire car's keys. She checked the drawers in the cabinets beside the bed and those in the dressing table until she realised, shame-faced, that she was deliberately trying to delay their departure. Straightening, she found Vivian watching her. But the woman's expression contained no reproach, merely concern.

'This is a good thing, right?' Jenna asked.

'Yes.'

She hesitated. 'Are you scared?'

'Of course.'

Hearing that admission, from someone usually so assured, frightened her more than the dream. '*Ériu* protects,' she murmured, opening the door to the suite.

'Ériu's dead,' Vivian replied. 'Don't deify her. She wouldn't have wanted that, and you know it.'

Jenna drove them west, through a dense mist that rolled out of the forest like an army of marching wraiths. She drummed her fingers against the Jeep's steering wheel until a sharp look from Vivian stopped her. All of her fingers bore silver rings, except for the one that might have worn a wedding band; that finger displayed a circlet of tattooed vines instead. The rings had always comforted Jenna – each signified a memorable episode from her life, its meaning coded into the maze patterns that twined across the metal – but they failed to comfort her now.

Beneath her seat lay a Beretta semi-automatic pistol loaded with nine-millimetre rounds. She feared, more than anything, that tonight she might have to use it. She hated guns, had hated them for as long as she could remember, and while her memories didn't span the length of time that Vivian's did, they still stretched far into the past. Yet despite her abhorrence of violence in any of its forms, she could not deny the value of arming herself against what she might face.

Although if I'm forced to use the pistol, I'll probably end up shooting myself by mistake.

On the back seat, fully loaded, lay a Blaser hunting rifle with a clip-on thermal scope. The women had a permit for neither the rifle, the pistol under Jenna's seat, nor the second pistol tucked under Vivian's. If their arsenal were discovered they would face serious trouble. Even so, being waylaid by anything as mundane as a Garda patrol seemed to Jenna the very least of their worries.

Vivian stared at the road revealed by the Jeep's headlights. Brow knotted, she fingered the edges of a bronze disc hanging from a chain around her neck. Between her feet was a canvas bag stuffed with books and trinkets. Inside it, a mobile phone began to buzz.

Vivian leaned forwards. Her girth restricted her, making her gasp, but she found the phone and held it to her ear. 'We're driving,' she said. 'Half an hour. West, that's all I know. You?' She listened, grunted in response and tossed the handset back into her bag.

Jenna's grip tightened on the wheel, her rings scraping. 'We're on our own.'

Vivian glanced across at her. 'There's someone down in Galway. And Keegan's in Dublin. They're moving now.'

'Galway's two hours away. Dublin's three.'

Vivian nodded. 'Looks like the honour's all ours.'

Jenna blew out a breath. If the pull westwards was legitimate – and she had every reason to think that it was – then the stakes were too high to contemplate. If the call had been loud enough even for Jenna, then others must have heard it too.

Others meant the *balla-dìon*.

She shuddered. Even contemplating that made her stomach burn with acid.

And now, everything might depend on you and Vivian.

They sped through the village of Killala, tyres kicking up standing water. The houses they passed looked empty, abandoned: no glow of lamplight within, no flicker of television. It felt as if the entire community had been bewitched into sleep, or else spirited away. Jenna knew it was a foolish thought, but those windows looked desperately dark, even so.

Twenty minutes later they passed through Ballycastle, which seemed equally devoid of life. The road was drawing them towards the coast, now. Jenna could feel the flat, dark presence of the Atlantic, even if she couldn't yet see it.

The weather began to worsen. A salt wind rose up, tugging the 4x4 on its suspension. They rounded a bend and a squall hit them, raindrops crackling off the windscreen like hail.

'At least it's isolated,' Vivian said. 'Not many people about.'

Jenna blinked, realised that her friend had been studying her.

'Lower chance of corruptions,' the woman added.

That word – *corruption* – made her flinch, chilled her to the core. 'What about wildlife?'

'Out here? Nothing but sheep. Sheep, grass and rain.'

'Wolves?'

Vivian barked a laugh. 'Two hundred years ago, perhaps. Not now.' She paused, frowned. 'You knew that, right?'

Jenna felt herself colouring. 'I think so.'

'Don't lose your centre. This is where you live now.'

'I won't.' In an effort to restrain her next question, she bit her lip. It spilled out anyway. 'What about bears?'

'Holy mother! We're talking *thousands* of years. Put it out of your mind. No bears, no wolves. Just sheep, and maybe a few dogs to shepherd them. Domestic dogs at that.'

'Dogs can be deadly. Sheep, too, if there're enough of them.'

Vivian's chest swelled. She held her breath and bent forwards, pulling her Beretta from beneath the seat. Its metal glinted green in the dashboard lights. Racking the slide, she tilted the barrel towards the road. 'Are you telling me you'd bet on the sheep?'

The sight of Vivian, wearing a matronly grimace and pointing the huge pistol at the windscreen, was too absurd to stomach. Despite her fear, Jenna found herself grinning.

'Only one wolf around here,' Vivian muttered. 'And that's me.'

They laughed at that, both of them, and it felt good, felt important. But still Jenna could not remember the last time she had seen a light out there. It was starting to feel as if they travelled at speed across a deserted isle.

Vivian's laughter faded. The woman put a hand to her head, winced. 'Up ahead . . . there's a turning. Take it.'

A moment later Jenna felt it too: a tugging sensation behind her eyes, as if a little-used part of her brain had just contracted. Soon after, she saw the turning appear on their right. A hand-painted wooden sign read STALLOCKMORE FARM. She slowed and pulled the Jeep around.

'Lights,' Vivian said.

Jenna extinguished them. The 4x4 rattled over a cattle grid and bounced onto a track wide enough to accommodate a single vehicle. Without moonlight to guide her, visibility was negligible. She followed the track at walking speed for almost a mile as it threaded north-west towards the sea, rising at a shallow gradient all the way. Dark fields lay on either side, but Jenna could see no livestock populating them. They were approaching the top of a slope now, still hidden in a shallow depression of land.

'Stop the car.'

Jenna eased off the accelerator. The Jeep rolled to a halt.

When she killed the engine, the wind's baying filled her ears. It made her think of spirits trapped in purgatory. She buried the thought; hardly the time to let her imagination run unfettered.

Vivian opened the glovebox and pulled out two identical MP3 players, complete with lightweight closed-cup headphones. She dropped a set into Jenna's lap.

Jenna eyed it with distaste. The music player would provide a measure of protection, but she hated the idea of stepping outside with one of her senses caged. 'Do we really need these?' she asked. 'There's hardly enough light to see as it is.'

'Your eyes will adjust. Do you want the *balla-dìon* inside your head?'

'Of course not. But unless we really are the only ones out here, I don't see how—'

'I'll take whatever advantage I can, and so will you. This is the first proper lead we've had since she disappeared.' Vivian tucked her MP3 player inside her blouse and donned the headphones.

Jenna watched her, heart beginning to thump anew. The prospect of conflict was anathema, a concept so alien that it threatened to suffocate her. She stared at the gun her friend clutched. 'Could you do it?' she asked quietly. 'Could you kill an innocent?'

Vivian strained around. She plucked the hunting rifle from the back seat. Her eyes, when she turned to Jenna, were dark with determination. 'When you consider what's at stake?' the woman replied. 'Yes.'

It was a moment before Jenna could avert her gaze. Chilled, she tugged the headphones over her ears and dropped the music player into her pocket. Reaching between her legs, she retrieved the Beretta from under the seat. Its metal was cold, the texture of its grip like snakeskin. The comparison made her flesh tighten into goosebumps. '*Ériu makes us strong*,' she whispered.

Vivian grimaced. 'Ériu makes us merciless, gun-toting bitches. If you need to use your weapon, don't hesitate. You keep moving, keep thinking. We don't know what we're up against here. If things go sour, they'll go sour fast.' She grabbed the door handle, indicating Jenna's headphones with a thrust of her chin. 'Time for some music.'

The dimple of land where they'd left the Jeep had protected them from the worst of the weather. The moment they crested the hill's summit the wind pounced on them, snatching at their clothes. Vivian's scarf fluttered like a kite until she re-knotted it. Jenna's hair whipped her face, obscuring what little view she had of the surrounding terrain. Cursing, she fumbled in her pocket for a band.

She could smell the sea from here, could taste its salt on her lips. Without the headphones she thought she might have heard the booming of the waves as they burst against the sea cliffs, but Keegan's music filled her head instead, cutting her off from the ocean's power. She trapped the pistol under her arm, tying back her hair and blinking away tears.

From the top of this rise they had a perfect vantage point over the land below. It sloped away at a gentle pitch, terminating at the hundred-foot cliffs that protected this stretch of coast from the Atlantic. A vortex of cloud hid the stars and moon, but the landscape was not completely dark. In a shallow dip of land a farmhouse sheltered, surrounded by a cluster of stone-walled sheds. The main residence blazed with light. Even from this distance, Jenna thought she could see dark shapes moving behind its windows.

Vivian stripped off her coat and spread it onto the grass. She dropped to one knee. After catching her breath, she lay down on the coat and aimed her rifle towards the house. She switched on the night scope and put her eye to its lens.

Jenna shivered. Inside her head, that feeling of tightness had returned. Earlier, she had wondered whether they could have made some mistake. Now that she was here, she knew they had not.

She fished a pair of binoculars from her pocket. When she trained them on the farmhouse she gasped at what they revealed.

A moment later the hillside, and everything upon it, turned the colour of blood.

CHAPTER 22

Stallockmore, County Mayo, Ireland

Edward lay on his back, arms outstretched, as the old farm-house seesawed around him. So violent was the shaking that he expected at any moment the walls to topple or the ceiling to come crashing down. He felt the vibrations in his chest, watched cracks race up the plaster. His bedside lamp clattered to the floor. All around him the floorboards bounced up and down like the keys of an old Pianola. They raised a choking cloud of dust that hung in the air like smoke. The hall light flickered frantically, as if the building tried to transmit a desperate message for help.

Downstairs, McAllister's two border collies, Muffy and Teak, began to bark. But however urgent the dogs' warnings, their noise was all but obliterated by the bass rumbling that rolled up like thunder through the foundations of the house. Edward felt himself sliding across the floor. He flipped onto his front, grabbed a metal bed post and anchored himself.

Glass shattered. It sounded like the ground-floor windows were imploding. He thought he smelled something now, over the tongue-sticking dryness of the dust: an ammonia sharpness, as if deep below him the earth had cracked wide to expel a poisonous mist.

Edward drew up his knees, gashing one of them on a lifted

nail. The pain was a bright shard of clarity in his head. He pushed himself to his feet, nearly fell as another shockwave hit. His ears popped, equalising with a roar. Turning, he lunged towards the bedroom door. He caught hold of the jamb, steadied himself, stepped out into the hall.

Above him, the trapdoor to the attic dropped open. Its leading edge caught him above the nose and knocked him off his feet. Pain exploded in his head, so monstrous that he kicked out his legs and felt the banisters disintegrate into splinters. He rolled over and blood ran into his eyes. His stomach clenched, threatened to purge itself. Pulling himself upright, he wiped away the blood, felt more of it seep over his eyelids. Half-blinded, he staggered towards Piper's room, one hand pressed in front of him. He touched her bedroom door, pushed it open, shouted her name.

Darkness inside. On the table beside her bed he saw the outline of the nightlight he'd bought her: a garish plastic fairy crouched over a mushroom. When he touched the mushroom's surface it glowed blue, illuminating the bed.

Piper lay on her back, in the same position he had left her. She clutched a wad of bedclothes in each hand, the skin of her knuckles tight. Whereas, before, her eyes had roved beneath their lids, now they remained still. She breathed slow measured breaths. 'Pie?'

Directly above her bed was the room's only window. A blast of wind rattled the pane, lifting the curtains. Blood trickled into Edward's eyes. He smeared it away with his arm.

The girl blinked, gazed up at him.

Edward stiffened.

By what strange intuition he could not guess, but he knew, immediately, that whoever watched him through those eyes was not the girl he knew.

'She can't hear you.'

Piper's tone was authoritative, deep. It woke a dread in Edward, rocked him to his core. He wanted to grab her by the shoulders, shake her until he dislodged whatever *wrongness* had taken root inside her head. But he couldn't bring himself to touch her, couldn't bring himself to do anything except stare into the dark eyes that studied him.

'What's happening?' he heard himself ask. 'What do you want?'

'I want to keep her safe,' the voice responded. It had a cello's resonance, a compelling richness. 'So if you love her as much as I think, you need to listen. Trust me and she survives what's coming.'

His head throbbed. A wave of dizziness rolled over him. He felt himself losing his balance. Edward planted his legs, gripped a side table for support. Forced himself to maintain eye contact. 'Talk.'

'Piper's having a nightmare, and she's not ready to wake up. Right now she's broadcasting a signal loud enough for anyone who might choose to listen.'

'What's coming?'

'You remember the night she was born? The red light?'

He nodded.

'*Cathasach*,' the voice said. 'The *balla-dìon*. If it finds Piper before she's ready, everything is lost.'

Edward stared, his eyes narrowing. The compulsion to shake that invading voice out of his daughter's head was overpowering. He clenched his fists, held them at his sides. 'Why should I trust you?'

'Because you know me, even if you think you don't. I've been with Piper since the beginning. You saved her, Edward Schwinn. I put my faith in you and you repaid it. You gave her a home. A life.'

He tore his eyes away. The first thing he saw, hanging over a chair, was Piper's grimy jacket. His throat ached at the sight of it. 'I've given her nothing.'

'You've given her everything. But she needs one more thing.'

He looked at her once again. Felt a cold, eely flicker of revulsion in his belly. 'What do you want me to do?'

'I'm going to slow her heart, kill the dream. It'll make us invisible for a while, but it won't help if the *balla-dìon* already has our location. You chose this place well, but we need to get out of here. I don't mean the farm. We need to get off this island, Edward. Right now.'

He stared in disbelief. How could he do that? He had worked at Stallockmore for just over a year, allowing McAllister to hold in trust what remained of his wages each month after deductions for food, lodging and Piper's lessons. If he skipped out now, he wouldn't see a penny. They would have nothing to their names except whatever meagre possessions he could stuff into a bag, along with whatever loose change he carried in his pocket. Another thought struck him, just as debilitating: he didn't even have transport. Was he meant to hike out of here carrying Piper on his back?

'Whatever it takes,' the voice responded. 'Find a way.' Piper's chest rose and fell. Her eyes dulled. A few moments later, the last of the aftershocks dissipated through the farmhouse walls and fled into the night.

For a minute or more Edward simply watched her. Then he picked up a blanket from the foot of the bed. He wiped his face, appalled at the amount of blood he saw. When he touched his head he felt a spike of agony like raw electricity. His gorge rose. He tasted bile in his throat. Grimacing, he stumbled to Piper's cupboard. From the top of it he dragged down a battered suitcase and flipped up its lid. He pulled open the drawers of a bureau, grabbed as much of the girl's clothing as he could: underwear, leggings, vests, tops. He flung in her books and the few belongings he knew she cherished: a wooden box decorated with seashells; a plaster of Paris cast of Minnie Mouse, badly painted by Edward and missing one ear; a medal she'd won at a village fair; a Roman coin; an old collar of Argus's. He scooped up Piper's jacket, raised her to a sitting position and eased her arms inside it. Lifting her off the bed, he picked up the suitcase and headed to the hall.

The case lodged in the doorway behind him. When he tried to tug it loose a sharp edge of the latch plate ripped a gash along the fabric. A spew of clothes fell out.

Edward swore, wanted to yell. Reversing his grip on the suitcase, bracing the punctured side against his leg, he walked it across the hall. His boots crunched over smashed picture frames and broken glass. He reached the top of the stairs. Above him the hallway light – a naked bulb hanging from a span of brown flex – swung to and fro, echoing the earlier tremors. It spawned an audience of shadows that rocked and swelled like horses on a carousel.

Clutching Piper with one hand, manhandling the suitcase with the other, Edward edged down the stairs. The ground-floor hall came into view. He saw an overturned console table, loose papers chasing in a spiral.

The front door hung ajar. Through it blew a bitter wind.

From somewhere deeper inside the house, Edward heard the dogs, their barking more frenzied now. He was nearly at the bottom of the flight. Glancing behind him, he noticed that the suitcase had spilled a trail of Piper's clothes down the stairs. When he turned back around he saw that the living-room door had opened. Old Man McAllister came through it. The farmer's eyes were bloodshot and wild. In his hands he held a shotgun.

CHAPTER 23

Stallockmore, County Mayo, Ireland

'*Beò-Ìobairt*,' the old man chanted. '*Beò-Ìobairt*.' He glanced up, and when he saw Edward on the bottom landing his grip tightened on the gun. 'I was dreaming,' he said. 'Of a dead thing. Walking.' Then he saw Piper. His jaw dropped and he took a step back. Shook his head, as if to clear it. 'She put it in my head, didn't she? To teach me a lesson.'

Edward kept his eyes on McAllister's face, refusing to let his focus wander to the shotgun. 'I don't think she meant to. She's scared. Having a nightmare.'

'Wake her up.'

'No.'

The farmer hawked. He braced himself to spit, and at the last moment seemed to remember where he stood. 'Always knew she were something different. Pair o' you aren't related. Truth, now.'

Edward paused, considering the question. Slowly he shook his head.

'Tricked me.'

'I had my reasons. None of them meant to cause harm.'

McAllister stared. And then he nodded. 'I been none too fair on you, Schwinn.'

'No matter.'

'Maybe. Maybe not.' Noticing the suitcase, McAllister jerked his shotgun barrels towards it. 'Where you headed?'

'Away from here.'

'Aye. That you are.' The old man nodded. 'The lass woke something, something down dark. And now it's coming.'

'How do you know?'

'Saw it, in my dream. *Cathasach*, they call it – one of the old names. Little more 'n a foggy memory round here, but I knows it. Wants to put an end to your little one, no doubt. With good reason, some might say. She'll be your death, aye. Plenty others, too.'

Edward ignored that. 'I need money,' he said. 'Transport.'

Incredibly, now McAllister really did spit, a thick lump that hit the newel post and clung there like yellow jelly. 'Can't help you with the money. But you can take Cribby. And what food you might need.'

It was a shameful offer, and they both knew it. Had it not been for the shotgun, Edward would have ransacked the farmhouse for the money he was owed and to hell with the old man. But he had no bargaining power in this exchange. Worse, he sensed he had no time even to pack the offered supplies. 'Keys,' he demanded.

'In her slot.' The farmer inclined his head, allowing the shotgun barrels to wander. 'You hear that?'

Edward frowned. 'Hear what?'

'Bells . . . like *bells*.' McAllister looked around the room, confused. 'Go on, now. Away with you both.'

In the kitchen, the dogs fell silent.

Edward shot a glance down the hall, the hairs on his forearms prickling. He hefted Piper from one arm to the other. Picked up the suitcase.

The old farmer licked his lips. He moved to the front door and opened it wide. 'Tell her she was right. About the lamb, I mean. Shouldna killed it.'

Edward stepped past McAllister. Outside, a caged bulb fixed

to the farmhouse wall threw a yellow semi-circle of light across the courtyard. It made him blind to anything that might lurk beyond its perimeter.

Wind snatched at Piper's hair, blowing it into his face. Edward heard the front door slam shut behind him.

The lass woke something, something down dark. And now it's coming.

Seven years had rolled by since the night at the rescue centre where four people had died. He had never seen the bodies of Terfel Williams, Beth Williams and Gruffydd Vaughn, but he knew that they were gone; knew, too, that by bringing Gráinne to their door that evening he had as good as killed them himself. How he had hoped against a repeat of those events. How vain that hope now appeared to be. At least tonight, out here on this remote farm, there was only McAllister to weigh on his conscience should history repeat itself. Considering that, Edward felt a sting of shame.

Focus on Piper, that's all you can do. Keep her safe, keep her alive. Forget everything else.

And yet even as he thought it, the farmer's parting words echoed in his head: *She'll be your death, aye. Others, too.*

One arm heavy with the girl's weight, Edward dragged the torn suitcase across the courtyard stones. Its wheels bumped and stuttered behind him.

Ahead loomed the nearest lambing shed. Inside he could hear the frenzied bleating of the ewes. Never before had they made such a racket. It was an abominable sound, caustic to his ears, as if the animals had smelled, out there in the night, a swarm of approaching predators.

Edward quickened his pace. Felt the skin of his scalp contract. Piper muttered wordless sounds against his neck. 'It's OK,' he told her. 'It's OK.'

Behind him, the caged bulb on the farmhouse wall exploded, plunging the courtyard into darkness. A second later the surrounding hills, and everything upon them, turned a hazy red.

* * *

Colm Berrit McAllister stood in the hallway of his County Mayo home, head tilted to one side, and thought he heard the scratching of mice inside the walls. He inserted a finger deep into his ear and rotated it. When he heard a pop of released air, he muttered an expletive.

Tucked in a corner by the kitchen door stood the Comtoise clock he had inherited from his father. While he could see its enamelled face, his eyes weren't sharp enough to show him the position of its hands. He heard its pendulum rocking, there in the shadows. And then it stopped. The infernal scratching ceased. Silence pressed, like a blanketing fog.

The Voice spoke to him, then.

It slid into his head, butter-soft, and talked in such a loving tone that tears sprang into McAllister's eyes. Emotions, of an intensity he had not imagined could exist, swelled in him. His fingers opened and flexed. Distantly he heard the clatter of his shotgun as it fell to the floor.

'*Yes,*' he whispered, so grateful for this sudden intervention that he thought his heart might burst inside his chest.

He rejoiced as he felt the Voice enter him. What began as a heaviness in his feet became a lightness, then a honeyed warmth. It lifted higher, starting to immerse him, as if he stood in the rising waters of a spa. His skin tingled, his heart began to race. All the while the Voice sang pellucid assurances of its intent.

And then its timbre changed. It spoke with greater urgency. It showed him something important about the girl.

Something monstrous.

'No,' McAllister moaned. 'No, she can't. I won't let her. I won't let her do it.'

His bowels loosened in terror. For a moment he thought he might soil himself, there in the hallway. To think that he had *sheltered* that abomination. To think that he had sheltered the man. To think that he had harboured such—

THE MAN?

Yes, the man. The man.

McAllister sensed his memories of Schwinn churning like the pages of a flicker-book, an insect-dry riffling: solemn, gullible Edward Schwinn; a drifter who had come to him a year earlier, desperate for work; a man who had tended the flock of Suffolks diligently and without complaint; a man ill-equipped to strike a bargain, or attend fully to his daughter's needs. Earlier McAllister had felt a pang of shame for exploiting him, and—

FORGIVEN, said the Voice. That single word pealed like a gong inside his head.

Such relief to hear it. *Such* relief. Now, as he bent to retrieve the weapon he had dropped on the hallway floor, as he heard his old bones crack with exertion, he decided that he would—

SUBMIT.

With a cough of yellow phlegm, and a few flung spots of blood, Colm Berrit McAllister smiled beatifically and did exactly that.

As the dome of red light swelled from the earth to envelop the farmhouse, Jenna Black dropped her binoculars and threw herself to the ground.

She had heard the stories, had tried to prepare herself as best she could. But watching that caustic light rise from the soft Irish peat glued her tongue to the roof of her mouth and made water of her insides. As if attuned to her dread, Keegan's music swelled in her ears. The random electronic notes were a horror all of their own. They made it difficult to think, difficult to do anything at all.

Jenna rolled onto her side, heedless of the mud that soaked her clothes. She sought the darkness for Vivian. The older woman lay ten yards to the left, rifle scope still pressed to her eye. Vivian's finger curled inside the trigger guard, her mouth a fixed scowl.

Recovering a scrap of her courage, Jenna scrabbled in the grass for her binoculars and raised them back to her face. Down in the courtyard, dragging a broken suitcase behind him, spilling a trail of clothes across the stones, hurried a lean stranger with an unkempt beard. Jenna's gut tightened when she saw his expression. It tightened further, hardening into a knot, when she saw whom he carried.

Keegan's music still played in her headphones, so when Jenna spoke she heard her voice inside her head, as if from the confines of a coffin.

It's her, she said. *It's Mórríghan*.

And it was.

No doubt about it.

From here, the child looked so unassuming, so vulnerable. So innocent.

Jenna looked to her left. Beside her, the barrel of Vivian's rifle bobbed as it settled on its target. She swung her head back to the view down the hill.

Something else, now, in the courtyard behind the man.

Beneath her, the cold earth hummed like a bowstring.

Colm Berrit McAllister rode the night as if he were a baby capuchin clinging to the back of its mother. He was weightless now, displaced, but his sense of exhilaration endured. In truth, his act of surrender to the Voice had felt inescapable, and yet his acquiescence to its demands had been so transforming – so utterly liberating – that he existed in a near-unbearable state of bliss. He had no body to experience sensation, no nerves or muscles to call his own, but that made the waves of pleasure he experienced no less affecting.

From his vantage point, just behind the eyes of his tired old skull, he saw two hands snake out and close around the weapon he had dropped on the hallway floor.

The shotgun's metalwork was cold to the touch. It ignited a shivery firework-burst of sensation in his fingers.

CALM, said the Voice. McAllister wanted to laugh with glee, but he did as he was told. While he had no control of his arms, he imagined wrapping them around his bony shoulders in self-embrace. The thought slipped out and he felt his mouth – the real one, this time – twitch in tandem with his mirth.

A moment later his brow furrowed.

PLEASE.

Unbidden, his hands turned the shotgun over, broke it. He saw two cartridges in the breech, brass heads winking in the hall's soft light. The gun snapped shut like a breaking neck. The safety snicked off.

McAllister's head turned, owl-like, towards the door. Something popped in his cervical vertebrae. He felt a distant prick of pain, a knife-tip puncturing a pillow to scratch him.

The Voice threw its focus inwards. A moment later the old farmer felt a surge of electricity through his tendons and muscles; a tightening and a toning. His head rolled in a lubricated circle.

HEALED.

The door catch was in his fingers. Slippery-cold-hard. Joyous. He tugged it loose, or perhaps the Voice did. Already they were so entwined that he struggled to distinguish himself.

The farmhouse door swung open and he stepped outside. A blast of wind scoured his cheeks, so gloriously visceral that he opened his mouth and moaned.

All over his body he could feel the changes. His heart clenched and unclenched like a fist; leathery old muscles filled with blood; nerve endings sizzled like frying bacon.

He took two steps before he saw Edward Schwinn hurrying across the courtyard. In one arm he held—

HER! IT'S HER! BEÒ-ÌOBAIRT! AN TOISEACH!

The caged bulb fixed to the farmhouse wall exploded. Glass rained down. McAllister – feeling, as the light receded, that he'd been dropped inside a well – began to scream. He tried to step backwards, took a step forwards instead. He closed his eyes and they opened. His face screwed itself up.

ENOUGH! the Voice admonished, and it was thunder

inside his head. A bloody mist had crept out of the ground, and that made no sense. He was scared now, overwhelmed.

ENOUGH! ENOUGH! ENOUGH!

The Voice coiled inside McAllister like a winding spring. It focused itself on Edward Schwinn and prepared to leap.

McAllister screamed again, desperate. He would *not* be abandoned. The years of loneliness stacked against him were too monstrous to relive.

But the Voice wasn't listening. It gathered its strength, latched onto Edward Schwinn's shape and—

CAN'T! WON'T LET! DOESN'T WANT!

CAN'T!

CAN'T!

CAN'T!

McAllister gasped as the Voice flooded back. Shaking, he felt his arms raise the shotgun.

The stock touched his cheek. Cold smooth wood. Earlier it would have detonated a glorious cocktail of sensations.

Not now.

Now all he felt was terror.

Schwinn had reached the side of the nearest lambing shed. His suitcase bumped and jostled, splashed in the mud. Mórrighan's head lolled, as if she were a dead thing transported. But she wasn't dead. McAllister knew it. Even though death was all she promised.

His right eye drew a bead in the darkness. It lined up the gun's sights to a spot between Schwinn's shoulder blades. No glory here. Take the man, finish the girl.

GOOD, said the Voice.

His trigger finger tightened. Light flared.

Ahead, Edward Schwinn dropped like a stone. Then a sledgehammer blow knocked Colm Berrit McAllister off his feet.

CHAPTER 24

Stallockmore, County Mayo, Ireland

Their only hope of getting out of here alive, Edward knew, waited out of sight up ahead. Behind the nearest lambing shed lay the patch of sodden ground where McAllister kept Cribby, the Volvo belonging to his long-dead wife.

The vehicle, a rusting metal nightmare with cracked windows and rotting seats, should have followed its owner into the ground years ago. McAllister had kept it functional through a mishmash of unsightly repairs. If Cribby managed to carry them to the next county before disintegrating, Edward would be amazed. He wondered if its tank held anything but fumes.

The lambing shed stood five yards away. Its walls and roof glowed red, hostage to that sullen light rising from the earth.

Piper was a deadweight now, impossibly heavy. Edward thought he heard her whisper something against his neck, but the wind whipped away her words. No mistaking the sound he caught next. From the summit to the south he saw a flash of fire – then the report of a rifle crashed between land and sky.

Edward ducked, even though it was already too late to react. As he fell he braced Piper against him. In the scarlet half-light he saw a blur of movement. It coalesced into a form he recognised: Old Man McAllister.

The farmer, wearing a euphoric smile incompatible with his

nature, staggered backwards and sat down hard on the courtyard stones. The impact loosened his grip on the shotgun and the weapon discharged with a roar. The muzzle flash illuminated him for a frozen instant, and Edward saw that the rifle round, delivered from the hilltop to the south, had taken him in the throat. One side of his neck looked as if a pack of dogs had savaged it. Ribbons of flesh hung from gleaming bone.

Their eyes met across the courtyard. Edward scrambled to his feet. He transferred Piper to his left arm, grabbed the suitcase with his right. Only three yards separated him from the corner of the lambing shed. He thought he saw McAllister spit at the ground, until he realised it was blood squirting from the farmer's ruined throat.

Shoulders raised, Edward turned away. He angled his body, made it a wall between McAllister and Piper. Up on the slope he saw another muzzle flash. Moments later, matching thunder rolled.

The ewes inside the shed began to panic. He could hear hooves drumming, the frightened bleats of lambs. Something metal overturned with a crash. Then, away to the south, came a woman's scream. It serrated the night, jagged with despair.

Cringing, Edward reached the corner of the shed and hurried around it. A wet clod of earth jammed in one of the suitcase wheels and the whole thing flipped, ejecting more of Piper's clothes. He cried out his frustration. Twisted the carry handle. Dragged the case after him.

Ahead, in the shadows between two outbuildings, waited Cribby. The car sat low on its suspension, victim of too many overladen trips along unpaved roads. Edward splashed through mud to reach it. He opened the boot, flung in his luggage. The suitcase had lost more than half its contents now, clothes he would have a hard time replacing. But he could not think about that, not yet.

Next to the suitcase lay a crowbar. He picked it up. Slamming the boot lid, he wrenched open the rear door. He laid

Piper in the back, then climbed behind the wheel.

The vinyl seat had lost so much foam that it offered him a child's-eye view through the windscreen. The car stank: rotten straw and mildew. He tossed the crowbar onto the passenger seat, started the engine, heard the pistons kick into life. Saw, through the rear-view mirror, a belch of thick black smoke.

The track leading up the hill from the courtyard offered the quickest route off the farm. But McAllister was back there, and even though the man had been mortally wounded, Edward sensed that he still presented a threat. He remembered how Terfel Williams had continued to attack Gráinne long after his injuries should have incapacitated him. Whatever phenomenon had been at work in Snowdonia was undoubtedly present here too.

Instead of reversing into the courtyard he decided to detour around the lambing sheds closest to the sea cliffs. From there he could join the track further up the slope. He slipped the car into first and released the handbrake. The front wheels spun, then they found traction.

As the Volvo squirrelled forwards, Edward flicked on the headlights and saw, blocking the exit between the two buildings, standing shoulder to shoulder in a shifting press of bodies, perhaps one hundred of McAllister's ewes. Their black eyes, as they regarded him, reminded him of the orphaned lamb he had decapitated and flung into the sea.

Colm Berrit McAllister watched, mesmerised, as his blood hosed the courtyard stones. He felt no pain, no trepidation at its loss. In its rawness the sensation delighted him.

The Voice danced fraught circles inside his head. McAllister felt a scratch in his memories, saw again the flash of flame up on the hill that preceded the opening of his throat. His thoughts skipped back. Played. Skipped back. Froze.

There. A bright flower of fire, etched into the night.

His legs unfolded and he felt himself stand, saw a pulse of

arterial blood splatter across the flagstones. He gazed up the slope, in the direction of that single flash of gunfire (*ah, so that's what happened. I've been shot*).

YES.

Up there on the ridge, McAllister saw a stealthy flicker of movement, a lighter shade stitched into the coal-dark cloth of the night. If only his eyes were better—

He screamed, delighted, as the Voice fixed that. Oh the sweet *pain*! His eyeballs felt as if they'd been nicked by fishhooks and torn from his skull. Everything clarified: a crystal sharpness, like the image on one of those fancy TV sets he'd seen that time in Ballina.

A fat woman lay up there on the ridge: a disgusting slug concealed in the grass. When the Voice leaped out of him to seize her, McAllister squealed in anguish, but within a second it boomeranged back. He thought he heard fading snatches of music, a grating medley of random notes.

ESCAPING!

Its tone was panicked now. McAllister knew that the Voice referred not to the fat woman on the hill, nor to the blood erupting from his throat in steadily diminishing pulses, but to that wordless abomination he had harboured at his farm.

His eyes strained further, and he saw that the woman – mid-fifties, ruddy face, grey hair streaked with purple – was aiming a rifle at him. As he watched, its barrel flared orange.

McAllister held up his hand to ward off the shot and saw his index finger disappear in a red spray. The round blew through his chest and burst out of his back. *What* a feeling *THAT* was! Needles and fireworks. Champagne through his heart. The force of it knocked him onto his side and he came to a rest with his face inches from the courtyard stones. He saw every detail: hairline cracks filled with grit, fragile lichen; the husks of dead insects. Such clarity! Such perfection! He opened his mouth, chuckled with glee.

Inside his head, the Voice sang a furious lament.

McAllister raised himself up. He opened his mouth to suck in air. It entered his lungs through his shattered throat.

KILLED YOU.

No bother, he replied in his bliss. *As long as you're with me.*

Again he felt its love envelop him, a warmth he'd never previously experienced. He grew pleased at his sacrifice. Proud.

On his knees, he looked up and saw the woman. His vision was a little grey around the edges but he noticed that she wore something over her ears. Headphones, perhaps.

He recalled the strange music. Was that what had made her invisible? It struck him, as he knelt at the centre of a spreading pool of blood, that he could sense the awareness of every living creature for miles around. *So* much stimulus: the cold pulse of earthworms in the soil, the tiny *scratch-flick!* of beetle brains; the grippy skittishness of the lambs in the sheds. With a sudden flash of insight he realised that the Voice linked them all. Not merely a Voice, nor a rising light, but a shepherd of insects, lambs and men.

The girl was here to destroy all that.

He had known her as Piper but he discovered, now, that she possessed a different name, an older name: Mórríghan.

She had allies, too. Not just the liar Schwinn – who had pretended to be her father, and likely misunderstood her true nature – but the woman up on the slope. That woman had been imperceptible before, but he had seen her now. She would not be able to hide again.

McAllister grinned.

He reached out, clenched his fist. Lifted his arm to the night.

Jenna Black watched through her binoculars, hardly daring to breathe, as the stranger cradling Mórríghan hurried across the courtyard. He was heading for the darkness behind the nearest outbuilding, but Jenna saw that he would never make it. The farmhouse's front door burst open and an old man staggered out. His movements were jerky, spider-like. In his hands he clutched a shotgun. When he saw the stranger and Mórríghan on the far side of the courtyard, he raised the gun to his cheek.

Jenna wanted to scream out a warning, but just then Vivian's rifle spat out an orange tongue of flame. The air fragmented, a sound like ripping linen. Thunder rolled among the hills.

In the courtyard below, both men fell and Jenna stopped breathing altogether. But a second later she saw the stranger, still clutching Mórríghan, struggle to his feet.

She panned the binoculars, shifting her view to the old man. He sat upright on the flagstones, shotgun lying discarded in front of him. Blood fountained from his throat in rhythmic pulses. For a moment he remained utterly still, as if transfixed by the severity of his injury. Then his head snapped up and he stared directly at the hill where she lay.

Jenna felt the air spool from her lungs. Over the meandering notes of Keegan's music came the hard clatter of a rifle bolt as Vivian reloaded.

As if the old man intuited what was about to happen, he raised a hand to shield himself. So frail he looked, so pitiful: another innocent caught up in something he could never understand.

The air reverberated with Vivian's second shot. Jenna saw a puff of dust from the old man's coat, saw him topple onto his side. There he lay, fingers uncurling; dead.

Except . . . that wasn't true. As she watched, he braced his hands against the stones and pushed himself back to a sitting position. He canted his head to one side. Then his eyes found the ridge once more.

Eyes still clamped to the binoculars, Jenna ducked her head. Had he seen her?

Again, the old man lifted his hand. Even from this distance, she could tell that he'd lost his index finger. Blood coursed down his wrist.

The bolt of Vivian's gun made the *wrap-snick* sound of a

reload. Jenna glanced left in time to see a brass shell spinning away into the darkness. The horror of what followed would remain inscribed in her memories for as long as she lived.

Down in the courtyard the old man closed his hand into a fist. In the long grass, Vivian convulsed. The rifle flew from her fingers. Eyes bulging, tongue protruding, she quivered like a dormouse seized by a raptor's claws.

The old man jerked his hand upright.

One moment Vivian was there in the grass.

The next she wasn't.

With a dry snap of breaking bones, limbs flailing uselessly behind her, the woman arced up into the night sky.

Jenna watched, dumbstruck, as Vivian's body, still gaining altitude, sailed high over the sea cliffs north of the farm and out across the ocean, and then she screamed. She was still screaming as her friend's trajectory found its peak half a mile out to sea and gravity began to pull her back towards the earth; still screaming as she lost Vivian to the darkness until, some moments later, she saw a distant burst of spray on the heaving black waters of the Atlantic.

Gone.

Just like that.

A life winked out before her eyes.

Jenna heard her breath rasping in her throat. She wanted to close her eyes, bury her head. Instead, she rolled onto her back. She fumbled in her pocket for the Beretta, hands shaking so badly she could barely close her fingers around it. At any moment she expected to experience the agony of her bones crunching into splinters, the sensation of her body catapulted heavenward.

Vivian was dead.

There was still so much at stake.

Clutching the Beretta like a talisman, Jenna jumped to her feet. Ran.

★ ★ ★

'Move!' Edward screamed. 'Get the *fuck* out of my way!'

The ewes watched him with eyes like ebony orbs. They moved towards the car, jostling each other in tightly packed ranks.

He slammed his hand on the Volvo's horn, toggled the vehicle's full beams, but the animals came on regardless, a living, moving barricade.

Cursing, he threw an arm over the passenger seat and peered out of the rear window. Blackness behind. He had wanted to avoid the courtyard and McAllister, but the approaching sheep blocked the only remaining exit. While he could grit his teeth and plough a path through them, he would not risk the prospect of a stricken animal gumming up his wheels and beaching the car.

Edward crunched Cribby's gears, found reverse. His foot slipped on the pedal and the tyres spun on the sodden grass. The car slithered backwards. He looped the steering wheel and the front swung to the right, the Volvo leaning like a trawler in a beam sea. Edward braked and scrambled the wheel into opposite lock.

Through the passenger window he spied movement. Hooves pounding, the sheep broke towards him. He crunched gears. Tramped the accelerator. Braced himself as Cribby slewed around the lambing shed.

The front wheels shrieked when they thumped onto the courtyard stones. The full beams doused the farmhouse with light.

Old Man McAllister lay on his back near the front door, eyes pointed at the sky. Edward got only a glimpse before the headlights veered away, but he would never forget the sight. The farmer's face was frozen in an expression of profound grief, as if in the moment of death he had been robbed of everything he had ever loved.

Recoiling, Edward peered at the road ahead. He found third gear, braced himself as the Volvo bounced over a rut and threw him up in his seat. The track narrowed and began to rise. It snaked up between the fields towards the top of the hill. Over the summit lay the public road that would take him and Piper out of here.

He blinked sweat from his eyes. Forced himself to breathe. He needed to be sharp now, needed to concentrate. He'd fled the farm without money or supplies. His bank account contained little more than spare change. He had no lines of credit, no ability to generate funds. He'd left his hunting rifle and crossbow under the bed in his old room.

Get off this island, Piper's interloper had told him. The urgency in that voice had been palpable. There were airports in nearby Sligo and Knock. From Rosslare or Cork on the southern coast, a ferry could take them to northern France. Ports to the west offered English and Scottish destinations. But all of those options required money. If getting Piper out of the country was his primary task, he had to find a source of funds; he could let nothing stand in his way. So intensely did he begin to consider the problem that he noticed the obstruction almost too late.

Edward stamped on the brakes, throwing an arm behind him to brace Piper against the seat. The Volvo's tyres locked, but the car had not been travelling fast. It shuddered to a stop within a few yards.

Blocking the track, headlamps extinguished, stood a brand-new Jeep Cherokee. Edward could see no one inside.

He stared at it through the windscreen, listening to the uneven rattle of Cribby's exhaust. He thought of the flashes of light he had seen up on this slope; recalled the peals of gunfire. At the time he had assumed that Piper was the target. Instead, McAllister had been hit.

He glanced up at his rear-view mirror. The kink in the road prevented him from seeing anything behind him. He didn't want to get out of the car and investigate the Jeep, but the hedgerows grew too close to allow two vehicles to pass.

On the back seat Piper slept on, oblivious. The girl hadn't stirred during the gunfire, not even when he had dropped to his knees while carrying her.

Edward cracked open his door, listened. Cribby's engine chugged and spluttered. Exhaust vapours rolled under the car and rose like steam in the glare of the headlights.

The crowbar sat on the seat beside him. He picked it up and climbed out. Atlantic wind snatched at his clothing. Ignoring it, he walked to the Jeep and put a hand on its bonnet. Warm. Which meant it must be the vehicle that had brought McAllister's killer here. It meant that the gunman was close.

Edward moved to the driver's door. He cupped his hands against the window glass and peered inside.

No one in either of the front seats. No one in the back.

He tried the door handle. Unlocked. When he opened it a ceiling lamp came on, revealing a spotless passenger cabin. The vehicle's keys were in the ignition.

It took him less than a second to make his decision. In another twenty he had transferred Piper and what remained of their luggage to the Jeep. Rather than laying the girl down on the back seat this time, he arranged her in a sitting position and secured her with a belt.

Slamming her door, he was about to climb behind the wheel when he realised that he'd left his crowbar on the driver's seat. Before he managed to remove it a voice said, 'Stop.'

CHAPTER 25

Stallockmore,
County Mayo, Ireland

Colm Berrit McAllister lay on his back, staring up at the sky. He would have liked to see the stars one last time before he died but the clouds swarming in a disorderly pack overhead would deny him that wish. Still, when he found himself swaddled in such perfect love what need, really, did he have of stars or moon?

He had not taken a breath in a minute or more, and he knew he would not take another. He sensed a growing tightness in his chest. But it did not pain him, did not concern him.

Had he done everything he could?

YES, the Voice assured him.

McAllister smiled. Such bliss in hearing that he had served his purpose. Such peace in knowing he was supported like this, at the end.

He felt the Voice send out strings of thought into the darkness and winced at their loss, a hoarder now of everything good.

CALM.

Hearing that, he grew content once more.

Those thought strings latched on, and now his vision swam with a hundred different images, like the pieces of a translucent jigsaw stacked before his eyes. He smelled damp wool, heard the soft braying of lambs. Somehow, through all that glorious sensation, he saw the dark outline of a car. And a man, silhouetted at the wheel.

The Voice spoke, and the kaleidoscope montage jostled, but the car was reversing now, and suddenly it disappeared. The Voice cried out in alarm. McAllister's knuckles cracked as his fingers curled into fists.

More strings of thought seeped out of him – one or two at first, growing to a torrent. He shook his head, frantic. *No!*

A stupefying effusion of love restrained him. For a moment he was too dizzied by its intensity to react. Yet even at its peak, he recognised it for what it was: a farewell; a doleful parting of the ways.

He screamed, even though the air escaping his ruined throat made no sound.

And then the Voice was gone.

Engulfed by terror, McAllister scrabbled his fingers across the flagstones, tried to fill his lungs. Where had it gone? *Where?* He couldn't be alone; not now, not here, lying beneath a cold sky with his life ebbing away. Where had it *gone*?

The tightness in his chest was an agony. He tried to seize onto something to sustain him but his thoughts were disintegrating. For the first time in his life he had been delirious with joy. And now . . . and now he was . . . he was—

She was perhaps five years younger than Edward. Pale hair. Frightened eyes. Over her ears she wore closed-cup headphones. In her hands she held a pistol, which she aimed half-heartedly at his chest.

Edward stared. He gripped the crowbar and lifted it from the seat. Eased the car door shut. 'Get out of my way.'

Despite her headphones, the woman seemed to grasp his meaning. She began to back away and checked herself, jaw tightening. Planting her legs, she locked her arms in front of her. When she spoke her voice trembled, but it was laced with determination. 'I can't let you take her.'

'Try stopping me.'

Behind her he saw the red dome hanging over the farm, a bloody beacon in the night. Further off, he could hear the crash of waves against the sea cliffs.

He recalled the conversation in Piper's bedroom.

Whatever it takes, the voice had instructed him. And while that exchange had disturbed him greatly, he knew he could not allow this woman to delay him.

'I'm leaving,' Edward told her. When he retreated a step towards the Jeep she raised the gun higher, aiming at his face.

No time now. He had to get Piper out of here.

The woman screwed up her face. 'Come with me.'

'No chance.'

'You don't know the danger you're in.'

'I've a fair idea.'

'You can trust me.'

Edward laughed. She had executed McAllister – shot the old man in cold blood – and now she solicited trust? He knew from bitter experience that he could trust no one but himself; he would not allow a stranger to jeopardise Piper's safety.

He tapped his ear, indicating her headphones. 'Take them off.'

She shook her head. A gust of wind blew strands of hair into her face and Edward swung the crossbar in a tight arc. It hit her arm halfway between elbow and shoulder, and he heard the cricket-bat *snap!* of her shattering humerus.

The woman collapsed to the ground with a grunt, the pistol tumbling from her fingers. Edward closed the distance between them. He picked up her weapon, pocketed it. Her eyes, as she watched him, were bright with pain and fear.

'I'm sorry,' he told her, and found that however insincere he might sound, he meant it. He gestured towards the Volvo. 'It's a heap but it goes. Don't follow me. If you're wise, you'll get out of here too.'

She clenched her teeth. Clutched her broken arm. 'Why?'

'Because she needs me.' Turning his back, Edward walked to the Jeep and climbed in. 'Not you,' he added. 'Not anyone else.'

And there, sitting behind the wheel of the 4x4, he realised, for the first time in seven years, that the words he had spoken were true. Piper *did* need him.

It felt like an epiphany. A lightness in his chest. And yet, and yet . . .

I'm your daughter. That's all that matters.

He started the car, turned on the headlights, saw the woman raise her good hand to shield her eyes from the glare.

He reversed along the track for a few hundred yards until he reached the main road, then accelerated away. He chose a route south, towards Westport and Achille Island. The roads were deserted, the hillsides dark. He drove ten miles before he saw the first light shining from a distant farmhouse window.

Edward glanced around the Jeep's interior: clean seats, no sign of clutter. The passenger-side sun visor displayed a rental sticker. The key fob bore a matching logo. He smelled a pleasant new-car aroma. A check of the instrument display told him the 4x4 had covered three thousand miles since new. Its tank was half full, which gave him a range of perhaps two hundred miles, enough to take him anywhere he wanted to go on the mainland: as far south as Cork; as far west as Dublin. He suspected that the woman would not report the vehicle stolen, which made it safe to use until the rental agreement expired. Even so, he knew he wouldn't keep it longer than a day, whatever the paperwork showed.

An hour later he diverted through the town of Castlebar, less from necessity than a desire to reassure himself that civilisation still persisted. He passed the illuminated signs of hotels and pubs and peered through their windows, envious of the welcome he might have received had he sufficient funds. One thing he knew with certainty: no comfortable bed awaited the pair of them at the end of tonight's journey.

He saw a handful of people out on the streets, but rather than finding reassurance in their presence he began to worry. Each stranger presented a possible threat, a weapon to be used against the girl. He thought of the red dome of light hanging over the farm, imagined the consequences of it appearing here and turning the entire town against him.

Haunted by the prospect, Edward steered the car west, heading towards Achill Sound and its road bridge to the island beyond. While he might be limiting his options in the event of a pursuit, he felt, instinctively, that isolation was his safest option.

An hour later he crossed the bridge onto Achill Island. The land was flatter here, the vegetation patchy. When, after a few miles, he saw on his left a hillock rising out of the scrub, he slowed the 4x4 and steered off the road. Stones crackled and popped beneath the Jeep's tyres. He nudged the vehicle in a wide arc until the hillock shielded him from the road. Satisfied that he was out of sight, he switched off the engine.

The interior lights came on, a soft yellow glow. Outside, the Atlantic wind rocked the vehicle on its springs. Edward unclipped his seat belt and popped the glovebox hatch. Inside he found the rental documents. They showed that the vehicle had been leased to a D. Kramer, and was due back at the company's Knock depot in two days' time. He wondered whether D. Kramer was the woman he had attacked at the farm.

Thinking of her raised a flush on his cheeks. He remembered her eyes, alive with pain and accusation. At the time he'd told himself he had no choice, but was that true? Could he have delayed for a few seconds, long enough to hear her story and learn how she was involved?

No. He'd done the right thing. The only possible thing.

I'm your daughter. That's all that matters.

Both of the Jeep's door cavities were empty. In the back, where Piper slept, the remaining seats were clear. He cracked open his door, slipped out and opened the boot. Inside he saw two cardboard boxes and a black travel case. In one of the boxes he found two sleeping bags rolled up in their liners, the retailer's tags still attached; in the other an unused camping stove, a plastic jerrycan filled with water and a selection of freeze-dried meals.

Seeing that bounty, Edward's eyes filled with tears. He unzipped one of the sleeping bags and used it to cover Piper. In the crook of a wheel arch he set up the stove, shielding it from the worst of the weather. The steady hiss of its burner was the most glorious thing he had heard in days. He listened constantly for sounds of pursuit, but save for the stove all he heard was wind.

It took five minutes for the water to boil. Soon afterwards he was back in his seat, tucking into a foil packet of rehydrated meat and potatoes. He scalded his tongue on the first mouthful, forced himself to slow down. Ravenous he might be, but with no source of money to sustain them, he'd have to reserve most of the rations for Piper. The food helped, though; it settled him.

After Edward had scraped the foil clean – first with his spoon, then with his tongue – he took out the Jeep owner's manual from the glovebox. Flicking through it, he located the storage compartments he had not known to investigate. Most of them turned out to be empty, but when he popped the release tab for the passenger seat base he discovered a cavity that relinquished a squat metal tin.

Edward lifted the container onto his lap and opened it, blinking in bemusement at what lay inside. Behind him, Piper stirred. When he turned he saw her watching him. And it *was* Piper now, he somehow knew, not the fleshless interloper that had addressed him back at the farm.

'We made it,' she said.

'Just about.'

'Too close.'

Edward nodded. 'Way too close.'

'Will we be all right?'

He took a long breath. Expelled it. 'We need to figure out some things, have a proper talk. But we'll get there. We always do.'

'Me and you,' Piper said. And smiled.

He grinned back.

'I'm hungry. Do we have any food?'

'Plenty.'

'Not porridge,' she said.

'You don't like porridge?'

'You *know* I don't like porridge.'

'Then I'll find you something else.'

'What have you got there?' the girl asked, craning her neck for a glimpse.

Edward lifted out the tin's contents: a neat shrink-wrapped parcel of banknotes. When he tore off the plastic, ten paper-wrapped bundles fell into his lap. Each bundle contained perhaps one hundred banknotes. The currency was euros, the denomination of the notes five hundred. 'Looks like travelling money,' he told her.

PART III

Nine years later

CHAPTER 26

Gorges du Tarn, Southern France

In late summer, nothing seemed more beautiful to Piper than the two minutes each day when the sun began to dip below the tall canyon walls. For a few precious moments beforehand, it appeared to balance on the limestone ridge; then, like a split yolk, it melted into the rocks until nothing but a golden shard remained.

Piper held her breath as that final sliver winked out. Around her the calls of stone-curlews, larks and tawny pipits stalled as the birds turned a wary eye west. Faces appeared in shadowed stone. The sliding waters of the Tarn – a rich emerald during the day – deepened to indigo. A chill seeped out of the surrounding rocks.

Beside Piper, on a blanket they'd laid across the flat boulders of the northern shore, Therron Vaux squeezed her fingers. 'Show's over, I think.'

'Maybe not,' she told him. Sometimes, around now, she would see the wide black shapes of griffon vultures riding the thermals back to their roosts. As the shadows lengthened she might hear the calls of nightjars, or the unworldly hoot of an eagle owl.

Therron raised an eyebrow. 'Have you planned something special for me?'

Laughing, Piper prodded him. 'Try not to be creepy.'

He bounded to his feet, grinned. 'The word you're looking for is *inquisitive*. Not creepy.'

She squinted up, admiring the hard curves of his legs. 'Where're you going?'

'Your dad asked me to man the office for the late shift. No sleep tonight for poor Therron.'

'Maybe I'll drop by later and cheer you up.' Piper saw his expression and rolled her eyes. 'Get out of here, creep.'

He blew her a kiss and sauntered off, sandals slapping the wet rocks. She watched him go, entranced by the way his muscles flexed beneath T-shirt and shorts. Although the craggy sun-bleached landscape of the nearby Cévennes was the most beautiful Piper had ever seen, it sometimes failed to distract her from the sight of Therron Vaux.

This was her fifth summer in the gorge, and it was growing difficult to imagine that she'd lived anywhere else. After fleeing Stallockmore Farm nine years earlier, her father had spent a few years driving them around Europe before purchasing this forty-pitch campsite south-west of Sainte-Enimie.

Joyau Caché, they named it: Hidden Gem. Edward took down the old sign and carved a new one from the trunk of a single beech tree. He hoisted it over the entrance and there it still hung, welcoming visitors to this section of the gorge from late spring to early autumn.

While Piper had found something to love in each of the region's seasons, the winter time reigned as her favourite. The tourists went home, the seasonal staff departed and she was left alone with her father and the frosted beauty of the gorge. It was all the company she had ever needed, or thought she would ever desire. Until, that was, Therron Vaux came looking for work.

He had appeared at Joyau Caché a year ago, a nervous stick of a boy who kept his shoulders raised and his eyes pointed at the ground. On the rare occasion that he smiled, his muscles tensed like those of a feral cat. He was fifteen at the time, a Lozère native and a refugee from abusive parents back in Mende. Edward, as was his way with all wounded creatures, had made it his task to rehabilitate the boy. He gave Therron a patched-up caravan in a quiet corner of the site and simple maintenance jobs away from the guests. Over the next twelve months they witnessed a transformation: a new Therron emerged, this one full of questions and quick wit. He put on weight. His smooth skin darkened to toffee in the French sun. And, by degrees, Piper fell in love.

Now, alone in the gorge as the evening sky darkened, she climbed to her feet and pushed her toes into sandals. After folding up her towel, she hopped across the boulders towards Joyau Caché's paved loop. She met Mórríghan on the scorched tufts of prairie grass at the top of the riverbank.

The woman stood beside a rusting canoe trailer, clad in her customary attire: a dark linen culpatach with a deeply recessed hood. Beneath it her skin seemed as pale as champignon mushrooms; her eyes were milk-white and blind.

While Mórríghan presented a compelling sight, Piper found, as always, that to stare at her too long made her feel uneasy, nauseous. She knew that Mórríghan was not physically present, that she had conjured this manifestation of the tenant inside her head, but the knowledge made the woman seem no less real.

'He's a fine boy,' Mórríghan said. Her voice was a penetrating contralto, as old as the rocks. It raised Piper's skin into goosebumps.

'Yeah. I like him.'

'More than that, I think.'

Piper glanced around. A line of trees screened the closest pitches from the bank. Satisfied that no one could see them, she perched on the hull of a beached kayak. 'Isn't this dangerous?'

'The longer we speak, the louder we shout. I won't trouble you long.'

'It's time, soon. Isn't it?'

Mórríghan inclined her head. Beneath the hood her features seemed to ripple, as if burrowing creatures moved beneath her skin. The surrounding air swarmed with shadow. 'Four weeks.'

Four weeks until the source of the red light Piper had feared all her life became, for a brief time, dormant: *cadalach*, in the old language. It would offer them the opportunity for which they had been waiting these last sixteen years. Piper still knew little of what that opportunity entailed. Mórríghan had been resolute in her refusal to offer enlightenment; but with the date fast approaching, soon that would have to change. 'Samhain,' she said quietly.

'As some call it.'

'All Hallows Eve. Hallowe'en.'

'A coincidence, really.'

'Is it?'

'The title matters not, nor the custom. The date is what's important. The alignment.' For the first time Mórríghan blinked. 'It's why you need to be careful now.'

'Of my emotions.'

'And of your priorities. You know what happened before. Cathasach's eyes will be everywhere, soon. We only have one chance at this.'

'Why do you call him that?' Piper asked. 'When it's not his name?'

The woman plucked something from the black fabric of her dress and discarded it. 'It's what he's been called for thousands of years.'

'Not by you,' she replied, and caught herself wondering: *Do I project her body language based on what I sense, or does she retain control of that?*

Abruptly, Mórríghan laced her fingers together in her lap. When she looked up, her eyes were clear. 'No. Not by me.'

For a while, neither of them spoke. A cool breeze rolled through the gorge, rustling the leaves of boxwood and juniper.

'You love him,' Mórríghan said. 'This boy, Therron.'

'Yes.'

'Then you have to send him away.'

'Why would I do that?'

'Because if you keep him close he'll die.'

Piper flinched at that, felt an ache in her chest that was difficult to bear. 'You can't know that.'

'I wouldn't lie to you.'

'What about Dad? Am I a danger to him, too?'

'You're a danger to everyone, Piper, but not in the way that you think. Your father made his choice long ago. We'd be wise to honour it. His future is bound to yours, it seems, and even I don't know the reason for that.'

'I won't involve him in this. Not after everything he's been through.'

To that, Mórríghan said nothing.

'I wish my mother was here.'

'It's hard for you. The fact that she's not.'

Piper shrugged. 'From what I hear, she was pretty messed up.'

'Hardly surprising, given her history. Your mother possessed a singular compassion for the world. Such depth of feeling has its burdens, and Gráinne didn't carry hers easily.' Mórríghan paused. 'Selflessness *in extremis* can often seem like cruelty. But your mother saw what needed to be done, and acted as only she could.'

'She gave me up so that you might return.'

'The hardest choice she ever faced, I'm sure. Gráinne weighed the needs of her only child against the needs of humanity, and made an extraordinary decision.'

'I'd always thought she was coerced.'

'There was never any coercion. She did it out of love, Piper, even if it was a form of love you might struggle to understand. Your mother loved humanity deeply but she knew that it suffered a sickness, a malady not of its making.'

'Cathasach,' Piper said. '*Balla-dìon.*' And in her head she thought: *The Wall.*

As she spoke those words she felt something wet on her upper lip, and touched her fingers to her nose. They came away bright with blood.

Mórríghan's eyes narrowed. 'I have to go.'

'But we've hardly—'

'This isn't safe. We'll do it in segments, you and I.' She indicated the blood gathering fresh on Piper's upper lip. 'You're not used to it. When I go it's going to hurt for a while. I'm sorry about that. In time you should get stronger.'

'Hurt?'

Mórríghan vanished.

Piper blinked, and her mouth fell open. As she stared at the empty patch of prairie grass upon which the woman had stood, a bright lance of pain speared her between the eyes. Crying out, she fell to her knees. Canyon shadows danced around her.

Her stomach clenched. She heard herself retch. The pain in her head was brutal, a rapier heat. By the time it began to subside, night had fallen.

CHAPTER 27

Labastide-Esparbairenque, Southern France

Jolyon Percival woke on the floor of his studio wreathed in sweat, throat so dry that the very act of breathing made him gag. His head thumped in time with his heart. '*Beò-Ìobairt*,' he spluttered, and licked his lips with a tongue like a stick of dried beef. '*Beò-Ìobairt*.'

Already the dream was fading, but its appearance had become routine, and Jolyon was well prepared. Pushing himself to his feet, ignoring the twin pops of complaint from his knees, he snatched an artist's pad from a bureau and began to sketch. Only when he had transferred every remaining image to the paper did he grab a water-filled carafe and lift it to his lips. He drank greedily, noisily. With every swallow he felt himself invigorated, a wrinkled desert seed swollen by unexpected rains.

Sated at last, he carried the pad to the studio's balcony. On the way he caught sight of himself in one of the many gilt mirrors Madame Bousin had hung from the walls. 'By gods, man,' he barked. 'As loathsome as a toad!'

His eyes, bloodshot and dry, peered out of a face treated unkindly by the French summer. Not always in this heat did he remember to wear a hat, and the sun had burnished his freckles and fried his skin.

His hair stuck up in ginger tufts. His belly, densely thatched and colossal in girth, had burst from the hem of his vest like over-proved dough. Of more concern was the expression of quiet bewilderment his reflection wore. At some point during the previous evening he had streaked charcoal through his beard. It lent him the look of a bleary-eyed Viking returning from a village-razing. The image cheered him, but he was not ready to rekindle his usual bonhomie quite yet. It would take a breakfast of Madame Bousin's fresh eggs and toast to do that.

At the balcony he pushed open the floor-length shutters and winced as the sky poured in. Already the sun was a merciless white disc. From its position he thought that it must be some time after nine o' clock in the morning.

The tiny community of Labastide-Esparbairenque perched high on a forested fold of the Montagne Noire range. South-west along the valley nestled the village of Roquefère; to the north-east lay Pradelles-Cabardès. Labastide-Esparbairenque itself comprised little more than thirty homes, most of them inhabited by artists like himself or those simply wishing for a more secluded existence.

Jolyon had arrived six months earlier, in a forty-year-old Citroën DS crammed with art materials and provisions. Here he had been when the dreams had intensified, and here he had been ever since.

He rented the studio from Madame Bousin, a thickset yet curiously birdlike woman ten years his senior. They had slept together only once so far, a bad-tempered liaison he'd been appalled to discover had won him zero concessions on his rent. Worse, the woman had interpreted their brief union as confirmation of her graduation from landlady to confidante. As a result he now heard her key in his lock more days than most, and would turn from his easel to find her fiddling with which-ever of his trinkets she had deigned to pick up.

Now, collapsing with a grunt onto one of the balcony's rattan chairs, Jolyon turned his eyes to the pad resting on his belly. 'What bloody mumbo-jumbo *is* this?' he muttered. On the pad, sketched in hurried strokes, was the image of a boy perhaps sixteen years old. When Jolyon saw the boy's eyes – two vivid black scratches – he shuddered, his skin suddenly cool. In the background of the picture, barely visible, he perceived the shadow of a girl he had drawn many times before. Above her, on wide wings, flew a bird. Below the composition Jolyon had scrawled a sentence: *Though they sink through the sea they shall rise again*. He recognised it as a fragment from a Dylan Thomas poem:

> *Though they sink through the sea they shall rise again;*
> *Though lovers be lost love shall not*
> *And death shall have no dominion.*

He had no idea why he had written it, but he felt that the line had risen out of his subconscious as an interpretation of what he had dreamed, rather than appearing in the dream itself. He wondered at its connection to the couple he had sketched. '*Beò-Ìobairt*,' he said once again, rolling the words around on his tongue. *Living Sacrifice*. But to whom did that ancient Gaelic phrase refer?

Jolyon strained to his feet and shuffled back into the studio. Placing the pad on the bureau, he went to his easel and loaded it with a fresh canvas.

He had seen the girl in his dreams before, the boy too, but the bird was new. He mixed oils, picked up a brush. Exhaling, he began to paint. The world receded, sound and smells, and for a while he existed outside of it, suspended somewhere between his painting and the dream. Slowly, from a seemingly random series of strokes and colours, the bird he had glimpsed began to emerge. Beneath its wings an arid landscape formed: snaking river, deep canyon walls.

So caught up was Jolyon in the act of creation that he failed to hear the rattle of Madame Bousin's keys in the door, or the sound of her boots on the stairs. Only when she arrived in the doorway, basket under one arm, did he put down his brush and turn around.

'*Ma chère Madame* . . .' Jolyon began.

The woman frowned, dismissing his words with a flick of her wrist. 'Elise, I have told you, Monsieur Percival. Elise.'

'*Ah, mais oui. Je m'excuse très humblement, Elise.*'

She sniffed at that, softened when he punctuated his words with a bow. Addressing her in French while she responded in English made no sense whatsoever, but it was a habit they found difficult to break.

'You've not slept,' she told him.

Jolyon grinned, felt the creases around his eyes deepen. 'Burden of the wicked.'

Madame Bousin tilted her head. After a moment's pause, she raised her basket. 'I will make coffee. Today I have ham from Monsieur Labelle. Eggs, too.'

'Most kind. Really, though, there's—'

But already the woman had disappeared. He heard the pipes rattling as she filled a coffee pot with water, and sighed.

They ate breakfast on the balcony, plates of ham and eggs balanced on their knees. The coffee was strong and sweet. After his third cup Jolyon began to feel human once more.

Madame Bousin ate slowly, chewing with small, suspicious movements, as if considering with each mouthful whether her food was safe to swallow. She studied him from the corner of her eye. 'I have a parcel for you.'

'Oh?'

'It was delivered to the house.' She dipped into her basket and removed a package wrapped in brown paper. 'The postmark says it's from England. No return address.'

Jolyon placed it on the ironwork table between them.

'You're not going to open it?'

He balanced his empty plate next to the parcel and stood. 'Madame . . . *Elise*, I should say. I'm very grateful. But now I think . . .'

She shot to her feet. 'Of course, Monsieur Percival, of course! An artist needs his peace. I shall leave you to the silence. I came only to bring your parcel, and tell you that Didier Guérin and his wife will be visiting tonight for a game of belote. You will be joining us?'

He smiled. 'I'd like nothing better. But of course that really depends on—'

'We will expect you at eight o' clock.' With that, Madame Bousin swept past him into the studio. At his easel, on which the new canvas stood, she paused. Jolyon moved to block her view but she slid around him, narrowing her eyes. 'A good beginning, I think. Although in reality the gorge is not as bleak as you portray.'

'The gorge?'

She turned from the painting, frowning. 'You do not know this place?'

'I saw a picture a while ago,' he said. 'I'd forgotten the location.'

Madame Bousin shrugged. 'Well, you've captured it from memory very well. It is the Gorges du Tarn, Monsieur Percival.'

'Here? In France?'

'*Oui.* And a place of great beauty. Except, of course, for those.' She pointed at the bird soaring over the canyon walls. 'Griffon vultures. They make their home there now. I do not know why we tolerate them. You know they ate a fallen hiker a few years ago. All of her gone in less than an hour.' Madame Bousin tutted, a loud clack that echoed off the studio's whitewashed walls. 'Horrible creatures.' She strode out of the room and clattered down the stairs.

The moment the front door slammed Jolyon returned to the balcony. He sat down in his chair and ripped open the parcel that had arrived from England.

Inside he found an invoice from the London dealer he had used and, within a layer of bubble wrap, a small book bound in black leather. The spine popped as he opened the cover, and when he lifted it to his nose he smelled aged paper and dust. At the base of its title page he saw an embossed Mottram–Gardner publisher's crest. Above that: *Notes on 'The Black Book': A Journey into the Celtic Apocalypse*. Its author was Patrick Beckett, a professor at Balliol College, Oxford.

The dreams Jolyon had experienced since arriving at Labastide-Esparbairenque had been increasing in frequency and intensity, but if the fragments that survived his waking were not captured immediately they dispersed like threads of woodsmoke. He had started to keep a pad by his bed, with plentiful others scattered throughout the apartment. Over the last few months he had amassed a large collection of images and words. Most of those images were of the girl he had glimpsed this morning. The words were Scottish Gaelic, a language he knew nothing about.

A few weeks ago he had hooked up his old Apple Mac to the studio's phone line. An afternoon spent investigating those phrases had led him to mentions of two ancient works of anonymous Celtic authorship, now lost. They had been dubbed, by historians and folklorists alike, *The Black Book* and *The Red Book*. Both works were apocalyptic in nature, although not in the modern sense of the word. In recent times, *apocalypse* had become shorthand for the destruction of the world and mankind, but traditionally it had been synonymous with *revelation*, pertaining either to the ultimate purpose of humanity or the divine.

Professor Beckett had collected hundreds of fragments from the lost texts. Through an extraordinary feat of patience and scholarship, he had reproduced the original works as closely as the evidence allowed. Copies of Beckett's lesser-known *Red Book* translation had been impossible to find, but Jolyon had tracked down the tome he now held to an antiquarian book dealer near London's Leicester Square. The volume had been published in 1968 and had received only a single printing. It had cost Jolyon the equivalent of a month's rent.

Turning to the first page he began to read, and what he discovered troubled him deeply.

Later that evening he capitulated to Madame Bousin's invitation. He played belote, drank too much Corbières wine and scared Madame Guérin with his impression of the French president. Stumbling back to his studio some time after midnight, he climbed the stairs, kicked off his flip-flops and fell upon his bed, alcohol-soaked and content.

He dreamed, once again, of the boy. This time the two of them were locked in an embrace, lips pressed together in passion. Although Jolyon blinked and kicked and tried to struggle loose, his strength failed him. When he looked into the youth's eyes he saw a reflection of himself and tried to scream; for it was not his own image he encountered, but that of the girl. Her face – *his* face now – was a monstrous shadow, even more terrifying for its lack of definition. She possessed no eyes, just ragged holes. '*Beò-Ìobairt,*' he moaned. '*Beò-Ìobairt.*' And, in doing so, thrashed so violently that he woke.

He lay there in the studio's boxroom, walls swimming around him, a scream lodged like a cockroach in his throat. For a while he thought he was going to be sick. As soon as that feeling passed he reached out and felt around in the darkness. When his fingers touched the sketchpad, he hauled it onto the bed. He found a pencil and worked blind, scratching hurried shapes.

After ten minutes of activity Jolyon cast down his pencil and levered himself off the mattress. He stumbled through the apartment to the kitchen, ducked his face under the cold water tap and drank until he choked. Returning to the bedroom he turned on the light, picked up the pad and looked at what he had drawn. This time, as well as a terrifying image of the girl, he saw three words. The first was *Piper.* Written directly below it was *Joyau Caché.*

Jolyon scratched his beard. He felt his heart labour in his

chest. Earlier that evening he had read Professor Beckett's *Black Book* translation in its entirety. While not all apocalyptic works ended in mankind's destruction, this one had. It prophesied the arrival of a young woman born in blood who, at a time of her choosing, would commit an atrocity so far-reaching it would herald civilisation's collapse.

Earlier, while the sloping sun had plated the studio balcony with copper, Jolyon had found *The Black Book*'s text peculiar, unsettling, but little more than that. He did not believe in prophecies, nor predeterminism.

Why, then, as he stared at the words he had scribbled in the dark, did he feel a chill deep in his marrow, and a sense of approaching calamity?

Piper.

A musical term, but also a name. Was there a clue in that, he wondered? He recalled the shadow he had seen in the boy's eyes and something *snicked* in his mind.

Jolyon Percival wrapped his arms around himself and shivered. Suddenly the forested slopes of Labastide-Esparbairenque seemed far too isolated for comfort.

CHAPTER 28

Gorges du Tarn, Southern France

Edward Schwinn was sitting at the front desk fiddling with the roster when the red-bearded stranger came in seeking accommodation. Outside, the fires in the western sky had faded to indigo, encouraging the first silver pricks of starlight. Inside the booking hut, the only illumination came from a single floor lamp. Jutting from a wall bracket, a fan chased lazy circles. In one corner a drinks fridge hummed.

The stranger wore cut-off jeans and flip-flops, a paint-splattered T-shirt riding high on his belly. He gazed around the hut's interior as if he'd stepped into a dream, his eyes moving over the colourful map of Joyau Caché's pitches, the rack of sun-faded tourist leaflets and the stencilled sign offering free Wi-Fi.

He turned his attention to Edward and his eyes narrowed. His voice, when he spoke, was a sonorous baritone. 'You're not another of these buggers who always insists on addressing me in English?'

Edward matched the man's stare. 'What would you prefer?'

'As if I were no more capable of learning a foreign language,' the stranger continued, 'than flapping my arms and trying to . . . what?'

'I speak English and French. About five words of Spanish. Take your pick.'

The man put his hands on his hips, exhaled explosively. 'Sorry,' he said. 'I'm being a shit.' He nodded towards the window. 'Driving that damnable disaster of engineering always crucifies my patience. Tried to fling me off the Millau Viaduct on the way here.'

Edward glanced outside. In one of the parking bays he saw an ancient Citroën. It hadn't been there five minutes earlier. The car leaned over on its side as if drunk, awning ripped, tyres virtually bald. No passengers sat inside. 'One for camping?' he asked.

The stranger scratched his head. 'What?'

'You're not towing a caravan. Did you want a camping pitch?'

'*Camping* pitch?'

'For a tent.'

'A tent! My God, man.'

Edward closed the cover of his roster. He laced his hands in front of him and took a breath. 'What is it you need?'

'This is Joyau Caché?'

'Yes.'

'Not exactly what I was expecting.' The man glanced again at the site map. 'This was all a bit spur-of-the-moment, if I'm honest. I don't have a tent. Nor a tipi or a yurt, or any damned thing.'

The admission hardly surprised Edward; the stranger looked about as far removed from a natural outdoorsman as it were possible to get. 'I've a couple of static vans, rented by the week. Pretty basic, but I could put you in one of those.'

'Does it have its own toilet?'

'Yes.'

'Not one of those squatting monstrosities, built for savages.'

'No.'

'I'll take it.'

'You want to see it first?'

The man shook his head. 'All I need to know, most urgently, is whether this place has a bar.'

Edward shook his head, glancing at up at the wall clock. 'Site shop's opposite, though. It's open for another hour.'

'Does it sell wine?'

'Both colours.'

'Then you, sir, have struck a bargain. Should we spit and shake?'

'Won't be necessary. How long do you want the caravan?'

'Bloody hell. How should I know?'

Edward nodded. 'I'll put you in for a week. If you want to change that, drop in here and let someone know. Just you?'

'Unless I strike it exceedingly lucky with your wine merchant.'

They completed the paperwork and Edward grabbed a key from the pegboard. Outside, he pulled a bicycle from the rack and instructed the man to follow in his car. The static caravans stood on the highest part of the site, boasting grand views of the gorge. He pedalled up the road, his path lit by the headlamps of the following Citroën. On the way he made a list of tomorrow's tasks: fix a broken pipe in one of the shower stalls; order groceries for the shop; drive into Florac and pick up some guitar strings for Piper. His daughter's birthday wasn't for another four weeks but he'd been planning it, as he always did, far in advance. She never asked for anything, and with the exception of books she seemed not to covet material things, but creating, each birthday, the perfect gift with which to surprise her had become one of Edward's annual pleasures. Last year he had built a five-pronged bird feeder, installing it outside her bedroom window so she could wake to the sound of birdsong. This year he intended to give her a handmade acoustic guitar. He had spent the last three months working on it, using Englewood spruce for the soundboard and Amazon rosewood for the back and sides. He'd fitted the bridge and the tuning keys. All he needed now were the strings and it would be finished. It made him smile to think of her playing it.

He could hardly imagine that Piper would shortly turn

sixteen. Nine years had rolled by since their flight from McAllister's farm. After such a narrow escape, Edward had been reluctant to lay down roots anywhere. As a result, they spent the next four years travelling around Europe in an old Fiat Ducato bus. Yet while Piper seemed infinitely adaptable, he had worried that the constant movement – and lack of any stability – was as likely to harm her long-term as the short-term consequences of being found.

They chanced upon Joyau Caché one evening after passing through the Cévennes. The campsite had a different name back then, of course: Hidden Gem could not have been a more inaccurate description. They were the site's only guests that night, and it wasn't hard to see why. The place was in a terrible state. Edward fell into a conversation with the elderly couple who owned it, and before he quite knew what he was doing he offered to buy them out. The next day they agreed a price that struck him as fair, and five years later struck him as exceedingly *un*fair.

The two years that followed were almost as tough as their twelve-month stint in County Mayo. With most of his funds depleted from the initial investment, Edward couldn't afford to recruit outside labour to assist with refurbishments, and until basic improvements were made, Joyau Caché's visitor traffic – even of the casual sort – remained minimal. It was a vicious circle that took him three years of heavy labour to break.

Slowly, as he toiled beneath the hot sun of the Lozère, he began to make a life for them both; an income and a home. The episode at McAllister's farm – and the more distant events surrounding Piper's birth – began to seem less like memories than bad dreams. Yet even as some of the details faded, Edward remembered with sombre clarity the voice that had addressed him through Piper's mouth that evening in Ireland, as well as the dead lamb she had returned to a brief yet horrifying parody of life.

Another thing he had trouble forgetting was the encounter

with the woman whose Jeep – and whose money – he had stolen during their escape. She had threatened him with a gun, and he had broken her arm in reply. If he had delayed a moment longer at the McAllister property, he knew that Piper would not have survived. Yet however much he tried to justify his actions against the woman who had tried to stop him, he still felt hollow when he recalled her face.

Although the nine years since had been as calm as he could have hoped, they had not been without incident. A handful of times he had witnessed something alarming enough in the girl's behaviour to seek out the notes he had kept during her early childhood.

The first of those episodes occurred when Piper was nine years old. They were travelling through the southern Alps on a circuitous route to Chamonix, where Edward intended to lay flowers on Laura's grave. He had been a young man at the time of her death; twelve years later he had grey in his hair and beard, and a body that ached more days than not. It was time to go back; time to say sorry all over again. Time, perhaps, to educate Piper in the dangers of youthful follies. It was a lesson he hoped she would learn well.

Their battered Fiat spent a week wheezing up and down the punishing Alpine roads before it finally broke down outside Grenoble. Edward booked the vehicle into a nearby garage and the pair of them into a nearby hotel. Piper used the opportunity to drag him around the city. They rode the cable car to the Bastille and visited the Musée de Grenoble. Surrounded by the paintings of Veronese, Canaletto, Renoir and others, the girl burst into tears, overwhelmed. 'We can be so beautiful,' she sobbed. 'I didn't know. I didn't *know*.'

While her words struck him as strange, her outburst was not out of character. He knew that she was an unusually sensitive child, and he had noticed that examples of beauty or barbarity in humanity affected her greatly. While Piper could appreciate the purity of an Alpine vista or the simple grace of a spider's web, it was always the fragility of human endeavours that brought her to tears. Edward did not know why such things affected her the way they did, and he did not feel equipped to enquire. He had made enough mistakes guarding her physical safety without blundering around in matters psychological.

However dramatic Piper's behaviour in the Musée de Grenoble, it was a mere precursor to what happened later that day. After leaving the museum they had lunch in a bistro overlooking the Isère. As they lingered over steak-frites, the bell above the door jangled. A woman walked in, taking a table near the window.

She was about as beautiful a creature as Edward had seen, and he could not stop himself from staring as he ate his meal. Her high cheekbones, accentuated by sharp emerald eyes and hair like spun sunshine, gave her an elfin look. It was wintertime in the Alps and the cold had buffed her cheeks with colour. She pulled a magazine from her bag and began to read, oblivious of her effect on him.

When Edward turned back to Piper he met a grin so wide it threatened to split her face in half. He frowned, puzzled by her sudden change in mood.

'You like her,' she said, tilting her head towards the stranger. 'Don't you?'

Edward glanced back at the woman, quickly averted his eyes. 'No, Pie. You're wrong.'

Her eyes sparkled. 'I saw the way you looked at her. You don't have to pretend with me.'

He shook his head, uncomfortable with the intensity of her gaze. 'The door opened and I looked up, that's all.'

Piper giggled. 'You're blushing.'

Irritated, Edward opened his mouth to rebuke her, then stopped himself. He would not respond harshly to a question that was, after all, entirely natural. He knew she craved a mother figure, knew that she wanted, more than anything, for him to find a partner – someone they could both love. It would never happen, of course; he did not deserve to be with a woman again, and he refused to exorcise himself of Laura's ghost.

For a moment, as the girl stared at him across the bistro table, he thought he felt a shiver of energy through the floor beneath his feet. Across the street, a flock of pigeons burst into the sky.

They finished their food. Edward looked around for a waiter so he could pay the bill. As he tried to attract attention he noticed the woman by the window turn in her seat. She stared at him, eyes wide. Unnerved by her scrutiny, he looked away. The waiter appeared, then. Edward handed him a sheaf of notes, anxious, all of a sudden, to get outside.

Piper looked at him askance. 'What's wrong?'

'Nothing,' he snapped. 'Let's go.'

He stood up too fast and his belt caught the table-edge. His empty water glass toppled onto its side and before he could stop it, rolled off the edge, smashing to pieces on the floor. He felt eyes on him now, from everywhere in the bistro.

Flustered by the attention, panic beginning to grip him, Edward seized Piper's hand. 'Outside,' he said. 'Now.' He pulled her towards the door, heartbeat thumping in his ears. He heard the girl's protests but the exact words she spoke were lost to him. Her cry of pain was not, and it seemed to rouse the other diners too.

As he threaded between the tables he saw the woman by the window rise to her feet. Just as he reached the door she moved in front of him. Her eyes looked wild: pupils dilated, sclera engorged. The cold-weather blush on her cheeks had spread to her throat.

She placed a hand on his chest and he felt her fingernails hard against his skin. '*Pardon*,' she said. '*S'il vous plaît ne partez pas.*'

Shaking his head, he pushed past her.

Sorry. Please don't go.

It made no sense.

Behind him he could hear chair legs scraping, strangers

climbing to their feet. Piper shook his arm.

Edward snatched at the door, yanked it open. In a breath they were on the pavement. Bright sunlight sparkled on the Isère. Suddenly he could breathe again, great lungfuls of frozen Alpine air.

'What *was* that?' Piper shouted. Tears gleamed on her cheeks. 'What's wrong with you?'

'Not now,' he hissed. He looked left and right, tried to remember where he'd parked the Fiat.

'Dad, you're hurting me. My arm—'

He hadn't parked the Fiat anywhere. It was in the garage, being repaired.

The hotel, then. Did it stand behind them? Across the river?

Edward felt the strength draining from his limbs. For a moment the people in the street canted and blurred.

'*English?*' asked a voice. When he scrunched up his eyes and squinted, he saw that the woman from the bistro had followed them outside. Condensation plumed from her mouth. She took quick shallow breaths, as if adrenalin had flooded her system, stranding her somewhere between fight and flight.

Edward glanced at Piper. His daughter looked abashed, now. Stricken.

You like her. Don't you?

In that moment, he realised what she had done.

'I can't help it,' the woman said, her teeth beginning to chatter. '*Je suis désolée.*'

Stepping forward, she gripped his face between her hands. Shocked, Edward jerked backwards, but she held on tight. The heat of her fingers seared his skin.

She kissed him. Hot mouth, wet against his lips. Hot tongue, pushing between them. She tasted of coffee and cinnamon and madness. Her eyes were inches from his own. He could see every detail, every whorl and fleck.

Edward put his hands on her shoulders and prised her away. 'I'm sorry,' he said. 'I'm sorry.'

'No,' the woman insisted. 'It's OK. Really, it is. I'm Brigitte. This . . .' She flapped a hand. Burst out laughing. Studied him and chewed her lip.

'I need you to listen,' he told her, as gently as he could. His chest was aching. He couldn't catch a breath. 'Brigitte, did you say? I need you to listen.'

To Piper he asked, 'Can you stop it? Can you get rid of what you've done?'

She swallowed. 'Oh, Dad, I don't know. I don't know *how*.'

Edward imagined that red dome rising out of the ground, imagined all the people in the street turning against them. 'Piper, please.'

'I don't know what to *do*!' she wailed.

He nodded, grimaced. Taking the woman by the arms, he forced himself to meet those wild eyes once more. 'Listen,' he said. 'You can fight this. Overcome it.'

Her lips formed a half-smile. 'Why would I do that?'

'We're leaving. Me and the girl. Don't follow us. Whatever you're feeling – it isn't real. Look at me. Really look at me.'

'I am,' she replied, eyebrows furrowing. 'I know what I see.'

'Go back inside.'

'I can't.'

Again, he thought of the red dome. This time it decided him. 'I'm telling you as clearly as I can,' he said. 'Don't follow us. Turn around and go back.'

With that, Edward grabbed Piper's hand and stepped into the street, dragging her across the two lanes of traffic flowing along the Quai Stéphane Jay; pause, sprint, pause, sprint. They reached the other side and he fought through a press of tourists.

Piper tugged his hand. 'No, Dad. It's this way.'

He looked and saw, of course, that she was right. Opposite the bistro, the Pont Saint-Laurent arced across the Isère. It was wide for a footbridge, the deck supported by heavy cables hung from two stone towers. Edward raced across, pulling Piper along with him. Their hotel was north of here, three blocks distant. They could walk it in twenty minutes, run it in ten. Would that be far enough away if this were the epicentre? They'd have to risk it. All their possessions were still in the suite. Even if they fled Grenoble, which they would surely have to do, he still needed to retrieve their passports from the safe.

On the pavement outside the bistro Brigitte watched, her breath steaming. After a moment she stepped onto the road.

'Shit.'

They were halfway across the bridge. The Isère glimmered beneath them. Ahead, rising up behind the shops and apartment buildings of Place de la Cymaise, Edward saw the Bastille's rocky outcrop.

He reached the far side of the bridge and paused, waiting for a break in the traffic passing along the quay. Piper glanced over her shoulder. 'She's coming, Dad.'

As they crossed the road and ran into the square, Edward tried to think. Two years had passed since Stallockmore Farm; two years since the red dome had brought violence and death to the place they'd called home. Piper's nightmare that evening had triggered the quake that hit the house, but how much time had elapsed between that seismic event and the arrival of what sought her? Five minutes? Three? How much distance could they cover in that time? Would they escape the dome's immediate perimeter? Would the woman chasing them allow it to follow?

The square was spaced with neatly cropped trees. Colourful plastic chairs – red and orange and yellow – stood outside the cafés. Edward and Piper raced past them, veering into an adjacent street. This one was narrow. Cramped parking, a single lane of traffic. Apartment buildings crowded close on either side, leaving a thin strip of sky. Edward checked that it still shone blue. He failed to notice that he'd strayed into the middle of the street until it was almost too late.

Ahead, a dark green delivery van was travelling far too fast down the slope towards them. He saw the driver's mouth open wide in shock, saw the man's hands scrabble at the wheel. The vehicle's tyres shrieked. It rolled on its suspension. Edward leaped to his left, yanking Piper after him. The van swerved past, clipping a parked car. It ricocheted away, see-sawing back across the street.

Brigitte ran out of the entrance to Place de la Cymaise, directly into its path.

Edward saw the van's brake lights flare red and its wheels lock, but it had barely a second to scrub off speed before it hit her. He heard a hollow-sounding bang as she folded around the bonnet, palms flat across its surface. Brigitte's eyes widened as the van carried her across the street, dulled as it mashed her against the side of a red-brick apartment block and came to a halt.

Steam vented. Brick dust rolled. Blood mixed with oil and flowed along the gutter.

Edward stared, unable to process what had happened. The van door opened and the delivery driver stumbled out. He fell to his knees, raked fingers through his hair.

Piper screamed. Raising her hands to her mouth, she screamed again.

It was the fillip Edward needed to break his paralysis. He lifted her up and ran.

'I killed her,' the girl moaned. 'I killed her. I killed her.'

'No, you didn't,' he said, bundling her away as fast as he could. And, in doing so, closed his mind to the darker thoughts that had bloomed like rich fungus inside it.

The girl's eyes glazed. Her head fell against his shoulder. She did not speak again.

How he managed it, he would never know, but he carried her through their hotel lobby only a few minutes later. Legs shaking, he climbed two flights of stairs to their floor. Inside their room Edward tried to lower Piper to her feet, but her eyes were closed now, her body limp. He shook her but she didn't respond. Changing his mind, he laid her on the bed.

He went to a fitted wardrobe and threw open its doors. At the back of a shelf, secured to the rear wall, sat the room safe. Edward keyed the code and scooped out their passports: two for him, two for her. He grabbed a money roll and stuffed it into a pocket. Beneath the shelf sat their bags, already packed. Edward dumped them on the bed. When he looked up he noticed that Piper's eyes were open. But it wasn't his daughter behind them.

A thrill of fear climbed his spine. 'Pie?'

The girl's eyes were fixed on the ceiling. Slowly they swung towards him. 'It wasn't her fault.'

And it was *that* voice again – the one that had spoken to him in Ireland the night he had slaughtered the resurrected lamb.

Warily, he approached the bed. 'If there's any blame, it's mine.'

'You did well to get her away.'

'The woman, Brigitte—'

'Is a tragedy. I'd reverse it if I could.'

His breath was coming back now, but his mouth felt as if it were lined with sand. He moved his tongue around it, worked up some spit. 'How much time do we have?'

'It depends how many people saw you. Not long. Change your clothes before you go back outside. Cover your face and hers.'

'It uses people. Doesn't it?'

'Yes.'

'The way you're using her.'

'No.'

'Don't lie to me.'

Piper's mouth became a tight line.

'How's she doing all this?'

No response.

'I've played along until now,' Edward continued. 'But we're at a crossroads, you and I. I'm your only route out of here, your one chance of escape. If you want my help, I need answers.'

'You're endangering Piper. If—'

'*You're* endangering her!' he roared.

'Edward, there's no time.'

'*Tell me!*'

The girl's eyes blazed. 'Piper is strong, clever. But she was never taught how to handle this. She should have been prepared, and she wasn't. It's become a little crowded in here. Sometimes the boundaries between us aren't as strong as we intended. Whatever Piper's qualities, she's still a nine-year-old girl. When she goes exploring inside her head, when she reverts to instinct or daring, or has dreams, she accesses parts of me that were never meant to be shared. Because she does it subconsciously, I have little ability to prevent it.'

He nodded, even though he didn't understand. 'Who are you?'

'I'm *An Toiseach*.'

Edward remembered the Gaelic phrases he had researched, and recalled what that meant: *The First*. He unzipped the bags he had thrown onto the bed, stripped off his clothes and changed into a fresh set. He peeled off Piper's jacket, swapped it for another. Her eyes followed him all the while.

'It wants you dead,' he said.

'Yes.'

'What is it? This thing hunting us?'

A pause. 'It's *An Toiseach*, too.'

'The same as you?'

'No. Absolutely unlike me.'

'Is it inside someone? The way you are?'

She shook her head. 'It's in the earth. It's everywhere.'

'Everywhere?'

Piper's eyes widened. 'It's coming.'

Edward cringed. He knew how tightly he was playing this. 'We're leaving,' he said. 'Right now. But there's one more thing. A condition.'

'We don't have time.'

He stared, resolute. 'A condition.'

'Go on.'

'I don't want her to remember. What happened just now, back at the bistro. It wasn't her fault and she doesn't need that. I know what that kind of guilt is like, what it would do to her. Piper wouldn't cope. She wouldn't.'

'I can't just erase—'

'I think you can.'

'We need to go, Edward.'

He hoisted the bags over his shoulder. 'Then give me an answer.'

'Yes.'

He went to the bed, picked her up. 'Smart choice.'

A minute later they were back on the street. A minute after that they were in a taxi heading north. Another ten minutes and they were at a car hire depot, where Edward rented the cheapest 4x4 they had.

If the red dome appeared over Grenoble, he never saw it. They made it to Chamonix without incident, approaching the town from the south-west. The snow-covered summits of the Mont Blanc massif loomed on their right. Edward pulled into a rest area and forced himself to look. Twelve years had rolled by since Laura had died up there in the clouds along with their unborn child, but the passing of time had made the memories no less savage. While Piper stared through the windscreen, captivated by the beauty of the peaks, Edward stumbled outside. He made it to the rear of the car before he vomited onto the tarmac.

Twelve *years*.

The baby, he had discovered following the postmortem, had been a girl. They would have called her Esme, after Laura's grandmother. Esme for a girl, Solomon for a boy. If Esme had survived, she would have been close to Piper's age by now. That thought, out here so close to where it all had happened, made his hands shake and his stomach clench. He vomited again, this time until he was purged.

Piper didn't look at him as he slid behind the wheel, and he didn't offer her any words. He started the car and they drove in silence to Chamonix's Biollay cemetery, where Laura's ashes had been buried. He found it hard to breathe as they walked the manicured paths. Twice the pressure inside his chest grew so intense that he thought he might have to stop, but he clenched his fists and persevered. All the while the mountains peered down. He wondered if they remembered him.

'It's beautiful,' Piper said, and he nodded, unable to speak. So many climbers were buried here, so many of his childhood heroes: Whymper; Rebuffat; Terray.

In a quiet corner of the cemetery they came across Laura's grave. Her headstone, like so many of the others, was an irregular lump of granite with a single polished face. Before it, on a neat square of gravel, a dwarf conifer in a plastic pot stood beside a bouquet of wilting flowers. The bouquet, Edward saw, had been sent from abroad. On the accompanying card he recognised Laura's father's handwriting. Seeing it sparked another electric shock of memory.

About the only thing Edward and her parents had agreed upon in the immediate aftermath of her death was that she should be buried here, in the town she had loved. Her mother made it clear that Edward was not welcome at the remembrance service, and he respected the woman's wishes, refusing to be the cause of any further grief. The night before they offered Laura's body to the flames, he visited the funeral home and spent a few hours in private at his wife's side.

That was the hardest time of all. He had only been discharged from the hospital earlier that day; he went from lying in a bed with bandages around his hands and feet, to sitting in a softly lit parlour beside an open coffin.

'I want to die, too,' he told her. 'But I don't know if I can.'

Laura stared up at the ceiling, her face impassive and

beautiful. He kissed her cheek, sobbing when he felt the coldness of her skin, and left Chamonix the same evening. He did not see his wife again until that night on the road in Snowdonia; when, for a few short hours, his hope had been rekindled.

'I'm sorry,' Piper said. And for a moment Edward wondered if she had heard his thoughts. 'You loved her very much.'

'I wasn't worthy of her.'

'Perhaps one day you'll realise just how worthy you were,' she replied. It was a strange thing for a nine-year-old to say, and Edward did not like to hear it. When Piper tried to slip her hand into his he shrugged her away. Such contact, standing as they did in front of Laura's grave, did not feel right. The girl bowed her head and hugged herself.

They did not stay in Chamonix, but booked a hotel in nearby Courmayeur. That night he and Piper shared an awkward meal in the hotel bar. He knew he betrayed the girl with his unwillingness to talk. She did not press him, and that made him feel worse. The next day they took an early breakfast and retraced their steps to Grenoble, where they picked up their motorhome. Edward was nervous of returning to the city so soon, but he could not afford to be reckless with their savings – the Fiat, even with the long miles on its odometer, still represented an important percentage of their capital. Reunited, they abandoned the Alps for Italy.

They had just passed the town of Donnas in the Aosta Valley region when he pulled over and switched off the engine. Piper looked up from her book and blinked in surprise. She was reading Thucydides' *History of the Peloponnesian War*, which was an insane choice for someone her age. Her eyes wandered to a stone campanile rising from the forested slopes. 'What's up?' she asked.

Edward opened his door and jumped out. 'Come on.'

'Where're we going?'

'It's cold. Grab your jacket.'

He slammed the door and waited, blowing onto his hands to

warm them. When Piper appeared she wore a fearful look. 'Dad?'

A few yards from where they had parked, a trail led up through trees to a picnic table. Edward led her over to it and sat her down. He stared at her a long while. Finally, he said, 'It's time we talked.'

'About what?'

He chose not to reply to that, merely watched her instead.

Piper, to her credit, held his gaze a long time before she looked away. The surface of the picnic table was deeply scarred. She ran her thumbnail along a groove. 'You're scaring me. I thought I'd never say that, but you are.'

He frowned. 'Why do you say it now?'

'Because it's true. You look at me differently.' Edward began to protest, but she shook her head. 'Ever since we got to the Alps. Ever since you saw that mountain. There's always been a piece of you that's needed fixing, but I never guessed how big it was till now.'

That such words could come from a nine-year-old girl was hard to accept. 'We can talk about that. We can talk about anything you want. But first this, OK? First this.'

Piper nodded, miserable. 'What do you want to know?'

He reached over the table and tapped her forehead. 'What's in there with you?'

The girl hesitated, frowned. For a moment he thought she wanted him to elaborate. But then, with a lurch, he realised that Piper was listening, as if somewhere inside her head a dialogue was taking place.

'Her name is Mórríghan,' she said. 'At least, that's what they called her. When she came here last.'

'They?'

'They're dead now, most of them. This was long ago. I mean a *long* time.'

He nodded, as if he understood. 'How long has she been in there?'

The question seemed to surprise her. 'Mórríghan's always been here.'

'Always?'

'For as far back as I can remember.'

'How far back can you remember?'

'I remember the night I was born.'

He felt the skin of his scalp crawl. 'Pie,' he said carefully. 'You must know that's an unusual thing to say.'

'Yes.'

'What do you remember about it?'

'I remember you holding me,' she replied. 'I remember being on the floor of a car, looking up at you.' She paused. 'I remember a man with a knife. And a woman, with lank hair. My mother, I think.'

'I've told you this story.'

Piper shook her head. 'That's not it. I know what you're thinking, but that isn't the answer. It's a memory, Dad. Clear as anything. I can prove it, too.'

'How?'

'Because however many times you told me the story, you always missed out the part about her breast-feeding me before she died that second time.'

Edward stared at her, dumbstruck.

'It's kind of creepy when you think about it,' she continued, 'but it doesn't freak me out. It's comforting, in a way. I get why you didn't tell me, though. And that's OK.'

'I knew her for a single night. We had a few hours. Then she was gone.'

'I can still see her face,' Piper said. 'She looked sad, didn't she? Tired. The same way you look sometimes. In fact, the way you look most of the time.'

'You're pretty good at changing the subject.'

'I wasn't trying.'

'How did this thing get inside your head?'

'Mórríghan, Dad. Not a thing.'

'How'd it get in?'

'I told you. She's been there since the beginning. Before I was even born.'

'Is it in you all the time?'

'*She.* Yes, she's always here.'

'Is she listening right now?'

'Probably.'

'Can we have a private conversation? You and me?'

'What do you mean?'

'Can you stop her from listening? Just for a little while?'

'I guess, Dad, but—'

'Will you do that for me? Just for a few minutes?'

Piper watched him. Her eyes clouded, as if she conducted another of those internal discussions. Then, finally, she shrugged. 'OK,' she said. 'It's just us.'

'Are you positive?'

'I cross my heart, Dad.'

As satisfied as he could be that he spoke privately, Edward took his daughter's hands. 'How do we kill this thing, Pie?'

Aghast, she tried to snatch her hands away, but he held on tight.

'You heard me. This . . . *intruder* . . . inside your head. You might think it's normal but it's not. It has no right to be there. It never asked your permission, did it? Never gave you a choice. All it's done, all it's ever done, is put you in danger.'

'Dad, Mórríghan is—'

'Don't. Don't call it that. Don't humanise it.' He paused, looked hard into her eyes. 'Maybe that's the reason you're OK with it being inside you – you think of it as a person, with real feelings, thoughts.'

'It does. *She*, I mean. She does.'

'You remember when we were living at Stallockmore, that time the flock had a tapeworm infestation?'

Piper shuddered. 'Yeah.'

'You could see little chunks in the faeces, tiny pieces.

Nothing too bad, really. But look inside one of those sheep and you'd have found a worm coiled up as tall as you are now.'

'Gross.'

He nodded, waited for that to sink in. 'How do we get it out?'

Piper bunched her shoulders. He could see that he had disturbed her with the image he had planted. 'We can't,' she said. 'And even if we could . . . I wouldn't let you. You're wrong about her, Dad, I promise you are. I know how this looks to you, what you think about her. But Mórríghan is here for a reason. And even if I don't—'

Abruptly, the girl shut her mouth. She pulled away from him, stuffing her hands into her coat pockets.

'Even if you don't what?'

She shook her head.

'Why is she here? What is she intending to do?'

Piper's lips were a tight line.

He leaned back, giving her space. Down on the main road a lorry blasted past, destined for France. 'You remember Grenoble?' he asked. 'The place we went a few days ago?'

'What about it?'

'What do you remember?'

'I remember the museum,' she said. 'Going up to the Bastille.'

'You remember the bistro, afterwards?'

'We had steak–frites.'

'You liked that place?'

Piper shrugged. 'It was OK.'

'Would you go there again?'

'I guess.' She scrunched up her face. 'But if you want a steak, it's cheaper to buy one and cook it yourself.'

Edward stood up. 'Let's get out of here.'

'Where are we going?'

'I don't know yet. Somewhere hot.'

★ ★ ★

And that's where they went, driving south down Italy's west coast. They lingered a while in Rome, so that Piper could see the sights. They visited the Colosseum, the Vatican, the church of San Clemente. But out of all the places the girl saw, the catacombs of San Callisto affected her the most. The tunnel complex, five levels deep and stretching for eleven miles, housed the skeletons of nearly half a million dead. Edward hated it – hated being underground, hated being so confined – but he stayed for Piper's sake.

She wandered in silence, pressing her hands to the walls. 'We so often look down, instead of up,' she said, once they had emerged into the light. 'Why do you think that is?'

'I don't know.'

'I don't like being underground.'

'Me neither.'

'When I die,' she told him, 'I want a sky burial.'

'What's that?'

'In Tibet, the ground's too hard to dig graves. There's not much wood for cremations, either. When somebody dies, their family takes them to the charnel grounds.'

'What are they?'

'Have you heard of Vajrayana Buddhists?

'No.'

'They believe in the evolving consciousness.'

'OK.'

'The transmigration of the spirit.'

'You're losing me.'

'They also think that a person's physical remains are simply an empty vessel, something to be offered back to nature. The charnel grounds are usually on a mountain-top, somewhere the dead are taken and left. After a while the vultures come. They strip the body of flesh, crunch up the bones until there's nothing left.'

'Sounds pretty gruesome.'

'I think it sounds beautiful.'

Edward had nothing to say to that, so he kept his mouth shut.

After Rome, they passed through Naples and reached Italy's southern tip. From Villa San Giovanni they took a ferry to Sicily where they spent the winter. When spring broke, they retraced their steps up Italy's western spine before turning north-east towards Austria. Two years later they stumbled across Joyau Caché after passing through the Cévennes.

They had lived here five years. Every few months he wondered whether he should sell up, move on. But the red light and its accompanying horrors had not made an appearance for nearly a decade. Since the tragedy in Grenoble, Piper had exhibited none of the behaviour that had previously disturbed him, and for the first time in her life she had found some stability – a small network of people whom she could trust. She would be sixteen in November, and then what? Would she stay with him? Move away? Maybe that would be the time to arrange a little sky burial of his own.

He had been twenty-eight when Laura had died on the mountain, thirty-one the night Piper was born. In three years' time he would be fifty, and he felt it far more than he should. The succession of menial jobs he had taken while Piper had been an infant had left their mark. He had started to suffer from arthritis in his knees and wrists, and it was a rare morning that he could climb out of bed without his back spasming. Even cycling was an effort these days, but he persevered at that; apart from swimming, it was the only exercise he could manage.

Now, on his bike, slogging up the hill towards Joyau Caché's row of static caravans, he knew that tomorrow's rising would be a difficult task. A muscle on the left side of his ribcage twitched repeatedly; his right knee buzzed every time he completed a revolution of the pedals.

Behind him, Jolyon Percival followed in the rusting Citroën. Edward's shadow preceded them, a spindly silhouette with distorted head and feet. When he reached the row of caravans, he dismounted and dropped his bike into the grass. He directed Percival to park outside.

Edward went up the nearest caravan's steps, opened the door and flicked on the lights. Percival followed him over the threshold and glanced around. Inside, the living area was simply appointed — folding table, sofa, narrow galley kitchen — but it was clean and well kept.

'How long have you been here?' the man asked.

'Few years.'

'Like it?'

'Nothing better.' Edward retreated to the door. He disliked small talk; had never been much good at it.

'Own the place, do you?'

He nodded. 'There's clean sheets on the bed. Reception number's on the card. I'll send someone up with spare linen.'

'Any family?' asked his guest. 'Kids?'

Edward stared, disquieted by the question. 'Just me.'

CHAPTER 29

Frank Irwin Center, Austin, Texas

On an evening like this, with temperatures outside the arena refusing to drop below seventy degrees, Pastor Benjamin D. Pope could lose seven pounds in a single performance.

Right now he was feeling that heat aplenty. Sweat rolled into his eyes as he crossed the stage. The spots blazing from the lighting rigs dissolved into a rhinestone shower. Caught beneath them, he felt like a bug frying on a griddle. Behind him Terrance LaDouceur's band belted out another refrain, the drummer setting a furious rhythm for the rest of the section to follow.

'*REACH OUT!*' the pastor yelled into his mike, and the crowd roared its approval. '*REACH OUT FOR THE HOLY SPIRIT! LIFT UP YOUR HANDS! LIFT UP YOUR HEARTS TO THE LORD!*'

Sixteen thousand voices sang out in exultation. To the right of the stage stood Wendy Devereaux's team of greeters, many of them shepherding those already healed back to their seats. To the left waited the dwindling queue of faithful still to be seen.

Pastor Benjamin spotted two sharp-suited attendants helping a black woman towards him from the front of the queue. He knuckled sweat from his eyes and tried to focus. Those damned lights! Ah. Here she was, now, swimming into view: late fifties; platinum pixie cut; thrift store clothes. Gold hoops hung from her ears but her fingers were free of rings. When she came closer, Benjamin saw why. Her hands were lumpy and twisted; twin horror shows emerging from grossly bloated wrists. Below her skirt, her stockinged legs flowed into ankles that looked as if baseballs had been sewn beneath the flesh. Mascara ran down her cheeks. She smiled at him, overcome.

At LaDouceur's prompting, the band faded to the chords of a single Hammond organ. 'What's your name, child?' Pastor Benjamin whispered. The radio mike picked up his voice and broadcast his words across the arena.

'Grace.'

'Ah, of course. *Grace.*' Benjamin raised his arms, turning in a circle for the crowd. He gloried in that sweet hovering of expectation. Sweat rolled down his spine, gathering in the waistband of his jockey shorts. The hairs of his forearms lifted. 'I don't need to ask, Grace – the Lord helps me see. I *see* that bad ole arthritis, Grace. I *see* what it done to you. There's a devil on your back; he's talkin' through your hands, he's dancin' through your feet. In Jesus' name I say, *DEVIL BE GONE!*'

With those words he swooped around and lunged. The woman fell backwards into the arms of the greeters. They lowered her gently to the floor. '*RAISE HER UP!*' he hollered, and they dragged her back to her feet.

Pastor Benjamin grasped her head in both hands and thrust it away from him. '*DEVIL BE GONE!*' Again she collapsed in a heap. '*RAISE HER UP!*'

This time, as she swayed in front of him, eyes rolling in her skull, the pastor turned his back. He felt his left arm beginning to twitch, heard a hi-hat start to hiss in time with his movements. Bless LaDouceur, he thought, for coming up with that.

A drum lick sounded; the crowd began to rock. Pastor Benjamin spun around. He threw out his hands as if casting bolts of lightning. '*HEALED IN JESUS' NAME!*' Again, Grace fell backwards but the pastor's team trampolined her. '*HEALED, I SAY, AS A FOLLOWER OF CHRIST! SHOW US YOUR HANDS, GRACE! OPEN AND CLOSE THEM LIKE THIS! LIKE THIS, GRACE! LIKE **THIS**!*'

Following his lead, the woman clenched and unclenched her fists, a nerve spasming in her cheek. 'Praise Jesus!' she cried. 'Hallelujah!' She faced the crowd and performed an awkward pirouette. Cheers and applause greeted her. LaDouceur whipped up his band with the enthusiasm of a racehorse jockey. Bass, guitar, organ, drums. The choir sang out a gospel fragment.

The energy was enormous. To Pastor Benjamin, rolling towards his grand finale, it felt like the entire arena had ignited. '*WHO HEALS?*' he bellowed, and the crowd chanted '*JESUS!*'

'*SAY IT LIKE YOU MEAN IT!*'

They howled their affirmations.

To his right, Wendy Devereux's team had finished assembling a group of twenty faithful. Pastor Benjamin ran towards them. He tore off his jacket, hurling it around his head. '*HEALED!*'

As one, all twenty collapsed to the floor. Two began to convulse. Greeters dragged them to the back of the stage.

LaDouceur offered up a trombone chorus. Salt sweat stung the pastor's eyes. He shook his head, squinted. Saw two greeters in the pit hoisting someone onto the stage. His right eye cleared for a moment and he perceived a young boy. '*BRING HIM! BRING HIM!*'

A figure close by shook its head. Started to wave its arms. Was that Wendy? He ignored her. They might be pressed for time but he knew a great close when he saw one. Again he knuckled water from his eyes and saw the lights fracture into sharp white shards.

The greeters led the boy closer and Pastor Benjamin turned on his smile. Wendy – it *was* Wendy, he was sure of it – was shaking her head furiously now. He felt a flash of irritation. Couldn't she see the crowd? Couldn't she *feel* this energy?

He chopped a hand towards the band and LaDouceur reined it in. A hush fell upon the arena. Benjamin lifted his arms and his face to the roof. The lights scorched his cheeks like burning pitch. 'Hold up your hands to heaven, brothers and sisters. You're going to see a boy saved.' He raised his voice a touch. 'I said, all of you, *hold up your hands to heaven.*'

Cries of *Amen!* and *Hallelujah!*

Pastor Benjamin opened his eyes and surveyed the crowd: a sea of raised arms; sixteen thousand expectant faces, many wet with tears. He smiled beatifically. His audience smiled back. Among them walked his administrative staff, taking credit card donations on hand-held terminals.

Once again the arena lights swam. Benjamin called out, 'Tell me how this child is afflicted.'

'His legs, Pastor.'

Not the voice of a greeter he recognised. The pastor turned his face towards the pair supporting the boy, but his eyes remained dazzled. He saw only coruscating shapes, faces devoid of features. The boy hung suspended between them. 'Tonight, in faith, you'll see him walk.'

'Praise the Lord!' the greeters cried.

LaDouceur's organ swelled. The crowd rocked on its feet.

The pastor had them, now. The arena balanced on the tip of his finger. He pointed at the boy and appealed to those watching. '*Witness* the power of the Holy Spirit! *Witness* the power of Jesus standing among us!'

Finally his vision started to recover. He saw four of his security staff, marshalled by Wendy Devereux, rushing across the stage towards him. Benjamin frowned, angered at the distraction.

Then he realised his mistake.

The faces of the pair supporting the boy coalesced. Neither belonged to a member of his team, but they did share a likeness with the youngster. The father wore his grey hair shaved close. The mother wore a wedding frock and scuffed heels. Their eyes were bright with hope. How had they circumvented security and got themselves up on stage?

To the boy's father, he asked: 'What's your son's affliction, friend?'

'Car wreck,' the man replied. 'Legs crushed.'

Benjamin felt goosebumps break out across his flesh.

'Paralysed,' the woman sobbed. 'From his waist right down to his feet.'

It was the pastor's nightmare writ large: a grand promise made in front of an expectant crowd, and one that could not be fulfilled.

Too late, now. Too late.

The boy stared like a captured bird. Benjamin began to take a backwards step, checked himself.

Wendy Devereux and her team swarmed behind the family but every eye in the house was on the boy, and the woman knew it. At the base of the stage Benjamin saw a security guy – external company, not part of his ministry – standing beside an empty wheelchair. The man gave him a *shit-happens* shrug.

As if sensing the pastor's distress, the band struck up. Trumpets, trombones. Organ, drums and guitar. LaDouceur's arms moved in a blur.

Benjamin's finger hovered over the boy. 'Will you tell these good people your name?'

'Jared, sir.'

'Jared. Can you feel the Holy Spirit here among us tonight, Jared?'

The boy didn't answer that, but it mattered little; his voice would have been lost in the cacophony of sound sweeping the arena. Some in the audience surged forward, desperate for a closer look. They pressed behind the wheelchairs of those watching from the front row.

Everywhere Pastor Benjamin looked, eyes glittered, hungry for a miracle.

'We can't know why these tragedies hit us,' he said, and winced at his choice of words. He felt his concentration unravelling. 'Jesus keeps those reasons to Himself. But the Lord does tell me this, young Jared. He stands here and tells me *He wants you to WALK*!'

Musical pyrotechnics from the band. On the arena floor, half the gathered crowd collapsed as if struck. Jared's parents clasped their hands together and sank to their knees. Unsupported, the boy keeled backwards. Two of Wendy's team made a grab for him. Both missed. Jared's shoulders slammed the stage and his head cracked the boards with an impact like a sniper shot. In a practised move, the greeters surrounded him and lifted him away.

Panic, now, in the eyes of many of his team. The band riffed like crazy. '*CHRISTI CRUX EST MEA LUX! CHRISTI CRUX EST MEA LUX! WHEN HE WAKES!*' Pastor Benjamin cried, winding up his fists and flinging them heavenward. '*THE BOY WILL WALK ONCE MORE! I GIVE YOU PRAISE! I GIVE YOU PRAISE! I GIVE YOU PRAISE! ALL OF YOU JOIN ME! I SAID ALL OF YOU JOIN ME! GIVE THE LORD OUR GOD YOUR PRAISE!*'

The crowd erupted.

Wendy Devereux tugged a finger across her throat.

Pastor Benjamin walked off stage, smiling, as thousands of flashbulbs strobed the arena. He smiled as his team led him through the barriers towards the exit. Smiled as he entered the corridor, tight with security staff, that led to his suite.

Wendy Devereux squeezed up close. Just like his, her lips were tight across her teeth. She ripped away her earpiece. 'Top job,' she said, and added nothing until they pushed through the door to the suite.

He could still hear LaDouceur's music and the whoops of the crowd, but it was muted here, a formless pounding. The room was large enough to sit fifty for dinner, but this evening it had been furnished with easy chairs and sofas. Tables dressed in white linen lined one wall, awaiting the buffet to be served to the VIPs. A few people milled around. He saw Ricky Delafonte, his accountant; Jocelyn Cayman, his physio; some of the guys from the ministry.

Wendy grabbed a towel from the back of a chair and tossed it to him. 'Kid has a knack for car crashes, I'd say.'

Benjamin blotted his face. He draped the towel over his head like a boxer. 'Pretty harsh.'

'Yeah. Maybe.'

'How'd they get past your crew, Wendy?'

Her face fell. 'Beats me. I'll check it out.'

The pastor nodded. 'Arthritis I can do. Lupus I can do. Mangled legs . . . did you *see* that kid? Parents must've been crazy, bringing him up there.'

'Desperation does funny things.'

'Is he OK?'

'Scott's with the family now.'

'I want to see them. See what we can do to help.' Benjamin held up his hands. 'Financially, I mean. Talking of that . . . Rick, how'd we do?'

Ricky Delafonte came forward, tapping on a tablet. 'Money's still rolling in. Best guess, maybe two-fifty k from the floor, on top of tickets.'

The pastor whistled. 'That's a hot night in Texas, folks. How many views via the simulcast?'

'Maybe half a million. PayPal numbers will be crazy. You nailed it, boss.'

Benjamin winced. He didn't like it when Ricky called him that. He opened his hands to the team. 'Good work, guys. Now, back to it. We've a meet and greet happening right here in less than thirty minutes.' To Wendy, he added: 'Find me that kid. And fix the security problem. We can't have another incident like that one.' Turning away, he headed across the suite to his dressing room.

Inside, the lighting was dim, the air a blessed fifty-nine degrees. Blackout curtains shielded the windows. Benjamin collapsed into a club chair. He thought about stripping off his sweat-soaked suit, then decided it could wait. Instead he pulled the towel over his eyes. Breathed.

'Quite a show.'

The pastor sat up with a start, tearing the towel from his face. For a few moments he failed to locate the voice's owner. Finally he noticed, across the room in a chair wreathed in shadow, a man's dark shape. Benjamin strained his eyes, but he could see little more than an impeccably creased trouser leg, and the outline of a torso.

He took a breath, tried to sluice the tension from his body. 'I don't know how you got in here, friend—'

'The door was open. I walked in.'

Benjamin squinted, puzzled by the man's accent. It sounded British to his ears, although there was something odd about it. 'Are you here with the VIP programme? Did Rick let you back here?'

'I don't want you to think me rude, Pastor, nor impose on you a moment more than I must. I give you my word that I'll be brief. I'm here on behalf of someone who very much wishes to meet you.'

'I'm sorry, Mr . . .' Benjamin began, and when the stranger didn't offer a name he carried on regardless. 'I hear that, I do, and I'm mightily grateful. But time is ticking on and I'm in sore need of a shower. I do appreciate you coming back here, and I'd truly love to help—'

'I just knew that you would,' the man replied.

'But it's ministry policy that all private appointments go through the phone line.' He grinned, tight-lipped. 'It's a toll-free number, if that's what you're worried about.'

There, he'd made a joke. Softened the mood a little.

'Benjamin D. Pope,' the man said. 'What does the "D" stand for, if you don't mind me asking?'

Offended now, deciding that he needed a lengthier talk with Wendy on the subject of security, Benjamin got to his feet and took a step towards the door. 'OK, friend, it's been fun. But now I'm gonna have to ask you to leave.'

'A minute of your time is all I'm asking, Pastor.'

Benjamin shook his head. He grabbed the door handle. Then, cursing with pain, he snatched his hand away. Confused, he reached out again, brushed the metal with his fingertips. Frozen: colder than ice. Examining his palm, he saw blisters beginning to form. 'Wendy!' he shouted. '*Wendy!*'

'She can't hear you,' the stranger said. 'And it really is important that we talk.'

The lights in the room seemed to brighten. Benjamin glimpsed his guest clearly for the first time.

The man looked seventy, perhaps older, but he possessed a wrestler's physique. He sat in the chair and studied the pastor with cool green eyes. His skin was lined and wrinkled, yet so supple it appeared as if he'd bathed in olive oil every day since birth. His silver hair was pulled tight against his scalp in a ponytail that trailed down his back like a bolt of silk. His teeth were porcelain-white. He wore a dark suit; in one ear, a single golden stud. On his head sat a wide-brimmed hat, of the type a missionary might wear. It frightened Benjamin, that hat, for reasons he could not fathom.

Where on earth was Wendy? Or Ricky for that matter? Hadn't they heard him calling? The man stood up and held out a hand. Benjamin flinched away. Would it be cold, he wondered? Like the door handle?

'My name is Aiden Urchardan, Pastor. I didn't mean to alarm you, and I do hope you'll forgive my persistence.' His lips spread wide. Those white teeth shone like icebergs. 'He can be a little demanding at times.'

'Your client, we're talking about.'

'I wouldn't describe our relationship that way.'

Benjamin eyed the door handle, thought he saw a rime of

frost around the brass. He shivered. 'Mr Urchardan, are you a believer?'

Beneath the missionary hat, the man's smile broadened. 'Oh yes, Pastor. Although, may I say it, I suspect the doctrines to which we subscribe somewhat differ.'

'How so?'

'Would you take a seat? I'll keep my promise. I won't trouble you more than a moment.'

Reluctantly, Benjamin returned to the armchair. He picked up the towel from the floor and wiped his hands.

'For as long as I can remember, I've served him alone,' Urchardan said. 'He prefers it that way, doesn't feel the need to recruit a following, the way others have. In truth, in all this time there's not been a great deal for me to do. He's *cadalach* only every eight years or so, and for such a short time, really, that you'd hardly notice.'

'Cadalach?'

'Forgive me. An outdated term, and somewhat inaccurate besides. Its meaning is immaterial. What *is* material is his need for someone like you. My skills are not altogether lacking, but sad to say, I've not been overly blessed with charisma.'

'I hadn't noticed.'

Urchardan laughed. The wide-brimmed hat trembled on his head. 'You, on the other hand, appear to have been blessed with a surfeit.'

'It's kind of you to say, Mr Urchardan, but—'

'Oh, come now,' the man chided. 'Two hundred and fifty thousand good American dollars *in addition* to gate receipts? It takes a rare man to achieve that. A rare man indeed.'

'Actually, all it takes is faith.'

'Then have faith in *me*, Pastor.'

'I don't know you, friend. And in any case, I believe I'll reserve my faith for the Lord.'

Urchardan's eyes sparkled. 'Encouraging to hear.'

Benjamin eyed the door handle. He saw a prickly beard of

ice crystals sprouting from the metal. 'Where is he, then – this client of yours . . . whatever?'

'He's here, right in this room. He's anxious to meet you. In fact, he thinks you're the very man he's been looking for, all this time.'

Benjamin glanced around. 'You got him hiding in the en suite or something?'

'Not exactly.'

'So you wanna bring him out?'

Aiden Urchardan steepled his fingers together. 'No, Pastor,' he said. 'I want you to invite him in.'

Benjamin sighed. He glanced at his watch. 'OK, listen. Because I'm gonna be clear about this, and I'm only gonna say it once. He's got two minutes, that's it. After that, I don't care if he's the—'

They were the last words Benjamin spoke for some time.

The Bliss entered him in a rush, a scintillating energy that soaked through his skin and raced along his veins like champagne. He opened his mouth, felt himself scream with joy, lost himself for a while in sheer ecstasy. Every nerve in his body chimed, a billion tuning forks resonating at exactly the same pitch.

His back arched. His toes curled. The room's sounds came to him in a sensory torrent: the machine-like *phum* of the air-con, the dry rustle of Urchardan's breathing, the crackle of nylon carpet as his shoes stuttered across it. His throat felt numb, a reminder of the bad old cocaine nights of his youth. Yet however fierce those sensory fireworks, they were a mere taster for what came next. The Bliss embraced him, and Pastor Benjamin felt himself immersed in a love of such purity that tears sprang into his eyes. 'Oh my,' he murmured. 'Oh my, oh *my*.'

He shivered, and the experience wrapped his nerve-endings in an electricity so delicious he feared that his balls might burst and his heart explode. The Bliss was sifting his memories now, reading and judging. Weightless, Benjamin thought of his many sins, and even in his delirium a deep shame confronted him.

He had little time. Panicking, he raced ahead of the Bliss, darting through the neatly ordered corridors of his mind. He twisted and turned, dodged and weaved, until finally he found the door to a small, dark room where he kept the bad things locked away.

His father was in there somewhere – the old man's corpse, at least. So, too, the drunk who had bounced Linda off his fender all those years ago. Many other nightmares and old bones. Benjamin threw open the door, his eyes squeezed shut. Into the room he unloaded every remaining regret, every duplicitous deed, every broken promise and boast and sinful thought. Then he slammed the door shut as hard as he dared.

Exhausted, he turned and opened his arms to the light rushing towards him. '*I'm here*,' he whispered, and heard himself laugh with glee. '*I'm HERE.*'

CHAPTER 30

Gorges du Tarn, Southern France

Once the campsite's proprietor had left, Jolyon turned off the lights and moved to the window. He watched the man pick up his bicycle and ride away down the hill. All the while he felt a curious scratching behind his eyes, as if somewhere inside his head an old memory strained against its leash. When the man pedalled around a bend and disappeared, the sensation vanished.

Jolyon stood at the window a moment longer, wondering what he had sensed. He felt tantalisingly close to a revelation, but it skipped out of reach every time he tried to approach it. Deciding that he might have more success by creeping up on it unawares, he went outside to his car. He was tired from the road, hungry and overwhelmed. With sleep and good food in his belly, he could consider his situation afresh.

Overhead a canyon moon sailed high, its light silvering the prairie grass. Jolyon opened the Citroën's rear door and began to unpack. He had not travelled light. The back seat was crammed: canvases, boxes, satchels, paintbrushes, clothes. While he hadn't emptied his studio back in Labastide-Esparbairenque, he had brought with him the vast majority of its contents.

Jolyon took the paintings inside first, along with his sketchbooks and easels. After that he carried in four crates of art materials, followed by his wash bag and clothes. Finally he retrieved Professor Beckett's slim leather-bound volume.

He would arrange his stuff later. Right now he needed food and a bottle of something restorative. He grabbed his denim jacket from the passenger seat and shrugged his arms into it. The day had been a scorcher but with the onset of night, the temperature in the gorge had dropped. Jolyon shuffled down the hill, flip-flops slapping the tarmac.

The campsite shop was a simple place, adequately stocked: fresh bread, vegetables and meat, chilled foods and canned goods, newspapers, alcohol and cigarettes. Jolyon took a basket and tossed in the ingredients for a simple meal, along with two bottles of Merlot and a lighter Bordeaux.

The woman at the counter was in her early sixties, a Lozère native who delighted in conversation. When she discovered that he was a painter she began to list the places nearby that he would no doubt wish to see, speaking so fast and with such sing-song enthusiasm that he struggled at times to keep up. After some gentle probing he found out that Edward Schwinn, Joyau Caché's owner, had owned the place for five years, building it up from the brink of bankruptcy. He also found out that Schwinn had lied to him. The man had a daughter.

Jolyon returned to his caravan and prepared a meal of pâté and fresh bread. He ate outside on the deck, washing down his food with one of the Merlots. The meal and the wine brought an anaesthetising drowsiness. Afterwards he struggled up from his chair and fetched the second Merlot. This one he drank with his head canted back so that he could watch the stars rotate. So many constellations up there, so many distant places. The darkness of the Cévennes gave the heavens a breathtaking clarity. There was Ursa Major and Ursa Minor; Cassiopeia; Draco; Cepheus. For a short period a few years earlier Jolyon had grown obsessed with the stars, the nature of the universe and its beginnings. He bought himself a telescope and spent three months pointing it at the sky. Up there he found a startling canvas, far too miraculous to define. After a while his desire to understand it faded, replaced with the simpler joy of contemplation.

Now, as he lazed on the deck with the cicadas serenading around him, he reacquainted himself with old friends and confidantes. 'Why am I here?' he asked them, filling his lungs with cool canyon air. 'What is happening to me?'

An hour later he rose from the chair and staggered inside. Navigating by moonlight, he found the caravan's single bedroom. Crisp sheets lay on the bed, onto which he collapsed. Within moments he was asleep.

He dreamed of the boy. It was not a darkly erotic dream, like the others had been. This one was marked neither by claustrophobia nor lust. Instead it threaded him with a terror so pure that he felt as if his insides had been rinsed through with bleach.

In the dream, he stood on a rock-strewn beach among straggles of seaweed like ripped-out hair. At his back a steel sea swelled. Waves smashed themselves apart in violent explosions of spray. In sand beds among the rocks, stiff clumps of marram grass grew. On either side of the bay, jagged sea cliffs climbed skywards.

Beyond the beach, in a steep-sided chine, stood a man without a face. His features were shallow depressions, like dimples in clay; no eyes, no mouth, no nose. Grey rags flapped around him. His head was twisted towards the nearest cliff.

When Jolyon followed the focus of that featureless face he saw something that terrified him: the boy, running up the slope, dodging rocks and boulders in his efforts to escape.

Hide! Jolyon cried. *Lie flat! Don't let him see you!*

The boy stumbled on a rock, recovered himself. He glanced over his shoulder and spied Jolyon, his eyes tight glints of fear.

In the steep-sided chine, the faceless man raised his right

arm, the fingers of his hand spread wide. Unaware, the boy continued to climb. He hauled himself onto a boulder, leaped to another.

LIE FLAT! Jolyon screamed. *DON'T LET HIM GET A—*

The rag-covered stranger closed his fingers into a fist and the boy spun around. His spine arched. His eyes bulged.

Caught. Like a mouse seized by a hawk.

The boy – *Therron, that's his name, it's Therron* – trembled inside that invisible grip. Back in the chine, the man without a face raised his left hand. With a pincer-like movement, he closed his fingers.

Jolyon could hear the crash of surf at his back, could taste the ocean salt on his lips. Somewhere overhead, gulls cried out their mercies. At the entrance to the chine, the featureless man flung out his pincered fingers to the sea.

With a violent ripping of fabric, Therron's clothes tore free. They sailed over the cliff, flapping like crows, trailing seams and threads. Jolyon opened his mouth, but this time no words would come.

Therron's face was mottled now, as if he struggled to draw breath. Down in the chine the featureless man lifted his head.

No! Jolyon screamed, his voice returning. *He's an innocent! AN INNOCENT!*

The man still held one fist aloft. With his other hand he re-formed the pincer. Despite his lack of eyes or mouth he exuded a malicious humour, a sadistic intent. Out to sea, Therron's clothes fluttered into the waves. They rolled on the swell like a waterlogged corpse.

Spray stung Jolyon's neck. Wind snatched at his hair. *Please don't*, he murmured, even though he knew it was a prayer without hope.

Please don't. Please don't.

In the chine, the featureless man once more flung his pincered fingers to the sea.

Up on the slope, in a single shocking separation, Therron's

flesh tore loose from his bones. It arced over the cliff, a glistening streamer of meat, and began to fall.

The boy's head remained cruelly intact. It bobbed on a blood-slicked skeleton. Down by the shore, the stranger wearing the grey rags opened his fist.

Therron blinked, once. Then his head tilted and his bones collapsed beneath him like a driftwood stack knocked loose by a stone.

Jolyon fell to his knees. Sharp rocks cut into his skin.

In the chine he saw the stranger's face begin to grow features, eyes and nose and mouth materialising out of formless flesh. He recognised them – *THE GIRL! THE GIRL! THE GIRL!* – and this time when he screamed the sound filled his head with nails and shook him awake.

He lurched upright on the mattress, thrashed free of the covers. '*Beò-Ìobairt,*' he moaned. '*Beò-Ìobairt.*'

For some moments he wondered where he was. Finally his eyes adjusted and he saw, through the window, the view down the hill. Even then he remained unsure of whether he was alone in the bedroom. It seemed quite possible that he had brought his tormentor out of the dream with him, that he might look up to see the girl standing by the door, ready to whip off his flesh and reveal the white glimmer of his bones.

He shivered, rolled out of bed. It was too dark in here, too claustrophobic. He stumbled through the caravan's living space and fled outside. Hands on his thighs, he gulped down lungfuls of air, waiting for his heart to slow.

The campsite seemed strangely silent. He could hear no spill of music from nearby motorhomes; no radios, no TV, no laughter. The cicadas had grown quiet.

Jolyon straightened, peered down the hill. He could see lights glowing inside caravans and tents, and in the booking office where he had met Edward Schwinn.

He returned to the static van's front door and locked it.

Pulling up his collar, stuffing his hands into his jacket, he began to walk.

Slowly the sounds of humanity returned. He heard low voices, the sudsy clatter of crockery being washed. He could see shadows moving behind windows, reassuring shapes. At the bottom of the hill he walked past the shop where he'd bought his supper, watching his reflection flitter across its windows.

Opposite it stood the booking office. Jolyon peered through the glass.

His mouth fell open and his heart began to race once more.

CHAPTER 31

Gorges du Tarn, Southern France

Teeth clenched, Piper clawed herself awake, fighting a bed sheet that had twisted about her in sleep.

Scrambling to her knees, she raised her hands to her face. Her fingers searched frantically: eyes, nose, lips. Only after finding all her features in place did she sag forwards on the bed and release the breath trapped in her lungs. Silent, she waited for her thoughts to clear.

'It won't happen,' said a voice in the darkness. 'Not unless you allow it.'

Piper's head snapped up. In a corner of the bedroom Mórríghan sat on a wicker chair, the black folds of her *culpatach* flowing into the surrounding shadows. Beneath her hood, the woman's eyes glinted like wet teeth.

'I . . . I killed him,' Piper said. 'I killed Therron.'

'No. You didn't. And you won't.'

As usual Mórríghan's voice – deep and resonant, and yet somehow strangely fleshless – imbued in Piper a deep disquiet. 'Don't tell me that was just a dream.'

The woman shook her head. 'Nothing so mundane.'

'Was it you, then? Teaching me a lesson?'

'Is that what you think?'

Piper flushed. 'No. I don't even know why I said it. But it made your point pretty well.'

'My point?'

'Therron,' Piper said. 'When all this starts, I can't take him with me.'

'That'll be your decision. Just like everything else.'

'In case you think that's reassuring, it's not.' An alarming thought struck her. She glanced through her window at the darkness outside. 'Did anyone hear?'

'No. I brought you out pretty quickly, I think.'

'So we're safe?'

'For now. I don't know if this is the *balla-dìon* seeking you out, or something else entirely. But we need to take steps, otherwise it's going to find us.'

'You need to tell me the truth, Mórríghan. All of it.'

The woman's eyes flickered. 'Let's walk.'

It was a short stroll to the riverbank. Piper hopped across spray-slick boulders until she found one that jutted into the water. There she sat, watching the Tarn carve the moon's reflection into milk-white slivers.

Like a black stain seeping out of the surrounding air, Mórríghan materialised on a neighbouring stone. She lifted away her hood and the moonlight touched her face. Silver hair, falling unbound, framed ageless Celtic features: high forehead, sharp chin, narrow, pointed nose. Her eyes were milky and wild, as hard as they were blind.

Piper stared, until a flutter of nausea made her look away. She felt something warm trickle down the inside of one nostril. When she wiped her nose she saw, on her sleeve, a dark smear of blood. 'The night before I was born,' she said, fixing her gaze on the Tarn. 'The night Dad found my mother. It should never have happened like that. Should it?'

'None of this should have happened the way it did. Ériu planned it so carefully. Everything was timed to perfection.'

'Timed for what?'

'Once every eight years there's a narrow window, a moment when the *balla-dìon's* power reduces and its vision is dimmed – *Cathasach* become *Cadalach*, as some might say. It offered me a chance to return here unseen.'

'But you were betrayed.'

'So it seems.'

'By who?'

'I don't know.'

For a while, neither of them spoke.

'Ériu,' Piper said. 'That's not a name I've heard before. Who is she?'

'Ériu.' Mórríghan paused, and Piper felt a tick-like scratching in her head as the woman searched for appropriate words. 'Ériu is a sister, a daughter, an ally; and more than all those things besides. She is one of my four *Triallaichean*, as once they were called.'

'The other three?'

'Their names would mean nothing. And to have them rattling around unguarded inside your head—'

'Their names are *already* rattling around somewhere inside my head. I'm sure if I tried hard enough I could dig them out. But who knows how much noise I'd make?'

Piper turned, focusing her attention on Mórríghan's face. It hurt her head to stare at the woman for long but she persisted, ignoring the pulse of blood that flowed over her lip. 'Their names.'

A shadow passed over Mórríghan. For a moment she appeared to join with the rock. 'Drustan,' she said.

Piper grunted, feeling as if she had been kicked. The name itself meant nothing; it caused no rush of memories or emotion, but she could not deny its power.

'Eber,' Mórríghan said. 'Orla.'

Pain flared inside Piper's mouth. She realised she was grinding her teeth and tried, in vain, to stop. Fresh blood flooded from her nose.

'Look away,' Mórríghan hissed. 'You'll harm yourself.'

Alarmed, Piper averted her eyes. The relief was immediate; the muscles of her jaw unclenched; the flow of blood over her lips began to subside. She spat a dark streamer onto the stones. 'The four *Triallaichean*,' she muttered.

And suddenly she knew: knew who they were, *what* they were, all without being told. The insights tumbled from her head like loosened rocks. 'You arrived first,' she said. 'You and Cathasach. The pair of you were . . .' Piper's mouth dropped open in shock. 'Together. Two parts of a whole. *An Toiseach*.'

Mórríghan raised bony shoulders, like the bunched wings of a carrion bird.

'You had an agreement,' Piper said. 'An arrangement between you. One of you sacrificed, one of you exiled. All for the sake of . . .'

She paused, struggling for an answer. And then she lurched forward as a revelation struck.

'Humanity, yes,' Mórríghan said. 'To safeguard you. To prevent your corruption.'

'Cathasach,' Piper continued, her words coming faster now. 'He gave himself up, sank himself into the earth.' She paused, remembering an old Gaelic phrase she had heard from her father. '*Beò-Ìobairt*. That's it, isn't it? That's him. *Beò-Ìobairt:* Living Sacrifice.'

'No,' the woman insisted. 'That was never him. Nor is it a phrase he would even comprehend.'

'He offered himself. Became the *balla-dìon*.'

'You need to slow down,' Mórríghan said. 'Don't try searching for the answers. Let me explain.'

Piper jumped to her feet. She faced Mórríghan, her gaze accusatory. Twin spikes of pain pierced her eyes but she ignored them. Her hands balled into fists.

'You made me believe he was a threat, but *he* was the one who gave everything up. And he did it to protect *us*. It was *you* that chose exile; *you* that sent back your *Triallaichean* to destroy him. And when that didn't work you came back to do it yourself. Not physically, this time, because that would be too much of a risk. But through me.' She shook her head. 'We're just puppets, aren't we? Puppets on invisible strings.'

'Nothing of the kind.' Mórríghan's face rippled, as if burrowing creatures squirmed beneath her skin. 'Some of what you said is true, I'll grant you, but your interpretation . . . it's about as far from reality as you could possibly get. Cathasach *changed*, Piper. He *is* a threat.'

Tears gathered in the woman's eyes, shining like liquid pearls in the moonlight. 'We involved ourselves in something we should never have touched. But we did so, the pair of us, out of love. We saw the potential, saw what might flourish if outside influence could be thwarted. But it was only ever meant to be a temporary measure, a little breathing space to ensure your future. When the time came, the *balla-dìon* – as Cathasach had become – should have faded, but instead it chose to remain. I sent messengers to inquire. They disappeared. After that – yes – I dispatched the *Triallaichean*. But not to destroy, as you have suggested, simply to seek answers. We did not know what had happened, nor why the *balla-dìon* remained intact.'

The pain behind Piper's eyes had begun to soften. As she continued to watch Mórríghan's image, she felt as if she stared too long into the sun: she knew she inflicted damage even though she could not feel its effects. With some effort she glanced up at the moon riding high above the canyon. For a short while she saw two of them up there, glistening side by side like monstrous twins.

'So what did they discover?' she asked, her earlier anger beginning to abate. 'Why is the *balla-dìon* still here?'

'Of that, you know as much as I,' Mórríghan replied. 'Were it not for the attack the night before your birth I'd have all the answers by now. It was only by sheer good fortune that Gráinne managed to escape. Luckily, your father found us. But exactly what happened that night – who was responsible, or even what became of Ériu and the other three *Triallaichean* − I simply cannot say.'

Piper sat back down on the rock. She picked up a stone and launched it across the water. It skipped seven times on the surface before it sank. 'Cathasach,' she said. '*Balla-dìon*. The red light that whispers. Three names for the same thing. Whatever it's called, you want me to destroy it. Don't you?'

Mórríghan stilled. For a minute or more she was silent. Then she raised her head. 'With me as your guide, yes.'

Piper closed her eyes. Opened them. 'Why me?'

'Because that's the role your mother ordained for you. Cathasach isn't *Beò-Ìobairt*. You are.'

For a while Piper was silent. She picked up another stone, hurled it into the Tarn. 'Come on. It's time, now. Really, it is. I don't think you can prepare me any more than you have. Most of what you've told me isn't new, even if you've never spelled it out. How do I do it, Mórríghan? How do I destroy this thing? And what's going to happen to the people I love when I do?'

Afterwards, she sat alone in the chiselled canyon depths and cried. While some of her tears were for the people she knew, most of them were for herself. Strange, but she had known what Mórríghan was going to say even before the woman said it. She had known for as long as she could remember. And yet hearing it was still a shock.

Piper thought of her mother, and when she considered what Gráinne had offered on her behalf she felt a stab of rage that she could not sustain. Instead, she found herself thinking of Edward Schwinn, the man who had become her father in every definition except blood, with no expectation of gratitude or reward.

Beò-Ìobairt.

A phrase now thick with meaning.

Some choice she had been offered. It was no choice at all.

Piper watched the moon's passage overhead; around her she could hear the river's gentle laughter: an abundance of beauty in every sphere her senses sought. Yet for all the bewitching magic her surroundings offered, the beauty she had always held most precious was that exhibited by the people she loved. Suddenly, more than anything, she needed to be around them.

Piper leaned over the boulder and washed her face. As she cleaned her mouth and chin of blood, she wondered what damage she had caused herself by contemplating Mórríghan's image for so long. Had a cancer now formed in some district of her brain? Was a tumour swelling behind her eyes? She grunted. Did it even matter?

Turning from the river, she picked her way across the boulders. It was a short walk along the campsite loop to Joyau Caché's booking office. From the pitches that lined her route she smelled the lingering traces of barbecue fires. She heard laughter, the strum of a guitar. In the centre of the road Piper halted and savoured it all: simple sounds and smells, made by strangers enjoying their short freedoms. How she wished to be among them, or at least like them – no cause of heartache to those around her, and with a future of her choosing, confined only by the limits of her imagination or talent.

Through the booking office windows, she saw Therron sitting behind the desk. His elbows were planted, his head bowed. Light from a single lamp fell across him. The hairs of his forearms shone golden.

The boy jerked upright when the bell jangled over the door. For a moment his face appeared strangely vacant. Then his eyes focused and he brightened.

Piper went and perched on the edge of the desk, glancing down at the book he'd been reading – a battered hardback, open at its quarter-point. Its corners were frayed, its pages foxed and tanned. She lifted it up, tilted her head: *The Count of Monte Cristo*. 'You're reading the translation?' she asked, eyebrows raised. 'That's insane.'

Therron shrugged. 'Improves my English and puts me ahead at the same time.'

'You're not ahead.'

'Will be once I finish it.'

Last New Year's Eve they had compiled, between them, a list of fifty books to read by the following Christmas. Piper had completed the challenge in March, but she wouldn't tell Therron that. She tucked her hair behind an ear, grinned. 'You've a way to go.'

He shrugged. 'I'm savouring this one. I can see why you thought I'd like Dumas. I don't know if I can see why *you* like him.'

'What's not to like? Hope, friendship, revenge, romance. He covers it all.' She bent over the desk and kissed him.

'I'd almost given up on you.'

'Never do that.' Piper slid off the desk and came to his side of it, positioning herself between him and the book. She lifted her legs and placed her feet, one on each arm of his chair. 'Do you love me?'

'You know I do.'

'Then tell me.'

'Pie, I love you.'

'Do you really?'

He laughed. It faded to a frown. 'Of course.'

'If I left France, if I ran away . . . what would you do?'

'If you ran away? From here?'

'Humour me,' she said. 'If I ran away from here, and if I needed to keep moving, forever . . . and if being together meant that we could do nothing for the rest of our lives except go from place to place, never putting down roots, never having children or friends or family around us . . . what would you do?'

Therron searched her face with his eyes. 'I'd confront whatever you were running from, and stop it from hurting you.'

'What if you couldn't?'

'If I couldn't?'

'What if that weren't possible?'

'Then I'd come with you.'

Piper swallowed. 'What if I couldn't even tell you what we were running from?'

'Is that likely?'

'Please, Therron.'

He leaned back in his chair. Appraised her carefully. 'Are you asking me if I trust you?'

'Maybe.'

'I trust you. With my life. Pie, you're everything I have. If something like that happened, I'd come with you. Of course I would.'

'Even if it happened tonight?'

'Tonight?'

'Now.'

'*Right* now?'

Piper studied his face. Gave him a lopsided grin.

Therron blinked, glanced past her to the booking-office windows that faced the main loop. He sat up, his expression darkening. 'What the hell?'

Piper turned, followed his gaze. When she saw the object of his attention the skin on her scalp contracted like a drawstring purse.

CHAPTER 32

Austin, Texas

Pastor Benjamin D. Pope returned to his West Lake Hills home around midnight, climbed from the back of the Lexus SUV and bade his driver goodnight. The scent of buddleia and sweet almond accompanied him up the drive.

The house was Spanish in style, American in vision, every inch of it purchased through mission funds. As he stepped onto the tiled porch, a maid opened the front door and welcomed him in. The pastor thanked her and instructed her to go home. He wanted solitude right now, some space in which to think.

But first he decided to visit his wife. Benjamin kept Linda on the ground floor these days; it was far easier, that way, to take her outside when he thought she needed sun. He reached her room via a softly lit passage in the north wing. Usually it was a journey that weighted him with sadness. Not tonight. He felt trepidation, yes, but none of his usual melancholy.

Benjamin paused at her door and listened. From the other side came the steady rasp-suck hiss of Linda's ventilator. Hearing it, he allowed himself to breathe once more. Even now, after all these years, he worried that in his absence the machine might fail. Every time he returned home he dreaded that he would encounter, instead of those bleak mechanical sounds, a deathly silence.

The ventilator, in truth, was virtually indestructible. The

house itself had its own back-up generator which, in the event of a general power outage, would kick in without any interruption to the supply. Linda's machine, in addition, had its own bespoke generator. If both those systems failed, it would switch seamlessly to a battery back-up. Computers constantly monitored patient and machine; if they recorded any irregularity, the system would send notifications to the household staff, Benjamin's mobile phone and a private hospital three miles away. Still, he worried. How could he not?

Gently opening the door, he slipped inside and raised the lights. At the far end of the room, his wife lay on an elevated push-button bed. Her eyes were closed. Her arms lay flat on the bed covers.

'I'm home,' he said, padding across the carpet to her side. He picked up her hand, marvelling, as always, at the smoothness of her skin. The care staff had washed her hair since he'd been away, and someone had applied make-up to her face: lipstick, mascara, eye shadow. Benjamin frowned at that. Linda needed no stylist's tricks to make her beautiful. Using a wipe from a box beside the bed, he carefully cleaned her face.

'Something happened tonight,' he told her. 'Something that might change everything for us. I can't say more than that for now, but I think I may have found . . .'

He stopped and thought about that a while. What exactly *had* he found? He recalled the enormity of his experience in the suite at the Frank Irwin Center. For so long his lack of faith had been a badge of defiance worn in secret, a middle finger thrust in the face of all those fools claiming to see the hand of God, instead of dice-roll randomness, in the world around them.

Back when he had founded The Church of the Holy Sacrament, his goal had been simple: raise money for the medical bills Linda's insurance failed to cover. But as Benjamin built a successful ministry, his anger at his wife's condition grew. That rage bred a passion that his listeners mistook for conviction.

The money poured in. He hired accountants, security, PR. For the rest of her life, Linda would receive the best care that medicine could supply, yet still Benjamin preached empty words; still he shouted down demons and cancers, and railed against the devil. Such theatrics, he discovered, had become the only tonic to his ire.

'I'll be back,' he said, kissing Linda's forehead, avoiding the depression in her skull that was the only visible evidence of her brain injury. He retreated to the kitchen, where he fetched a carton of salted caramel ice cream from the walk-in freezer. Sitting on a barstool at the counter, he prised off the lid and began to eat. He managed perhaps four mouthfuls before he heard a knocking behind him – knuckles on glass.

He wheeled around and saw, peering through the window, Aiden Urchardan. Half the man's features were hidden beneath his missionary hat. Benjamin's pulse quickened. He went to the sliding door, deactivated the alarm and pulled it open. 'How'd you slip past security?'

Urchardan removed his hat and stepped inside the house. 'People see what they choose.'

'Uh-huh. I get you a drink?'

'Brandy, please. If you have any.'

'I don't keep alcohol in the house. Not unless you count communion wine. Something else?'

'Coffee, then. Thank you.' The man walked to the counter and hauled himself onto one of the barstools. 'How are you feeling?'

'I'm not sure,' Benjamin replied, as he busied himself with the espresso machine. 'A little like the rug's been pulled out.'

'I can appreciate that.'

'And a lot like I need answers.'

'Which is exactly why I'm here.'

The machine dispensed its shots into two white mugs. Benjamin topped them up with frothed milk and sugar. He slid one in front of Urchardan before realising that he'd forgotten to ask the man his preference. 'What I did before,' he said. 'What you saw tonight, at the arena.'

'Was wrong, yes.'

'Am I damned?' he asked, and winced. So strange to be using such terms in earnest.

Urchardan smiled. 'For that, no. We're all sinners, Pastor. Every one of us. I'm sure you've worked some good, amid the lies you've spun.'

That stung. And it made him feel afraid. 'You don't seem to like me very much.'

'Do you? *Like* yourself?'

He found he couldn't answer that. Found he couldn't maintain eye contact, either. 'Please. This is all so confusing. I know you have the answers, but I don't even know what my questions should be.'

'Are you still an atheist?'

'Of course not.'

'Well, that's a start.'

'Is He here? Now?'

'He's always here,' Urchardan replied. 'His attention isn't always on us, but He walks among us nonetheless.'

'That doesn't exactly sound like Scripture.'

'That surprises you?'

Again, Benjamin had no answer. He opened his mouth, closed it.

'I imagine,' Urchardan said, 'that you're wondering, part-icularly, why you were chosen. That you're wondering why such a pedlar of lies should be selected to do the Lord's work.'

'I remember you mentioning a need for charisma. And I've gotta say that the longer we talk, the more I'm beginning to see what you mean.'

Urchardan grinned, picked up his coffee mug. He took a sip, waited.

'What does He want of me?' Benjamin asked.

'Something evil is coming; something definitive. It hides in plain sight, protected by innocents unaware of its intentions. *Lupus inter oves*. A wolf among sheep.'

The man had an unusual way of speaking. Benjamin picked through his words. 'Those intentions are?'

'To destroy,' Urchardan said. 'To ransack everything He has built. It's why He has a need of you now, Pastor. It is why the world has a need. For right or wrong, when you speak others listen. When you lead, others follow.'

Benjamin stared, frightened by what he heard. 'Will He forgive me?' he asked, gesturing at his surroundings. 'Will He forgive all this?'

'Why don't you ask Him?'

'Now?'

For the first time, Urchardan's face softened. 'Open your heart and ask.'

Benjamin watched his guest a moment longer. Then he closed his eyes and lifted his hands, palms-up.

The Bliss entered him in a rush, so forcibly that he cried out. His skin felt as if it had unzipped from his flesh, releasing a billion particles of light. He sensed every nerve ending in his body spark and pop and zing. And, amidst all that pure and glorious sensation, he felt a divine love begin to swaddle him, a feeling for which he had thirsted ever since encountering it at the arena.

FORGIVEN, spoke a voice, deep inside his head.

Benjamin sobbed. *For everything?*

FOR ALL.

And Linda?

BLESSED.

It was too much. He heard himself cry out, felt the years of pain sluice from him in a single, incredible instant.

When he woke he found himself on the kitchen floor. Aidan Urchardan was cradling his head.

'I take it you conversed,' the man said. His eyes, now, seemed to brim with compassion.

Benjamin nodded through his stupor. 'What does He want from me? I'll do anything. What does He want?'

The emotion drained from Urchardan's eyes and his expression hardened. 'He wants you to build him an army.'

On the porch's front steps, Aiden Urchardan bade the pastor goodnight, fixed his hat upon his head and strolled down the drive. He knew the man watched his departure, but he did not look back. He walked two blocks to his hire car and climbed behind the wheel.

Earlier that evening, at the Frank Irwin Center, he had watched Pastor Benjamin's performance and despised what he saw. Yet during their conversation inside the house, his animosity towards the man had softened.

Was I any different? he asked himself. *Was I any less flawed?*

It seemed cruel to use the man's faith – or lack of it – as leverage for his support, but Urchardan knew that time was running out. Despite everything, the girl had not been found. Eight years ago she had been too young to act against them. This time around, she would be sixteen. Old enough, by far, to wreak the destruction she had planned.

What was one man's life against such a threat? Urchardan would sacrifice a thousand men. A million. Besides, was the pastor's interpretation of what he had experienced this evening any more wondrous than the reality?

Four weeks remained.

Twenty-eight days. Twenty-eight nights.

Samhain approached, an onward-rushing darkness. Urchardan wished he could see beyond it.

Pastor Benjamin walked through the rooms of his West Lake Hills home, turning out the lights as he went. At a bay window in its dining room, he stood in a pool of moonlight and looked out at the garden beyond. He saw dark, manicured lawns and the silhouettes of ornamental trees: dogwood, tulip poplars, weeping cherry.

So often he had been made miserable by the knowledge that Linda would see none of these riches. Now, as he contemplated how they had been won, he found himself grateful. 'It goes,' he whispered. 'It all goes.'

He thought of that sonorous voice, deep inside his head – *FORGIVEN* – and smiled. How lucky he was. How blessed.

Slowly, he began to undress. He folded his trousers and draped them on a barstool, took off his shirt. He kicked off his shoes and stepped out of his underwear. Naked, he walked back to the kitchen and searched the cupboards until he found what he was looking for: a gallon jar used to hold cut flowers. At the sink he filled it, waiting as the water sloshed and hissed. Once it was full he lifted it out.

With difficulty, he raised the jar above his head. He held it there for a moment, muscles shaking with the effort. Then he up-ended it.

Benjamin gasped at the water poured over him. He spluttered, shivered, laughed. Water dripped from his hair, his skin. He blinked it from his eyes. Placing the empty container at his feet, he splashed across the kitchen tiles to the door. A minute later he was standing at Linda's side.

So beautiful, she was. Even now, years after the accident that had left her in this catatonic state, his breath caught in his throat when he looked at her.

With the lights dimmed, he watched her chest rise and fall. The ventilator sucked and hissed. The lights winked on its control panel.

He had been told, so many times, that the chances of her waking were nil, that keeping her in a vegetative state could be considered a cruelty of sorts. But while Benjamin had known he would not talk again with Linda in this life, he had known, just as firmly, that no opportunity for reunion waited beyond it.

He would not cast her into a vacuum, would not release her to a place where he could not follow.

Now, all of that had changed

Benjamin touched Linda's cheek, her lips. She ignored him. Around her neck hung the gold locket and chain he had given her on their wedding day. Gently he removed it. He bent and kissed her mouth, put his nose against her hair and breathed.

Finally, he turned his attention to the ventilator. It was a moment's task to disconnect it from the network. He methodically deactivated the failsafes and unplugged its back-up power sources. For too many years this machine had dictated the rhythms of his life. He discovered, now, how deeply he hated it.

Benjamin waited until its pump filled his wife's lungs a final time, and then he switched it off. At her side, he took her hand once more and closed his eyes.

After a minute, he thought he felt Linda's fingers twitch, as if she tried to communicate a goodbye. A tear rolled down his cheek. It clung to his jaw for a while, then dripped to the floor.

Look after her.

YES.

Benjamin smiled. His chest swelled.

Tell me what to do.

CHAPTER 33

Gorges du Tarn, Southern France

Edward drove his utility truck up Joyau Caché's hill with the windows down, the warm night air drying the sweat on his forehead. The day had been as long as any other, but he felt this one more keenly than usual. The pain in his knee was so bad that he hissed each time he operated the truck's clutch. He could have delegated this last task to Irène Duberry, the woman who ran their campsite shop, but Irene worked long hours for little pay, and Edward was loath to impose upon her more than he must.

He had another reason for delivering the stranger's spare linen personally. In the hours since Jolyon Percival had appeared in the booking office, Edward had been gripped by an uneasiness he could not dispel. There had been something odd about the man that he had not liked at all. '*Any family?*' Percival had asked, as they stood in the caravan at the top of the hill. '*Kids?*'

The questions jolted Edward, set his head ringing with alarms. While they could, quite easily, have been nothing more than a device for filling the silence between two strangers, he had sensed a purpose in the man's probing, and over the years had learned to trust his instincts.

Back at the booking office he typed Percival's name into his laptop's search engine and was rewarded with a number of links, including one to a short Wikipedia entry. The man was an artist by vocation, and appeared to have amassed quite a following. Several galleries throughout Europe and North America featured his paintings. His pieces sold for more money than Joyau Caché turned over in a year.

Personal information was sparse. Percival had been arrested three times: twice for drunk and disorderly and once for releasing five hundred helium-filled balloons outside the perimeter of a military air show. He had, for a time, posted comments to an amateur astronomy forum, going by the username *Eyeslookingup*. The posts themselves were unremarkable, but they drew blood from Edward's stomach as he read them.

Something about the man felt wrong. Dangerous.

At the top of the hill, Edward parked next to Percival's rusting Citroën. He grabbed the spare linen from the passenger seat, climbed the steps to the deck and rapped on the caravan's sliding door. No lights shone inside.

Overhead, clouds raced east towards the moon. Somewhere, out in the gorge, he heard the bleat of a mouflon.

No one responded to his knock. Edward tried again, waited.

Turning, he gazed down the hill. The campsite loop was deserted; no vehicles, no people. He moved his weight from side to side, relieving the pressure on his knee. Finally, he gripped the door handle and gave it a tug. Locked.

Edward pulled a bunch of keys from his pocket, unlocked the door and opened it. There was nothing wrong, he reasoned, with dropping off the man's linen; it was something he did routinely for many of the guests.

In the main living space, shadows pooled. A pale strip of moonlight bisected the darkness and crept halfway up the far wall. On the kitchenette counter he saw the remains of a simple meal: a tub of pâté, half-eaten; the nub of a baguette. Beside that, two empty wine bottles. Plastic packing crates covered the breakfast table but the light was too dim to reveal their contents.

A stack of canvases leaned against the sofa. More canvases were propped against the seat backs.

'Hello?' he called. He recalled the man's irritation at being addressed in his native tongue. 'Monsieur Percival?'

The caravan rang with silence. Edward balanced the linen package on top of the crates. Reaching into his back pocket, he pulled out a wad of Post-its and a stub of pencil. He scrawled the artist a message and stuck the note to the linen before pausing again to listen.

A canyon breeze pressed the caravan walls. The floor creaked beneath him.

Edward straightened. He put a hand to his spine and massaged the spot that always gave him grief. He was about to retreat to his truck when something caught his eye. Moving towards the sofa, he took a closer look at the nearest canvas. The strip of moonlight only illuminated a fraction of it but something there looked familiar. Edward lifted the artwork and angled it towards the light. The subject of the painting was Piper.

At first he was so surprised by his discovery that he could do little except stare at what his eyes showed him. While he knew nothing about art he saw, immediately, why Percival's talent was so revered. The man had captured the girl perfectly – not just her image but her essence: an amorphous quality Edward had never managed to define.

He stood there, motionless, the portrait tilted towards the light. Slowly the magic of that image began to fade. Edward blinked. He dropped the canvas and grabbed another from the sofa, lifting it into the oblong of moonlight. This painting featured Piper, too. But the image was hardly recognisable as the girl he knew. Her eyes blazed with savage intent. Her lips curled back from her teeth in a vehement sneer.

The next canvas featured yet another image of Piper. This one had only been sketched roughly in charcoal before Percival had driven the point of a pencil or blade through the girl's eyes, leaving ragged punctures.

Edward moved to the wall and flicked on the lights. Now he saw what the shadows had hidden. Stacked canvases filled every available space. They leaned against the gas cooker. They lay on stools beneath the breakfast counter. They lined the narrow hall leading to the bedroom. Edward worked his way through them, growing steadily more appalled. Every single portrait featured his daughter. Worse, none of them – apart from the first he had found – depicted the girl in a way that was remotely sympathetic.

When he reached the stack in the hallway, the subject of Percival's obsession changed. Not Piper, now, but Therron. In each case the boy's expression was terrified, his eyes dark holes.

At last, lodged in the gap between the sofa and the wall, Edward discovered a huge paper-wrapped package. He lifted it onto the breakfast counter and tore away the paper.

It took him a moment to work out what he was seeing. Most of the canvas had been daubed with thick black paint, but in the centre, lit by what, in the image, appeared to be the beam of a dying flashlight, he recognised two people. The first was Piper. The second was himself.

The painting possessed an almost photographic realism. Its importance to Percival was clear – the man had invested an extraordinary amount of effort on its creation. In it, Piper sat on her haunches, face marked with blood and tears and dirt. Edward was bending over her. They seemed to be in a mineshaft, or some kind of cave – although one with smoothly excavated walls that tapered like a pyramid above them. The floor was stone, carved with intricate patterns. This time Piper's features contained no malice, merely fear. Her eyes were fixed on a knife that Edward held towards her throat.

Suddenly he could not contain his rage. He punched his fist through the canvas, picked up the frame and hurled it against the wall, smashing it into splinters.

Outside, he started his truck, slammed it into gear and reversed onto the loop. With the lights set on full beam, he accelerated down the hill. If he saw Percival, he would run the man down without slowing.

Five years of hard work he had sunk into Joyau Caché, all of it designed to give Piper a shot at normality, a stable environment in which to flourish. In the last twelve months he had dared, at last, to believe he might succeed. Now, this stranger had appeared and shattered those hopes.

Edward braked hard outside his chalet and leaped out. The impact with the ground detonated a firework display of pain in his knee. He cursed through clenched teeth, staggered up the front steps.

The door was unlocked. Inside, the rooms were dark. 'Pie!' he called.

No answer. From the living room he heard the tick of a wall clock. Nothing else. Edward limped through the chalet. He shoved open doors, flicked on lights, banished shadows.

Piper's room was empty. On her bed, the covers were rucked. She usually dumped her sandals in the corner when at home, but he couldn't see them. Her favourite hoodie wasn't on its peg. So where was she?

Unless the girl had gone out to the canyon, Edward could think of only one place. Earlier that day he had asked Therron to work the office late shift. The boy would be there right now. Sometimes Piper liked to join him.

Contemplating that led Edward to his second question: where was Jolyon Percival?

Moving as fast as his knee allowed, he fled his daughter's bedroom and went into his own. The bed was a divan without wheels. He grabbed the mattress and hurled it to one side, grunting from the electric spark of pain that flared between his shoulder blades. He pulled the divan's two halves apart, reached down and retrieved the rifle he kept hidden there, checking that it was still loaded.

Clicking off the safety, he went into the bathroom. From the back of a wall cabinet he grabbed a zippered vinyl bag.

Inside were six passports – two each for him, Piper and Therron – and five thousand euros in cash. He stuffed the bag into a pocket and retraced his steps outside.

The moon was still up, shedding a soft light. Edward walked down the centre of the track, rifle held before him. Every hair on his body stood erect, as if currents of energy surged beneath his feet. He moved with shoulders raised, wondering what he would do if the night sky turned scarlet and the dome reappeared here, now.

It was a short distance to Joyau Caché's main loop, and a few hundred yards to the booking office. Through its windows Edward saw Therron sitting in the chair. Piper perched on the desk, her legs straddling him. Both of their faces were turned towards the glass, but neither saw Edward. Their attention was concentrated entirely on Jolyon Percival.

The man, still dressed in shorts and flip-flops, stood with his palms pressed against the windows. His eyes, as he peered inside, looked stricken. His body trembled like a spider's web caught in a storm.

CHAPTER 34

Rame Peninsula, Cornwall

Deep inside the thick stone walls of Crafter's Keep, the woman who called herself Orla stood on the floor of her bower, eyes locked on the flickering image before her. 'It's starting,' she said, and watched keenly for a reaction.

The room was opulently furnished. Wall-hanging tapestries depicted scenes from Ovid's *Metamorphoses*. The artworks were sixteenth century in origin, commissioned in Italy; likewise, the suit of Milanese armour in one corner.

Ériu had mocked her for the armour, of course. And then, on Orla's next visit to Aberffraw Hall, she had seen an identical set on display in Ériu's own bower. They had both raised smiles at that.

On a bearskin rug in the centre of the room stood Eber, second of the four *Triallaichean*. His representation was uncannily authentic. Orla watched his eyes carefully, looking for any indication of suspicion.

'The dreams,' Eber said, with his thick Highlands burr. 'You're having them too?'

She nodded.

'The *balla-dìon*,' the old man continued. 'Time's growing short and it's trying tae seek her out.'

'How do you know this is the *balla-dìon*?'

'What else could it be?'

'The girl herself?' Orla suggested.

'If the girl were the source, or if she responded, we wouldhae sensed something. Ye were always the most attuned. Have ye felt her?'

'Of course not.'

With a jolt, Orla realised how closely the old man was studying her.

Careful now.

'If ye know something,' he began.

'We're four weeks away from what could be the biggest event in our history, and still the girl hasn't been found,' she snapped. 'Do you really think I'd keep anything from you at a time like this?'

Eber stared, his eyes unreadable. 'Not knowingly, maybe. But if ye had a hunch, even if it were something ye were reluctant to—'

'Then I'd tell you straight away. Why ever would I not?' Angered, she strode to a table, snatched up a carafe and filled a glass with wine. 'Why are you still hiding away up in Caledonia?'

'We call her Scotland these days.'

'Call her what you like. You should be on the road. Leading the search.'

'I've done better than that. I've put Cameron in charge. If my son can't find the girl, no one will.'

Orla took a sip of wine, forced herself to swallow. 'I wish Drustan were here.'

'Aye.' Eber paused. 'You're certain ye havenae a lead?'

'I'm going now,' she said, and flicked her hand.

His image vanished.

Scowling, Orla turned to the bower's darkest corner. 'What do you think?'

Nora Kinraid, most senior of Orla's followers, stepped into the light. 'He suspects.'

'Yes. But I think we're closer to finding the girl than he is.'

'Strange that he's put Cameron in charge.'

Orla examined Nora carefully. 'Are the pair of you still estranged?'

The woman averted her eyes. 'Cameron's a good man. I just . . . what's coming is too important to allow our marriage to jeopardise it.'

'The location I gave you. The one in France.'

'I've dispatched someone to check it out.'

'Who did you send?'

Nina told her.

'She's lying,' Cameron said, rising from a stool in his father's cottage. He moved to the fireplace and held out his hands to the flames. It was early October in Argyll, but a fierce north-easterly had been blowing all week. The cottage's thatch sang like a flute. 'She knows something. Or thinks she does.'

Eber stared at the bricks of burning peat. 'If there was one thing I never wanted tae believe,' he said. 'It was that Orla was involved in what happened.'

'What will you do?'

'Well, I can't sit up here with a rug on my knees any longer. Orla needs watching and ye have your hands full already.'

'When will you leave?'

'Tonight. Ye better arrange transport.'

Cameron peered out of the window at the wind-ruffled night. 'Do you really think she could have betrayed us?'

'I hope not.'

'If it *was* her,' Cameron said, 'if she was responsible for Ériu's death, for everything that's happened since, do you think . . . I mean, do you have enough strength . . .' He stopped, licked his lips.

'Enough strength for what?' Eber demanded.

When Cameron remained silent, the old man rose to his feet. His eyes narrowed into slits. 'Are ye asking whether I have enough fight left in me, boy? Do ye *doubt* me?'

'I—'

'I stood with Áedán mac Gabráin!' Eber roared. 'I fought with Bruce! I've *waded* through blood, *bathed* in it. If Orla stands against us, I'll bathe in her blood too. I'll wash my face with the blood of *any* who oppose us.'

A muscle in his jaw began to twitch. His fingers flexed, curling into fists.

Cameron watched, keeping his face impassive. He had hoped to provoke his father into rage and, in so doing, stir him into action that was long, long overdue. By the looks of it, he had succeeded.

CHAPTER 35

Gorges du Tarn,
Southern France

Edward jammed the rifle stock hard into his shoulder and placed Jolyon Percival in its sights. 'Away from the glass.'

Thirty feet away, the artist stood with his palms spread wide against the booking office windows. Percival's face, as he turned, captured reflections from a loop of coloured fairy lights hung across the road. They gave his features an eerie, carnivalesque look.

'*Beò-Ìobairt*,' he murmured. His voice sounded strange, suffused with morbid fascination. He blinked once, head still canted towards Edward. An awareness began to creep back into his expression. 'It's her, isn't it?' The man grimaced, as if he attempted to extirpate a rotten memory. 'It's Piper.'

Hearing his daughter's name spoken with such enmity sharpened Edward's anger into rage. He recalled the portraits in Percival's caravan; unjust images of the girl, delusory and dark. His finger tightened on the trigger. 'You don't worry about her,' he said. 'You just worry about me.'

Inside the booking office, Piper slid off the desk and approached the windows. Edward caught her eye for a moment before returning his attention to Percival. 'I told you once. Back away from the glass.'

This time, the artist lifted his hands and kept them raised.

Carefully, he stepped towards Edward. 'If you fire that rifle,' he said, 'everyone on this campsite will hear it.'

'And you'll be dead.'

Percival stared. Then, incredibly, he laughed. His eyes shone, their vigour renewed. 'A valid point,' he said. 'Worthy of note.'

Thrown by the man's reaction, Edward kept the gun trained on his chest. 'I haven't killed for her yet,' he said. 'Not directly, at least. But I *will* shoot you if you don't do as I ask. I will. Now come over here towards me, and keep walking, away down the loop. Don't think too hard about whether I mean what I say. Because I do mean it. I promise you.'

'By the gods,' Percival replied. He remained motionless a moment longer, then took a slow step forward. 'I've a feeling that might be the longest speech you've ever given. Bravo.'

'Move.'

Edward swung the sights of his rifle around as Percival passed him. The man walked with a casual shuffle, flip-flops slapping the road surface. His gargantuan belly preceded him, a ginger-fuzzed crescent of it poking out from under his T-shirt. As he moved beneath the fairy lights, a chameleon spread of colours danced across his skin.

Edward fell in step behind him. He threw a glance back at Piper. *Stay*, he mouthed. To Percival he said, 'Road curves to the right. Then there's a turn. Take it.'

They came to the fork and the man obeyed Edward's instructions, stepping off Joyau Caché's main loop. The path was unpaved here, a cracked mud track dotted with the crisp carcasses of weeds. At its terminus, surrounded by trees, stood the simple chalet in which Edward had lived with Piper these last five years.

His legs felt heavy when he saw it. The building was pre-fabricated, squat and unremittingly ugly; but he had worked so hard to make it a home, and for a time it had become exactly that.

'Door's unlocked,' he said, as Percival reached the chalet's front steps. 'Living room's out the back. Go straight along the hall. Don't think about a way out of this. There isn't one. I know the house, know its layout. You don't.'

In single file they reached the living room. It was a simple space, sparsely furnished. Cheap plywood bookcases lined one wall, filled with Piper's collection of second-hand literature. An old cathode ray tube TV set stood in one corner; Edward's armchair was pulled up in front of it, near the couch where Piper liked to read. French windows opened into a weed-choked garden. A single reading lamp, its bulb still lit, made dark mirrors of the glass. Already the room exuded a forlorn, cast-off look: a place where two people had found comfort, and would find it no longer.

Jolyon Percival came to a halt and turned, eyes moving over the bookshelves and their contents.

'Sit,' Edward told him.

The man complied, lowering himself onto the couch. He peered up at Edward and his ginger eyebrows tented. 'This will probably strike you as impertinent,' he said. 'But do you have any wine? Red, preferably. Although, quite frankly, any old plonk would do. In fact I'd—'

'Don't,' Edward said. 'Don't do that.'

Percival hesitated. 'What?'

'Don't make light of this. Don't make the mistake of thinking this isn't serious. You're in trouble, now. Here. With me.'

'I can see that you're upset.'

'No,' Edward replied. 'That's not what you see. What you see is someone trying to think of a single reason not to put you in the ground. You'd be wise to start talking, help me out.'

Hearing that, the artist seemed to lose a little of his composure. 'What's our topic?'

'Start with the paintings. The ones in your caravan.'

'Ah.' For a moment Percival was silent. Then, slowly, he

nodded. 'All this aggression – I'd been trying to work it out. But if you've seen the paintings, that explains a lot.'

'How did you know her name?'

The man winced. 'I warn you, it won't make easy listening. It doesn't make easy telling if I'm honest. I dreamed her. In fact, you could say I've been dreaming her for years, on and off. Believe me that I know just how bats-in-the-belfry that sounds. Frankly, if I heard this from anyone else I'd be inclined to lock them up somewhere quiet and confiscate their cutlery. Not,' he added hastily, 'that I'm suggesting you adopt such a course.'

'The dreams.'

Percival shrugged. 'They started innocently enough. Snatched images, really, nothing very distinct. In the beginning I never glimpsed her face. First time I ever saw her clearly she was in the passenger seat of some kind of motorhome. There were white mountains in the background, I remember that. She happened to glance up at a mirror and bang, there she was. She seemed sad. Lonely.'

Edward thought of the trip he had taken with Piper through the Alps when she was nine. His skin prickled.

Percival laughed. 'You know what's ridiculous? For a while I actually considered her my muse. The dreams didn't happen often back then, but each time afterwards I saw a noticeable improvement in my work. Then, in my studio about a year ago, I blacked out. When I came to hours later I saw that I'd painted her. Best thing I'd ever produced. Incomparable, really. Frightened the hell out of me, I can tell you. Everything stopped soon after. I thought I was over it. But six months ago, the dreams came back. This time they were different. *She* was different.'

The man's expression was hollow. 'You've seen the paintings. I can't tell you what it's like to have such ghastly stuff in your head every night. Getting it down on canvas – it became a kind of therapy. Catharsis, if you will. If I hadn't had that as a safety valve, I'm not sure I'd still be here. The dreams – they got worse and worse. Pretty soon the sleep-talking started. I'd wake up muttering words I didn't understand, phrases I'd never heard. Convinced myself I was on the long road past bonkers. Either that or possessed.' He laughed again, but it contained little humour. 'Alzheimer's or the Devil – and I gave them equal consideration. Shows how bloody decrepit I'd become.

'I tried everything to make it stop. I must have drunk half the wine stocks in the Languedoc. Once I stayed up for four days straight, simply to see if exhaustion would keep it at bay. If anything, that made it worse. Eventually I just started writing things down. Phonetically, of course; I had no idea how any of that stuff was spelled. But once I had some of the words on paper, it was easy enough to work out their root.'

'Gaelic,' Edward said. He recalled how long it had taken him to make the same connection and grimaced.

'Scottish Gaelic,' Percival said. 'The language of old Alba. Look. It's obvious you've got a head start on me. Why don't—'

'Keep talking.'

The man sighed, shrugged. 'The same phrases kept coming up. *An Toiseach*; *Beò-Ìobairt*; *balla-dìon*.'

'*The First*,' Edward said, watching closely as he translated. '*The Sacrifice; The Wall*.'

'*Barrier wall*, that's right. Then there was *Triallaichean*, which translates as *The Travellers*, and two more: *Cathasach* and *Cadalach*. The first of those is a name, or was before it fell out of use. It's Irish in origin – the Scottish equivalent is *Caithriseach*. It means *vigilance*. *Cadalach* is a word used to describe drowsiness, or sleepiness. You could say the two are opposites.'

'*Cathasach* becomes *Cadalach*,' Edward said, and wondered where he had heard it. For a while, neither man spoke. 'How did you find us?'

'A few nights ago I woke up and scrawled down *Joyau Caché* on the pad I keep near the bed. Earlier that day my landlady recognised a place I'd painted from a dream – the Gorges du Tarn. There's only one Joyau Caché in the gorge and it's this place. I hopped in my car and drove down here.' He eyed Edward's rifle and screwed up his face. 'I'm beginning to think that might have been a poor decision.'

'Why did you come?'

'You'd have to be suffering from a pretty terminal lack of curiosity to stay away, don't you think?'

'That's not the reason.'

'No.' Percival took a breath. He trapped it inside his chest a while before releasing it. 'Once I had the translations, I did a little more research. You're streets ahead of me so you won't be surprised to see it, but that's when I found this.' He dipped two fingers into the pocket of his shorts and pulled out a small book, bound in black leather.

'What is it?'

'Surely you've come across it.'

'If I had, I wouldn't ask.'

The man frowned. 'Edward – it is Edward, isn't it? Edward, if you've really never seen this before, if you haven't read it, then that makes me very worried indeed.' Percival tapped the book's spine with his finger. 'It's an apocalypse text. You know what that means?'

'Yeah,' Edward said. 'Judgement Day. The end of the world.'

'Not quite. That's a New Testament association: the words of John the Apostle, the Book of Revelation. When you go back to the original Greek, *apocalypse* is simply the word for an *unveiling*, or *uncovering*. Before its biblical connotations became commonplace it was used to describe any work that claimed to disclose hidden knowledge. This one was written by a man called Urchardan some time between the fifth and sixth century. We know little about him, except that he was probably a monk and most likely lived on Skye, or possibly the Western Isles. It's not even clear whether Urchardan was the original author. He might just have been preserving the words of an earlier scribe. We'll never know for sure – no complete work has ever been unearthed. This,' he said, holding up the book, 'is an interpretation stitched together from a number of secondary sources, all of them fragments. It's a piece of speculative non-fiction, if you like, but an authoritative one even so. What complicates things further is that none of those fragments are written in the original language, which is thought to have been Common Brittonic, or perhaps Pictish.'

'What did this Urchardan have to say?'

'A lot of old claptrap, you might think. He starts with a creation myth of sorts, as many of these things do. This one is innocuous enough, although it pre-dates Christianity by at least a few thousand years. Unfortunately, Urchardan assumes a great deal of familiarity on the reader's behalf, which means much of the detail is omitted. He talks of six warrior tribes united by two lovers, Mórríghan and Cathasach, who appeared out of the sea one day on the western coast of Scotland near Loch Broom.'

Edward thought of his conversation with Piper's interloper seven years earlier. An insight struck him. 'The *An Toiseach*.'

'How did you know that?'

He waved Percival's question away. 'Go on.'

'Apparently this Cathasach feared for the tribes' survival in the face of outside corruption. Wanted to do something about it.'

'What kind of corruption?'

'Frustratingly, Urchardan never explains. I can only think he meant outside influence or expansion. Either way, Cathasach pledged his life to protect the tribes. According to Urchardan, he descended into the earth to create the *balla-dìon* . . . or *barrier wall*, as the term translates. Mórríghan, mad with grief at his sacrifice, fled into the sea; but not before she killed half the tribes' children in a jealous rage.

'That's about all we get as an intro. The meat of Urchardan's writings narrate events from his own time. He talks of the *balla-dìon*'s continuing vigil over the land, uninterrupted for millennia until the arrival of the *Triallaichean*.'

'The Travellers.'

Percival nodded. 'Four of them, sent by Mórríghan in secret, tasked with destroying Cathasach's legacy. But Cathasach – our good guy in all this – managed to outsmart them. Using the power of the *balla-dìon* he scattered the *Triallaichean* to the four isles.'

Edward stared. The rifle was heavy in his hands. 'What's any of this got to do with Piper?'

'The last part of Urchardan's text is a warning. It foretells a future attempt by Mórríghan to destroy the *balla-dìon*, describing the consequences if she succeeds.' Percival flicked through the book's pages until he came to a section he had marked. He began to read: '"*Guard well, be vigilant. For if the balla-dìon fails, all of humanity will be eaten by those who pour through.*"'

The man snapped the book shut. 'Look, I have no truck with this kind of thing. Ancient prophecies, mystics, seers . . . it's all horse-shit if you ask me. I don't believe in fate, warrior gods, predestination – any of that crap. But I can't explain why I've been dreaming about your daughter, or why my head's been filling up with Gaelic phrases. And I can't tell you why every single one of those phrases appears in a text written by a monk some fifteen hundred years ago. I do know one thing: it freezes my balls. I don't think this Urchardan, whoever he was, had the full truth of it, but it seems the guy had *some* kind of clue.'

Percival raised his eyes to Edward. 'I'm worried that Piper is going to do something. Something very bad indeed. And if she succeeds, if any of Urchardan's predictions in this book come true—'

'They will.'

Piper's voice, that one.

Percival glanced towards the doorway and his expression changed. So far, even with the gun trained on his chest, his demeanour had been calm. Now, the blood drained from his face.

Edward turned his head and saw, standing in the doorway, with Therron hovering behind her, Piper.

The girl's eyes burned as she studied Percival. 'They *will* come true,' she repeated. 'But not in the way that you think. And not without your help.'

CHAPTER 36

Gorges du Tarn, Southern France

For a moment it looked as if Jolyon Percival would try to struggle up from the couch. His eyes flickered between Edward's rifle and Piper's face. '*Beò-Ìobairt*,' he stammered, and immediately looked stricken, as if the phrase had slipped past his lips unbidden.

Piper winced. 'Yeah, I'm not really sure how much I like that as a name.'

'You'll kill us,' he said.

The girl stepped further into the room, and to Edward it seemed as if every lamp in the house had momentarily brightened. She seemed to inhabit a nimbus of light almost of her own making.

The artist's words echoed in his head: *I'm worried that Piper is going to do something. Something very bad indeed.*

She approached the sofa, keeping her focus on Percival. 'Not all of us.'

'Is that meant to reassure me?'

'Once you've remembered everything, you won't need reassurance.' Turning to Edward, she laid her hand on his rifle and guided the barrel towards the floor. 'You won't need that. He's not going to harm us.'

'Pie,' Edward began. The gun barrel bobbed, caught in

conflicting currents. 'You heard what he said.'

'And he's half right. But he's half wrong, too.'

'I don't understand.'

'Dad, listen to me. I'm so grateful for everything you've done. But you don't need to involve yourself in this. Not in what happens next.'

Edward's mouth fell open. Pain flared in his chest: as real as the ache in his joints.

His daughter returned her attention to Percival. 'It's a pity you chose Urchardan's account. From what I understand, he was hardly impartial.'

The man's breathing grew ragged. 'Why do you say that?'

As Piper moved towards the couch, Percival pressed his spine into it, but she skirted him, going to the French windows and throwing them open. 'It's a warm evening,' she said. 'We shouldn't be cooped up in here. Let's do this outside, you and me.'

The artist opened his mouth, stared. 'I've been called many things,' he replied, appearing to recover some of his bluster. 'Knave; philanderer; fool. But if you think for one minute I'm going outside, alone, with you—'

'How old are you, Jolyon?'

He flinched. 'What?'

'It's a simple enough question.'

'I'm fifty-three.'

'Really? Where were you born?'

'Where?'

'How about your mother's name?'

Percival frowned. 'My mother?'

'You do have a mother?'

'Of course.'

'So what's her name?'

'I . . . I can't quite recall.'

'You can't quite recall? Isn't that a little . . . odd? Where did you grow up?'

He swallowed. Took a gulping breath. 'Wiltshire.'

'Which town, Jolyon?'

'What?'

'Which street?'

'I . . .' The artist stared at her, perplexed. 'Damndest thing.'

'Name three of your childhood friends,' Piper said, the pace of her interrogation increasing. 'In fact, name one. Did you ever have a dog? A favourite book? A first kiss?' She raised her eyebrows. 'Are these questions bothering you? Are you wondering why you can't answer them?'

Sweat began to bead on his forehead.

'Is Jolyon your real name? Is that, really, what you are called? Or do you have a different name?' Piper's eyes narrowed. 'An older name, perhaps?'

The man's fingers loosened and his book tumbled to the floor. He shifted his weight, face sallow as he contemplated her. 'What are you doing to me?'

'I'm asking you simple questions.'

'If you have answers . . .'

In reply, Piper gestured towards the French windows.

Percival stared a moment longer. Shaking, he pulled himself to his feet and shuffled outside. The girl followed without looking back.

For a minute or more Edward remained motionless, too paralysed by his daughter's words to move. Gradually he became aware of Therron. The boy hadn't spoken throughout the exchange.

He engaged the rifle's safety and leaned the weapon against the wall. 'Want a drink?'

'Yeah,' Therron said. 'I think so.'

Wincing from the pain in his knee, Edward limped into the hall. He hadn't touched a drop of alcohol since he'd discovered the smashed convoy in Snowdonia nearly sixteen years earlier, but he had long since ceased to fear it. At the back of a cupboard he found a dusty bottle of Calvados left by the previous owners. He poured two glasses. Back in the living room, he handed one to the boy and eased himself down into his chair.

Therron perched on the sofa and sipped from his glass. 'She's not who we thought.'

Pointless to deny it. Edward shook his head.

'Is she even your daughter?'

'What do you believe?'

'I think you love her that way,' Therron said. 'But I don't think you're her father by blood.' He raised his head. 'Are you?'

'No.'

'Who is she?'

'I don't know.'

'That man,' the boy continued. 'He's here for her, isn't he? He's come to take her away.'

Edward knocked back his Calvados and waited for the burn, but it never came. 'I think so.'

In truth, it might be the best thing ever to happen to her. When he thought of the life he had given the girl, his guilt overwhelmed him. For the first seven years they had survived on a pauper's wage. He had regularly gone without food, simply so that Piper might eat. He had moved her from town to town, too fearful for her safety to stay anywhere long, too scarred by Laura's death to hold down anything but the most menial of jobs. They had fared better these last few years, admittedly, but only thanks to the cache of money he had discovered during their flight from Stallockmore Farm. When he looked around him, little of what he saw was the result of his own toil. It was a testament to Piper's strength that she had not allowed his many failures to affect her more acutely than they had.

'I knew this couldn't last,' Therron said. 'All my life – something good happens, something bad happens to counter it.'

Edward glanced up, dismayed to see such misery in the boy's

expression. He got to his feet and limped back down the hall to the kitchen. Returning with the Calvados, he topped up Therron's glass. 'Whatever happens,' he said, 'you've got a home. Whether it's here or some other place, I don't know. But I won't abandon you.'

The boy rubbed his eyes with the back of his hand. 'I don't want *her* to abandon *us*.'

Edward knocked back his drink, bit down on it.

He had no more words.

Jolyon followed Piper to a plastic picnic table surrounded by chairs. Overhead the moon still sailed an easterly bearing, but everything else in his world had changed. He heard an echo of the girl's voice as she had addressed him:

What was your mother's name? You do have a mother? Are these questions bothering you?

He could feel something swelling inside his head. But whether it was physical – a tumour readying itself to burst – or purely psychological, he could not begin to guess.

Piper sat down, gestured at a vacant chair. She drew up her legs and wrapped her arms around them. So relaxed she seemed, and yet in some strange way so vulnerable. She appeared the very antithesis of the dark creature he had painted. Why, then, did he feel an insectile skittering across his skin each time he met her eyes?

'I do remember my mother,' he blurted, collapsing onto the seat she had indicated.

'Oh yes?'

'Yes.'

Piper nodded. 'That's good. Father?'

'What?'

'You had one, I presume? Most people do.'

Jolyon opened his mouth, found he could not formulate a reply.

'Look,' she said. 'I'm sorry for what happened in there. But we don't have time for subtlety. I need you to remember who you are.'

'Why don't you tell me who you think I am?'

'Because I don't know why you've forgotten. Until I do, I'm not sure I want to go blundering around inside your head. I'm no psychiatrist.' She licked her lips, shot him a look. 'Nor am I the nasty little hussy that Urchardan makes out.'

'You've read him.'

'Of course. Read him and dismissed him. Aiden Urchardan was in awe of Cathasach from the start. No wonder he took the view that he did. You should have picked up Mac an Làmhaich.'

'*The Red Book*,' Jolyon said. 'I couldn't find a copy.'

'Pity. Làmhaich gives a far more balanced account.'

'From whose perspective?'

'There *is* that,' she admitted. 'But I have a copy upstairs. You can read it if you like – make up your own mind.'

'I think we're a little beyond that, don't you think?' He paused, forced himself – however unsettling – to hold her gaze. 'Look. I can't explain any of this. I don't know why you're in my head. And I don't know why this guy Urchardan was writing hate mail about you over a thousand years before you were born. You've got to admit it's a little off-putting.' He paused. 'But just as I said to your father, I don't believe in prophecies. I don't believe in Celtic polytheism, Bigfoot, hobbits, unicorns, any of that stuff.'

'Nor do I.'

'But something odd is going on here. Whatever it is, like it or not I seem to be a part of it, so you—'

'Would you like me to tell you?'

'—might as well spill the beans and to hell with the—'

'Drustan,' Piper said, leaning across the table to touch him.

And everything in Jolyon Percival's world changed again, this time irrevocably.

★ ★ ★

Edward lurched out of sleep, tumbling into his first hangover in sixteen years. His tongue felt so dry that merely touching it to the roof of his mouth made him gag. His head swelled with each beat of his heart.

Disorientated, it was a moment before he saw his daughter's silhouette beside his chair. He struggled upright, screwed up his face. His voice cracked when he spoke. 'Where's Therron?'

'Asleep upstairs.'

'Time is it?'

'Late.'

'That guy still here?'

She shook her head. 'He was pretty shaken up. He's gone back up the hill.'

'Do you trust him?'

Piper placed her hand over his. 'Yeah. I do.'

'When I was up there,' Edward said, 'earlier tonight . . .'

'The paintings.' She nodded. 'He told me.'

'It doesn't worry you? The way he depicted you?'

'I don't like the idea of you seeing me like that. But it wasn't me, Dad. And it's never going to be.'

'Are you friends now, the pair of you?' The edge of bitterness he heard in his voice embarrassed him.

'He's got some thinking to do, but yeah. I think we are.'

'And you're OK?'

It was a while before she spoke. Then: 'Come on. Let's get you upstairs. You look kind of dreadful.'

She helped him out of his chair, and, for the first time in his life, he allowed himself to lean on her. Piper slung her arm around his waist and guided him towards the stairs.

Edward cleared his throat. 'When are you leaving?'

'Let's not talk about that yet.'

'So it's true.'

'Dad . . .'

She sounded so forlorn that he could do nothing except nod in mute agreement. Side by side, they climbed the stairs.

In his bedroom, he lay down on the mattress and kicked off his boots.

Piper pulled the covers up to his chin. She kissed his cheek and retreated.

The door snicked shut, leaving Edward alone in the silence.

CHAPTER 37

Cévennes Mountain Range, Southern France

Jenna Black sat in the passenger seat of the Mercedes Vito next to Sabine Estrella and watched the French autoroute disappear beneath the crew van's wheels. The moon had dipped below the horizon an hour ago, leaving a black bowl of stars. Among them she saw Mars, Jupiter and Saturn engaged in their eternal transits across the heavens. As always they imbued a sense in Jenna of the fundamental rightness of her mission. Yet however reassuring those planetary titans were, they could not offset her growing disquiet as the distance to her destination shrank.

Beside her, Sabine Estrella peered at the road past a nose that emerged from her face like the prow of a Viking longship. She was a pale slip of a thing, long-boned and fragile, the nose a striking flaw in an otherwise matchless countenance.

'How much further?' Jenna asked.

Sabine glanced at the sat nav. 'Twenty minutes. If we keep up this pace.'

'That's no good. Go faster.'

The woman shot her a look, but she pressed her foot a little harder to the floor.

Their flight had landed in Montpellier two hours earlier. Had they left the airport on time they would have reached their target by now. But Keegan, for reasons he had failed adequately to explain, had met them with the rental van an hour later than planned. Considering the stakes, his behaviour was unforgivable. Jenna, much to the man's chagrin, had installed Sabine behind the wheel, relegating Keegan to the Mercedes' second row. Hardly a promising start to the most dangerous situation they had faced in years.

Not since Ireland, nearly a decade ago, had Jenna experienced dreams like those that had plagued her these last few weeks. Back then they had culminated in the disastrous encounter at Stallockmore Farm. Even now, nine years later, she could recall with dreadful clarity the deadwood crack of Vivian's bones as her body was sucked heavenward.

'These mountains – the Cévennes,' Sabine said, after another mile had slipped by. 'Do you know much about them?'

'Only what I read during the flight.'

'Are they populated?'

'Sparsely.'

'Wildlife?'

Jenna glanced to her left. She saw the woman's throat bob as she swallowed.

Go easy on her. You were just the same.

'No bears,' she said gently. 'Not here; not any more. You'd have to go as far as the Pyrenees for that.'

'What else?'

'Sabine—'

'There's boar,' Keegan said, from the back seat. 'Nasty tusks and teeth. Couple of corrupted boar could kill you pretty quick. Then there's wolves to worry about. Lynx, vultures, mouflon, deer.'

Sabine's mouth dropped open. '*Wolves?*'

Jenna scowled, angry at the man but unwilling to destabilise things further by admonishing him. 'A handful of sightings at most,' she said. 'Keegan's talking about a few rogue migrants out of the southern Alps. This range covers three hundred and fifty square miles. That's a lot of ground, even for a wolf. Put it out of your mind, Sabine. We've far more pressing concerns.'

The woman blinked. '*Ériu protects*,' she whispered.

'And I told you to stop that. Ériu is dead. She's no deity, no good-luck charm to be muttered as a ward. I need you focused, sharp.'

She saw Sabine's face tighten at the rebuke and winced. She was no good at this. She lacked the skills to motivate others, the confidence to make tough decisions. Why anyone had wanted her to lead what remained of Ériu's followers, she could not begin to fathom. For all his faults, Keegan had been the natural choice. He would have been *her* choice. She could feel the burn of his resentment, and had no idea how to handle it. The man had been difficult enough for Vivian to contain. For Jenna, he was an impossibility.

Ahead, the road veered south and began to descend. Within a few miles, they hit the first of the switchbacks that would take them to the canyon floor. Unclipping her seat belt, Jenna climbed into the second row, feeling Keegan's eyes rove over her as she scrambled onto the seat beside him. 'Let's go over the gear.'

He nodded, face immediately serious. He unzipped a holdall and rummaged inside. From it he retrieved a couple of drawstring bags. 'Here,' he said, upending the contents of one of them into her palm: two silver pellets with rubberised caps, and a separate metal tube the size of a triple-A battery.

'What is it?'

'Wireless player. Best you can get.' He gestured with his finger. 'Earbuds, controller. Simple as that. It's Bluetooth tech, limited range, so don't drop the stick.'

'What's on it?'

'Same patterns you've heard before, with a few tweaks. If I'm right it means you won't need the volume as loud.'

'And if you're wrong?'

Keegan arced his hand upwards towards the ceiling, making the sound of a rocket motor.

'You're unbelievable.'

'You're pretty special too.'

'Vivian was wearing her headset when she died. It didn't protect her.'

'Then she must've been spotted. If she'd kept out of sight she'd have been safe.' Keegan tapped the MP3 player. 'I've preset it, so no need to fiddle. Screw the buds into your ears. Press once, here, for music. Press again for silence.' He slipped his hand beneath her palm and closed her fingers around the device. 'Ériu protects,' he added, and grinned.

Jenna shook her head. 'How many sets do you have?'

'One for each of us. Six spares.'

'Six?'

'Playing it safe.'

'OK.' She paused, dreading the question she must ask next. 'What about guns?'

'Ah, the main course. What's your preference?'

'You know my preference, Keegan.'

'Yeah. Somehow I don't think kind words and prayer are going to cut it.' He delved back inside the holdall and removed a moulded plastic box trailing nylon straps. 'Tactical holster. Holds a semi-automatic. Keeps your hands free for when you need them. These straps go around your thigh.' Keegan's teeth glimmered. 'If you open your legs I'll show you.'

'I'm wearing a dress.'

'So hitch it up.'

'Not going to happen.'

Shrugging, he tossed the holster into the bag and pulled out a firearm instead, turning it over in his hands. 'Glock 17. Slide-stop's here if you need to reload. Seventeen rounds in the mag, and that's—'

'I've used one.'

He raised his eyebrows. 'Bad girl. What about one of these?' Eyes shining, he grabbed another bag from the footwell, unzipped it. He pulled out a brutal-looking piece of hardware.

'Heckler and Koch UMP. On full auto it can fire—'

'Forget it.'

'This'll punch through—'

'I don't *care* what it can punch through, Keegan. *Look* at me. I could barely carry that thing, let alone use it. I'll take the pistol as a last resort, but only because I've no choice.' She stared at him, appalled. 'You live for this stuff, don't you?'

The man's eyes grew flat. 'What I live for,' he said, 'is the prospect of revenge. Of getting even for what they did to Ériu. Of stopping this thing dead and reversing all the damage it's done.'

The passion in his voice surprised her. For all Keegan's flaws he had loved their *Triallaiche* mentor more fiercely than anyone. He wore his grief openly, even now: scars of battle, defiantly displayed. She wished she could summon the same rage.

'Jenna.' In the front seat, Sabine tilted her head. The van began to slow. 'I think this is it.'

CHAPTER 38

Gorges du Tarn, Southern France

After helping her father into his bed, Piper tiptoed down-stairs. No lamps burned in the living room now, but enough light spilled from the hall to define Mórríghan's shape.

The woman stood by the French windows, her face as pale as tallow. Its surface shifted restlessly, as if a community of beetles and blowflies scurried beneath. Her image, usually so immutable, swelled and shrank; it flickered dark around the edges.

'No,' the woman protested. Her voice sounded like it came from a tunnel. It crackled and popped like an old phonograph. 'I know what you intend to do. You can't—'

Piper held up a hand and Mórríghan's image froze. Its defining edges began to bleed into the surrounding shadows. 'This is the price,' she said, thinking of the boy. 'This is *my* price.'

As if jerked unwilling through an old cine projector, the woman grew animated once more. She raised her arms, opened her mouth. 'Wait, *please*. Think this through.'

'I already have. This is for me and him alone, no one else.'

'If you do this, there's nothing to stop—'

Piper gritted her teeth and closed her hands into fists, crying out with the effort it cost her. Abruptly, Mórríghan's silhouette folded in on itself and winked out. Piper fell to her knees, hands braced on the carpet. The pain was like a heated needle in her skull. Blood burst from her nose. She rolled onto her side and curled into a ball. The pressure inside her head was unbearable. Her ears roared, as if waves crashed onto a shore mere yards from where she lay. Her lungs grew tight. She tasted blood in her mouth, felt it trickle warm down her throat.

Finally, after what seemed like long minutes of paralysis, her agony began to subside. She raised herself to all fours, blinking as her vision returned. A dark stain blotted the carpet where her head had lain. She felt a steady seep of blood from her left ear. It rolled down her cheek and dripped from her jaw. More blood flowed from her nose, salty over her lips.

Finally she staggered to the kitchen. At the counter she grabbed fistfuls of kitchen towels, clamping a wad to her ear and another to her nose. Holding herself together that way, she climbed the stairs. When she switched on the bathroom light its brightness speared her, but she forced herself to hold her eyes open. In the cabinet mirror she inspected her reflection.

Piper had expected the sight to be unpalatable, but never as bad as that which greeted her. She looked like she'd been in a car accident. One side of her face was dark with clotting blood. Fresh blood flowed from her nose in steady pulses.

She stripped off her vest and wadded it into a ball. Using strips of toilet paper, she made plugs for her nostrils and ears, screwing them in as deep as they could go. Then she turned on the shower above the bath and stripped off her remaining clothes.

It took her a minute or two to rinse away the blood. She washed her hair and soaped her body, watching the suds swirl into the plughole When she climbed onto the bathmat her vision swam, forcing her to perch on the side of the bath until it cleared.

Back in front of the mirror, she removed the plugs from her ears and nose. She waited anxiously, but no blood reappeared.

'What a catch you are,' she muttered. It was far from the truth. Her eyes looked lifeless, her lips pale and blue.

From the cabinet where she kept her paltry collection of beauty products, she removed a tub of scented body lotion. She prised off the lid, scooped out some cream and rubbed it into her skin. Next, she found her tester bottle of Chanel Coco Mademoiselle. She spritzed herself sparingly: throat, navel, breasts. When the fragrance reached her nose it revived her. Squaring her shoulders, examining her reflection again, she sighed at what she saw.

On the back of the door hung her robe. Piper shrugged into it, tying it loosely at her waist. Out in the hall the house was still dark.

Somewhere, a tap dripped. Other than that, silence.

She moved across the landing to her room, eased the door open and slipped inside.

A lamp glowed beside the bed. Under a cotton sheet, Therron lay sleeping. How beautiful he looked, how enduring. She knew he was as temporary a creation as any other, a fleeting construct of flesh and thought, but she drank him in regardless, hoping that the image might sustain her now that she had decided her course.

The boy stirred as she closed the door, raising himself up on one elbow. He blinked, rubbed his face. 'You OK?'

'It's time,' she replied.

Therron sat up and the sheet fell into his lap. He searched her expression more closely. 'Time?'

Piper nodded, smiled. Her hands moved to her gown and untied it. The garment slipped to the floor.

The boy's eyes grew round. 'Oh,' he said. His Adam's apple bobbed. When he reached out a hand to the lamp, Piper shook her head.

'I want to see you,' she said, walking to the bed. 'I want to experience everything.'

★ ★ ★

Jolyon Percival burst through the door of his caravan and slammed it shut behind him. Canvases cluttered the floor space. Wherever he looked, Piper's eyes measured him: unblinking, unrelenting. He heard the girl's voice, inside his head:

Is Jolyon your real name? Is that, really, what you are called? Or do you have a different name? An older name, perhaps?

With a roar, he snatched up the nearest portrait. Raising it above his head, he dashed its frame against the wall. He wadded up what remained of the image and flung it across the room. He grabbed a second painting, smashed that one too. Put his foot through a third. Destroyed six more.

Jolyon tore through the living space, wrecking everything in his path, growing more frenzied with each act of violence. Only once he had annihilated every remaining frame, shredded every canvas, obliterated every single one of the portraits he had brought with him from Labastide-Esparbairenque did he collapse among the ripped linen and splinters, his knuckles bloody, his fingertips sore. He burned for a drink, for the anaesthetising oblivion it would bring.

Haven't you pursued that course long enough?

With a second anguished cry, this one from the very depths of his chest, Jolyon pulled himself to his feet. He staggered to the kitchen counter and prised off a packing crate lid. Inside he found oils, brushes, solvents, rags. Not what he was looking for. Frustrated, he overturned the crate, heedless of the contents as they clattered to the floor. He tore open another container, another. None contained what he needed.

Jolyon stormed outside and wrenched open his car door. On the passenger seat lay an untidy pile of satchels and bags. He rifled through the first one he saw, pulling out fistfuls of receipts, museum tickets, napkins. He tossed them into the air, scattering them like confetti. He upended the next bag, raked through its treasures. Ransacked another. Shook his head. Swore.

Finally, a shard of clarity pierced his madness and he hurried to the Citroën's rear. With his palms pressed against the boot, he lifted his face to the heavens. There was Ursa Major. Ursa Minor, too; Draco; Cepheus; Cassiopeia. So long their lights had sustained him.

Or had they?

Could any of what Piper had suggested be true? Could he even *begin* to give her words credence? He thought he felt a shiver in the metal beneath his fingers, a vibration transmitted through the Citroën's chassis from the earth beneath. As he contemplated those distant constellations, as his earlier frenzy began to subside, another thought occurred to him: Did he really want to *know*?

Jolyon laughed out loud at that, heartily and from the belly. Within his grasp, quite literally, might lurk the answer to every question he had ever asked: questions about himself; about creation; about destiny. What did he have to lose except his history . . . and possibly his sanity?

He guffawed once more. Tears sprang from his eyes and rolled into his beard. His hands fumbled with the boot catch and he lifted the lid. Inside, amongst twine-bound stacks of old newspapers, magazines and music scores, rested a battered steamer trunk banded with elmwood and finished with a scuffed houndstooth fabric. Jolyon wrestled it over the boot-lip and let it tumble to the grass. Lifting one of the handles, he dragged it inside the caravan and dumped it on the floor. He knelt down beside it, fingers hovering over its catches. There he paused, puffing and blowing from his exertions.

Jolyon popped the trunk's catches and raised its lid.

Underneath was a fold of tartan. He pulled it back. Beneath, lay his history: papers, medals, school exercise books, trinkets, photographs.

He picked up one of the exercise books and flicked through it. Inside, he found pages dense with handwriting: pencil diagrams depicting glacier formation, plate tectonics, the Gulf Stream. Here was the proof he had been seeking, the evidence that made Piper's words a lie. As his heart began to slow its frantic rhythm, he closed the book and spied the name on the cover.

It wasn't his.

Jolyon snatched his hands away.

Nausea rolled in him. He retrieved the book from the pile, studied the name again, passed a thumb over the words: *Clive Marchant*.

He picked up another. This one was different to the first: a different school crest, a different name on the cover: *Nicholas Short*.

In the trunk, a handful of exercise books remained. He examined them one by one, unearthing a clutch of meaningless names. Beneath the layer of books, he found a cardboard folder of photographs. Fingers trembling, he opened it. A few hundred images spilled out. Some were colour shots but most were monochrome. This was the clearest evidence he possessed of the life he had lived; and yet he recognised none of the faces he saw in those prints, none of the locations.

He heard a rattling and glanced up at the door. But it was only the sound of his teeth clattering together in his mouth. He burrowed deeper through the chest, finding keepsakes that raised no memories in him, and plucked no chords. At last he found his birth certificate and unfolded it. There it was in faded typescript; incontrovertible proof:

```
Jolyon Linus Tobias Percival
```

But the space allocated for his birth date was blank, as were those left for his parents' names.

Drustan, she had called him.

Overcome, Jolyon collapsed into the detritus he had created, birth certificate clutched to his chest. He drew up his legs and lay in a foetal curl, listening to the rasp of his breathing. Only one question occupied him.

If Piper had been right about this, could she have been telling the truth about everything?

Against his leg he felt the hard edges of the *Black Book* translation he had ordered from England. In it, Aiden Urchardan offered a distressing counterargument to the girl's claims.

CHAPTER 39

Austin, Texas

Pastor Benjamin D. Pope sat in the back of the Lexus SUV as it crawled up the hill towards Mercury Hall, fiddling with the locket he had taken from his dead wife's throat.

Wendy Devereaux had selected the venue, and it was just about perfect. A century earlier the building had served as a church for the frontier town of Mercury, a community formed by the expansion of the Fort Worth and Rio Grande Railroad. A few decades ago it had been dismantled and reassembled here, on this wooded Austin hilltop. Lavished with money, it functioned, nowadays, as a wedding venue and music hall. Tonight it would host the pastor, his security team and one hundred hand-selected members of his flock.

The Lexus crawled along the white-gravel drive towards the entrance. Benjamin saw Wendy waiting for him out front, dressed in her signature trouser suit. Two security personnel flanked her.

The sun was sinking in the west, a last celebration of tangerine fire. He saw it burning in the windows of the hall's clapboard frontage. Glancing down at his lap, he snapped open the locket's clasp. The wedding photograph had faded over time, but the intensity of the smiles worn by bride and groom endured.

One of the security men opened the Lexus's door, and

Benjamin emerged from cool air-con into the dry heat of a Texan evening.

Wendy came forward and kissed his cheek. 'Right on time.'

'Are they here?'

'Full house.'

Benjamin nodded at that, relieved. The invites had been mailed a fortnight earlier, but you could never be sure. 'Security?'

'All our own people, and I do mean *all* our own, just as you asked. Not a soul from outside. And no band, no sound system. No fancy lights. Building's gonna be locked down the moment we're inside.'

'Caterers?'

'Sent home ten minutes ago. Everyone's been fed and watered. It's just you and your flock, Pastor.' She tilted her head. 'So . . . you gonna spill the beans for me? Tell me what this is all about?'

Benjamin gazed past her to the building, at the candles burning inside. He reached out and took Wendy's hands. 'It's been a pleasure working with you; you know that. A real treat.'

'Been?' Frowning, she pulled her hands away. 'You're not planning some kind of Jonestown-style massacre in there, are you? Should I frisk you for weapons?'

He smiled, and then a thought occurred to him. 'All these years you've been with me, looking after my interests, the interests of our church, and I've never even asked you the question outright.' He paused, waiting until she looked at him. 'Are you a believer?'

Wendy held his gaze for less than a second before she glanced away. 'I believe in *you*, Pastor. Always have. Now, come on. There's an audience waiting. Let's get you inside.'

The room – clean and bright and minimally dressed – buzzed with conversation. Tall arched windows, their borders decorated with blocks of pastel glass, let in what remained of the day's copper light.

Arranged on seats in ten neat rows sat his congregation. Necks craned as he walked to the front; conversation died. Benjamin took his time, pausing to press hands, squeeze shoulders. He did not recognise every face in the room, but he knew the vast majority and had personally vetted them all. Each had been chosen according to specific criteria. One face he did recognise was Aiden Urchardan's. The man sat in the front row, dressed in a white shirt and black suit. Beneath his missionary hat, his silver hair flowed liquid down his back.

Benjamin cleared his throat. He opened his hands to his audience. 'You might expect me to begin with a prayer. But tonight I'm not gonna do that.'

Some in the crowd raised eyebrows, but fewer than he expected. *Are they that used to my theatrics?*

'In fact, I'll start with an apology.' He waited for that to sink in. Then: 'I'm sorry. About as sorry as a man can be. I preached to you, in the past, even though my own faith was weak. Not just weak, but non-existent. A man such as that – a man without faith – has no fear of damnation, no hope of salvation.' He paused. 'But I have it now, praise Jesus. I have it now, and I won't ever lose it.'

Outside, the sun had begun to melt into the trees. Inside the room, the one hundred patrons of his church listened in silence. 'I know that many of you have been asking, these last two weeks since your invitations arrived: "Why me? Why have I been chosen? What's our pastor want with *me*?" Well, take a good look round at each other.' When nobody moved, he opened his arms and gave them a little of the homespun they always liked to hear.

'Go on, now,' he urged them. 'Have a good ole gander. Size each other up, that's it. There's something you might notice if you're sharp enough, something the eagle-eyed might already have figured out.'

He waited and watched, saw their heads turn, their foreheads crease. 'Not many womenfolk among you tonight, are there? Oh, I know there's a few. We couldn't do without our dear Ladell, our dear Terri or Deana. Nor, especially, without our Wendy.' He paused, seeking her out, and spotted her by the door at the back, her arms folded and her eyes narrowed.

Benjamin smiled, then returned his attention to his flock. 'And why *couldn't* we do without them? Because they're warriors, that's why. Just like the rest of you. Warriors ready to do God's work, to fight God's fight, to stamp out evil wherever it's found.'

The room was silent and the Pastor could feel a gathering tension. He jived off it. 'How many of y'all brought your bibles here this evening?'

In the audience, perhaps seventy hands raised.

'I want you to take 'em out. Hold 'em up.'

A few moments later he saw them raised aloft: compact bibles, study bibles; NIVs, NABs, KJVs. Some were finished in leather, some in cloth. Some had no covers at all. 'Put 'em on the floor,' he told them.

A shuffling of feet while they complied.

'You can leave them here tonight, because you won't need them again.' Benjamin waited for the gasps, surprised when the silence endured. He saw plenty of frowning faces, but he heard no voice of protest, no mutterings of disapproval.

'You don't need to *read* the Word, my friends, when you can *receive* the Word directly. I give you a promise: before you leave this building tonight you'll *hear* the Word spoken in your heart, as clear as you hear me now. Earlier you listened to me talk about a fight, about being a warrior for God. We're so used to those tired old phrases that they become muzak after a while, empty noise. But tonight I'm not constructing a metaphor.'

Benjamin raised his hands to his flock. 'Folks, in a matter of weeks a battle will be fought that will make widows and orphans both. A battle that must be won, whatever the costs. It will be fought many thousands of miles from here, many thousands of miles from your homes, from your loved ones. It will be fought in a place long-forgotten, in a part of the world very different to the one you know. And, God willing, every single one of you here tonight will be coming with me to fight it.'

Silence, in the room.

Two hundred eyes regarded him.

In the second row, Billy Gosselin, a gap-toothed high school janitor with a ginger goatee and wiry physique, scratched his head. 'Are you shittin' me?'

The pastor smiled, the tension draining out of him. 'I know how it sounds, Billy. Believe me. Which is why I won't seek to persuade you a moment longer. Look around at each other, ladies and gentlemen. See your brothers and your sisters. Now, lift up your hands.'

He waited, counted to three. '*I said lift up your hands! That's it! Now open your hearts and LET HIS WORD FILL YOU!*'

The Bliss entered Pastor Benjamin then, with an intensity that was tenfold his previous experience. He opened his mouth and stammered his delirium. The waves of sensation assailing him were simply too powerful, too intoxicating. His skin felt as if it had been stitched together from a million flickering fireflies. His vision skipped and jumped. Colours swam before his eyes. His testicles clenched like buffalo hearts.

GOOD, spoke the Bliss.

Such love he felt enveloping him, such depth of compassion. As his vision began to clarify, he saw that his congregation had been similarly affected.

Mouths hung slack. Cheeks glistened with tears. Every pair of eyes in the room stared, enraptured. Eventually, as Pastor Benjamin knew they would, those eyes switched their focus to him.

LEAD.

Again, at the back of the room, he noticed Wendy

Devereaux. She stood awkwardly, one of her stilettos discarded. A bead of saliva elongated from her lower lip, forming an unbroken bridge to her blouse. Bubbles glistened along its length, descending with elevator smoothness to darken the silk. Her chest rose and fell in snatched bursts. She seemed caught halfway between ecstasy and pain. When Benjamin smiled at her she moved her lips, shivered. The saliva string snapped.

ONE, spoke the Bliss.

Wendy's eyes flared, as if in recognition. A moment later, the pastor summoned enough control of his thoughts to shepherd the members of his congregation. He opened his arms and surveyed their faces, sharing a silent communion with each of them. 'Brothers and sisters,' he said, 'in less than a week from now, a private aircraft will take off from Austin-Bergstrom and fly across the Atlantic. That aircraft has seats enough to accommodate every single one of you. I will be on the flight.' He paused, filled his lungs. 'You have questions, I know. I have only one. Will you follow me?'

Nobody moved. He could hear soft inhalations and exhalations, nothing more. Time seemed to elongate, taut as a guitar string.

In the second row, Billy Gosselin jumped to his feet. He clenched his fists and his eyes darkened. 'I'll follow you!' he shouted. 'Man, I'll do anything you fuckin' ask!'

Deana Taylor and Terri Freedman, two large women in their thirties, were next. They held fast to one another as they pulled themselves upright. 'I'll follow,' Deana said. Terri echoed her.

Chair legs scraped. Within a few seconds the entire gathering was on its feet. Seeing that reminded Benjamin of the bad old antics from his past. But this was different. This was *real*.

At the back, unable to take her eyes off him, Wendy Devereaux flexed her shoulders, rolled her neck. *I'll follow you*, she mouthed, and he felt a pulse of desire that shocked him with its intensity.

He slid a hand into his pocket. Tightened his fingers around his dead wife's locket.

GONE.

Benjamin blinked. Frowned. He had been thinking of something, and now—

Across the room, Wendy Devereaux slid her bare foot into the discarded stiletto. She walked up the aisle towards him, heels clacking on the floor.

CHAPTER 40

Gorges du Tarn, Southern France

As the Mercedes crew van rolled to a halt on the side of the road, Jenna Black climbed into the passenger seat beside Sabine and peered through the windscreen.

The turning was on the right, twenty yards from where they had stopped: a single-lane track twisting into a forest of dark pines. Above it, suspended by thick ropes, hung a single tree trunk. Its facing side had been carved with two words: JOYAU CACHÉ.

Jenna felt her palms grow slick. She had seen those words in dreams, had been pulled here with the instincts of a migrating bird. That, in itself, was inexplicable. But what she could not begin to understand was the reason she seemed – out of all Ériu's surviving devotees – to be the only one affected.

'Is this the place?' Sabine asked.

Jenna glanced to her right, saw the woman mouthing the words on the sign as if committing them to memory. 'Yeah. This is it.'

From the back seat, Keegan stirred. 'Looks kind of basic.'

'She's spent the last sixteen years in hiding. What did you expect?'

He shrugged. 'I guess. What's the plan?'

Jenna cringed at the question. How unnatural it felt to be

asked that, how unwelcome. She peered again through the window, at the dark path through the trees. No moon brightened the skies overhead. No lights illuminated the road. She could see no signs of human habitation in any of the directions she looked. 'It's a campsite, we know that much. Which means the van won't seem out of place.'

'You want to just drive in there?'

Jenna scowled, angry at Keegan for second-guessing her, but his challenge was reasonable enough: get this wrong and all their lives might be forfeited. Not for the first time she found herself wishing that Vivian, her old mentor, was still alive. 'Pass me a few of those music players.'

Keegan dropped two of the MP3 sets into her palm. She screwed a pair of buds into her ears and handed a second set to Sabine, along with a controller. 'We should all wear these from now on. You know what happened last time we were this close – things could turn sour fast. We'll drive in, get an idea of what we're dealing with, drive out.'

She stared at Keegan, daring him to disagree, but the man remained silent. From his holdall he retrieved one of the Glocks. 'Just in case,' he said, passing it between the seats.

Jenna took it from him, grimacing at the weapon's cold weight. After checking that Sabine had donned her earbuds, she activated her own player. At once, Keegan's eerily discordant music filled her ears. It spawned dark memories of Stallockmore Farm, stirred her grief. She clasped her hands in her lap, mouthed a prayer. 'All right,' she said. 'Let's go.'

The van nudged forward and swung onto Joyau Caché's private road, its headlights swabbing the trees. They were on the canyon floor now, with the Tarn river on their left; she could see the silhouette of a canoe trailer and a line of beached kayaks. The campsite rose in a shallow gradient, abutted on the right by an impenetrable shadow that must be the canyon wall. Ahead, the tarmac road split into a loop the shape of an athletics track. Around its perimeter she saw neatly hedged pitches of gravel and prairie grass. In some stood caravans, motorhomes or tents. Lights glowed in a few, but most of them were dark. Halfway along the loop rose a cluster of single-storey buildings.

Sabine turned in her seat. 'What do we do?'

'Take it slow,' Jenna told her. 'Follow the road around.'

They pulled onto the loop in a clockwise arc that drew them closer to the Tarn. Beneath the stars the river was a black tongue, revealing its strength in the white breakers it stacked against the boulders lining its banks. Jenna could hear it from here, an anxious chattering that harmonised uneasily with Keegan's music.

Leaning forward, she turned off the sat nav screen, not wanting her face revealed to anyone watching outside. 'Let's try those buildings.'

Sabine nodded, coaxing a little more speed from the van. Ahead, a string of coloured lights looped across the road between two buildings. The first was a shop, its interior dark. Outside, a brightly lit Coke vending machine stood beside an ice dispenser. Across the road was an administrative office with floor-to-ceiling windows along its frontage. Inside, Jenna saw the muted glow of a laptop screen. 'Pull over.'

Sabine frowned. 'You're getting out?'

'These places usually have someone on hand, even at this time of night.'

'But I thought you said—'

'Change of plan. I think we'll look more suspicious if we don't inquire.'

The van rolled to a stop. Jenna put one hand on the door handle.

'You sure you're up for this?' Keegan asked. 'You want me to go instead?'

She hated him for that, for offering her a way out. 'No.'

'Need some company, then?'

Again, Jenna shook her head. She tucked the Glock into her pocket and slipped outside.

The canyon temperature was colder than she had expected; the night air was chill against her skin. She crossed the road to the booking office and put her hands against the glass.

Shadows wreathed the interior. The laptop screen illuminated an empty desk and chair, the moving blades of a fan. She went to the door and turned the handle.

Unlocked.

Jenna swung it wide. Stepped across the threshold. '*Bonsoir?*'

No answer. No movement within.

Strange to leave the place un-staffed and unsecured. Her stomach lightened. Something felt wrong here, sour, like something bad had happened, and recently. Abruptly, she turned and retraced her steps to the van. 'Drive,' she told Sabine.

'Was anyone there?'

'No. And it's pretty weird that they left it unlocked.'

They followed the loop, peering at darkened caravans and motorhomes. 'She could be in any of them,' Jenna said, trying to contain her frustration. 'There's just no way of knowing.'

Keegan snorted. 'You want to start knocking on doors?'

She closed her mind to him. As the Mercedes reached the western end of the loop she spotted a track leading off into the trees, and immediately felt a tightening sensation in her head, as if a fish hook had snagged her brain and was beginning to pull. When she squinted up the path, she saw lights shining from a chalet half-obscured by trees. 'Stop the van.'

Sabine complied.

'That's it,' Jenna said. Her heart began to race. 'She's in there.'

Keegan frowned at her through the rear-view mirror. 'How do you know?'

'The same way Vivian did, back in Ireland. I had it then, too: this feeling, I mean. But last time it wasn't so strong, so focused.'

'You're some kind of psychic, now?'

'I . . . I don't know. Not exactly. Maybe it's something Ériu passed onto me before she died.'

His eyes narrowed. 'I don't feel anything.' He turned to Sabine. 'You?'

The younger woman shook her head.

Jenna put her hand on the door handle. 'I'm going to check it out. While I'm gone, I want you to—'

'Hang on,' Keegan said. 'What do you mean you're checking it out? I don't like this, not one bit. You say you're *feeling* something? Feeling what?'

'I can't explain.'

'It could be a trap.'

'No. I'm certain it's her.'

'Fine.' He slung the UMP's strap over his head. 'Then I'm coming with you. If what you're saying is true—'

'Keegan, I want you to stay here.'

'What kind of—'

Sabine Estrella twisted round in her seat, her cheeks mottled with anger. 'Will you *stop* challenging her!' she hissed. 'Ever since we met you at the airport you've been picking away, second-guessing her. It's like having a twelve-year-old along for the ride, and a bad-tempered one at that. Jenna was chosen, you weren't. *Deal* with it.'

Silence, punctuated by the electronic notes of Keegan's music. In the rear-view mirror the man's eyes glittered. He blinked, licked his lips. 'You're right. You're right, of course, and I'm sorry. This is too important to let personal enmities get in the way.'

'I don't feel any enmity towards you,' Jenna told him. 'I never asked for this responsibility, never coveted it. I'm just trying to do my best, and figure things out as I go.' She met his eyes once more. 'What I'd like is your support, as much of it as you can give.'

'You have it.'

She held his gaze a moment longer, then turned to Sabine.

'Take the van around the far side of the site. Keep your phone handy in case I call. I won't be long.'

The woman nodded. 'Don't take any risks.'

Just being here was a risk, but Jenna wasn't going to highlight that. She jumped down onto the tarmac. The van pulled away, edging out of sight.

Jenna crossed the road and stepped into the undergrowth. No lights brightened the dirt track leading to the chalet. She kept as hidden as possible, weaving between dark trunks of pine.

Nine years since she had been this close. Last time the hunt had ended in the narrow lane leading from Stallockmore Farm. A man had been protecting the girl that night, determined and ruthless. He had broken Jenna's arm in three places before stealing her car and leaving her to die. Just thinking of him made her teeth clench and her mended bone throb.

Ahead, the chalet lights glimmered. A light canyon breeze raised whispers from the surrounding forest.

Sabine Estrella drove the Mercedes van around Joyau Caché's tarmac loop, hands tense on the wheel. After her outburst, she had never expected Jenna to leave her alone with Keegan.

'This is fine,' he told her. 'Pull in here.'

They were now on the far side of the loop, closer to the canyon wall. Sabine spotted a section of unbroken road and brought the van to a stop. She switched off the engine and headlights.

Keegan's randomised notes played in her ears. Under them she heard the nasal rasp of his breathing. The man rested his chin on her seat-back. 'Going out for a smoke,' he whispered, lips inches from her ear.

Keegan's door opened and he stepped out. He passed her window and kept walking. Twenty yards from the van he shook a cigarette from his pack and lit up.

Sabine watched, intrigued at how agitated Keegan appeared.

He inhaled through clenched teeth, spat out smoke. From his pocket he took a mobile phone and checked its screen.

Seeing that, Sabine retrieved her own phone from the door well and checked the time.

Four forty-seven a.m.

Inside Mercury Hall, Aiden Urchardan watched Pastor Benjamin's performance and could not help but be impressed. By degrees, and much to his surprise, he felt himself softening towards the man. He did not approve of the pastor's past actions, nor the power he wielded over his congregation, but his charisma was infectious, his usefulness beyond doubt.

Benjamin stood at the front of the hall, fielding questions from an audience both anxious and overcome. And while his answers were based on doctrines that inaccurately portrayed the forces at work, their assurances were no less powerful as a result. Urchardan struggled to keep his face impassive as he listened. If there was one thing that bothered him about this, it was the mass deception he was witnessing in pursuit of a greater good.

GREATER GOOD, YES.

He lurched forwards, shocked that his thoughts – even now – were being monitored. *I'm loyal*, he replied. *I know what's at stake.*

ALL WARFARE BASED ON DECEPTION: SUN TZU.

Urchardan smiled at that, but he could not ignore the goosebumps spreading across his skin. He looked around him at the bright-eyed members of Pastor Benjamin's church. How many of them would survive the decisions taken on their behalf?

HOW MANY OF THEIR DESCENDANTS WILL SURVIVE OTHERWISE?

As a rebuttal it was unassailable. At least the pastor had been helping to stack their odds of survival as favourably as possible. In advance of tonight's meeting, Urchardan had seen the invite list. Half of this audience had military experience. A good number were serving police officers or firemen. Many others were recreational hunters, familiar with firearms. The list also boasted three doctors and seven nurses. There were plumbers, electricians, chefs.

Urchardan's mobile phone began to vibrate. He drew it out, keeping the screen shielded from those sitting nearby.

Found. Joyau Caché cmpsite, Gorges du Tarn, FR.
Nrst town: Severac-le-Château. Be quick and url kill her.

He shuddered, flung back in his seat as the Bliss drained out of him. Through his feet he felt the ground rumble as if with departing thunder.

CHAPTER 41

Gorges du Tarn, Southern France

Edward woke a few hours later. His head crashed in protest at the alcohol he had drunk. His stomach needled and rolled.

Outside, the first grey fingers of dawn were creeping over the gorge. He climbed out of bed, wincing at the complaints his body raised. His left knee throbbed. His back ached. A muscle in his neck twitched spasmodically.

Downstairs, the aroma of coffee hung thick in the hallway. When he opened the living-room door he saw Piper curled up on the sofa, the French windows ajar behind her. The girl wore a baggy T-shirt, the hem pulled over her knees. She cradled a coffee mug, and smiled as he came in. 'Hey,' she said, untucking her legs. Her voice sounded scratchy, fatigued. 'Want a cup?'

Edward nodded, looked around the room. His hunting rifle stood against the wall where he'd left it. A canyon breeze blew through the windows, lifting the drapes.

Piper returned with a mug of coffee and handed it to him. 'Hungover?'

'A little.'

'First time I've seen you drink.'

'Bad timing's my speciality. How come you're up?'

'Needed to think about some things. Wanted to get stuff straight in my head.'

Edward nodded, his throat tight. He had hoped that she would decide to outrun her past; now he saw she meant to confront it. 'If I came with you,' he began.

Piper shook her head. 'I think I have to do this alone.'

He took a sip of coffee. 'Can you tell me what it is?'

'I have to put something right. Something that went wrong a long time ago.'

'That's pretty vague.'

'You'll understand once it's done.'

'Why don't you want me with you?'

Piper's face creased. 'If there are two people in the world I want with me right now, it's you and Therron. Which is exactly why you have to stay away. I've no right to involve you in this.'

'You've every right,' Edward said. 'I'm your father, Pie. Not by blood, I'll admit, but in every other way.'

'Dad . . .'

'I know it hasn't been easy for us. I never managed to give you a fraction of the things I wanted to, any of the things you deserved. But I did one thing – I kept you alive. I've not achieved much in the years we've been together but I've achieved that, at least.'

'Dad, I could sit here for the next six months listing the things you've achieved.'

'You don't have six months,' said a voice. 'You barely have one.'

Edward glanced over at the French windows, to the figure that stood outside them.

Jolyon Percival shuffled down Joyau Caché's paved loop, flip-flops slapping the tarmac, hands stuffed into the pockets of his denim jacket. For the last few hours he had lain on the floor of his caravan, crippled by the discovery that he did not own the history he had claimed. Curled up among the detritus of his art, he had worked back methodically through his memories, testing each for its strength. A shocking number of them failed.

His recollections from a year ago (living in Paris, dating a woman called Sapphira from the Greek island of Náxos) seemed sound. From there he could skip back another ten years without issue. The women's names during that period – Diane, Francine, Niamh, Phoebe, Drew, Tamika, Luisa – changed more frequently than the locations, but every one of those relationships felt real. In all cases he could recall their first meetings, how he had romanced them and how, eventually, he had disappointed them. He remembered meals shared, galleries visited, conversations and arguments and laughter. Regressing ten years further back proved more problematic, but it was difficult to know whether that was due simply to the passage of time, or something more sinister. Distressingly, every memory more than two decades distant, including those of his childhood and his teenage years, collapsed to dust when he tried to examine them.

The evidence was as inescapable as it was harrowing: despite possessing the body of a fifty-year-old, he owned memories that reached back less than twenty years.

Where had he been before?

Who had he been?

Piper had offered an answer to those questions last night, but her story was so fantastical – and yet, in a way, so utterly beguiling – that he would have feared for his sanity had he accepted it as fact. Instead he escaped to the caravan, where the apparel of a counterfeit past confronted him.

Now, in an effort to break his paralysis, he decided that the only way forward was to question the girl more closely, analyse her claims more critically, and in that way attempt to separate what kernels of truth lay concealed among the deceits.

The approaching dawn had sketched the canyon in vague grey shades. Jolyon walked passed a row of motorhomes, their windows misted by those slumbering inside. Around him he heard a chorus of morning birds far too sharp for his ears. Each chirrup and whistle felt like a tattooist's needle pressed to the inside of his skull.

Overhead, he spotted the wide black shape of a griffon vulture. It hung motionless, as if the sky was a glass dome on which the bird's outline had been engraved. Jolyon stopped and watched it, remembering the painting in his studio at Labastide-Esparbairenque. Three more carrion birds flew out of the east and began to spiral. A strange feeling overcame him. He tucked his hands deeper into his jacket and continued to walk.

The road swung to the right. Parked on one side he saw a silver Mercedes van. That, in itself, was no surprise. But then he saw the man, and he saw the woman, and what was about to happen.

Edward recognised her immediately, although he could hardly believe what he was seeing. Nine years had passed since the woman with the headphones had intercepted him at Stallockmore; nine years since he had attacked her with a crowbar and escaped in her Jeep, leaving her to the mercy of whatever horrors lingered at McAllister's farm.

He watched her enter the room and pull the French windows shut behind her. As she came fully into the light he saw that she had changed hardly at all. Her skin was as smooth as it had been nearly a decade earlier. Her beechwood hair shone like gossamer. Two metal lozenges plugged her ears – some kind of wireless receiver system he had not seen before. Silver rings encircled each of her fingers, except the one on which she might have displayed a wedding band; there, instead, he saw a vine wreath tattoo.

Over a floral print dress, she wore a thin cotton cardigan. She could have been a librarian or a minister's wife had it not been for the pistol she clutched. It looked oversized in her delicate fingers, but no less deadly. He remembered the way she had handled her gun nine years earlier: warily, hesitantly, as if she were more frightened at what it might destroy than what protection it could offer. She did not hold this weapon the same way.

'You broke my arm in three places that night,' she told him. 'I won't let you hurt me again.'

Edward strained to keep his eyes from wandering to the rifle propped up against the wall. 'I never wanted to hurt you.'

'You did a pretty good job.'

'I took no pleasure from it. You forced my hand, that's all.'

'Forced your hand? I'd just watched my friend die.'

'I'm sorry.'

'And then you attacked me.'

'You were aiming a gun at my chest,' Edward said.

'I was scared.' Her throat bobbed with the memory. 'I had to *crawl* into that crap-pile Volvo you left behind. The entire time I thought I was going be the next one to die, that I was going to—'

'What's your name?' Piper asked, from the sofa.

The woman jumped as if she had been bitten. She shot a glance in Piper's direction, but could not bring herself to meet the girl's gaze. Instead she took a steadying breath. 'Jenna. Jenna Black.'

'Why are you here, Jenna?'

She paused, licked her lips. 'I'm here for you.'

'Are you alone?'

Jenna shook her head.

'How many with you?'

'Two others. Outside.'

'How did you find us?'

'Orla sent me.' Jenna cast another furtive look in Piper's direction. 'But I've been dreaming of you for weeks.'

'Seems like you're not the only one around here doing that,' the girl said. 'Listen to me, Jenna. We're going to have plenty of time to talk this through, you and I, and once we're done I'll come with you to wherever you want to go. But until then, I need to tell you something about my dad.'

The woman frowned. 'Your dad?'

'It'll take a while to explain. But trust me, he's my dad in every way that counts. Now, please – sit down here and put that ugly piece of metal away until there's a reason to use it.'

Jenna's eyes moved to the gun and her cheeks flushed. After a moment's hesitation she lowered it and perched awkwardly on the sofa, putting as much distance between herself and Piper as possible.

Odd, Edward thought, that while the woman seemed unconcerned at confronting him, she seemed so nervous around the girl. Even as he thought it, he realised that *nervous* was the wrong word for what he was seeing. Jenna appeared *reverential*, to the point of awe.

'Dad told me all about that night in Ireland,' Piper said. 'I can't imagine how it must have felt for you, being abandoned like that. But what you have to understand is this: he's the very reason I can't imagine it. Because he never *has* abandoned me. He's the only reason I'm still here, talking to you now.

'That night . . . so many things went wrong. If you'd found us in different circumstances, maybe our meeting would have gone better. I don't know anything about the friend you lost, and I'm sure Dad doesn't either. One thing I do know: everyone at Stallockmore Farm that night was terrified out of their wits. People made split-second decisions, my dad included. I need you to trust him, Jenna.'

The woman cast her eyes towards Edward, her mouth a thin line. She took a breath, let it out, started to rub the part of her arm he had broken, checked herself. Finally, she refocused her attention on Piper. 'I can hardly bring myself to ask. But . . . are you still one with Mórríghan?'

The girl smiled. 'It's getting a little crowded in here – especially these last few weeks – but we're managing, just about.'

Jenna closed her eyes. The tension seemed to leach out of her. As her face relaxed, Edward realised with a jolt just how beautiful she was. For the first time in years, he felt his heartbeat quickening for reasons other than fear.

'Where is Orla now?' Piper asked.

'The same place as always.'

'You'll have to forgive me. I'm relying on memories that are a few thousand years old, and geography that's just as out of date. We're talking about England, yes? Cornwall?'

Jenna's eyes widened, but she composed herself quickly. 'Crafter's Keep, on the north coast.'

'And Ériu went to Wales.'

'That's right.'

'Eber? Still up in the Highlands?'

'He's been a little more visible lately, helping with the search. But that's where he bases himself.'

'And Drustan,' Piper said. 'We know all about him.' Jenna cocked her head, but Piper continued without explanation. 'Mórríghan and her four *Triallaichean*. Reunited after all this time.'

At that, the older woman's face fell. She balanced her pistol on the arm of the sofa and fiddled with one of her rings. 'Three *Triallaichean*,' she said. 'No longer four.'

'Three?'

'I'm sorry to be the one to tell you this. But Ériu lost her life the night we brought Mórríghan back.'

Piper turned ashen. 'Ériu's *dead*?'

'When the attack began, a few of us managed to smuggle your mother out. But everyone else at Aberffraw Hall was killed, Ériu included. We still don't know who was responsible. Somebody betrayed us, which makes no sense when you think about what we were trying to achieve.'

Edward watched his daughter carefully while she digested the news. Piper sat rigid, her eyes vague, as if she conducted a silent conversation inside her head. Finally, she looked up. 'Dad, I need to have a proper talk with Jenna. Fully understand all that's happened.'

He nodded, levered himself out of the chair. 'I'll put on more coffee,' he said. 'Feels like we need some.' He limped into the hall and from there into the kitchen. He opened the fridge, blinking at its harsh white light, and took out the milk. At the sink he filled the kettle. He opened the door to the cupboard where he kept the crockery, and froze.

Inside, instead of the deep shadows he might have expected, he saw a row of chipped china mugs lit by a scarlet glow. Edward stared. He shut the cupboard. Opened another.

A chrome toast rack. Stacked crockery. A glass cafetière.

The toast rack glowed cherry red. The crockery looked as if it had been dipped in blood.

Edward put out his palms to the countertop.

He could still hear Jenna's voice as she talked. Pivoting away from the counter, he limped back to the living room. Jenna glanced up as he came towards her but she read his intentions far too late. He snatched up her pistol and backed away to the room's furthest corner.

'Dad?' Piper asked. 'What's going on?'

'We're leaving,' he said. 'You and me. Right now.' He turned towards the hall, bellowed Therron's name.

'Dad, what's happening?'

'It's here,' Edward told her. 'It's found us.'

CHAPTER 42

Gorges du Tarn, Southern France

Sabine Estrella sat behind the wheel of the Mercedes crew van and watched Keegan as he stood by the side of the road and smoked. The man kept his back to her, head bowed as he fiddled with his phone. The soulless oscillations of his creation – she would not call it music – murmured in her ears. The randomised notes made her want to grind her teeth or scream. In an effort to ignore them she examined again the weapons he had given her: a Beretta semi-automatic, and a wickedly sharp bowie knife.

Sabine had spent many days practising with the handgun, firing and loading, firing and loading. At first she had concentrated on distance work, until Keegan had explained that most gun fights occurred at a distance of ten feet. After that she concentrated on her close-up accuracy. She had not gained as much experience with the bowie knife, except for the killing of a few pigs, the purpose of which had been to accustom her to the sight of blood.

Outside, Keegan took a last drag and ground his cigarette butt into the dirt. Slipping the phone into his pocket, he walked towards the van. Sabine climbed out. Six hours of driving had compressed her spine and stiffened her shoulders. She arched her back, stretching her arms behind her. 'Oh, please stop that,' she muttered, catching where Keegan's eyes went. Then she wrinkled her nose. 'Can I steal a smoke?'

He stared, eyes appraising her. Finally, he pulled out a pack of Gitanes. He proffered it, just beyond her reach. 'Hadn't pegged you for a bad girl.'

She waited for him to tire of his game but he held his ground, teasing her. With a sigh, Sabine snatched the pack off him. She shook out a cigarette and put it between her lips, allowing him to touch his lighter to the tip.

Taking a drag, she turned her back, walking to the base of a nearby tree. When she leaned against its trunk, she saw that Keegan had followed. 'Do you think Jenna's right?' she asked, blowing out smoke. 'About Mórríghan, I mean. Do you really think she's here?'

Keegan glanced towards the path leading into the trees. 'One thing I'll say about that,' he said, and before he could finish his sentence, Sabine stabbed him in the chest with the bowie knife.

It slid into him with the merest of resistance, finding a route between two ribs.

Keegan grunted in surprise. 'What?' he asked.

As Sabine pulled the blade out of him his eyes widened in recognition of what she had done. Telling herself that this was no different to the pigs she had slaughtered in rehearsal, she plunged the knife in and out as quickly as she could. It *was* different to the pigs, she found, but not by much. In Keegan's eyes she saw the same stunned question.

Her task complete, she retreated to the van. Behind her, over the electronic notes of what she liked to consider his funeral dirge, she heard the thump of Keegan's knees hitting the dirt.

She grabbed his UMP from the van and slung its strap over her head. From the holdall she took two spare clips and stuffed them into her jacket. She retrieved her Beretta from the door cavity and tucked it into her waistband. Wedged beneath the back seats she found two Mossberg pump-actions. She took one of those, too.

Through the van window she glimpsed Keegan kneeling in the scrub, as if in prayer. In the dawn's half-light the blood draining from his injuries looked like black treacle. He pressed his hands to his abdomen, trying to stem the flow, but whatever reserves of energy had kept him upright so far now abandoned him. He keeled forwards, planting his face in the soil. Knuckles flat at his side, arse pointing at the sky, he did not move again.

Sabine heard other sounds now, from all around. Across the campsite, the doors to motorhomes and caravans were banging open, their occupants stumbling out.

She smiled. Reaching up, she pulled her earbuds free and discarded them. 'Where are you?' she whispered.

HERE.

In the double bunk above the driver's cabin of his parents' Fiat Autotrail, Matthais Hossner blinked himself awake. At first he could not work out what had woken him. When he rolled onto his side and saw his sister, he cried out in surprise. Kerstin lay on her back, her gaze fixed on the ceiling. The girl's eyeballs seemed to be vibrating, as if powered by tiny springs. Her pupils were grossly dilated, the capillaries of her sclera engorged with blood.

'Kerkie?' he whispered.

Her knee twitched, knocking against his leg. '*Töte sie,*' she wheezed. Her breath came in shallow gasps.

Matthais shrank away from her. 'That's not funny.'

Kerstin's mouth widened into a grin. Still she stared at the ceiling. '*Ja. Ich verstehe.*'

'Stop it. You're not allowed to tease me.'

Matthais heard movement, down in the motorhome's main living space. He twisted around in time to see his father emerge from the rear bedroom. Reynaud Hossner wore a pair of boxer shorts hitched up on one leg. Matthais's mother followed close behind, and he saw that she was naked; her breasts hung low on her chest like two deflated tyres. The boy had never seen her without her clothes. The sight terrified him.

'Mama? Papa?'

His parents ignored him, and as they came closer he noticed that they wore the same fixed smiles as his sister.

Reynaud Hossner went to the cutlery drawer and opened it. A faint scarlet light glowed within. He removed a carving knife and carried it to the motorhome's side door, where he studied the latch as if seeing it for the first time. Moments later, he whipped out a hand and unlocked it.

The door swung wide. A cold breeze swirled in. Reynaud stood on the threshold, unmoving. Then he climbed down the portable steps and disappeared outside.

In the bunk beside Matthais, Kerstin rolled onto her stomach. '*Töte sie*,' she repeated, pushing herself up on all fours. A line of drool swung from her lips. Eyes quivering like eggs in a pan, she slithered over him.

Matthais screamed, pressing his head against the mattress, but his sister seemed unaware of him. She clambered down the ladder and went to the cutlery drawer. Waiting until her mother had armed herself with a filleting knife, Kerstin reached in and selected a pair of scissors.

Mother and daughter moved to the door. Together, they stepped out into the grey dawn.

Inside his specially adapted Niesmann and Bischoff RV, Bendt Friis sat at the breakfast table and thought about the day ahead. He had been an early riser since his time in the *Sjællandske Livregiment*, and even though his army days were long behind him the habit had followed him into retirement.

Later this morning, after his wife, Inga, had showered and breakfasted, they would leave Joyau Caché and drive to Toulouse. From there, depending on how tired he felt, they would press on to the Spanish border. Inga did not like driving the motorhome anywhere except Denmark, and even with its modifications Bendt could not pilot it for long periods.

Still, they were in no hurry. A warm welcome awaited them in the Pyrenees, whatever time they arrived: they had friends in the Principality of Andorra whom they had not seen in years.

When Bendt heard, from the back of the motorhome, the sound of his wife getting dressed, he levered himself along the bench seat and switched on the kettle. Inga would need at least two cups of strong coffee before she was ready to face the day.

The door to the bedroom opened and Bendt smiled in expectation. 'Good morning, my little flower.'

Inga appeared in the doorway, still wearing her nightdress. Her eyes looked red-rimmed. '*Javel, javel,*' she muttered.

Only then did Bendt notice what his wife clutched in her hand: his old M62 bayonet blade. He frowned. 'Inga?'

'*Javel, det gør jeg.*' She sidled into the main living space and moved to the motorhome's door. With one hand she unlocked it.

'You will do what?' he asked.

Ignoring him, Inga opened the door and stepped outside.

Bendt peered through the window, trying to see where his wife had gone. What he saw distressed him greatly.

CHAPTER 43

Gorges du Tarn,
Southern France

In the living room of the tiny chalet where they had lived these last five years, Edward Schwinn met his daughter's gaze and saw the bewilderment it contained.

For a moment the girl stood motionless. Her eyes seemed to swell. Then she turned to Jenna and said: 'He's right. Look.' Piper pointed to the recess beneath their old TV. A reddish luminescence gathered there, as if a candle had been lit deep within its depths. It possessed a strangely hypnotic quality; terrible yet compelling.

Overhead, the floorboards of Piper's bedroom thumped.

The girl cast her eyes towards the ceiling. Her mouth fell open. She tensed, grabbed Edward's arm. 'Oh shit. *Shit!*'

'What is it?'

'He's not immune, Dad! Therron! He's not *immune!*'

Edward looked up, saw the ceiling shade vibrate, heard the boy charge across the bedroom floor and onto the tiny landing. Therron reached the top of the stairs and thundered down them. The entire chalet seemed to shake with his footsteps.

Moaning, Piper dived towards the wall. She snatched up Edward's rifle. 'We've got one chance!' she screamed. 'Whatever happens, don't let him see your face, don't let him! Turn his head away!'

Edward twisted away from her, his thoughts reeling. He recalled Terfel Williams, eyes not his own, driving a blade into Gráinne's belly. He thought of Old Man McAllister, the way the farmer had burst from the farmhouse with his shotgun raised, intent on killing Edward and the girl he tried to protect.

However nightmarish those incidents had been, until now those used as pawns had never been people that he loved.

Therron's footsteps reached the bottom of the flight. Linoleum floor squealed with skidding feet.

A wild thought struck Edward, in the seconds before the living-room door crashed open, that it was not Therron who charged towards them, not the boy at all, but something so monstrous, so godless and unworldly – something comprised less of flesh and blood than spines and mandibles and carapace – that it would reduce his mind to wordless insanity should he glimpse it.

Perhaps, in a way, his subconscious attempted to forewarn him, because when the hall door burst open and its assailant barrelled through, Edward recognised the shell of the boy he had come to know but little else.

Moving with a predator's speed, Piper lunged forwards and slammed the rifle stock into the side of Therron's head. The boy cartwheeled across the coffee table like a wounded spider, a maelstrom of scrabbling limbs. He bounced off a bookcase and clattered to the floor.

Edward leaped onto his back. Mindful of Piper's warning, he grabbed a fistful of Therron's hair and thrust his face into the carpet. The boy bucked and writhed. A dreadful keening came from his throat. Veins as thick as pencils throbbed in his neck. He strained his head around, teeth snapping at the air. Edward slammed an elbow into his ribs, hearing the crack of bone. Therron thrashed even more violently after that, as if the injury had served merely to enrage him. He tore his head free, leaving Edward with a handful of bloodied hair.

Suddenly Jenna was between them, lending her weight to

the struggle. With her knees pressed against the boy's shoulders, she screwed two of the silver lozenges into his ears and rolled clear. 'Hit him again,' she urged. 'Knock him out.'

'No!' Piper yelled. 'You'll kill him. Let me.' She sank to the ground, casting the rifle aside. Pressing her fingers to Therron's temples, she gritted her teeth.

The boy went loose.

Abruptly, all Edward could hear was the rasp of his own breathing. He looked from one frightened pair of eyes to another.

A torrent of blood burst from Piper's nose. Gasping, she wheeled backwards, pressing her hands to her face.

Edward felt his heartbeat pulse in his ears, a pressure wave of adrenalin. 'Pie? What the hell? What's wrong?'

She waved his concern away, but her eyes looked hollow. She spat blood onto the carpet. When she turned her attention back to Therron, she seemed to recover her senses. Her lower lip trembled. 'Is he alive?'

The boy had ceased his struggles the moment Piper had touched him, but his carotid artery still pulsed. Edward nodded. 'Is he a threat?'

'Dad, it's Therron.'

'Whatever came through that door wasn't Therron Vaux.'

'He'll be himself when he wakes,' Jenna said. She gestured at the lozenges she had forced into the boy's ears. 'He can't be corrupted while he's wearing those.' She took a slim metal cylinder from her pocket and tucked it into Therron's jeans. 'That's the transmitter. It needs to stay with him. All times.'

Edward retrieved his rifle from the floor and checked it over. He picked up Jenna's pistol and stuffed it into his waistband. 'We're leaving.'

'Let me call the others,' she replied. 'I'll get them to—'

Edward shook his head. 'No one else.'

'But they're—'

'I don't care. No strangers. No one but the four of us. You come alone or you stay here.'

The woman gave Piper a pleading look, but the girl moved to Edward's side. 'My dad's right, Jenna. We do it like he says.'

Edward turned to his daughter. 'Grab the keys from the kitchen. The panic bags, too. I'll go out first, carrying Therron. You unlock the truck and open the doors. We'll put him on the back seat.'

She nodded.

'Go.'

The girl raced into the hall. Edward glanced around. On the shelves he saw Piper's collection of second-hand books, neatly ordered, and thought of all the evenings he had spent in this room, listening to her read to him. She had been at her happiest here; Joyau Caché had offered her five precious years of sanctuary. Somehow he doubted she would ever find such peace again.

Piper reappeared a few moments later, and her expression confirmed his worst fears.

'Dad,' she said, her face draining of colour, 'it's too late.'

CHAPTER 44

Gorges du Tarn, Southern France

Piper led him down the hall and into the chalet's kitchen, keeping close to the wall. Near the window stood a narrow breakfast bar. The girl had drawn back the drapes beside it, leaving the net curtains in place.

Outside, a lavender dawn wove indigo clouds. While the rising sun had all but banished the red dome from the sky, Edward could see its spectral light glowing on the tips of tree leaves, on stems and on stones. It was a funereal sight, darkly beautiful and wholly terrifying, yet for all the attention it demanded, Edward saw that it was not the only arrival the dawn had brought; because on the track that led through the woods, connecting their chalet to Joyau Caché's main loop, he saw a woman walking.

She was long-boned and slender, her features bisected by a nose too large for her face. Over black combat boots she wore olive cargo trousers and a maroon leather jacket. In each hand she carried a pistol, barrels pointed at the ground. From a strap around her neck hung a sub-machine gun; over her shoulder, a pump-action.

Following close behind her, spread out across the width of the track, walked what Edward thought must be every able-bodied resident of Joyau Caché.

Among them he saw Inga Friis, the Danish woman who had arrived days earlier with her army veteran husband; she wore a white cotton nightdress, her pendulous breasts swinging freely beneath. He saw Kerstin Hossner, side by side with her parents. Reynaud Hossner wore a pair of boxer shorts. His wife, Maritza, wore nothing at all. Behind the Hossners walked an old man in a bathrobe whose name Edward could not recall. Beside him came a teenage girl in jogging bottoms and vest; three barefoot young men in T-shirts and shorts; too many others.

Between them they brandished a gruesome collection of makeshift weapons: kitchen knives and scissors, cricket bats and hammers, barbecue forks, golf clubs, knitting needles and hatchets. The old man carried a snapped broom handle. The teenage girl in joggers clutched two aluminium awning spikes.

Jenna had followed Edward into the kitchen, and when she saw the woman at the head of the group she gasped. 'That's Sabine Estrella.'

'One of yours?'

'Yes.'

Edward checked his rifle for the second time in as many minutes. One round in the chamber, three in the magazine. He felt in his breast pockets for his two spare magazines and stacked them on the breakfast counter. 'I'm sorry,' he said.

Jenna turned to him. Her eyes clouded. 'Sorry for what?'

He flicked off the rifle's safety. If he thought too hard about what he was about to do, he might lose the courage. But however brutal the act, the alternative was worse.

Piper stepped forward. 'Dad?'

Edward clenched his teeth. He wanted to look at his daughter, but right now he could not bear to meet her eyes. 'My truck's outside,' he said. 'It's our only route out of here. They're in the way.'

The girl caught his sleeve. 'We can go through the woods,' she said. 'Outrun them.'

'And Therron? Are we going to just leave him?' He shook his head. 'We won't lose them on foot.'

Tears stood in Piper's eyes. 'We can *try*, Dad.'

Edward steeled himself, and then looked at her. He saw the dawning horror in the girl's expression, refused to let it weaken him. Her survival depended, now, on his ruthlessness. 'We have to go through them.'

'He's right.' Jenna's face was paper-white. She lifted both hands to her mouth, as if she yearned to claw back her words. 'We can't let them near you, Piper, and we have to get away.' To Edward, looking as though she might be sick, she added: 'Whatever you're going to do, you'd better do it now, before it's too late.'

'No!' Piper cried. She tried to insert herself between her father and the window.

Jenna intercepted her, grabbing the girl's shoulders. '*Listen* to me!' she shouted. 'I know how this must feel. I *know*. Those people out there – they're innocents. They'll give up their lives without even knowing why. It's brutal, unjust, but it won't be in vain. It *won't* be. You're Beò-Ìobairt, Piper. People have been dying for you since before you were born. You have to see this through.'

She turned back to Edward, and he saw what effort those words had cost. 'Keep out of sight,' she urged him. 'Don't let them see your face.'

He nodded. Reversed his grip on the rifle.

'Please,' Piper moaned. 'Not because of me. *Please* not because of me.'

Jenna pulled her away from the window. She placed her hands over the girl's ears, angled her face away.

Edward smashed his rifle stock against the pane, shattering it. He raked the weapon back and forth, showering the floor with glass. Stepping to one side, he slid the barrel through a gap in the net curtains, jammed the stock into his shoulder and put his eye to the scope.

This was it, then. The crossroads. The point at which keeping Piper alive no longer meant concealment and escape, but the taking of life. So often he had tried to anticipate his reaction when this moment finally came, and now that it was here, all he could honestly say that he felt was shock: shock that such a thing could creep up on him unawares; shock that as he prepared himself for the task, he felt nothing but a grim determination, and the certainty that however damned he might have been before, he was doubly damned now.

He put his eye to the scope. It took him a moment to find his first target. Emerging from a blur, Sabine Estrella filled his field of view. She appeared to look straight at him, eyes narrowed as if in recognition.

Edward placed the scope's red dot in the centre of her face. His index finger curled around the trigger.

He felt his heart beat a sluggish rhythm in his chest. His breathing slowed.

Stopped.

Strange, but he found himself wondering, in that last frozen moment, about the history of the woman he was about to kill: how she had lived, whom she had loved; what she had believed. Would he have liked her? Hated her? What would she have thought of him in return?

He forced himself to meet her eyes for a few seconds longer and then he shot her. The rifle kicked against his shoulder but not hard, like a shotgun; more like a chastising tap. The air rang with the blast and Piper screamed into Jenna's neck.

Edward grimaced. Kept his eye pressed to the scope. He pulled back the bolt. Chambered another round.

Outside, Sabine Estrella fell dead. The others kept coming.

One of the young men in T-shirts bent to the woman's corpse as he passed, stripping it of the sub-machine gun without breaking stride. The old man threw away his broom handle and snatched up a pistol. Maritza Hossner discarded her kitchen knife and claimed the pump-action. Another of the young men took Sabine's remaining pistol.

Edward shot him next, cringing at the sound of the rifle's report. His victim spun as he fell. Piper screamed again, but the tone of her protest had changed, stunned acceptance replacing denial.

Edward reloaded, a machine now, traumatised by his actions but unable to stop. Before he could settle on a new target he saw the old man raise the sub-machine gun. Edward threw himself back from the window as the weapon stitched a seam of destruction across the front of the house. A round punched through the fridge. Another shattered a clock hanging from the wall.

Edward returned fire, missing with all three of his shots. Cursing, he ejected his spent magazine, snatched up a spare from the breakfast bar, reloaded.

He put his eye to the scope. Swept over the targets. Found Maritza Hossner. 'Goddamn this,' he said. 'God*damn* this.'

Maritza raised the pump-action and Edward shot her through the head, taking off a sizeable chunk of her skull. She dropped the shotgun, falling first to her knees, then her face. Her daughter, Kerstin, bent to retrieve the weapon, straightened. Edward lined up the shot. He felt himself grow cold. Before he could pull the trigger Kerstin broke left, disappearing into the undergrowth beside the track. Simultaneously, the old man with the sub-machine gun slid into the trees on the right.

Edward knew the consequences of that, but he refused to let it paralyse him. He centred his scope on the last young man in the group. Fired. Saw a glistening loop of ejecta fly from his victim's head. He found a new target. Took it out. Lined up another.

More of Joyau Caché's residents peeled into the trees. Edward yelled his frustration. He tried to concentrate his fire on those who carried arms, but it was a pointless strategy – every time a weapon fell, fresh hands retrieved it. He ejected his second empty magazine and snatched up the last of his spares.

Six bodies now littered the track. He couldn't think of them as people, merely targets. Ten were still advancing down the middle of the path. He'd lost some in the undergrowth, but how many? Three? Five?

Four rounds left in the rifle. Four chances to save his daughter's life.

Snarling, he pressed his eye back to the scope. Those on the track were closer now. Heads and bodies filled his view. He found Reynaud Hossner, placed the scope's red dot in the centre of the man's face.

Reynaud grinned, raised an arm towards the house.

Instantly, Edward felt as if a giant hand had wrapped around his torso. He managed to pull the trigger and the rifle kicked, but its barrel had already dropped. The round took Reynaud in the chest, knocking him off his feet. The man rolled in the dirt, pushed himself to his knees, raised his hand again. This time Edward shot him in the face.

His ears were ringing; whether from the gun's reports or the horror of what he was doing, he did not know. He fought to control a tremor in his fingers. Fought to steady his jaw.

Breathe in. Breathe out. Locate a target. Fire.

His heart seemed like it was shrivelling inside his chest. With each pull of the trigger he felt more of his humanity slipping away. Still he kept his eye pressed to the scope.

He killed an overweight man in boxer shorts next. Then a young woman in a hoodie and bikini bottoms. When he put his crosshairs over Inga Friis and thought of the woman's husband, his resolve nearly abandoned him, but when he glanced across the room at Piper he knew, at once, that whatever scales he used to weigh his daughter's worth, he would never find her balance. Summoning the last reserves of his strength, Edward re-acquired his target and pulled the trigger. This time the rifle dry-fired.

It took him a moment to accept what that meant. Including Inga, seven people still approached along the track. With them they carried guns, hammers, scissors, hatchets, blades. He had lost count of how many had disappeared into the trees. No doubt they were flanking the chalet even now, closing from every direction.

Jenna lifted her head towards him. She said nothing, but in her eyes Edward saw her despair.

He threw down his rifle, drew the pistol from his belt. 'If I don't come back—' he began.

Piper's head snapped up. 'Dad, no way. No *way* you're going out there.'

'We can't let them get inside.'

Eyes wild, she shook her head. '*No*. You can't do this.'

Edward hesitated, glanced back through the window. They had half a minute at best before the chalet was overrun. He went to his daughter, embraced her. 'Listen to me. What Jenna said, it's true. It won't be in vain. It won't be. I have to keep you alive.'

Piper screamed, tried to push him away.

He held her a fraction longer, turning his face towards Jenna. 'Keys are on the counter. You have somewhere to take her?'

The woman nodded, hollow-eyed.

'You keep her safe.'

'I will.'

Edward kissed his daughter's hair, released her. Piper tried to grab onto him but Jenna enveloped her, trapping her arms. He ran to the chalet's front door, the girl's shrieks ringing in his ears. Sixteen years ago he had promised not to abandon her. As much as breaking that vow pained him, her life took priority.

In the front door, a panel of frosted glass admitted an oblong of the dawn's pale light. He checked the pistol. A Glock semi-automatic. He wondered how many rounds it contained.

Seven walkers on the path. Perhaps another five in the trees.

From the kitchen he heard his daughter's sobs. Convinced that he would not see her again in this life, Edward Schwinn opened the front door and ran outside to meet his fate.

CHAPTER 45

Gorges du Tarn, Southern France

On a patch of scrubby weeds to the left of the house stood his truck. Keeping his body as low as he could, Edward sprinted towards it. His knee screamed in outrage at every footfall. He knew his body could not accept much more abuse. Likely, it would not have to.

He heard the chatter of gunfire somewhere close. Saw the *chk!-chk!-chk!-chk!-chk!* line of detonations across the ground behind him.

Pebbles flew. Dust sailed.

The shots had come from the trees on his left. Edward leaned around the truck's front wing and saw, just inside the woods, the glimmer of an old man's pate.

From the opposite side of the path, he heard the blast of a pump-action. One of the truck's tyres exploded with a hiss.

Edward winced, ducked down. When he looked back to the trees he saw that the old man had revealed himself. He brought up his pistol, squeezed off a shot. Fired three more rounds.

The last one blew through the old man's left cheek, sending blood and bone fragments flying.

Four shots. One kill.

He had to do better than that.

Across the path, the shotgun roared again. Another of the

truck's wheels disintegrated, rocking the vehicle on its suspension. Instead of targeting Edward, the shooter was concentrating on the intended method of escape. In quick succession, three more shotgun rounds tore through the truck's radiator grille.

He risked a glance down the track and saw the seven Joyau Caché residents swarming towards the house. They were moving faster now, their actions more coordinated. One of them – a middle-aged man wearing a plaid shirt unbuttoned to the navel – saw him and raised his hand, fingers pincered.

Edward ducked out of sight. A moment later he felt the surrounding earth shiver. One of the truck's windows shattered. He heard a groan of metal, a protesting creak. Another window imploded. The roof pillars began to deform. A dent, like an oversized thumbprint, appeared in the passenger door. He watched, aghast, as a crease raced along the side panel. Then, with a tortured squeal, the vehicle began to fold in on itself. The headlamps blew out, followed by the indicator lights. The remaining tyres burst apart. The chassis crumpled, twisted.

Beneath him, the ground shivered again. This time the truck moved too. It swung sideways, wheel rims ploughing dark furrows. Finally, it tipped and rolled.

Edward was exposed, now, crouching on open ground: nothing shielding him from those on the track and no hope of getting to the trees unseen.

Seven walkers remained visible. Morning sunlight glinted on hatchets, scissors, bats and blades.

Grimly, he wondered how many he could kill before they fell upon him. The man with the unbuttoned shirt made a chopping motion with his hand and the pistol flew from Edward's fingers.

There was his answer.

Tears streaming down her cheeks, Piper watched Jenna shrug her arms into one of the backpacks. The woman ripped open a kitchen drawer. From it she grabbed two carving knives. 'We're leaving,' she said. 'Right now.'

Piper shook her head. 'I can't. I won't.'

'You know what's at stake,' Jenna hissed. 'Don't let his sacrifice go to waste.'

Piper peered through the window. Outside, her father crouched behind his truck.

She saw gunfire erupt from the tree line, saw the vehicle rock on its suspension. One tyre blew out. Another. Then, as if clutched and squeezed by an invisible fist, the bodywork began to crumple. Panels popped and sheared. Glass shattered. Struts deformed. Within seconds, the truck had compacted to a fraction of its original size.

Piper felt the ground shudder, felt the chalet shift on its foundations. A cupboard door banged open. Crockery fell out, smashing to pieces on the floor. Outside, her father's truck slid away from him and rolled onto its roof.

Further up the track, the remaining seven residents of Joyau Caché, their faces split by mirthless grins, charged towards Edward Schwinn.

Piper screamed out her panic. '*No! NO!*' When Jenna slid an arm around her she tore it away. 'I won't let them! *I WON'T!*'

She tried to run into the hall but Jenna pulled her back.

'Look, Piper!' the woman yelled, pointing through the window. '*Look!*'

Jolyon Percival watched from the tree line as the woman with the flaxen hair killed the stranger who had given her a cigarette. She slid her blade in and out, eviscerating him as casually as a butcher might gut a pig. Blood fell in ropey splatters.

Her act of savagery complete, she walked back to the van, not even waiting for the man to collapse. Eyes wide with horror, her victim pressed his hands to his abdomen, trying in vain to hold himself together. He fell to his knees and keeled forwards onto his face.

Shocked by the violence he had just witnessed, but unsure how to react, Jolyon switched his attention to the woman. She was inside the van, now, unscrewing something from her ears. A moment later he saw her spine arch and one of her palms press flat against the window glass. Shortly after that, he felt it himself.

It was the worst thing he had experienced: a sensation like a thousand locusts scuttling over his skin. They whickered and ticked, crisp in his ears and nose. He felt one work its way behind his eyes, whirring and fluttering, and he shook his head, desperate to dislodge it. He could feel something in his mouth, something in his throat. In his chest; in his gut; in his crotch.

A handful of seconds it lasted and then, just as he thought he could bear it no longer, the sensation took flight as quickly as it had arrived. Nauseated, disoriented, Jolyon sat down hard on the prairie grass. He spat into the soil, wrapped his arms around his shoulders and began to scratch. He felt violated; defiled.

Behind him, from individual pitches all over Joyau Caché, he heard sounds of movement: doors opening, awnings unzipping. When he turned to look he saw something that made no sense.

They emerged from motorhomes, caravans and tents: men, women, youths. Some were clothed, some not. All wore the same gruesome smile. They moved as a single mindless entity – except *mindless*, Jolyon saw, was not really the word. Between them they displayed a unity of purpose that suggested a sole, subjugating mind.

He counted eight, then fifteen, then twenty. They came along the road towards his hiding place, clutching among them a macabre collection of weapons, and when they reached the Mercedes van the woman climbed out and joined them. Her own arsenal was far more sophisticated: two semi-automatic pistols; a sub-machine gun hanging from her neck; a pump-action shotgun over one shoulder. She crossed the road to the track that served Edward Schwinn's chalet and led the rest of the group down it.

The moment they turned the bend, Jolyon clambered to his feet. Sweat, cold and greasy, laddered his back. Whatever strangeness had tried to invade his head moments earlier had abandoned him, but it seemed to have found plenty of alternative victims. He thought of Piper and her father, thought of that silent horde descending on them unawares.

Jolyon lifted back his head and roared. He strode towards the Mercedes, threw open its door and got in. Its keys still hung from the ignition. On the back seat he saw a sports holdall filled with guns. From it he retrieved two semi-automatic pistols, tossing them onto the passenger seat. In the footwell he discovered a pump-action shotgun. He took that too and laid it beside him. He'd never fired a gun in his life, but a conviction seized him, pin-sharp in clarity: no matter the cost, the girl must live.

From inside the woods, he heard the supersonic crack of a hunting rifle.

Jolyon started the engine, found first gear, slammed his foot on the accelerator. The front wheels whistled as they spun. When they found traction he hauled the van around, bumping up onto the track that served the chalet. He crunched into second gear, then third. Bracken and trailing vines snatched at the tyres.

Jolyon gripped the wheel tighter, changed up another gear. The van hurtled along the track. If he struck any of the trees lining it, he knew the impact would kill him. But his sole concern was what might be happening deeper inside these woods, and the consequences of him arriving too late.

In recent months his dreams of Piper, and this tucked-away corner of France, had begun to obsess him like nothing else. Urchardan's words, in Beckett's *Black Book* translation, had sharpened his fears about what the girl represented, but once he had met her at the chalet and looked into her eyes he had seen, first-hand, her intentions. Too many lies had been told about her; too many obstructions placed in front of what she hoped to achieve. He still found it hard to accept much of what Piper had told him, but he no longer thought she was lying: merely that he could not grasp fully the magnitude of her revelations.

'*You won't find an answer down here, where you live now,*' she had told him in the chalet's tiny garden, turning her face to the night sky. '*It's up there you should look.*'

'*What are you saying to me?*' he had asked her, bewitched. '*What are you saying?*'

'*Do you really not remember, Drustan?*'

The track curved to the right. The van's back end swung out, tyres scrabbling for purchase. He controlled the slide as best he could, determined not to lose unnecessary speed. Ahead, the road straightened, and what it revealed made him howl.

CHAPTER 46

Gorges du Tarn,
Southern France

Across the track, Jolyon saw bodies strewn like broken mannequins. Among them he recognised the woman whose van he drove. She lay face-down, hair matted with blood. In front of her he saw eight more corpses, all of them head-shot.

Appalled, both by the sight, and the knowledge of what he must do, he accelerated. He could not afford to stop, and there was no way to avoid them. The van's front wheels thumped over the first corpse and Jolyon's teeth clattered together. When he struck the others, the vehicle shuddered and bounced. The steering wheel ripped loose from his hands and he fought to regain control.

Ahead, he saw the rest of the group. They were racing down the track in loose formation. One of them – a man in a plaid shirt open to the waist – had his hand raised towards the chalet.

Outside the building, beside the twisted wreckage of his pick-up truck, knelt Edward Schwinn. A gun lay at his feet. He stared at the man in the plaid shirt, chin thrust out in grim acknowledgement of his fate.

'*No!*' Jolyon cried. '*No, you filthy swine! You whore-son!* Cùm air falbh bhuaithe!'

The van's engine screamed. He hunched over the wheel, knuckles white. Ahead, the chalet door opened and Piper ran outside. The girl dropped to her knees beside her father, flung her arms around him. Edward Schwinn stared at her in horror.

Jolyon crashed the van through the swarm of Joyau Caché residents, breaking bones and cracking skulls. A man's head shattered the windscreen, leaving a scarlet print. The Mercedes rodeo-hopped over those who tumbled beneath its wheels. Jolyon slammed his foot on the brake, holding on tight as the tyres locked and the nose dived. The vehicle wallowed from side to side. The moment it came to a halt he kicked open his door and jumped out, pulling the shotgun from the passenger seat.

The man in the plaid shirt lay on his back, his pelvis turned at ninety degrees. He glared at Jolyon in cold-eyed fury. His left arm was trapped beneath him, his right snapped back at the elbow. He tried to raise it, dragging the limb like a broken stick.

Jolyon put the shotgun to his shoulder, aimed its barrels and pulled the trigger.

Nothing.

Not even a click.

Outside the chalet, Edward Schwinn shook off his daughter's embrace and retrieved his pistol from the ground. He pointed it at the man in plaid and fired once, dropping him. 'Behind you!' he shouted.

Jolyon pivoted. Pinned beneath the van's front wheel was a young woman. One eye had collapsed inside her skull. The other swivelled towards Jolyon. Her mouth gaped wide and her arms flapped. He raised the shotgun and pulled the trigger. Nothing. Again.

'*HOW THE BLOODY HELL?*' he roared.

Edward snapped off a shot. The woman twitched and lay still. Incensed, Jolyon turned the shotgun over in his hands. On one side of the trigger guard he saw a black button. He depressed it, revealing a red circle.

A few yards away lay another of Joyau Caché's residents, this one a middle-aged man; his jaw worked silently, fingers clawing at the earth.

Edward went and stood over the man. He aimed his pistol and dispatched him. Then he circled the front of the van, methodically putting a bullet in each of the residents who had survived the crash. His face was deathly white. His shoulders shook more with each execution he performed. But he did not stop, did not slow. He turned towards Jolyon. Indicated the shotgun. 'You figure it out?'

'Yeah.'

'Good. Because this isn't over. Keep an eye out.'

Jolyon tried to speak, and found that he could no longer make the words − as if his body had climbed the peak of its adrenalin and now plummeted down its slope. His body felt so insubstantial he thought he might float away. He took great lungfuls of air, but they seemed to do nothing to sustain him. How contemptible, he thought, to pass out just as he was needed most.

His eyes found Piper. The girl knelt on the ground, her head bowed, her hands pressed to her ears. The sight of her, so vulnerable, renewed Jolyon's strength. He squared his shoulders, straightened his spine. Behind her the chalet's front door banged open. A pale-haired woman came out. In her arms she carried a boy he recognised from his dreams.

Edward helped the woman lift Therron into the van. While they were doing it, Jolyon spotted movement in the nearby woods. A teenage girl bobbed into view, her face scratched and bloody. Her smile revealed two rows of perfect white teeth. As she emerged from the trees he saw that she held a shotgun. She swung the weapon towards Piper, eyes gleaming.

Jolyon sidestepped, using his body as a shield. He lifted the barrel of his pump-action and pulled the trigger. The Mossberg discharged with a roar, punching his collarbone with almost enough force to fracture it. The girl staggered, but she kept hold of her gun. Jolyon pumped the Mossberg's forestock, fired again. This time the blast knocked the girl off her feet. He advanced to the spot where she lay. Pumped. Fired. Pumped. Fired. Realised, dimly, that he was yelling. Yelling and crying. Ears ringing.

The shotgun barked its fury, slammed his shoulder. Again. Again.

Soon, the girl was little more than a red streak in the grass. Jolyon felt a hand on his shoulder, shrugged it off.

Edward caught him by the arm, firmer this time. 'She's dead,' he said. 'Don't waste ammo.'

He nodded, panting, too tormented by his own savagery to speak. He met Edward's gaze and saw his own emotions reflected: abhorrence, competing with grim resolve.

He put his back to the girl he had killed, thinking that he might be sick, and stumbled to the van, where he found the woman from the chalet shepherding Piper onto the rear seat.

'I'll drive,' Edward said.

Jolyon nodded, opening the passenger door and climbing up inside. He gripped the Mossberg between his knees, tasted bile in his throat. Shivered.

The engine woke with a rattle. Edward reversed in a tight circle. He found first gear and dumped the clutch. The van lurched forwards, gathered speed.

Jolyon turned in his seat. Behind him sat the pale-haired woman from the chalet. 'Jolyon Percival,' he said, and wanted to laugh aloud at the absurdity of such formality.

'Jenna Black.'

The Mercedes rounded a bend in the track, its engine beginning to misfire. Edward changed up a gear, feathered the throttle. Trees blurred past on either side.

Eyes still on Jenna, Jolyon indicated the shotgun. 'You know how to load one of these?'

'Yes.'

'Can you show me?'

She nodded. Then she looked past him and her eyes widened. 'There!' she screamed.

Ahead, half hidden by undergrowth to the left of the road, stood a muscular young man in shorts and running shoes, his left arm raised.

The van slammed sideways as if broad-sided by a train. It lifted clear of the track, losing none of its forward momentum. Jolyon saw a line of tree trunks rushing towards the windows. He closed his eyes, braced.

The impact was monstrous. Metal twisted and sheared. Trees splintered. The van bounced free and slid across the track, chassis shrieking and sparking. It hit an earth mound and flipped high into the air. Jolyon's world rotated, curiously free of gravity. Then, as if a switch had been pressed, that world winked out.

CHAPTER 47

Gorges du Tarn, Southern France

Edward Schwinn came awake in a world choked by dust and steam. The right side of his face felt loose. His tongue was gritty with pieces of broken tooth. He sensed a spreading coldness beneath him, heard fuel pouring from the Mercedes' ruptured tank. Diesel fumes bloomed in his nose.

He blinked, tried to orient himself, discovered that his right eye was gummed shut. The van had come to a rest on its roof. His chest pressed against the ceiling. Beside him, Jolyon hung upside down in the passenger seat, legs wedged beneath the crumpled dash. A dark line of blood ran from the man's jawline to his hair, where it dripped with a steady *plik-plik-plik*.

'Puh?' Edward croaked; swallowed and tried again. 'Pie?'

She lay in an awkward heap behind him, head resting against Jenna's leg.

Her chest was still.

Beside Piper, Jenna Black slumped with her eyes closed, unconscious or dead. Her right forearm was horribly bent, a shard of white bone protruding from the flesh. A deep gash ran across her forehead from eyebrow to hairline.

Behind the woman lay Therron. The boy's head was angled towards the back of the van. Blood dripped from his earlobe.

'*Pie!*'

This time the girl's eyes snapped open. A moment later she lurched upright, knocking her head against a seat back. She gazed around the wreckage with eyes that rolled in their sockets. Finally, she found Edward's face. He held out his hand but she was too far away to reach.

The girl's chest heaved. She began to gasp. 'Coming,' she whispered, and her awareness seemed to sharpen. She stared at him with renewed panic. 'Dad, it's *coming*.'

A pall of smoke rolled through the passenger cabin, bitter and dark. Edward held his breath until the wind dispersed it. Twenty yards away he noticed movement in the undergrowth. The upturned driver's console blocked most of his view, but he saw a pair of muscular legs, and recalled the young man in shorts and running shoes.

Beside him, Jolyon groaned. The artist twisted his shoulders and thrashed in his seat, trying to work himself loose.

The stench of diesel was stronger now. Edward realised that the coldness soaking into his clothes was fuel from the ruptured tank. He thought of the smoke that had stung his eyes seconds earlier, wondered how long before the wreckage became an inferno. Outside, the muscular legs bent at the knee and a man's face appeared, inverted. His eyes were ice chips. He wore a mirthless smile.

Edward drew up his legs. Would he have time to extricate Piper before the van was crushed into scrap? Even if he did, what then?

Abruptly Jolyon dislodged himself, collapsing onto his back with a grunt. Debris rained down: coins, sunglasses, binoculars . . . and two semi-automatic pistols.

Edward snatched one up and aimed through the window. His first two shots went wide. With his third shot he did better, striking the muscular stranger in the chest. His fourth permanently dropped the man.

In that same instant, a hot wind tore down the track; stones and grit rattled through gaps in the broken windscreen. In its wake the ground shivered, as if their wrecked vehicle lay on a fault line between two plates.

'What in God's name?' Jolyon muttered.

Edward shot him a glance. 'Let's not hang around to find out.'

The artist hoisted himself onto his hands and knees. 'Agreed. Can you move?'

'Just about.'

'Anything broken?'

'Not that I can tell.'

Through his shattered window, Edward heard commotion. He turned in time to see the talons of a large bird appear on the ground nearby. It flapped dark wings, and when the air moved Edward smelled the sweet-rotten smell of carrion. The bird lowered its head, revealing the hooked beak and flat amber eye of a griffon vulture. Four more vultures landed beside it.

Now, Edward heard something else; an insect-dry whispering. The earth on either side of the hard-packed track began to seethe, as if it were boiling. But the phenomenon, he realised, was caused not by heat nor ground movement, but by the surfacing of a million soil-dwelling creatures. He saw the glutinous bodies of earthworms and larvae, squirming as if in a delirium. He saw the hard gleam of beetle carapace; ants; earwigs; woodlice, slugs and snails. Their frenzied thrashing suggested the earth had ceased to be a sanctuary and had turned, instead, into a place to be reviled.

From the gorge all around came a dreadful chorus of sound: barks, cries, howls and shrieks; the proclamations of wild animals stirred to rage.

Hearing it, Edward's skin shrank on his flesh. An insight struck him, terrible in its significance. 'Get out!' he shouted. 'Now! Out of the van!'

Joyau Caché's human residents had been deployed as foot soldiers, and had been defeated. Now, the canyon's wildlife would form a second line of attack. Edward kicked the remaining glass from his side window. Outside, the animal cries intensified. From the woods he heard the thump of hooves over pine needles. Snapping boughs.

Piper scrabbled forwards and Edward grabbed her hand. He indicated the nearest window but she shook her head. 'We can't,' she said. Her eyes were livid. 'If we go outside . . .'

Beside her, Jolyon peered through the shattered windscreen, eyes red-rimmed. 'They'll kill us,' he said. 'We can't go out there.'

Edward stared at them, incredulous. 'You mean that's it? We're just going to *wait*?' A fury ignited in him, incandescent. The thought that their lives could end here, huddled inside this diesel-soaked wreck, seemed like the most appalling travesty.

Jolyon shot him a wild look. A pulse throbbed in the man's forehead. '*Ní bheidh mé,*' he spat. Fresh blood dripped from his beard. His chest heaved and he shouted again. '*Ní bheidh mé!*'

Edward did not understand the words, but he recognised defiance when he heard it. He gathered Piper into his arms.

Around them the woods fell silent: a shocking, crypt-like stillness.

A breeze stirred the hairs on Piper's head. Somewhere above them, the last drips of diesel plinked from the tank.

In response to a signal that Edward neither heard nor felt, those who had answered the *balla-dìon's* call began to pour from the woods, a scampering, leaping brown tide.

The smaller denizens came first: rabbits, squirrels, weasels. They raced through the trees towards the van, bounding over tussocks and boulders. Gaping pink mouths revealed tiny white teeth.

Following behind them came a rising wave of rats, voles and mice. Accompanying that furred carpet, running amongst it, Edward saw mouflon, deer, three frenzied boar. Bright blood ran from their snouts. Their eyes bulged. Their ears lay flat against their heads.

Piper wailed, clutched at her father. 'Oh shit, Dad. Oh *shit.*'

Behind the ground-swarming vermin, shadows flickered, as if deep inside the woods a zoetrope rotated, on which the silhouettes of nightmares had been etched. A moment later those furtive shadows coalesced into a single onrushing cloud.

Bats.

They arced and flittered through the trees towards the wrecked Mercedes, silent and unassailable, a maddened host of tiny claws and teeth, far quicker than rats or mice. Almost before Edward managed to process what he was seeing, the first outriders flew in through the shattered windows. They smashed into Piper: nipping, flapping, writhing. The girl began to scream. Edward tore a bat from her hair. Mashed it against a doorpost. Grabbed another and hurled it outside.

Six more dive-bombed her. Others slammed into him now, too. He felt teeth bite his ear, his cheek. Saw a frenzied fluttering of wings in front of his eyes.

'*Ní bheidh mé!*' Jolyon roared.

Edward could no longer see the man, could concentrate only on protecting his daughter. He felt more teeth slice his face, his neck. Piper screamed and thrashed, manic. Never had he heard such terror. He ripped bats from her scalp, crushed the bodies of those he could not displace. She was buried, now, beneath a crawling coat of furred bodies and membranous wings. Everywhere he looked he saw glinting teeth, pink gums, eyes like tiny black seeds. The stench was caustic, abhorrent.

Edward felt teeth sink into his ankle, from an animal far larger than a bat. He kicked out his legs. Shouted his revulsion, his rage. A creature scurried up his chest and pushed into his mouth.

'*NÍ BHEIDH MÉ A CHUR FAOI BHRÁID!*' Jolyon bellowed.

There came a sound like water rushing into a vacuum.

White light.

CHAPTER 48

Austin, Texas

Pastor Benjamin D. Pope stood in the nave of the Church of the Holy Sacrament where he had preached these last ten years, and marvelled at its transformation.

The pews had been removed to the sacristy, leaving a wide, deep space. Through the vestibule came a steady stream of people carrying all manner of equipment and supplies. He saw metal crates, plastic packing cases, huge canvas bundles. Along the back wall leaned rows of shovels, axes, sledgehammers and saws. On the main floor space lay lengths of timber, carpentry tools, bed rolls, clothing, musical instruments, toilet rolls and a seemingly limitless amount of food.

'We're building a small city,' he said.

Wendy Devereaux flashed her eyes at him. Since the night of revelations at Mercury Hall, the woman had ditched her trouser suits in favour of a more casual look. Right now she wore sweatpants, pumps and a faded Indiana State tee, her ponytail pulled through the back of a blue and yellow Pacers cap. For some reason, Benjamin found that the new look accentuated her sexuality tenfold. He could smell her perfume, too, a compelling muskiness that triggered in him alternate bursts of excitement and distress. Wendy had never worn fragrance before. He wondered what it meant.

'We're building a garrison,' she replied. 'And not a damned thing is gonna get through it.'

The pastor turned in time to see Billy Gosselin drag a dolly stacked with pallets of salt beef through the main doors. In one corner, Deana Taylor and Terri Freeman inventoried the food mountain, checking off items on their clipboards. On the far side of the church, four volunteers unrolled and repacked a large marquee.

'You wanna see something cool?' Wendy asked, her voice laced with the merest hint of lasciviousness.

Intrigued, Benjamin raised his eyebrows. 'Why not?'

'This way.'

She led him down the nave and deep into the north transept. With the overhead spots switched off, little light penetrated, even at this time of day. In the shadows along the back wall he saw a row of black plastic shipping cases. Wendy went to the nearest one. Snapping open four metal latches, she raised the lid. Hard grey foam filled its interior, into which had been cut four lengthwise channels. Lying inside he saw what appeared to be assault rifles. A series of four smaller depressions held semi-automatic pistols.

'Look at this stuff,' Wendy said, keeping her voice low. She reached into the case and removed one of the larger firearms. 'M4A1 carbine,' she told him. 'Just like the SEALs use.'

Benjamin stared, Wendy's earlier words echoing in his head: *You wanna see something cool?*

'Where did we get all this?'

'Eric organised it.'

'Is it legal?'

She shook her head. 'Not unless you've got a class three permit. These are military grade, fully automatic.'

'How many do we have?'

'A hundred. One each for every man and woman.' Wendy grinned. Her teeth shone with saliva. 'How's that for equality, Pastor? Here.' She held out the weapon to him. 'Try it.'

'What?'

Her eyes glittered. 'Go on. Hold it in your hands. You'll be surprised what you feel.'

Reluctantly, but fearing she might drop it if he refused, he took it from her. The gun was heavier than he had expected, an ugly piece of engineering with a vile purpose, and yet . . . when he pointed it at the far wall and pushed the stock into his shoulder, he could not deny the power it transmitted. The feeling thrilled him. Disgusted him.

'See?' Wendy asked. She was closer, now. Her scent clogged his lungs. He noticed a dark diamond of sweat on the T-shirt across her breasts. Tried to swing his eyes away.

She touched his arm. 'You know what else we have? Fifty Beretta M9 pistols and ten M240 machine guns. Best of all, Eric managed to source us a few of these.' She led him to another case, opened it. 'We don't have many,' she told him, 'but we don't *need* many.'

'Dear Lord,' he said. 'What are they?'

She pulled one from the packing foam. 'Looks kinda like a giant vibrator, doesn't it?'

Benjamin stared, shocked by her description. To his eyes it looked nothing of the sort, but he had little experience of such things. He caught himself wondering if Wendy did. When he saw her watching him he blushed.

'M203 grenade launcher,' she told him. 'Snaps under the gun you're holding. We got five in total. Twenty anti-personnel rounds to go with them.'

You're Adam and she's Eve. And you're standing in the Garden of Eden just before the Fall. Or perhaps Wendy's not Eve at all. Perhaps she's the serpent. And instead of an apple she's arrived bearing crates of black-market military hardware.

He flinched, wondering why such a dark thought had struck him. Until now he had compared his task, somewhat grandly, to that of Moses leading the children of Israel out of Egypt. Or perhaps to David, second king of the Israelites, facing the Philistines near the Valley of Elah.

YES.

Benjamin staggered under the intensity of the rapture that filled him. He dropped the carbine and clenched his teeth, felt fireworks detonate in his mouth. The edges of his vision flared with colour, a coruscating rainbow. Throughout his body, nerve endings discharged shivery bursts of sensation. 'Oh my,' he said. 'Oh my.'

Wendy dropped the empty launcher tube to the floor. She gripped Benjamin's arm for support. 'Fuck,' she croaked. 'Ohhh *fuck.*'

For a minute or more, neither of them managed another word. Wendy panted for breath beside him. Finally, through her exertions, she managed to recover enough control of her face to throw him a smile. 'We're gonna do this, Pastor. You and me, we're gonna get it done.'

Benjamin knew that she referred to their mission. But he half wished that she meant something else entirely.

CHAPTER 49

Gorges du Tarn, Southern France

For a while the white light inside Edward Schwinn's head was so intense that it obliterated all thought. It sluiced him of sensation, holding him in a place as silent as it was bright.

At last it began to recede, revealing a world far stranger than the one he had left. His pain returned, too – shrieking, insistent, across every inch of his skin.

Something warm, furred and foul-smelling lay upon his face. He levered it off. Elbowing himself up, he tried to rid his airways of its corporeal stink. Everywhere he looked he saw the rigid carcasses of woodland creatures: bats, mice, voles, rabbits, squirrels. They had died, all of them, with eyes and jaws agape. He saw pink snouts crusted with blood. Tiny claws, ripped wings. Revulsion filled him. He began to dig through the bodies, repulsed by the heat they still radiated.

Edward burrowed through a twelve-inch depth of rodents before he found her. The girl's neck was a bloodied mess of bite marks. He rolled her onto her back, knowing that her face would have fared worse. The sight that greeted him made him cry out.

Piper's cheeks were a patchwork of chewed flesh. A strip of skin the width of his thumb had peeled back from her chin. A piece of her nose hung loose. She blinked up at him, and in the wildness of her gaze he saw his own horror reflected. 'What did they do to you?' he whispered, knowing that his words were the worst possible choice, and wishing he could claw them back.

Piper trembled, eyes fixed on his face. Edward put his arms around her, and for a while it was enough for them both. He could have remained for hours like that, but he knew he had to get her away from here.

Releasing his daughter as gently as he could, he dug through a press of dead vermin to reach the window. Careful not to cut himself further on broken glass, he edged out feet-first, pulling Piper behind him.

The pain from his own bites was beginning to overwhelm him, making it difficult to concentrate. His face was sticky with blood, his hands a cross-hatch of open wounds. Cringing, he thought of all the infections the creatures must have carried among them.

Inside the van, Jolyon Percival groaned. Edward was grateful to hear that he was still alive; whatever the artist had done, it had doubtless saved them. He dragged Piper free of the wreckage and helped her to her feet, appalled at the scene that greeted him.

In a wide circle around their upturned vehicle lay thousands upon thousands of lifeless animals, so numerous that Edward could hardly see the ground beneath them. Among the mice, rats and squirrels he saw grey-furred rabbits and hares, limbs stiffening in death. A mouflon lay with its head canted back, pink foam speckling its teeth. Further away lay three dead boar, their trotters pointing like way markers. He saw the broken wing of a griffon vulture, the rest of the bird buried beneath a knot of brown fur.

On the other side of the van Jolyon appeared, a dead bat tangled in his T-shirt. He brushed it off, staring at Edward in sickened incredulity. 'I thought we were goners.'

'What did you do?'

'I've no idea.' He stared again at the carpet of dead rodents. 'But it seems to have worked.'

Piper touched the bloodied flap of skin hanging from her chin, winced. 'We haven't won. It'll just start recruiting from further afield. We need to get out of here before it does.' She glanced back at the van. 'Therron's in there.'

'I'll get him out,' Edward said.

'Jenna, too. We can't leave her. Not again.'

With Jolyon's help, working slower than he would have liked but as fast as his injuries allowed, Edward cleared a space at the rear of the van and kicked out the window glass. Within a few minutes he had dragged out Therron. The boy was unresponsive, but his chest rose and fell in a steady rhythm. Piper knelt beside him, the blood on her cheeks mixing with her tears. 'Mórríghan warned me,' the girl whispered. 'I should have listened.'

Edward crawled back inside the van. He retrieved the rucksacks, and one of the pistols. Then, as carefully as he could, he extricated Jenna. The woman was unconscious – a mercy considering the extent of her injuries.

'Can you fix that?' Jolyon asked, pointing to the shard of bone that poked like a pale spearhead from her forearm.

Edward turned to his daughter. 'How much time do we have?'

'I don't know. Not long.'

'Both of you, find me something to splint this with. I'll need a dressing too.'

Jolyon grimaced. 'What about infection?'

'This'll be temporary. Just while we get her out of here.'

'Have you done it before?'

'No. But I think I know how.'

The man nodded, disappearing into the undergrowth. He came back a minute later with two stout sticks. Piper took a T-shirt from one of the rucksacks and used a sharp piece of wreckage to cut it into strips.

Mindful of the consequence if he severed a blood vessel, Edward gripped Jenna's elbow and pulled down on her hand. The bone shard sucked and grated, disappearing back into her flesh. He bound the wound tightly and made a makeshift splint. When she woke, the pain would be monstrous. 'Can you carry the boy?' he asked Jolyon.

The artist nodded, lifting Therron onto his shoulder.

Edward stuffed the pistol into his belt. Bracing himself, he picked up Jenna. She was lighter than he had expected, but her weight still punished him. Piper gritted her teeth and hefted the rucksacks onto her back. She stumbled, and for a moment he thought she was going to pass out. Instead she planted her feet and straightened. Together, they limped up the track to Joyau Caché's main loop.

For the first time since he had lived here, Edward heard no birdsong in the nearby trees. He tried not to think about that, tried to keep his eyes and his thoughts focused on the path. Overhead, the sky had deepened to a rich blue. Around them the canyon's limestone walls shone gold.

They emerged from the woods and stepped onto the tarmac loop. All across the site he saw motorhomes with doors hanging open, tents with their entrances unzipped. It was a poignant sight, one that forced him to consider anew the atrocities he had committed. While the residents of Joyau Caché would have killed Piper had he not intervened, they had been wholly innocent of any crime.

'You had no choice,' Jolyon told him.

'Still doesn't make it right.'

'No. But the alternative was worse.' A bead of sweat ran down the man's face, mixing with the blood. 'What now?'

'We get out of here.' Edward said. 'Take one of these vehicles and go.'

On a nearby pitch stood a huge six-wheeled Frankia with German plates. Its side door gaped. 'Let's try that,' he said. He laid Jenna on the grass and drew the pistol from his jeans. Going to the Frankia's side door, he climbed the steps.

The interior was luxuriously appointed: dark wood, aluminium, cream leather. Edward swept through it, checking the main living space, the bathroom, the rear bedroom. All deserted.

On the main galley table sat a laptop. Coloured images scrolled across its screen. Edward touched the trackpad and the images disappeared, replaced by a webpage from a German route-mapping site.

He clambered into the driver's seat and twisted the keys in the ignition, watching the needle on the fuel gauge rise until it stopped at the three-quarters mark. Back outside, he disconnected the hook-ups for power, water and waste.

They laid Therron and Jenna on twin beds in the rear bedroom. Piper elected to stay with them. Edward shut and locked the side door before sliding back behind the wheel. Jolyon took the passenger seat.

The vehicle pulled out of its pitch and bumped up onto the roadway. Edward upshifted, passing Joyau Caché's booking office and site shop. Off to the right sparkled the clear waters of the Tarn. He could hardly bear to look. As the Frankia gathered speed down the hill, he spotted two figures at the side of the road, beside a Niesmann and Bischoff RV. The taller of the two was Bendt Friis. The old war veteran wore prosthetic legs under his shorts. His arm was slung around a young boy, Matthais Hossner.

Bendt had been travelling across Europe with his wife. Matthais had been holidaying with his German family: two parents, one older sister. The Frankia drove past them, rolled beneath Joyau Caché's hand-carved sign and out onto open highway.

They drove for two hours without a break, picking up the A75 autoroute towards Clermont-Ferrand. With Edward settled behind the wheel, Jolyon searched the motorhome, checking every cupboard, locker and hatch. In the bathroom he found antibiotics and painkillers; in the kitchen, a fridge-freezer fully stocked with food. In one of the overhead compartments he discovered a case of red wine and hurriedly uncorked a bottle. Retaking his seat, he kicked off his flip-flops and put his bare feet on the dash. 'I don't know the names of our benefactors,' he said, lifting the bottle to his lips. 'But I'm grateful to them.'

'Joseph and Martina Kinski,' Edward said. 'Austrian couple from Salzburg, late fifties. Grown-up daughter in Vienna. You ran them down. I shot them.'

The artist rubbed his face and stared through the windscreen. After a moment's pause he lowered his side window and tossed the bottle into a field rushing past on their right. 'Thanks for enlightening me.'

They parked in a rest area on a quiet road outside the city, pulling down the vehicle's shades to afford themselves a measure of privacy. Edward went aft to check on the others.

Piper had washed the blood from her skin and had wound a bandage around her forehead. The rest of her face she had patched as best she could. Her nose wound looked brutal but there was little they could do about it yet. At least the bleeding had slowed to a steady trickle.

Therron and Jenna were both awake. The boy began to gulp when he saw Edward, his eyes filling with grateful tears.

Edward put a hand on his shoulder, squeezed. Then he turned to Jenna. 'How's the arm?'

'Bad,' she said. Beads of sweat glistened on her brow. He handed her three painkillers and a bottle of water. 'This'll help a little. I want you to take some penicillin, too. We've all been bitten. God knows what infections those creatures were carrying.'

'I need to make a phone call, bring in some help,' she said. 'We have to get Piper out of France. There's a campsite full of dead tourists back there, and we're driving around in one of their vehicles. You can't do this on your own any more.'

He weighed her words, glanced across at Piper. 'Is that what you want?'

The girl nodded. 'It's time to confront this thing, Dad.'

'People will die.'

'People already have.'

You might die, he wanted to add. Instead he gave her a brusque smile. 'We'll find somewhere secluded. Somewhere we can eat, sleep, maybe take a shower and get clean.'

Jenna opened her mouth. 'Before you go . . .' She hesitated. 'Thank you.'

'For what?'

With a drop of her head she indicated the splint. 'First time we met, you broke my arm. This time round you fixed it. I'd call that progress.'

Edward saw something in her eyes that surprised him. Turning away, lest he show his thoughts too plainly, he retreated to the driver's seat.

They drove for another hour, delving deep into the Auvergne's rural heart. In a valley screened by trees, Edward found an abandoned farm and parked beside a weed-choked field bordered by a drainage ditch. The water was silty, but adequate for their needs. With Jolyon's help, he jury-rigged a supply line to the Frankia's water pump, allowing them all to take a shower. The scent of bath gels and shampoo replaced the stink of rodent and bat. Plundering the possessions of those who had died felt distasteful, but Edward could see no alternative. Afterwards, they swapped what clothes they could with those they found in the Frankia's wardrobes and in the rucksacks they had brought along. Jenna made a series of brief phone calls.

'We'll hole up here,' she told Edward afterwards. 'They'll evacuate us in the morning.'

Exhausted, they folded out extra beds and slept. Edward took the first watch, setting up a picnic table and chair outside.

Jolyon relieved him four hours later. At sunset they lit a barbecue and cooked a meal.

It was a clear night. Stars twinkled on a satin backcloth. Jolyon reclined in his seat and gave the group a meandering tour of the heavens. Swigging from a freshly uncorked wine bottle, he pointed out the constellations and the planets, and told the story of their creation. Edward listened half-heartedly at first, unable to detach himself from thoughts of the slaughter back at Joyau Caché. But slowly, inexorably, he felt himself drawn in by Jolyon's words until his own eyes, too, lifted to the stars.

Once the artist finished his tale, Edward cleared his throat. 'It's a good story, told well,' he said. 'But it's not the whole of it.' He looked around the table, pausing to study each member of the group in turn. 'I think it's time we heard the rest.'

For a minute or more, nobody spoke. Finally, Piper raised her head. 'I'll tell it,' she said. Her gaze moved to Jenna. 'Although I might need a little help.'

CHAPTER 50

Auvergne, Central France

'All those stars up there,' Piper said. She gestured at the platinum rash that spilled across the heavens above their heads. 'Maybe three hundred billion in our galaxy alone. Three hundred *billion*. It used to be that we thought only a few of them hosted planets. Nowadays we think nearly all of them do. There are eight planets in our solar system alone. Multiply that by three hundred billion and you have a very large number indeed.

'All those places that might support life – that might nurture and develop it. And yet our skies are strangely silent. I know the distances are huge, but we're a relatively young planet. If something was out there, we should have heard it by now.'

'Some say we have,' Jolyon said.

'And it's a nice thought, but they're wrong. There hasn't been so much as a blip in recorded history.'

'Fifteenth of August, 1977,' he replied. 'I'd call that a blip.'

Piper smiled. 'The "Wow" signal. Jerry Ehman at the Big Ear radio telescope in Ohio. Detected once and never again, despite hundreds of attempts. Hardly convincing. No, it's as quiet as a grave up there.' She paused to sip from a can of Coke. 'And yet the universe is teeming with life. Overflowing with it.'

Therron shifted in his seat. 'What makes you say that?

Piper gave the boy a smile of such tenderness that Edward found his chest swelling with love for her. 'Because we were visited, once,' she told him. 'So long ago now that hardly any evidence remains. But it happened, just the same.'

'The *An Toiseach*,' Jenna said.

The girl nodded. 'That's our name for them, but it's one they adopted readily enough. Translated, it simply means *The First*. The first ones to reach us; the first ones to make contact.'

Therron glanced back up at the sky. 'You mean . . . from up there?'

Piper laughed. 'Pretty funny, don't you think? The single most important event in our history, and only a few people alive know anything about it. The two that arrived here – the ones we named the *An Toiseach* – came from a race that called itself *The Gardeners*; or at least that's the closest approximation. They were nomads, really. Pioneers on a grand scale. From the moment they developed the technology, they began to send out explorers, messengers. In fact, they were doing it before the technology was even fully tested. Hardly any of their earliest travellers survived long enough to discover anything at all, and yet none were ever deterred. This compulsion to make contact – it seems to have been an impulse experienced by the entire race, a kind of religion, if you like; a cosmic obligation. They had few successes, millions of failures. And a couple of thousand years later, as their understanding of the galaxy – and those who lived in it – began to grow, their emphasis changed. They began to apply themselves to an even harder task: seeking out civilisations too young to broadcast their whereabouts, so that they could be saved.'

Edward frowned. 'Saved from what?'

'Outside influence. It's not exactly a Ridley Scott horror movie up there, but bad things happen, and not always by design. When disparate cultures collide there's usually a loser. Think about how the Mayans fared after their discovery by the Spanish. Look at what happened to the Native Americans, or the Aborigines, after their contact with a so-called civilising race – pretty catastrophic, even if things went well at the start. *The*

Gardeners, during their explorations, saw even more extreme examples. Eventually they dedicated themselves to their prevention.'

Edward stared at his daughter, unable to shake the impression that he had fallen into a dream. 'You know all this how?'

Piper had avoided looking at him so far. Now her eyes met his and she flushed. 'We'll get to that,' she replied. 'But let me tell you first about the two that arrived here. Mórríghan and Cathasach, we named them. Again, those names are Celtic in origin, or perhaps even earlier, but the *An Toiseach* were happy enough to take them. I can't give you accurate dates for their arrival, but we're talking at least a thousand years before the birth of Christ, possibly even earlier. And while we might not know *when* they arrived, at least our two scribes – Urchardan and Mac an Làmhaich – agree upon where. They both describe the *An Toiseach* appearing out of the sea somewhere along Scotland's west coast near Loch Broom, although their initial landfall would have been somewhere else: likely one of the nearby archipelagos or outlying islands. They weren't here very long, a few seasons at most. But their influence during that time was considerable.'

'Urchardan talks of them uniting six warrior tribes,' Jolyon said.

'Piper nodded. 'Mac an Làmhaich describes similar interventions. None of that would have been sanctioned, of course. On arrival, the *An Toiseach* should have quietly set up their technology and left without being observed. But once they were here, they found the lure of contact irresistible. Hardly surprising, I guess, considering their heritage. Still, when they realised the tribes had begun to worship them as gods, they feared they might trigger the very outcome they sought to prevent. Their task had been to protect emerging cultures from outside influence, and yet here they were, influencing one directly. As their final act, they activated the *balla-dìon* and then they disappeared.'

'The *balla-dìon*,' Jolyon repeated. 'Urchardan references it constantly in the *Black Book*, but he never really explains it. I know the term translates as *Barrier Wall*, but that's all I ever found out.'

'Mac an Làmhaich mentions it too,' Piper said. 'And he's a lot more explicit. The *balla-dìon* was what the *An Toiseach* created to safeguard humanity's development and shield it from outside influence. They'd brought the technology with them, but for it to work successfully it needed to develop sentience. To achieve that, one of the *An Toiseach* had to forfeit its life and meld with the machine.' The girl paused, her brow furrowing. 'Imagine plugging yourself into a permanent virtual reality system. That's what the *balla-dìon* required.'

'Some sacrifice,' Edward said.

'For us, maybe. As individuals we have a pretty powerful self-preservation instinct. Most of the time it even overrides our sense of duty to others. Not so for the *An Toiseach*. Their compassion for the cultures they discovered outweighed any concern they had for themselves.'

From his pocket, Jolyon retrieved the black book he had brought to the chalet. He flicked through it to a page he had marked, and began to read: '"*For a moon's span they toiled, creating the balla-dìon, the like of which none had ever seen. In a flash of fire Mórríghan ascended and Cathasach descended. Beneath the earth he gave his life, joining to what they had built and securing for us our future. How we rejoiced! How we grieved!*"'

Piper nodded. 'It's about the only part of the story Urchardan narrates with any shred of impartiality. But he can't really be blamed. It's clear the guy never even met Mórríghan. The *balla-dìon* recruited Urchardan at least a thousand years after she left.'

'What happened to her?' Therron asked.

Piper cast a look towards her father, offering him the smallest of smiles. 'After Cathasach became one with the *balla-dìon*, Mórríghan left in the same vessel that brought her. Over time their names and their deeds faded, just as they had hoped. In the meantime, the *balla-dìon* continued to operate, out of sight and memory.'

'What does it do?'

'Don't ask me to explain the physics of it, because I can't,' she replied. 'But from the moment Cathasach gave it sentience – again, time-wise, we're probably going back as far as the Neolithic, or New Stone Age – it made us invisible. After that, if any outsider ever tried to monitor our little corner of space they'd see nothing, hear nothing, measure nothing. No gravity, no radiation, no chatter. It was never intended to last forever; just long enough to give us a little breathing space, a fair roll of the dice. Once we'd progressed a little further along our path, the *balla-dìon* should have switched itself off.'

'But it didn't.'

'No. And that, right there, is the single biggest tragedy of our history. Because we're simply not supposed to believe we're all alone. It's unnatural, and it doesn't suit our natures.' Piper glanced around the table. 'Look at us – how we live, how we seek comfort. We take partners, we surround ourselves with friends, we crave the stability a family can bring. We organise ourselves into tribes, communities, nations. We do whatever we can to reject the solitude of our individual existence. And yet for all that, we've been denied one of the most fundamental comforts we could have in this life: the knowledge that up there it's not all just empty space, and that we're not as alone as we fear.'

The fire popped, releasing an explosion of red sparks. 'You can see the effects wherever you look,' Piper continued. 'How much of our popular culture seeks to answer that very question? How many of our movies, books and TV shows explore that theme? Yet when you consider our investment in ESA, NASA, SETI and all those other organisations we've founded over the years and then allowed to flounder, it's as if we've already resigned ourselves to failure. We look down these days rather than up, inward rather than outward. And then we fall back on story-telling to fill the void.'

'So what went wrong?' Edward asked. 'Why is this *balla-dìon* still operating?'

'I don't have a concrete answer for that, but there's a theory. I told you how the *An Toiseach* feared their presence on earth might begin to corrupt us. It's possible that over the centuries the opposite happened. The *balla-dìon* is a machine, but a sentient one. After all these years among us, it may have learned our instinct for survival.' She grimaced. 'Which meant that when the time came for it to bow out gracefully, it stuck around instead. Not only that, it could have picked up our knack for self-deception, too – convincing itself that it's working in our interests while actually preserving its own.

'Sticking around past its sell-by date has caused it problems, even so. To start with, it had to reinvent itself as a two-way filtering system. Our explorations up there might have been paltry so far, but things like Voyager have given it a headache, and as a species we're getting noisier each year that passes. Meanwhile, down here it's had to use its defences far more aggressively than ever before.'

'The red light,' Edward said.

'Yeah. It's how the *balla-dìon* exerts its influence,' she replied. 'It throws up that red dome you've seen, kind of like a fishing net. Everything inside falls under its spell. People are its preference, but in a pinch it can use most forms of intelligent life.'

Edward thought of the animals pouring from the woods back at Joyau Caché, their jaws hinged wide in frenzied anticipation. He scowled. 'It can do more than just turn people against us. It managed to crush my truck. Flipped that van.'

'It still needed eyes on us first.'

'So it has limits.'

'Some,' she replied. 'Not many. It's managed to maintain the status quo all this time, after all, and with very little effort.

Just imagine how different the last five hundred years might have been had Galileo pointed his telescope at the heavens and seen them as they truly are, rather than what the *balla-dìon* wanted him to see. Imagine what might have happened if we'd switched on the first radio telescope back in the thirties and heard something other than static.

'Luckily, the fact that Cathasach's machine kept operating didn't go entirely unnoticed. Mórríghan might have left, but she kept tabs. It was clear that our little corner of space remained dark. She sent messengers to investigate, but they never reported back. Finally, in desperation, she dispatched her four closest allies. We know them, through Urchardan and Mac an Làmhaich, as the *Triallaichean*.

'The *balla-dìon* allowed the *Triallaichean* to land, but it wouldn't let them leave, nor allow them to transmit a message out. Worse, they stood no chance of destroying it themselves. Only Mórríghan retained the power to do that, and by now she was too far away to make the journey. An uneasy truce ensued, and it might have lasted forever. But Ériu – always the most insuppressible of the four – never gave up. After centuries of studying the *balla-dìon*, she discovered a potential weakness.'

'Which was?'

'You might not have heard of it, but every eight years the earth passes through what scientists call the Ookater Cloud. It doesn't do us any harm; in fact we hardly even notice it. But for a short window – so short you could probably blink and miss it – the *balla-dìon*'s systems are scrambled. Ériu discovered that if she timed it right, Mórríghan might be able to return, after all.'

Piper paused. She took another sip from her drink and looked directly at her father. 'Not in person, this time. But through a host.'

CHAPTER 51

Auvergne, Central France

'You,' Edward said, and found he did not know how to feel.

Piper nodded. 'Yeah. Me.'

Cicadas chorused in the surrounding darkness. For the first time, Jenna added her voice. 'You can't imagine how long it took Ériu and Mórríghan to arrange that,' she said. 'All those calculations and adjustments, a minimum eight-year gap between every burst of communication. Centuries of effort in total, before they were finally ready to begin. Gráinne, who was Piper's mother, and one of the most selfless creatures I ever met, offered herself as host, but the process required a mind uncluttered by experience.'

'It turned out an unborn child was the perfect solution,' Piper said. 'The night before I was born, the earth passed through the Ookater Cloud and Mórríghan' – at this the girl tapped her forehead – 'took up residence as planned.'

'We would have protected Piper until she was old enough,' Jenna said. 'With Mórríghan's guidance, she could have shut down the *balla-dìon* before it even became aware of her presence. Unfortunately, things didn't happen like that.'

Her face tightened. 'Ériu was betrayed, killed alongside nearly everyone I ever loved. A few managed to break Gráinne out of Aberffraw Hall before it was overrun, but when the *balla-dìon* came back online it immediately intervened, destroying the convoy that helped her escape.' She glanced across at Edward. 'You stumbled across the wreckage minutes later. The rest of the story you know.'

'Actually, I don't,' he said. 'Not at all.' He looked at Jolyon. 'For a start, I don't have the first clue about your connection to all this.'

Jenna glanced across the picnic table at the artist. 'Once the four *Triallaichean* discovered they were stranded here, they went to ground pretty fast. They lacked the power to destroy the *balla-dìon* and yet their lives hung on its whim. While Eber stayed in Scotland, close to where they'd made landfall, Ériu escaped to Wales. Orla went to Cornwall and Drustan headed across the sea to Ireland.

'Over time, three of the four amassed small followings from the local populace; disciples, you might say. It's not quite how I'd describe my relationship with Ériu, but there's really no better word. Drustan was the exception. He was by far the youngest of the *Triallaichean*, and he couldn't accept that he was trapped here without a purpose. Eventually he sought out Ériu and asked for her help. If he was fated to make this his home, he wanted to experience it as a native. Ériu tried to change his mind but Drustan was adamant. He wrote himself a backstory for the man he wished to become, and handed her all his memories for safe-keeping. Then he went out into the world and forged himself a life.'

'Hang on. You're saying . . .'

'I'm saying that Jolyon Percival is the latest in a long line of personas our friend here has created for himself. I'm saying that whether he remembers or not, the man sitting opposite you is one of the four *Triallaichean* that arrived here, all those years ago.'

Edward stared.

He opened his mouth. No words would come.

'"Is it true?"' Jolyon asked. 'Is that your question?' The artist kicked off his flip-flops, leaned back in his chair and scratched his beard. 'It might be. I know it sounds crazy that I wouldn't know. But last night, after Piper and I had our conversation, I went back to the caravan and had a little wander through my head. My memories aren't what I thought. The last twenty years are sound, but if I try to go back any further, I draw a blank.' He scowled. 'And the memorabilia I've been carrying with me – it's all fake.'

'And you think, because of that . . .' Again, Edward felt himself running out of words.

'If you're asking if I trust what your daughter is telling me, I'll turn the question around: Do you?'

Edward blinked. He looked from Jolyon to his daughter and back. 'I trust her completely,' he said. 'When I think of everything that's happened over the last sixteen years I can't imagine a better explanation. It certainly explains how you saved our skins while we were trapped inside that van.' He gazed around the table at the members of the group. 'So to put this in some kind of order,' he said. 'Either Piper keeps running from the *balla-dìon*, the way we've been doing since the day she was born—'

'With the likelihood that one day it'll catch up with her,' Jenna added.

'Or . . .'

'Or,' Jolyon said, 'we go along with the original plan, help Piper kill this thing, and along the way give humanity the biggest mindfuck since Atari invented Pong.'

'All I care about is my daughter,' Edward said. 'If we destroy the *balla-dìon*, what's the catch?'

Jenna hesitated, glanced across at Piper.

'No catch,' the girl said.

They sat outside for another hour, listening to the cicadas and watching the stars. Jolyon retired first; Piper and Therron soon followed. Jenna disappeared inside the motorhome and returned with two cold bottles of Grolsch. She offered Edward one. He hesitated before accepting it.

'I know,' she said. 'It feels wrong, doesn't it?'

'We killed them. And now here we are, eating their food and drinking their beer.'

'And Piper's alive.'

Edward watched Jenna take the deckchair opposite. In the moonlight her hair shimmered like spun silk. He waited until she took a swig from her beer and then he asked: 'Are you telling me lies?'

The bottle clicked against her teeth. She swallowed, wiping her mouth. 'If there are a handful of people in the world I'd say you should trust, I'm one of them.'

'That's not an answer.'

'I'm not telling you lies.'

For a while neither of them spoke. Then Edward said: 'The music on those headphones you wear. It's a way of preventing the red light – the *balla-dìon,* I mean – from seeing you. Or using you.'

'Yes.'

'I get why Piper's never needed it. Jolyon, too, based on what you said. But why am I immune? There's nothing special about me. By all accounts it should've been able to do the same thing to me that it did to those people back at Joyau Caché.'

'You're right. Only the *Triallaichean* have any kind of natural immunity to the *balla-dìon*. But that night, sixteen years ago, when you stumbled across the convoy in Wales, Mórríghan took a chance on you. She made a huge amount of noise reaching out, and the effort she expended nearly killed Gráinne, but the situation, at the time, was pretty desperate.'

'So you're saying I was coerced?' he asked, frowning. 'Because if that's true, it makes Mórríghan no better than—'

'There was no coercion. And you were never a puppet. She gave you immunity, that's all. All the choices you made were your own.' Jenna swirled the contents of her bottle. 'Pretty incredible choices, I have to say.'

For a while he said nothing, unsure of how to respond. Then: 'Something else I've never understood.'

'Shoot.'

'The things Piper did when she was a child,' he said. 'Unnatural things. Stuff no other child could have done, or should.'

'Like what?'

Glancing up at the motorhome in which his daughter slept, Edward shared the story of the lamb resurrected at McAllister's farm, and the incident at the bistro in Grenoble that had led to a stranger's death.

'When you have two personalities knocking around in the same head, it gets crowded,' Jenna told him. 'If everything had gone as planned, Piper would have been taught control, separation. But that never happened. Mórríghan retained her ability to do those things. It seems Piper found ways to tap into that at times.' She paused. 'Almost like a teenager snatching the keys to her parents' car.'

They sat in silence, listening to the crackle of the campfire's flames. Jenna arched her back and yawned. She turned to him, her head tilted. 'Do you really, honestly, believe that?'

'Believe what?'

'That there's nothing special about you?'

Edward pulled himself to his feet, his cheeks darkening. He chugged the rest of his Grolsch and placed the empty bottle on the table. At the motorhome door, he muttered: 'Night.'

The helicopters came at dawn, appearing like two mosquitoes on the northern horizon. Their engines were a soft chatter at first, growing in power until they filled the sky. They swept low over the campsite, peeled apart and flew back in from the south.

Edward stood beneath the Frankia's awning and watched them land in the opposite field. Piper stood beside him, eyes narrowed against the dust and leaves the rotor blades whipped up. He put his arm around her shoulder and she smiled up at him, but he sensed her nervousness, wondered what thoughts were rushing through her head. Against his spine he felt the hard shape of the Glock. Last night, before catching a few hours' sleep, he had cleaned the weapon thoroughly. Three steel-jacketed hollow-point rounds remained in the magazine. Nowhere near enough to reassure him.

The helicopter doors sprang open and two men emerged, visoring their eyes with flattened palms.

Jenna turned to Edward. 'Time to go.'

Ducking his head, he led Piper and Therron to the nearest helicopter. A sandy-haired stranger wearing fatigues hustled him inside. Edward clipped himself in near the window, grabbed a set of headphones from a ceiling hook and pulled them on. The others found their seats and the doors closed.

Piper's hand sneaked into his. He glanced across at her, realising with a jolt that she'd never flown before. Some initiation. He squeezed her fingers.

Opposite, the man who had greeted them donned a headset. His voice was tinny in Edward's ears. 'I'm Mike O'Shea. We're going to get you out of here, Edward. There's a lot of people wanting to thank you for what you've done.'

He winced at that, looked around the passenger cabin. 'What's the range on this thing?'

'Three hundred miles, give or take, but we aren't going that far. Just to the nearest airfield.' O'Shea turned in his seat and signalled to the pilot. The rotor whine intensified and the ground began to recede. Piper's fingernails dug into Edward's palm.

They banked and flew north, rapidly gaining height. The sun was a white disc in the east, the sky pale with promise. Below them rolled soft Auvergne countryside. From such a vantage-point it was difficult to believe that the horrors they had so recently experienced were real. Once more Edward found himself thinking of the men and women who had died at

Joyau Caché. He cycled through the names of those he could recall, and the faces of those he could not. He had damned himself in those woods, had lost so much of his humanity he could never claim it back.

Edward watched his daughter as she gazed out of the window. To keep Piper safe, he would do it all again in an instant.

Forty minutes later they landed at a private airstrip. A medium-sized jet stood on the runway, its airstairs lowered. O'Shea led them across the tarmac. A minute later they were cocooned inside. This time Edward found himself beside Jolyon, in a row behind Piper and Therron. The jet's engines began to whistle and it rolled along the runway.

Jolyon's fingers sank into the grey leather armrests. 'Can't stand flying,' he muttered.

Piper glanced over the back of her seat, her expression mischievous. 'Kind of ironic.'

The man grunted, clenched his eyes shut. A few seconds later the jet was airborne.

Once they reached cruising altitude, Jenna unclipped her seat belt and came down the aisle. Edward looked at her splinted arm. 'How is it?'

She shrugged. 'O'Shea gave me some pills. Not sure what they were but they helped.'

'What's our flight time?'

'Hour, maybe. Hour and a half, tops.'

'Is there any wine on board this thing?' Jolyon asked. His fingers still gouged the seat leather. 'Whisky, vodka? Gin?'

'I'm sure there is.'

'Then would you please save my life and ask someone to locate it?'

'You know it's eight in the morning?'

'And I've hardly slept,' the artist replied. 'Which means for me it's still last night, and a very long one at that.'

Jenna smiled. 'We'll turn the place upside down for you.'

Jolyon watched her retreat up the aisle and scratched wistfully at his beard. 'Good hips.'

Edward ignored him.

'Ah,' the man said, rocking back in his seat. 'Knew it. Saw it last night, when we were sitting round the fire. Saw it again this morning, too.'

'Saw what?'

'Don't be coy, man. It's as clear as Jupiter.'

Edward flushed with irritation. 'If you think, for one minute, that after—'

'What I *think*,' Jolyon hissed, keeping his head low, 'is that you should take your comforts where you find them. We don't, any of us, know how long we've got left.'

Within an hour they ran out of land. The English Channel slid beneath them. Across its surface, yachts, passenger ferries, trawlers and freighters carved sharp white lines. From the position of the sun he saw that the aircraft followed a north-westerly bearing. Soon England's coastline loomed into view: rocky cliffs and sand beaches defending patchwork farmland. The jet banked west and began to lose height, pushing into Cornwall. Edward's ears popped with equalising pressure.

They landed ten minutes later, within sight of the jagged northern coast. Their airfield, a single strip that looked hardly long enough to accommodate their jet, seemed devoid of life. Someone must have been manning the tiny control tower but Edward saw no ground crew, no immigration officials or security. The jet taxied to a stop and its airstairs deployed. A damp wind coiled in, ruffling napkins and papers.

Jenna led them outside. Three black SUVs waited on the runway, their doors slung open. Edward slid into the back of one of them beside Piper and Therron. Moments later the convoy swept out of the airfield, following a road that looped north towards the coast. Every now and then he caught sight of the emerald ocean, opposed by limestone outcrops and granite bluffs and raked by white breakers.

Ten minutes later the vehicles turned a bend and Edward saw, on a dramatic peninsula linked to the mainland by a sea-battered razor of slate, the ancient fortification known for eons as Crafter's Keep.

CHAPTER 52

Crafter's Keep, Cornwall

The castle's outer walls rose from the peninsula like a dark fossil chipped from the surrounding rock. One of its four drum towers had long ago collapsed into the sea, but those that remained looked formidable. Climbing high inside the fortified walls rose the inner keep itself. Its crenellated battlements lent it the appearance of a lower jaw thrust aggressively towards the mainland, but the defiance of its expression had been visibly abraded by time. Some of its merlons had crumbled like rotten teeth. Others appeared wind-pocked and raw.

It was, nevertheless, an edifice of undeniable grandeur. A narrow bridge of stone connected it to the headland, arcing over a three-hundred-foot drop to the fin-shaped rocks below. A stout barbican of grey stone defended the bridgehead, itself accessed by a chained drawbridge spanning a deep ravine. The flag of St Piran – a white cross on a black field – fluttered from a pole on its curtain wall.

'Scary,' Piper muttered, staring at the drum towers. Edward glanced at his daughter and saw at once that her comment belied her mood. Her eyes were bright, more with excitement than apprehension.

He shifted in his seat and felt the butt of the Glock pressing against his spine, a silent reminder of his task. He had not forgotten the story Piper had told around the campfire. Working together, three of the *Triallaichean* had arranged Mórríghan's return, choosing a date and time that should have guaranteed the safety of everyone involved. And yet it hadn't. Ériu, architect of the plan, had been murdered, along with most of her followers. Sixteen years later, the traitor had still not been found.

The cars stopped close to the barbican's entrance. Before Edward climbed out he leaned over to Therron. 'It's up to us to keep her safe in there,' he muttered. 'You see anything that alarms you, you let me know straight away.'

The boy nodded, his mouth a firm line.

'If you'll follow me,' O'Shea said. He led them through the barbican, a roofed passage between fortified walls punctuated by murder holes and arrow slits.

'How old is it?' Piper asked, her voice echoing off the stones.

'There's been a fort here, of some kind or another, since the Iron Age,' the man told her. 'The Romans occupied it for a while. After that it became a stronghold for Dumnonian royalty, but a lot of what you're seeing now is Norman in design, built on Anglo-Saxon foundations. Bits and pieces were added in the twelfth century. Fourteenth, too.'

They emerged into strong daylight. Ahead, the slender bridge Edward had seen on arrival linked the barbican to the castle's main gatehouse and the peninsula on which it stood. A slip over the side would result in a plummet hundreds of feet to the rocks below. As they approached, a salt wind snatched at their clothes. Around the peninsula's base the sea swelled greedily. Waves burst apart in glorious explosions of spray.

On the far side of the bridge, standing with her back to Crafter's Keep, stood a woman all alone. Edward's skin raised into goosebumps when he saw her. He suddenly felt very insignificant indeed.

CHAPTER 53

Crafter's Keep, Cornwall

She was, without doubt, the fiercest and most coldly beautiful woman Edward had ever seen. Orla stood as tall as he, her body framed by the gatehouse arch behind her. Even from this distance, her eyes froze him with their intensity. Her features were Celtic and sharply defined: high forehead, oval face, narrow, pointed nose. She wore her hair in a simple braid, the tails of her frock coat flickering behind her like a serpent's tongue.

Edward straightened his spine, forcing himself to endure her examination and conduct one of his own. But he was no equal in that contest, and her attention lingered on him mere moments before it locked, in its entirety, on Piper.

On seeing the girl, the ferocity in the woman's expression took flight, replaced by unalloyed joy. Her arms opened wide and her eyes filled with tears.

Edward felt a shiver of movement through the stones at his feet. Piper's hand slipped from his own, and when he looked at her face he saw an expression like none he had previously encountered. Breaking from his side, the girl bounded across the bridge with no regard for the winds that assailed it. She ran into Orla's outstretched arms and they spun around, locked together.

Jenna appeared beside Edward, threading her hand through his arm. She tugged at him. 'Come on. Let me introduce you.'

Together they crossed the bridge, cormorants crying and wheeling beneath them. He tasted salt on his lips, smelled seaweed and damp rock. Ahead, Orla and Piper stood with their foreheads touching in silent communion. They parted as he reached them, and Orla faced him.

This close, the woman's scrutiny was almost too much to bear, and in enduring it he acknowledged that everything Piper had told him about her must be true. He felt his cheeks colouring; he dropped his head.

'Edward Schwinn,' Orla said. Her voice was mellifluous, deep. 'I won't offer you my gratitude because I know you wouldn't accept it, but you have my admiration.' She examined him a moment longer. Then she leaned in and kissed his cheek. This time, when she spoke, her words were breath in his ear. 'Your role in this isn't over.'

With that, Orla stepped back and smiled. She turned to Jolyon and her smile grew wider still. 'Brother,' she said. 'Can we dare to hope that your wanderings are at an end?'

Jolyon blinked. 'Brother?' he repeated. His eyes travelled over Orla's face, drank in every inch of her body. He scratched his beard and sighed wistfully. 'By Jupiter that's unfortunate.'

They were given quarters in the upper levels of Crafter's Keep. Edward found himself in a tower room with palatial views of the sea. Four hundred feet below his window, the Atlantic smashed itself against the peninsula's rocks.

The room boasted a four-poster bed and an enormous carved oak chest. Edward ran his hands over the wood, and through his fingers felt the memories of its making. For a while he simply stood there, communing through touch. Then he thought of the guitar he had been making for Piper's birthday – and had been forced to abandon back at Joyau Caché – and his pleasure waned.

He heard a knock at the door. Jenna walked in, clutching a wash bag and a bundle of white towels. She looked scrubbed and clean, a fresh cast on her arm. Two men followed her, carrying between them a copper tub. They set it down on the flagstone floor and returned with pails of steaming water.

Jenna offered him a half-smile. 'We're a little medieval around here, but I thought you might appreciate a soak. Someone's organising new clothes for you. I had to guess your size.' She turned up her nose. 'I think they're burning what was left of mine.'

'Thanks.'

Jenna nodded, shrugged, caught herself and laughed. 'I'll leave these on the bed,' she told him, indicating the wash bag and towels.

Edward soaked himself for twenty minutes. In the bag he found a razor and tiny mirror and shaved off his beard. Outside his door he found a pile of fresh clothes: underwear, belt, jeans, shirt and boots. He dressed quickly, tucked the Glock inside his waistband and struck out in search of the armoury.

At the top of Crafter's Keep, Piper stood between two crumbling merlons and stared out to sea. From such a lofty position it was a compelling sight, but Piper's attention wasn't really on the view.

'How's your head?' she asked.

Therron touched a finger to the bruising near his right ear. 'Think it'll be a while before I can concentrate on Dumas.'

Piper grinned. 'Strictly Dr Seuss from now on.'

'Remind me what you hit me with.'

'The stock of Dad's rifle.'

'You don't mess about.'

'I'm a knock-out kind of girl.'

Therron screwed up his face. 'Did you just think of that?' he asked. 'Or have you been working on it?'

'Spent about a day on that one. Was it worth it, do you think? Was it funny?'

He tilted his head. 'I think it could be. If you improved the delivery a little.'

Piper leaned forward and kissed him, and for a minute or two they stayed locked together that way, while the wind tried to separate them. Finally, she pulled away and stared back out to sea. 'What was it like, at the chalet, when the *balla-dìon* took you?'

'I've never known anything like it,' he said. 'It felt . . . it felt like I was touching God, in a way. I know that's a terrible thing to say, considering what it tried to make me do. All I wanted was to please it, to give myself up to it. I didn't care about you, about Edward, about anything.'

'What did it want?'

Therron grimaced. 'It wanted to kill you, Pie. Wanted to stop *you* from killing *it*. Funny thing is, it seemed almost sad about it. But it's convinced that what you're doing is wrong. And not just wrong but fatal. For you, for it, for everyone it's tried so hard to protect.'

Piper was quiet for a long while. 'And what do *you* think?'

'I think, when the time comes, you'll do the right thing.'

'You really believe that? Even after having the *balla-dìon* in your head?'

He shrugged. 'I love you. I trust you. What else is there to say?'

'I wish I had your confidence in my fundamental goodness.'

Therron followed her gaze out to sea. 'I'm not sure I said anything about your fundamental goodness.'

'You didn't?'

'Pretty sure I didn't.'

'Oh,' she replied. 'That was me?'

Solemnly, he nodded.

Piper waited, counted to ten. 'Was *that* funny?'

Her throat constricted as she watched him. She knew their time together was running out.

★ ★ ★

Jolyon Percival stood in the Great Hall beside its vast oriel windows and watched the woman who claimed to be his sister pour him a goblet of wine.

The room was so splendidly appointed that he struggled to contain his awe. Its floor was laid with encaustic tiles that looked medieval in origin; they displayed a repeating heraldic motif in red and white clay. Stone walls rose thirty feet to a barrelled roof of oak. Alcoves displayed armour suits polished to a mirror shine. Behind them hung tapestries so old that their subjects could hardly be grasped. At one end of the hall stood a feasting table with three branching extensions, like the tines of a fork. On a dais, Jolyon saw a row of intricately carved chairs. None was more impressively decorated than another.

He took the goblet from Orla and tipped its contents down his throat.

'That's Chateau Latour, 1961,' she told him. 'You're meant to savour it.'

Jolyon held out his empty goblet. 'I'll definitely go slow with the second bottle.'

'It's eleven o' clock in the morning.'

He belched. 'Very slow.'

'It's good to have you back, Drustan.'

Jolyon waited while she topped him up. He took a sip this time, before knocking back the rest of it. 'It's a lot to take in.'

'I can imagine.'

'You've lived here how long?'

'For most of its history.'

'You're looking good for it.'

Orla smiled, wryly. 'Thank you.'

'What I don't understand – you say I've been here as long as you.'

'You, me, Ériu, Eber.'

'Which means, presumably, I could have had something just

like this.' He used his empty goblet to gesture around him at the Great Hall. 'My own castle, suits of armour, wine cellars.' He paused, scratched his beard. 'And instead of all that, I've been living out of a tatty suitcase, slopping around France like some witless hobo. Am I a complete and utter buffoon?'

'Come with me,' Orla told him.

He followed her through the keep, along dark corridors and down spiral stairs. With each level they descended, the walls and ceiling grew closer. Finally they arrived at the mouth of a claustrophobic passage without any light at all. Orla flicked on a penlight torch and led him down it. By now they were deep inside the peninsula rock itself. The floor was uneven, slick with water; the air smelled of minerals and damp.

At last they arrived at a squat iron-banded door, rust-flecked but solid. Orla produced a key and unlocked it. The door groaned as it swung open. She beckoned him inside.

It was a tiny space, with just enough room for a man to lie down. On a stone shelf in the far wall, Jolyon spied a long mahogany case. Orla closed the door and drew him towards it. 'You don't remember this, I know, but when the four of us began our journey at Mórríghan's request, our instructions were simple: discover why the *balla-dìon* continued to operate and report back. When we arrived, we made contact with it as planned. Cathasach's personality seemed intact. We even conversed. Later, without warning, or any provocation, he destroyed our ship. We had no way of leaving after that. We lacked the means to broadcast a message out, or destroy the *balla-dìon* itself.'

Orla paused. 'I can't begin to explain what it felt like, knowing that we were stranded. Shortly afterwards, we went our separate ways. Ériu fled to Wales. I came here. Eber retreated to the Highlands.'

'And me?' Jolyon asked.

'You were the worst affected of all.' She laid a hand on his arm. 'Perhaps it was harder because you were so much younger than the rest of us.'

'Younger?'

Dismissively, Orla gestured at herself. 'Don't let this deceive you. The *balla-dìon* is a curse for the planet and for humanity, but by tapping its power we have, at least, kept ourselves young.' She squeezed his arm. 'You didn't want that, Drustan. You wanted to escape and you couldn't, and yet you refused to be a prisoner.'

'Which is why I went to see Ériu with that tomfool idea.'

She bit her lip. 'Checking up on you became quite the sport. That first life, you ended up living with a madwoman called Ezredith on the coast of what became Norfolk. Nine kids, if I remember correctly, five of whom survived infancy. You spent forty years digging the same strip of land and trying rather unsuccessfully to grow turnips.'

'Sounds delightful,' he muttered.

'Trust me,' Orla replied. 'In the early years that rated as one of your better experiences.' She led him closer to the mahogany case. 'Each time your life was drawing to its natural close, Ériu arrived and revealed the truth to you. She stored the memories of the life you'd lived and helped you begin again.'

Orla opened the case. On a bed of blue silk, Jolyon saw what looked like fifty or sixty mason jars. Their contents swirled, emitting a soft amber light.

'The night Ériu was murdered at Aberffraw Hall, I rescued these. I thought you might want them.'

'Want them?' Jolyon began, unable to take his eyes from the case's contents. 'How do I . . . What do I . . .'

'You just need to touch them,' Orla told him.

Jolyon reached out his hand. He hesitated, then snatched it back. 'I'm not sure I can.'

'This is who you are,' she said. 'Earlier you asked me why you hadn't lived as one of us. Here's your answer. This is what you did instead. Every one of these casks holds a life full of memories; people, places, passions. I joked about it earlier, but you've lived more richly than any of us.'

'I don't know where to start.'

Orla pointed. 'See the lighter one? That's the most recent. Perhaps it might be easiest to start there and work back.'

Jolyon licked his lips, stared. Then he reached out his hand to the jar. Touched its surface.

Returned.

They ate dinner that night in the Great Hall. It was not an occasion that Edward enjoyed. Beforehand he gathered with Piper, Therron, Jolyon and Jenna in one of the galleries over-looking the Cornish coast. A woman joined them, dressed in the same quasi-military garb that many of the keep's inhabitants seemed to favour. She carried herself confidently but with no hint of arrogance. On the way to the Great Hall she introduced herself as Nora Kinraid.

'Most senior of Orla's followers,' Jenna whispered to Edward, as they walked.

Nora reached a pair of tall oak doors, which opened at her approach. Inside the Great Hall, flames danced in three huge fireplaces. Chandeliers and candelabras glittered with candle-light. Around the three-pronged banqueting table sat far more of Ériu's retinue than Edward had expected to see. His discomfort increased tenfold when they stood as one and began to applaud.

Red-faced, he took a seat beside Piper. But however much he hated all the attention focused on his party, he could not help but be moved by the majesty of what he witnessed. It felt, in a way, as if he had been transported back in time one thousand years.

They dined first on lobster; after that, on roasted peacock. The birds had been stuffed with fowl in ever-decreasing size: goose, pheasant, chicken, duck, partridge, quail, squab, snipe and finally an ortolan stuffed with a single oyster.

Beside him, Jolyon dug into his platter with the relish of a man long-starved. The artist threw down glass after glass of red wine, wiping his beard on the back of his hand and greedily eyeing the assembled women.

Edward ate in silence, conscious at all times of the pistol he wore on a holster strapped to his leg. His visit to the armoury had yielded both the holster and a full reload for the Glock. As well as the gun, he also carried a boot knife, and three spare magazines in pouches on his belt.

After the meal Orla gave a speech, formally welcoming her guests to Crafter's Keep. She spoke more loosely about their task and what must happen next, but Edward saw that everyone in the room knew the significance of their presence. They filed from the Great Hall a few hours later, retiring to a well-appointed chamber dedicated to the observation of the stars. Doors opened onto a broad balcony, where a huge motor-driven telescope pointed at the heavens.

'I know you found that uncomfortable,' Orla told Edward. 'But the people in there have been searching for you and Piper for sixteen years, and they'll have a huge role, too, in what comes next. It was important that we recognised that tonight.'

'You still haven't found your traitor.'

'No. But I don't believe that anyone you'll meet at Crafter's Keep has anything but good intentions for the pair of you.'

Edward said nothing in response. Orla's admission was all the justification he needed for his unease.

Cameron Kinraid, first son of Eber, crouched behind a tree on the south bank of the Tarn river and watched the gendarmes pour into Joyau Caché. Two helicopters hovered overhead, their searchlights providing illumination to those on the ground. Emergency vehicles parked nose to tail, lights flashing. A line of private ambulances moved slowly along the loop.

Cameron had arrived half an hour before the first responders, witnessing for himself the massacre that had occurred here. With each new victim he discovered, he grew more convinced that he would find the girl for whom they had searched for so long. But somehow, as he walked among the bodies, that most gruesome of discoveries never came. Slowly, Cameron's dejection transformed into quiet hope.

Yet if Mórríghan's host *had* survived, as he was beginning to believe, then where had she gone? He watched two paramedics lift the corpse of a middle-aged woman into a body bag and grimaced. Such was the scale of the tragedy at Joyau Caché that the search would now be joined by those with no clue what the girl represented. If she were to stand any chance of surviving long enough to complete her task, then Cameron had to find her, and soon.

Thinking of the girl's vulnerability led him, inevitably, to thoughts of his own children; and they, in turn, led to thoughts of his wife.

Cameron found himself dialling her number even before consciously retrieving his phone from his jacket.

Nora Kinraid answered on the seventh ring. 'It's late,' she said.

'You don't sound tired.'

'I am.'

He paused, sensed the conversation already spiralling beyond his control. 'How are the kids?'

'They're not kids,' she said. 'You could speak to them yourself.'

Cameron watched the two paramedics zipper the body bag and lift it onto a gurney. 'I'm bound to ask. Have you and Orla had any success? Any hint of the girl's whereabouts?'

'No.'

'Nothing at all?'

'Do you think I'd lie to you about that?'

He filled his lungs. Sighed.

'Where are you?' Nora asked.

Cameron watched the paramedics unfurl another body bag and thought: *I'm in hell, that's where I am; I'm in hell, cut off from my wife and kids, and from the sound of her voice, there's no way back.*

A pause, on the line. 'Cam?'

'Yeah?'

He heard Nora's quiet breathing. 'Nothing.'

The line went dead.

Cameron closed his eyes and leaned back against the tree, clasping the phone to his chest. So long since she'd called him that; but he had learned to avoid looking for hopeful signs where none could be found.

Next, he dialled his father.

'Tell me,' Eber said.

'Something bad happened here, but I can't find the girl among the dead.'

'I knew ye wouldn't.'

'Why not?'

'Because I know where she is.'

Heart beginning to thump, Cameron pushed himself away from the tree. 'Where?'

'Ye won't like it.'

'If you've found her, I won't care.'

Eber told him.

Cameron listened. Then he shook his head. 'That's impossible.' But as his father talked he began to realise that nothing, any longer, was impossible. 'Why would Orla lie to us?' he asked. And, in his head, he added the question he could not bear to voice: *Why would Nora lie, too?*

The answer to *that* was too dreadful to contemplate.

A few hours later, Edward found himself alone inside the chapel at Crafter's Keep. After the meal – with Piper immersed in an impenetrable conversation with Orla – he had stepped outside for some air. His hosts seemed happy for him to wander the castle grounds unaccompanied, so he decided to investigate the cluster of buildings that stood inside the fortified perimeter wall.

When he came to the chapel and found its doors unlocked, he slipped inside.

In an alcove, a rack of votive candles offered the only illumination. Their tiny flames bobbed and weaved, hostage to the draughts that twined through the building. At the far end, in what would usually be a chancel, he saw an apse complete with stained-glass windows, lit behind by stars and moon.

Edward recognised none of the imagery he saw etched upon the glass; but such was its beauty that he felt himself drawn closer. Near the altar, he squeezed into a pew and sat there gazing up at the iconography. For a while his head emptied and he existed untroubled by thought. Gradually, he became aware that he was alone in here no longer. He glanced around, and saw that Jenna had entered the chapel and was standing, now, in the nave on his right. His heart beat a little faster at the discovery, but it was neither fear nor shame that drove it.

Jenna offered no words of greeting as she slid into the pew beside him. She bowed her head, as if in prayer. After a while she took his hand.

That gentle sharing of touch seemed the only communication that either of them needed. Edward felt the warmth of her skin, felt her thumb trace patterns along his index finger.

Finally, she lifted her head. 'I didn't expect to find you here.'

'I'm not even sure why I came.'

'Really?'

Edward's gaze remained on the apse window, at the figures etched upon the glass. 'This church,' he said. 'It seems a little out of place.'

'Why would you say that?'

He shrugged.

'You think because we're not alone in the universe there's no room for God?'

'That's not what I meant.'

'What, then?'

'I don't know.' He took a breath. 'This isn't like any other church I've seen.'

'It isn't, not quite. And yet in some ways it's exactly the same as all the others.'

'I don't recognise any of the imagery.'

'You won't.'

'Did we have it all wrong?'

She moved closer, and Edward felt the warmth of her body against his. There was an inevitability to her, now. When Jenna pressed her mouth to his, he did not pull away.

High above the peninsula, the moon shed its light on a restless ocean.

Eber – second eldest of the four *Triallaichean*, and the only one to have produced offspring – hurried across the unlit road to the barbican of Crafter's Keep. He knew his approach was observed by the two guards he had seen on the battlements, but that did not bother him. As long as he was quick.

He met the first of Orla's guards just beyond the drawbridge. '*Trobhad*,' he whispered, '*Trobhad*.'

The guard shook his head as if he sought to ward off a wasp. Eber crept forward and touched the man's forehead. '*Caidil*,' he said. When the guard went limp, Eber eased him down onto the cobbles.

Above him, murder holes permitted a little of the moon's light. He concentrated, muttered a word and heard two bodies on the ramparts fall with a thump.

A fourth guard – this one a woman – came out of the darkness just as he emerged from the barbican. '*Trobhad*,' the old man whispered. '*Trobhad*.' When he touched her face she collapsed as if her strings had been cut, so quickly that he failed to catch her. Her skull cracked against the cobbles; blood began to fill the spaces between them. Eber regretted that, but he could spare no time to tend her.

Looking back through the shadowed passage, he cupped his

hands around his mouth and called. From out of the darkness they crept. First five, then ten, then thirty. He passed a hand across his brow, surprised to find it beaded.

He wouldn't save everyone, but he'd save as many as he could.

Chapter 54

Mid-Atlantic

Pastor Benjamin D. Pope sat at the back of the Boeing 747 beside Wendy Devereaux and watched the Atlantic Ocean sweep by thirty thousand feet beneath him.

They'd been in the air seven hours now, taking off from Austin-Bergstrom earlier that day. Wendy had raided the Church of the Holy Sacrament's bloated savings account and chartered the entire flight, meaning that three-quarters of the four hundred seats were empty.

While most of Benjamin's volunteers had chosen to travel in first class or business, he had decided that it would be inappropriate to join them, preferring to sit here in coach and set them the example of austerity. Over the last forty-eight hours he had witnessed behaviour – displayed by both himself and by some of his flock – that had begun to concern him. The church's members seemed energised by their task, excited beyond measure, and of course that was entirely natural. What worried Benjamin was how frenzied some of that enthusiasm had grown, how – in some senses – animalistic.

The pastor heard laughter peal out of business class, followed by the tinkle of broken glass. He frowned, sat up in his seat. 'What's going on up there?'

Wendy smiled. 'They're just blowin' off steam. Havin' a little fun.'

He glanced across at her. She had arrived at the airport

wearing a denim skirt cut to mid-thigh, a white cotton top and sneakers. Her legs were tanned to a hazelnut shade; the skin looked as smooth as toffee.

Wendy slanted her head. 'Pastor, are you checking me out?'

Benjamin jumped in his seat. 'I was just thinking that it's October. Where we're going it's likely to be cold.'

'I've got warmer things, don't worry.' She crossed her legs, smiled. 'Appreciate you thinking of me, though.'

Wendy pressed the button on her seat and reclined it a few inches. The angle revealed more fully the slopes of her breasts. Benjamin swallowed hard. When his gaze fell on the hand she had draped over the seat rest, he saw that she had painted her fingernails with tangerine lacquer. A thought bloomed, shockingly explicit. He grunted, shook his head free of it.

Ahead, the curtain partitioning business class trembled and two people spilled through: Lila Ruiz and Mike Zawisza. They seemed unsteady as they walked up the aisle. Mike dangled a bottle of Coors from his fingers. He tossed the pastor a grin and Lila giggled. They disappeared into the back of the plane. Benjamin heard the snick of the toilet latch, followed a few moments later by the steady thud of the concertina door rocking in its groove.

Wendy glanced up at him. 'Just blowin' off steam,' she repeated. When she licked her lips, he stared in fascination at the bead of saliva left by her tongue.

He closed his eyes. Counted to ten. 'I think,' he said, 'I'm going to go up front.'

'What for?'

'I believe it's time we all prayed.' Sliding into the aisle, he dipped his hand into his pants pocket. His fingers found the locket he kept there and, for a brief moment, he found peace. But whose jewellery it was, and why it brought him such relief, the pastor had long since ceased to remember.

* * *

Three hours later, they landed at Glasgow airport. Benjamin had expected to leave the aircraft and file through customs with the rest of his congregation. Instead, four glaze-eyed immigration officials boarded the aircraft. They checked passports wearing vacant expressions and left without speaking a word. Urchardan had handled all destination-side arrangements; Benjamin saw that the man did not intend to leave anything to chance.

Outside, two motorised boarding ramps moved against the exit hatches. A belt loader appeared, a cargo truck following behind. The pastor watched a group of ground staff begin to transfer luggage from the aircraft's hold to the waiting vehicle. He saw a dolly loaded with cases containing the M4 carbines. Within a few minutes he was standing on the tarmac, waiting as three tour buses pulled up beside the aircraft. A ring of emergency vehicles, lights flashing, maintained a secure perimeter. Every time Benjamin spied an operator's face he recognised the same vacant smile.

Is that how I look? When it's in me?

He flinched at the thought, steadied himself.

Wendy frowned. 'What's up?'

'Just tired.'

But it wasn't that. For the first time since his experience in the Frank Irwin Center he had thought of the Bliss not as a *He*, but an *It*.

'I don't know where we're going,' Wendy muttered, rubbing her arms, 'but I sure hope they have a sauna.'

The door to the lead coach hissed open. Aiden Urchardan stepped out. His hair, beneath the missionary hat, glimmered silver in the airport lights. He walked over, arms outstretched.

Benjamin accepted the older man's embrace, unaccountably relieved to see him. 'We need to talk,' he said.

'Of course,' Urchardan replied. 'How was your flight?'

'Eventful.'

'In a good way, I hope.'

'For some of us.'

'Well, no sense in dawdling. Let's get these good folk loaded. Then we can have our little chat.'

'Where are we headed?'

'All in good time, Pastor.'

The man turned to Wendy, flashed white teeth.

CHAPTER 55

Crafter's Keep, Cornwall

Edward Schwinn woke with a gasp, heart clattering in his chest. He could not see the ceiling from where he lay, but he could see Laura's face, even as the dream faded. Her eyes – the last things to disappear – seemed to beseech him.

He rolled onto his side and noticed, immediately, Jenna's shape. A spill of moonlight had fallen across the bed, revealing the milk-white curves of her ribs. Her chest rose and fell in slumber.

Edward turned his face away. Was the dream simply penance for souring Laura's memory with intimacy? Perhaps.

He swung his legs over the side of the bed, grimacing at the old pain in his knee. The flagstones were cold beneath his feet. He retrieved his clothes, pulling them on as quietly as he could. On a side table lay his pistol in its holster. He picked it up, carrying it with his boots to the door of Jenna's room. Casting a last look back at her, he slipped into the corridor. He passed Therron's room, then Piper's, and crept into his own. At the window, he peered out over the Atlantic. White breakers surged beneath a hunter's moon. He could hear the crash of surf against the peninsula's rocks.

Listening to it, Edward felt the skin on his forearms pucker into goosebumps. He wondered why he felt his muscles swelling, his abdomen draining of blood. Was it an after-effect of the dream, or something far more sinister? He listened to the silence inside the keep.

Something's wrong.

A thought with no evidence to sustain it. But Edward had learned, long ago, to trust his instincts.

Going to the chest opposite the bed, he retrieved the spare magazines he had taken from the armoury and clipped them to his belt. He stepped into his boots and laced them. Strapped on his holster. Let himself out of the room. Hurried to Piper's door. Opened it.

Inside, the girl had shuttered the windows, banishing the moonlight. Edward felt his way towards her bed. 'Pie,' he whispered. 'Wake up.'

No answer.

He found the edge of the mattress, moved his hand across it.

Empty.

Orla stood beside the window of her solar and stared up at the ancient tapestry sewn into the heavens. She could not see her home among the stars, but the possibility that one day others might filled her with hope.

She sipped from her wine and stepped back from the window. Frowning, she raised her glass and studied the reflections in its facets. Behind her, something detached itself from the darkness and slipped closer.

Orla took a breath, captured it in her chest. 'How did you know?'

'I put a watch on the place.'

Hearing his voice, she closed her eyes and let the air trickle from her lungs. 'It grieves me to know that I was right to keep the secret.'

'It grieves me to uncover it.'

'Ériu loved you,' she said. 'You more than any of us.'

'I loved her, too.'

Orla turned. When she saw the old sword Eber wore at his side, she smiled despite her grief; he looked faintly ridiculous. 'I recognise that blade.'

'It's the one Drustan forged, during that life he lived as a blacksmith.' The old man unsheathed the weapon, angling it. 'I wielded this beside Áedán mac Gabráin,' he said, and in his eyes Orla saw a glint of pride.

Too human, she thought. *All too human. That has become our fate.*

'You never could resist a fight,' she told him.

'Aye, true enough.'

'Back then you fought for what was right.'

'The world is safer as it is. We don't need it changed.'

'That's not your reason.'

'Don't do this,' Eber said. 'It isnae too late.'

'Not too late for what?'

'For ye. Ye don't want to die tonight.'

Orla's eyes flashed. 'You think I care about such a trifling thing?'

'You've lived here too long. I wullnae believe it's left nae mark.'

'We *agreed* to this, Eber. All those years ago, we *agreed* to bring her back.'

'No, we didnae agree. You and Ériu agreed. Ye heard my objections, chose to ignore them.'

'But the alternative—'

'Is what? This? Life? Peace? Ye would jeopardise all that for an idea? Maybe Ériu could have done so, but not ye.' His eyes flattened. 'Ye know why I'm here. The girl dies tonight. Quietly and without pain. I'll do the deed myself, take the burden as ma'own. She wullnae suffer, I promise ye.'

'No,' said a voice from the darkness. 'She won't.'

A stiletto blade appeared against Eber's throat, nicking the pouched skin. A bright bead of blood swelled on steel.

Orla covered her mouth with her hands. Of all the deaths

she could have suffered, this one, she knew, would be the cruellest.

Edward moved from the bed to the windows and threw open the shutters. Moonlight poured in, silvering the stonework. It revealed a room empty of Piper and her clothes. He pivoted on his good knee and limped into the corridor. It was so dark he could barely see. He worked his way down it, one hand pressed against the wall. The next room along was Therron's. He felt for the door, opened it. Stepped inside.

Therron's shutters were open to the night. The boy lay on the canopy bed, asleep. Beside him lay Piper. She blinked and sat up, clutching the sheet to her throat.

'Get dressed,' Edward told her.

'What is it?'

'I don't know. Bad feeling. We're getting out of here.'

Piper remained still for less than a second. Then she slipped out of bed, sheet wrapped around her. 'Can you give me a second?'

'I'll be outside.'

The girl emerged moments later, fully dressed.

'Where's Therron?' he asked. 'Didn't you wake him?'

Piper's voice cracked. 'He stays.'

Edward frowned. 'Pie, we can't leave him. I gave him my word. I promised him I'd never do that.'

'Dad, if he comes with us, he won't survive.'

'How can you—'

'Dad, *please*. You've got a bad feeling. So have I. It's worth a broken promise to save his life.'

Edward weighed that. Silent, he took her hand. Together they hurried up the corridor, using what little light spilled from Therron's room to guide them. They reached a corner and swerved around it. Ahead stretched a long gallery. Windows along one side offered a view into the keep. Edward saw black-clad figures down there, darting among the buildings. As he watched them he heard movement from the far end of the gallery. Looking up, he saw the silhouettes of two men emerge from the gloom.

Orla stared, mesmerised, as Nora Kinraid emerged into the light.

The woman kept the point of the stiletto blade pressed to her father-in-law's throat. 'It was you,' Nora said, addressing the old man. 'The attack on Aberffraw Hall, Ériu's killing, all those others deaths.'

Eber lifted his chin. '*A ghràidh*,' he said. 'Whatever it is that you're thinking, it's important that ye listen tae me right now.'

'Does Cameron know?' she asked, her throat bobbing. 'Is my husband in on this, too?'

The old man stared, and now his eyes filled with pain. 'Cameron's innocent. Of everything.'

'I don't understand,' Nora said. 'After all the years that have passed, what possible reason could you have for aligning yourself with the *balla-dìon*?'

Eber held his daughter-in-law's gaze for a long moment. Then he switched his attention to Orla, and his mouth hardened. 'She doesn't know,' he said. 'Ye havenae told her what will happen if the girl succeeds.'

Lips pressed together tightly lest his harried breathing give him away, Edward backed behind a stone pillar, pulling Piper with him. They stood in the darkness, silent, listening for the intruders' approach. Footsteps as soft as slippered feet whispered down the gallery towards them.

Edward put one hand on his pistol, ready to draw it, but the weapon would be a last resort. He had seen perhaps twenty black-clad figures outside; he had no wish to alert them to his position.

The two intruders padded towards the pillar and froze, so close that Edward could smell their sweat. He heard one of them breathing, a shallow nasal rasp. They must be standing right beside the large gallery windows, looking down into the quad.

Edward's left knee popped.

The sound was a rifle-crack in the silence. He winced, both in pain and in dismay. Heard the scrape of leather on stone and wondered if his adversaries were spreading out around him. His fingers tightened on the pistol's grip.

No safety switch on the Glock, he reminded himself. Aim, pull, fire.

From the other side of the pillar he heard movement: the sound of the two intruders walking along the gallery in the direction Edward had come.

He allowed himself a shallow breath. Then, still clutching his daughter's hand, he edged out from behind the pillar, crept past the gallery windows and turned the corner. There he saw a row of doors, some closed and some hanging ajar. As he passed the first open doorway a pair of arms shot out, dragging him and Piper inside.

'Tell me what?' Nora asked, her eyes fixed on her father-in-law.

Despite the blade held at his throat, Eber ignored her. He kept his focus on Orla. 'I take it from that,' he said, 'that ye have not.'

'Have you told your son?' the woman countered.

He shook his head. 'Until now there's been nae need. After all, I'm not the one who's been pressing for this outcome. I've been fighting tooth and nail against it.'

'Tell me what?' Nora demanded, glancing between the two *Triallaichean*. 'What is it I don't know?'

'Have ye really become that arrogant,' Eber asked, his attention still on Orla, 'that ye would solicit support from your followers without even explaining tae them the consequences?' He turned to his daughter-in-law, and his eyes narrowed. 'She lied to ye, *a ghràidh*, by omission if nothing else. Let me answer your question with another. For how long have ye allied yourself to Orla?'

'You know the answer to that.'

'Of course I do. What I'm wondering is whether *ye* remember. Because it's *hundreds* of years, isn't it? And do ye think that this remarkable longevity of yours, since Orla plucked ye from obscurity, is a coincidence? No. You're not that stupid. Nobody ever talks about it but the inference is clear enough. It's a reward for your loyalty. Now, let's consider your children's longevity. Those glorious bairns ye delivered, men and women grown: Adeline, Simon, Kyla, Megan.

'Orla never approved of me fathering children, ye know. Neither did Ériu. And do ye know why? Because she worried I would grow too attached to them: that when the time came I'd put their safety above all else.' He grunted. 'They were right, of course – that's exactly what happened. I *do* put their safety before all else. Cameron's life, your life, the lives of your children. I come from a race that values *society* above individuals and family, but I share that outlook nae longer.

'What Orla hasnae told ye is that there's a rather important consequence for all of us, if the *balla-dìon* is destroyed. You see, the energy it creates to maintain our privacy is the very manna upon which ye and your family rely for your life support. The *Triallaichean* aren't immortal, far from it. And while you're still as pretty as a seashell to my eyes, you've walked this earth a good long time. If the *balla-dìon* fails, so do I, so does Cameron, so do ye. Likewise, most important, your four lovely bairns.'

The point of the stiletto blade wavered. Nora's eyes flickered to Orla's. Widened.

'And not just the six a ye,' Eber continued. 'But all the surviving *Triallaichean*, myself included, along with the remainder of Ériu's followers, and all the many residents of Crafter's Keep.' The old man grimaced. 'If the girl survives long enough to complete her task, Nora, every one of us dies. Every *single* one.'

'It's not true,' she whispered.

'Oh, but it is,' Eber replied. 'The girl you're trying to protect is planning a massacre on a scale unimaginable.'

Edward allowed himself to be dragged inside the room with Piper, and then he drew his pistol and shoved the barrel into his assailant's side.

'For pity's sake put that thing down,' Jolyon hissed.

Edward lurched backwards in disbelief. 'What the *hell* are you doing?'

'The keep's under attack,' the artist said. His eyes looked wild.

Edward nodded. 'We're leaving.'

'Follow me,' Jolyon replied. 'I know a way.' He led them back into the passage and down three flights of steps, descending through forgotten rooms and damp-riddled chambers. From his pocket he took a torch and switched it on. He arrived at a steep spiral stairwell and clattered down its steps. Lower and lower they dropped. Edward began to smell seawater, rotten seaweed. At last they came to a heavy iron door set directly into rock. Jolyon unlocked it with a key hung around his neck. The door shrieked open; cold Atlantic wind gusted through.

'How did you know about this?'

'Got my memories back,' Jolyon replied. 'And Orla gave me a key.' He led them outside, onto the razored causeway that linked the peninsula to the mainland. All around, black waves pounded the rocks. Moonlight glittered on surf. Anchored twenty yards out, a sleek white yacht rolled on the swell. Behind it bobbed a small dinghy.

High up on the peninsula, inside the walls of Crafter's Keep, a bell began to toll, its urgency palpable.

Jolyon cringed. 'We'll have to swim for it,' he said.

CHAPTER 56

Crafter's Keep, Cornwall

Trapped between the two *Triallaichean*, Nora Kinraid felt herself cut loose from every certainty she had ever known. To her left stood Eber, father of her estranged husband, grandfather to her four children. Holding a blade against his throat felt so outrageous an act, so monstrously disloyal, that she struggled to keep her arm locked in place. And yet opposite Eber stood the woman to whom Nora had dedicated her entire life.

'Is it true?' she asked.

Orla's eyes brimmed. 'Yes.'

Daggers of grief pierced her, then. She felt her strength begin to wilt. 'Would you have told me?' Nora waited for an answer that she knew would never come, and that she did not need to hear. 'You'd decided against it.'

'Would it have made a difference?'

'Perhaps, perhaps not. It would have given me a little time, at least. Time with my children, with Cameron. An opportunity to say . . .' Her throat closed up. She shrugged.

'I never imposed on you any standard I wouldn't impose on myself,' Orla told her. 'You heard what Eber said. I die too.'

Nora laughed bitterly. 'That's what? A consolation?'

'If we succeed in this, you'll have traded your life for something world-changing.'

'It's not just my life you're asking me to trade, is it?' She thought, again, of her children: Adeline, Simon, Kyla, Megan. Her shoulders trembled, and when her blade dipped from Eber's throat the old man lunged forward and cut Orla down with a savagery astonishing to behold.

Jenna Black woke to the sound of a bell intruding over Keegan's music. For a moment she struggled to recall where she was. Then her memories of the previous night surfaced: memories of Edward Schwinn.

She rolled over and snaked out a hand, felt cold sheets. His absence so surprised her that for a moment the bell's tolling – and Keegan's discordant notes – faded entirely from her awareness. Jenna sat up. When she saw that she was alone in the room she slid out of bed and stumbled into her clothes. Pulling on boots, she grabbed her music player from beneath the pillow and clipped it inside her shirt. From the nightstand she snatched up a pistol and torch.

In the corridor she discovered Therron. The boy, barefoot and bare-chested, wore a pair of jeans, his hair sleep-tousled. 'What's going on?' he asked.

'Get back to your room,' she told him. 'Lock the door.'

'Where's Pie?'

'Therron, get *inside*!'

Eyes wide, he retreated. Jenna passed his door, went to Piper's. Darkness within. She snapped on the penlight, aimed its beam: empty bed, no sign of the girl.

The bell continued to peal. Over it Jenna heard shouting, and then a burst of gunfire so shockingly out of place that it made her stomach clench like a fist. Behind her Therron reappeared, fully dressed. In his hands he held a gun of his own.

'I told you stay back!' she whispered, furious.

'Yeah, *fuck* that,' the boy replied. He ducked his head inside Piper's room. 'She was with me,' he said. 'Not more than an hour ago.'

Jenna moved to Edward's door. Like Piper's, it hung ajar. A

quick swab of her torch confirmed his room was empty. 'Gone,' she muttered, more to herself than the boy. The knowledge that he'd left without her hit harder than she'd anticipated.

Therron shook his head. 'They can't have. Not without me.'

Jenna glanced at his pistol. 'You know how to use that?'

'Aim. Shoot.'

She checked his ears. Both were plugged. 'You have your music player?'

He tapped his jeans pocket.

'OK. You do as I say, and you point that gun at the floor. Let's go.'

They raced along the corridor, following the beam of her torch. Lights were coming on all over the keep, now. Jenna heard another burst of gunfire outside. An even fiercer burst answered.

They reached a wide staircase and threw themselves down it. Arriving on the next floor, they sprinted along a gallery towards the Great Hall. As Jenna turned the corner, she ran headlong into a man coming the other way. She grunted, wind knocked from her lungs, and almost dropped her pistol.

The man was O'Shea. 'Where's Piper?' he shouted.

Alarmed, Jenna backed away.

'We're under attack,' he said. 'I don't know who from. You can come with me or go your own way. Your choice.'

Dangerous to trust him; and yet so was indecision. 'Where are you headed?'

'The solar. It's the last place I saw Orla.'

Jenna glanced at Therron, then back at O'Shea. 'OK.'

They doubled back to the stairs and this time took a different route, passing a column of armed men and women whose grim faces Jenna recognised. Outside, the exchange of gunfire intensified. She wondered how anyone could have broached the keep's defences. When she arrived in the solar a few minutes later, she found her answer.

The room was grandly appointed, designed for private reflection and counsel. At one end stood a huge stone fireplace.

In a corner, Nora Kinraid, rendered almost unrecognisable by grief, clung to a bell rope that disappeared through a hole in the ceiling, hauling on it with all her strength.

Across the room, Orla lay in a spreading pool of blood, cleaved from shoulder to hip. A longsword lay on the flagstones. Beside it, an old man. With a gasp, Jenna recognised him. Protruding from Eber's neck, angled upwards, she saw the hilt of a thin-bladed knife. His eyes were open but sightless.

Moaning, O'Shea collapsed at Orla's side, reached out his hands to her.

Incredibly, the *Triallaiche* woman managed to turn her head. She coughed up a thick clot. 'Jenna,' she spluttered. Blood ran down her chin like a dark yolk. 'I must speak to Jenna.'

Edward squinted at the black swell as it surged, foaming, all around him. A sliver of rock linked the peninsula to the mainland but it offered no means of escape, terminating at the base of a vertical cliff face besieged by the sea.

He studied the yacht as it pitched and rolled out there in deeper water. Loose halyards rang against the mast. Waves slapped the hull. Edward asked Jolyon: 'You know how to sail her?'

'Sort of.'

Piper glanced across at him. 'What does *that* mean?'

'I was a sailor, once,' he said. 'Worked on a brig called the *Bacchus*.'

'When was that?'

Jolyon trawled his memory. 'Eighteen thirty or thereabouts.'

'I'm no expert,' Piper replied. 'But things might have moved on a little since.'

'I did some crewing around the Maldives a few years ago,' the man added. 'If we can get aboard we'll be OK.' Jolyon moved to the edge of a rock. Kicking off a flip-flop, he dipped his foot into the water. 'Gods alive,' he muttered. 'This is going to be brutal.'

High up on the peninsula, a salvo of gunfire lit the night. Edward grimaced. 'If we're going to do this,' he began.

Piper dived into the water. The girl surfaced ten yards out, shaking seawater from her hair. Without a backwards glance, she swam towards the yacht.

Cursing, Edward braced himself and leaped into the sea.

The shock of it, ice-bath cold, crushed the air from his lungs. He kicked to the surface, coughing and gasping, and saw a black wave bearing down on him. He ducked his head, powering beneath it with all his strength. The rocks at his back were as sharp as kitchen knives. If the wave caught him they would slice him apart.

Edward broke the surface and gulped down a breath. He searched the sea for Piper. Ahead, the yacht yawed violently in the swell. 'Pie!' he yelled. He kicked off again, propelling himself arm over arm through the waves. Salt water stung his eyes and throat. Already the cold was dragging at him, stiffening his muscles, numbing his limbs.

He saw movement on the yacht's transom ladder and realised it was Piper pulling herself out of the water. Such was his relief that the next wave caught him unawares, breaking over his head before he could snatch a breath. He kicked hard. White-hot pain flashed through his knee. When he cried out, water surged into his throat.

Edward surfaced into a trough, saw yet another wave bearing down. He coughed seawater, tried to fill his lungs before it hit. It broke over him and he clamped his mouth shut, refusing to surrender his breath. The moment he was clear he swam for the yacht, using the last remains of his strength.

His fingers found a ladder rung, but the swell ripped them loose. He seized it again, this time with both hands. Waves battered him, but he clung on. Somehow, he hauled himself up and collapsed onto the deck.

For a moment he just lay there, on his back, staring up at the moon as it rolled back and forth in the sky. He shivered violently, heart beating so hard that he could feel its movement in his throat. Angling his neck, he saw Jolyon appear at the top of the ladder.

The man shook his head, shedding seawater from hair and beard. 'Hell's *teeth*,' he gasped.

Too exhausted to respond, Edward rolled onto his side and looked around. The yacht's open cockpit housed two huge wheels and an extensive array of high-tech equipment. A T-shaped deck led to a companionway hatch offering access below decks. 'How do we put up the sails?'

'We'll worry about that once we're off these rocks,' Jolyon said. He glanced around the cockpit, taking stock of the various switches and screens. Dipping his hand into a recess, he twisted a key.

Beneath them, a diesel engine thrummed into life. A couple of screens winked on. Jolyon studied them. Then he grabbed a handheld device connected to a console by a coiled lead and activated it. At the bow, something bumped and rattled. 'Anchor chain,' he said. The rattling intensified, and then it locked. Jolyon pushed forward on a short stick between the two wheels and the engine note rose in pitch. White water foamed behind the transom. The artist spun one wheel to port as the yacht began to nose through the waves.

Edward glanced about him, trying to familiarise himself with the boat's operation, but in the dark it was an impossible task. Instead, he checked on Piper. The girl gripped the starboard rail and gazed up at Crafter's Keep on the peninsula's summit. Lights blazed in its windows. Flashlight beams danced across its walls.

'Therron,' Piper said miserably. Water dripped from her nose and hair.

Edward laid his hand on her back. She turned, clung to him. Together, as the wind sawed in their ears, they watched the coastline recede into the darkness. Soon they were surrounded by inky sea.

PART IV

CHAPTER 57

Open Sea

Once Jolyon had decided that they were far enough from shore, he switched on the navigation lights and pointed the yacht into the wind. With Edward's help he stripped off the sail covers, and hoisted the mainsail and jib. 'Where are we headed?' he asked.

'Out to sea,' Piper told him. 'As far from the shipping lanes as possible.'

'West, then.' He spun the wheel and the boom swung around. The mainsail flapped once in hesitation, then it filled. Edward felt the yacht come alive beneath him. Soon they were knifing through six-foot waves beneath a glittering curtain of stars. For a while he simply stood beside his daughter, hugging her close, grateful for her proximity. He listened to the creak of the rigging and watched the pitch and roll of the sea. As their distance from the mainland increased, he began to draw breath a little more easily. They had escaped without injury, and although Crafter's Keep had been attacked, the red dome had not appeared within it. He feared for Therron's safety, Jenna's too; but Piper, at least, was safe.

Moving to the front of the cockpit, he opened the companionway hatch and led his daughter below decks. The stairs opened into a saloon far more expansive than he had expected to find. A central aisle split a wide seating area served by a table that could be unfolded to unite both halves. A long galley kitchen housed a four-ring stove, double sink, inbuilt microwave and fridge-freezer. Astern, he discovered a master bedroom complete with en suite. In the bow was an en suite guest cabin, and a smaller cabin on the port side.

Back in the master bedroom, he located towels and fresh clothing for himself and Piper. The clothes were a little tight on him, but they would suffice until his own were dry. In a locker he found lifejackets and handed one to Piper. Then he carried fresh towels and clothing up to Jolyon. After that he spent ten minutes investigating the rest of the yacht and inventorying its supplies.

The galley kitchen was fully stocked with canned goods and freeze-dried meals, and the fridge was filled to capacity with fruit and vegetables, meat and cheese. The vessel carried seven hundred litres of fresh water, and the means to produce more. The fuel gauge indicated they sat on nearly nine hundred litres of diesel. The battery packs were fully charged.

'She's called the *Saoradair*,' Piper said, looking up from a sheaf of papers.

Edward glanced over. 'Bit of a step up from our chalet,' he replied. 'You want a brew? Something hot?'

'I'll do it. I need a job, something to keep me busy.'

He nodded, keeping his eyes on her as she filled a kettle and searched the cupboards for mugs.

They drank their tea up on deck with Jolyon. The artist used the opportunity to give them a lesson in seamanship. He explained how to read the sails, pull in the mainsheet and check off depth, speed and course. 'Speaking of courses,' he said, 'it might be an idea to plot ours soon.'

'Keep heading west for now,' Piper said. 'We'll need to turn north eventually, but I'd rather sail up Ireland's west coast than the east.' She shivered. 'It would be good to see a map.'

'What's our destination?'

'An island,' she replied. The girl stared across the yacht's coach roof to the empty night beyond. '*The* island.'

CHAPTER 58

Open Sea

Jolyon took the first watch. It was a decision that Edward accepted reluctantly, even though he knew it was right. The man was the only one among them with any seafaring experience; far better that he should remain at the helm through the hours of darkness.

Claiming exhaustion, Piper retired to the *Saoradair*'s forward guest suite. At the sink in the galley kitchen, Edward stripped his pistol and cleaned it as thoroughly as he could. With a J-cloth he buffed each of the weapon's seventeen rounds and slotted them back into the magazine. He didn't know if they would work after their immersion in the sea, but he resolved to test-fire the gun at first light.

In addition to food and water, his search of the yacht had yielded a stash of emergency signalling equipment: one twelve-gauge launcher and a bandolier containing six aerial flares, ten rocket-propelled parachute flares and three floating smoke packs. In the smallest cabin he discovered scuba gear, including four titanium knives and sheaths. Whether such a makeshift arsenal would grant them any protection at their journey's end he had no clue.

After returning his pistol to its holster, Edward switched off the light. Dawn was a few hours away and he needed to get some rest. He lay on his back, closed his eyes and listened to the creak and clank of the yacht as she rocked on the ocean. The conditions were not rough. Through a hatch in the coach roof he could see the sky, as black as obsidian now they were out of sight of land. He thought of all that water beneath him, all that empty space above; and, in every direction of the compass, a dearth of humanity. His eyes grew heavy and he slept.

When Piper closed the door to the forward cabin she found Mórríghan standing beside the bulkhead. As usual, the woman's image made her stomach flutter with nausea. She turned away, not wanting to risk a nosebleed or a migraine, and sat cross-legged on the narrow bed. 'So here we are.'

Mórríghan nodded. 'How are you feeling?'

'Scared, sad. Wallowing in a huge, filthy puddle of self-pity.'

'Leaving Therron was hard.'

'The worst. I'm guessing you're going to tell me it was the right thing to do. But you can't know that. Before we left Crafter's Keep I heard gunfire. Therron −' her voice cracked − 'would have been in the middle of it.'

'You gave him a chance, Piper. I know that must be little consolation, but you know what would have happened had you brought him along.'

Piper slumped on the mattress. 'I think I need to sleep.'

'First we have things to discuss. We're close, now. I need to tell you what must happen once we arrive.'

'You'll be with me, won't you?'

'For most of it. If we time things correctly I'll help you bypass the *balla-dìon's* outer defences. But for the last task, I'm afraid you'll be on your own.'

'The last task?'

'That's what I'm here to explain.'

CHAPTER 59

Open Sea

Edward relieved Jolyon at dawn. He donned an oilskin and emerged from the companionway hatch to find the artist at the wheel with a tarp wrapped around his shoulders. It was raining now, a fine cold drizzle that dripped from the man's beard and hair. Overnight the wind had freshened, blowing steadily from the south-west. The swell had heightened, too. Each new wave foamed white at its crest.

While Jolyon went below decks, Edward maintained a westerly course. He saw a tanker or two, but otherwise the seas were his own. After a few hours, Piper emerged. She brought a flask of coffee and sat with him a while, watching the horizon as it rose and fell. 'I never realised how big it was,' she said.

'The ocean?'

The girl nodded.

'How're you feeling?'

'A little teary earlier, but I had a word with myself. I'm fine, now.'

'You're worried about him.'

Piper laughed, a hard sound in her throat. 'Yeah.'

Jolyon reappeared mid-morning, grizzled from sleep. 'I figured out the autopilot,' he said. 'We should test it while there's still light.' They spent the next few hours fiddling with the system until they satisfied themselves as to its operation.

For lunch, Edward cooked steaks, wanting to use up the fresh meat before it spoiled. Afterwards they gathered around the map table, where Jolyon had unrolled a chart. 'We're here,' he told them, pointing to a cross he had made along a pencil-drawn line. 'And that,' he added, his finger moving to a spot on Cornwall's north coast, 'is where we were.'

Piper indicated Ireland's south-west tip. 'We should head towards here. How long?'

'Mizen Head,' Jolyon said, pursing his lips. 'We've been averaging around five knots since last night. If we keep that up, it'll take us a day or so.'

'Then let's do it,' Piper replied. 'After that we can turn north. Follow the coast.'

The artist nodded. 'With a decent south-easterly we'll be able to let her run a bit. But if you want me to plot a course and give you a realistic timeframe you need to show me our destination. Last night you mentioned an island. Which one are we talking about?'

'Do you have a map that shows the Hebrides?'

'I think so.' He returned with another admiralty chart, which he unfurled, weighting its corners with coffee mugs.

Edward watched his daughter hover over it. She was silent for a minute or so, eyes narrowed. Finally, she placed her index finger on an empty spot near the chart's left-hand edge. 'Here,' she said.

He frowned. 'There's nothing there.'

'Trust me.' When the girl looked up and saw his expression, she laughed. 'Dad, the *balla-dìon* was designed to make an entire planet disappear. Hiding an island in the North Atlantic is a card trick by comparison.' She turned to Jolyon. 'How long will it take us to reach it?'

'If we sailed an average of eight hours a day we'd be looking at six weeks.'

'Six *weeks*?' Piper repeated, her face blanching. 'We need to do it in half that.'

The artist shrugged. 'With good winds, sailing twenty-four hours a day, we could do it in two.'

At that, she recovered some of her composure. 'Three weeks should be our guide. We can't arrive too late, but getting there too early would be just as dangerous. Do we have supplies enough to last that long?'

'Better ask our quartermaster.'

'Three weeks is doable,' Edward said. He saw his daughter nod, and thought she had never looked so anxious.

They spent the afternoon receiving intensive instruction in seamanship from Jolyon. The man was a capable teacher, and the amount of knowledge he could impart in an hour of tuition was formidable. Edward had never been a fast learner, but he found himself retaining far more of the artist's advice than he might have otherwise expected. That night they slept in shifts, letting the autopilot maintain their course while one of them kept watch.

Early the next morning they saw Ireland's south-west tip appear on the horizon: towering sea stacks smashed by waves; a debris of tooth-like rocks. They kept their distance as they rounded them, wary of the white water that gathered there.

That afternoon, as they sat together on the deck, a pod of fin whales appeared. Piper laughed in delight as the huge creatures began to swim alongside the *Saoradair*. Edward watched them snail through the water and could not help but feel awed. If the whales were somehow turned against their yacht, the consequences would be catastrophic, but in the presence of such grace it was impossible to dwell on dark thoughts.

'After the blue whale, they're the largest animals on earth,' Jolyon said, handing Piper a pair of binoculars. 'They grow up to ninety feet in length. Live for over a hundred years.'

'There's a baby with them.'

'Looks like two.'

Piper turned to her father, her eyes shining. 'It's a beautiful world. Don't you think?'

Edward flinched, and then he laughed. 'Your mother told me exactly the same thing, the night you were born.'

The girl's mouth dropped open. 'You never told me that.'

'Only just remembered it.'

'Did you believe her?'

'At the time? No.'

Piper looked at him thoughtfully. 'Do you believe her, now?'

He screwed up his face. 'Ask me again, once this is all over.'

The whales trailed them for two hours before finally turning west. Piper tracked them with the binoculars until they disappeared from view. That night, the wind slackened and the sea grew calm. Above them the clouds separated, offering a startling view of the sky. They sat beneath it, dressed in every item of warm clothing they could find, slaking their thirst with hot, sweet tea.

Edward gazed up at the stars. 'You remember everything yet?' he asked Jolyon.

The artist shook his head. 'Not quite. So far, it's been like looking into a tunnel that's constantly expanding. Damned frustrating, really – I want to know it all.'

'How far back can you go?'

'Right now I could recount to you, in explicit detail, the consequences of marrying into eighteenth-century French aristocracy.' He paused. 'I always hated rococo art. Now I'm beginning to understand why.'

'Tell us,' Piper pleaded, and at once Edward saw that her reaction was exactly the one the man had hoped to inspire. Jolyon talked for two hours straight. At one point, as he relayed a particularly graphic sexual encounter and its unfortunate medical repercussions, Edward escaped below decks. He could hear Piper's laughter, and it made his ears burn.

Each day that passed, Jolyon seemed to remember a little

more, and each evening he entertained them with tales of calamity and adventure. Edward wondered how far back he would go before he began to access memories that were no longer human at all.

'You know the question that's been troubling me the most?' the artist asked one night, as they sat around the map table tucking into pancakes. 'What kind of cretinous oaf willingly – *willingly*, I'll stress – decides to embark on life saddled with a name like Jolyon Linus Tobias Percival?'

Piper snorted, nearly choked on her pancake. 'You must have been very bored.'

'Either that or exceedingly drunk.'

A week passed. They spotted Achill Island, the place to which Edward had fled with Piper the night the *balla-dìon* found them at Stallockmore Farm. West of the Mullet Peninsula, he recognised the Inishkea islands. Soon after, he saw County Mayo's northern coast slide by to starboard. He spotted the Stags of Broadhaven rising from the waves like velvet-topped pyramids. Through his binoculars he saw the extraordinary sea stack of Dún Briste.

'Feels a little like a homecoming,' Piper said. 'Don't you think?'

Edward could not help but scowl. Despite its beauty, the place spawned dark memories. Their time in Mayo had been characterised by poverty, fear and exhaustion. Somewhere along that stretch of coast stood Stallockmore Farm. When he thought about how Old Man McAllister had exploited him, his knuckles tightened on the guardrail; but the farmer, in the end, had suffered a fate far worse than he had deserved.

'It wasn't all bad,' Piper told him, laying her hand on his fist as the land began to recede. Edward remembered the decapitated lamb he had tossed into the sea from Stallockmore's cliff face. He shuddered, and turned his face north.

Later that day a storm blew in from the west. They were

well prepared: Jolyon had been monitoring the surface pressure updates on the *Saoradair*'s tracking systems and the messages from the Inmarsat since mid-morning. But even with all their preparation, the weather front surprised them. Winds battered them with a savagery Edward had not contemplated. The sea became a landscape of mountain peaks. The waves were enormous; house-sized wrecking balls stacked against them. For the next three hours, with their harnesses tethered to the deck, they battled to tackle those monstrosities head-on. They lowered the mainsail and raised a storm jib, lashed down everything as securely as they could. The ocean pulverised them, regardless. Edward lost count of the times he thought a breaking wave, like a looming tower of marbled glass, was going to swamp them.

That night, exhausted, they retreated below decks and laughed hard at their triumph. With the autopilot engaged, Jolyon fetched an artist's pad and pencils that he had discovered in a forward locker. 'I feel like I need to do this,' he told Piper, lifting the pad's cover. He paused, waiting for her permission. 'I understand if you'd feel uncomfortable.'

The girl shrugged. 'I think it'd be fun,' she said. 'Can Dad be in it?'

'Of course.'

Nobody asked Edward if he would feel uncomfortable — and of course he did — but he sat beside his daughter and tolerated the artist's attention. Jolyon sketched and smudged; he frowned and smiled. And as he worked he told them of a woman he had once known in Hungary, a tale so strange that Edward grew convinced the man was spinning them a yarn.

Afterwards, Jolyon turned the pad around and revealed the image he had drawn. Piper gasped when she saw it, and her eyes filled.

Edward could not hide his confusion. He recognised his daughter well enough, but not the man beside her. 'Why have you drawn me like that?' he asked.

Piper rolled her eyes at him. 'Because that's who you are.'

Embarrassed, he went up on deck. That night he found himself contemplating Jolyon's sketch and asking himself questions he could not answer. He retreated to his cabin, where he checked over his arsenal of weapons, examining the pistol for signs of damage.

Ten nights later – three weeks after setting out from Crafter's Keep – the *Saoradair* reached her destination.

CHAPTER 60

Dìdean, North Atlantic

Pastor Benjamin D. Pope stood on a narrow beach amidst clumps of marram grass and watched the Sikorsky cargo helicopter recede into a granite sky.

While most of the volunteers from the Church of the Holy Sacrament had arrived by boat, Aiden Urchardan had wanted Benjamin and Wendy to see the island from the air. It was an experience from which he was still recovering. The helicopter had carried them a hundred miles west of the Scottish coast before it began to descend into what, to Benjamin, looked like open ocean. He gripped his seat with one hand, braced himself against a strut with the other. His throat closed up until he couldn't breathe.

SEE.

A single command, spoken inside his head. Immediately, the scene below him blurred, shifted. The pastor found himself staring not at wild sea but rock and earth, grass and sand. Urchardan turned to him and smiled. 'Welcome,' he said, 'to Dìdean.'

The helicopter banked and Benjamin pressed his forehead to the side window. Through the glass he saw an extraordinary land mass, from which rose a dramatic peak shaped like a shark's dorsal fin. Moss felted its anterior slopes; its concave southern face, in stark contrast, was a towering expanse of bitten rock climbing hundreds of feet. He saw a colony of black-winged birds circling the summit.

To the south, in the shadow of the peak's sheer escarpment, lay a desolate beach. A crescent-shaped reef, from which rocks rose like broken teeth, protected the shoreline from the worst of the Atlantic's fury. To the north, vertical cliff faces defended the coast. Westwards, the sea was a graveyard of shattered stacks and foaming surf. He thought he saw the rusted skeleton of a warship among the debris.

On a flat expanse of grassland, in sight of the southern beach, stood the camp. Eric Bocanegra had been tasked with building it, and Benjamin saw that the man had done a good job. Already, a neat row of canvas tents had been erected. Beside them stood a number of larger marquees. Latrines had been dug at the northern perimeter. Benjamin saw smoke rising from cooking tents, and members of his congregation emptying from the marquees to gaze up into the sky.

The helicopter descended to a patch of scrub landing with a bump. Urchardan rolled the door open and climbed out, gesturing at Benjamin and Wendy to follow. Seconds later the pastor found himself on Dìdean's soil, watching as the Sikorsky rose back into the sky.

'Will the pilot remember?' he asked.

'Not a thing,' Urchardan assured him. 'Nor the ground crew, nor anyone else we met.'

Eric Bocanegra, flanked by Billy Gosselin and Marcus Dyke, strode across the grass to greet them. All three men wore combat fatigues, with carbines slung over their shoulders and pistols holstered on their hips. Benjamin didn't know what to think about that – supposed he would have to get used to it. Incredibly, when Eric stopped in front of him the man snapped off a salute.

'Welcoming you to Camp Faith, Pastor.'

Benjamin smiled despite his fatigue. 'Camp Faith?'

Eric's face tightened momentarily. 'Just an idea Billy had. We kind of like it, but of course it's up to you.'

'No, no,' he replied. 'I think it's a great idea. I'm mightily impressed with what you've done here, Eric. Would you mind assembling everyone?'

The man glanced sideways at Marcus Dyke, blinked. 'You want to see everybody?'

'I'd like to lead us all in prayer.' Benjamin paused, raised an eyebrow. 'Is that a problem?'

'Not at all, Pastor. I know folks would sure appreciate it. Gotta few guys out on patrol, is all.'

'Well, I certainly don't want to disrupt that. Let's just gather everyone who's free.'

The prayer meeting went ahead in the large marquee twenty minutes later, and it was like none Benjamin had ever conducted. He felt like one of the circuit riders of the Old West, delivering ministry to some far-flung pioneer outpost; yet this was not Nevada or Arizona or New Mexico, and his congregation hailed not from the eighteenth century, nor the nineteenth, but the beginning of the twenty-first.

He stood before them, joining his voice to theirs as Terrance LaDouceur led a recital of 'We Shall Overcome'. Every face in the crowd shone with faith, and with the conviction of what they were all here to do.

AMONG YOU.

Benjamin smiled. He saw, in the eyes of those gathered before him, that the Bliss had spoken, simultaneously, to every single person in the tent.

He flung open his arms, witnessed his action mirrored wherever he looked.

IN YOU.

With those words Benjamin felt it enter him, and through his delirium he saw it enter his congregation. Many of those it touched could not hold themselves upright. Bodies tumbled to the marquee's rubber matting. Spines arched, necks twisted, jaws gaped and clenched. He heard moaning, blissful keening. Beside him, Wendy Devereaux grabbed his hand, and when he looked at her he felt as if a firework had detonated inside his brain.

The woman shuddered, pulled him close, pressed herself against him. 'I need you, Ben,' she hissed. 'I *need* you.' Blood leaked from her nostrils, leaving vivid scarlet splashes on her white cotton top. It aroused him, that blood, in ways he would never have imagined possible: aroused and appalled him in equal measure. When Wendy's lips spread wide he saw blood on her teeth, and cringed at the hunger it stirred in him.

Finally, perhaps mercifully, the Bliss began to recede. It left Benjamin shaking, both with repressed desire and deep disquiet. 'I have to address them,' he murmured. He eased Wendy away from him, unable to look at her while such libidinous thoughts still echoed. 'I need to explain why we're here.'

'Perhaps *I* should do that,' Urchardan said. 'Pastor, you look a little overcome.' The man smiled, indicated the nearest tent flap. 'Why don't you take a tour of the camp instead?'

Suddenly Benjamin wanted nothing more than to be free of the marquee's claustrophobic interior. He nodded, breaking for the exit as fast as his dignity allowed. Outside, with his back to the canvas, he filled his lungs with cool Dìdean air.

After five minutes of deep breathing he felt somewhat better. When he noticed movement in one of the cooking tents he decided to pay it a visit; he hadn't eaten for at least eight hours and his stomach was starting to protest. Inside, he found rows of trestle tables supporting propane-fuelled stoves and griddles. He smelled Creole gumbo, saw five huge cauldrons of it bubbling away. At a prep area stood Terri Freedman, slicing bread.

'Hey, Terri,' he called.

The woman flinched, relaxing when she saw who it was. 'Pastor.'

Benjamin stared. 'My gosh, what *happened* to you?' Terri's left eye was closed, the centre of a large bruise. As the question left his lips, he understood what had been bothering him at the prayer meeting. He had not seen Terri among the worshippers, and neither had he seen Ladell Williams, Deana Taylor or many of the other female volunteers. Unlikely, he figured, that Eric had sent out an all–female patrol.

'Terri?' Benjamin asked, moving closer to the prep table. The woman's hand, as it gripped the bread knife, was shaking.

CHAPTER 61

Open Sea

Piper had sketched out a map of the island far in advance of their arrival, but she worked off memories supplied by Mórríghan that were several millennia out of date. 'A lot can happen to a place over that amount of time,' she pointed out, as they pored over it. 'I don't know how much of this still exists.'

Jolyon scratched his beard. 'Well, it's better than nothing. What's our deadline for getting this done?'

'Today's the twenty-ninth. In two days' time the Earth passes through the Ookater Cloud. When it does I need to be on the island, ready to go.'

'What time is this thing due to hit?' Edward asked.

'Four twenty-five in the afternoon.'

'Around sunset. How long will the *balla-dìon* be out of action?'

'Its primary systems, only fractions of a second. Its external defences will be offline longer.'

'How much longer?'

Piper grimaced. 'Half an hour, max.'

'Does that give us enough time to get ashore, find it and pull the plug?'

She shook her head. 'Far too tight. I think we have to go in tomorrow night. Hunker down until it's time.'

'With the *balla-dìon* still on sentry duty?'

'It's the only way.'

'What kind of defences does it have?'

'You saw what happened back at Joyau Caché – it uses intelligent life to its advantage. Saying that, we're talking about a remote island in the North Atlantic. Apart from birds, which it tends to have difficulty subverting, I wouldn't expect to find much to be concerned about. A few grey seals, maybe. Mice.'

'But any eyes are bad eyes.'

'Yeah.'

Edward turned to Jolyon. 'How do we get ashore?'

The man grimaced. 'Assuming the map's still valid, we've got major problems in every direction. Those cliffs rule out the north. South and west we've got half-submerged reefs, sea stacks, debris. Looking at this, only the eastern approach seems navigable, but I still wouldn't want to take the *Saoradair* anywhere near it. Not only are those waters uncharted, but we'd also be running at night, without lights. She's a big girl; by the time we saw any rocks it'd be too late. We could use the RIB as a lifeboat, but at first light you'd have expensive pieces of yacht washing up all over the beach. Hardly subtle.'

'What's the alternative?'

'Use the RIB to take us in. It's far more manoeuvrable, and once we get ashore we can drag it out of sight. But that gives us another problem. At the moment we're over an area of ocean called the Rockall Trough. I've been checking the depth finder – these waters run deep. If we moor up too close to shore the boat'll be visible come daylight. But any further out, we likely won't have enough cable to drop anchor.'

'So we scuttle her,' Edward said.

Jolyon reared back from the map table. 'By gods, man. That's *sacrilege*.'

'It's our only option. We transfer what we need to the RIB, then we send the *Saoradair* to the bottom.'

'And in the process, wave goodbye to our ride home.'

It was an important point, to which Edward had no reply.

That night, in contrast to what he might have expected, the atmosphere on board grew buoyant. During the afternoon, Jolyon had baited fishing lines and landed three large cod. In the galley kitchen he whipped up a batter and fried them on the gimballed stove. They ate them at the table, with tinned potatoes and peas. Jolyon told outrageous stories of his former lives and Piper laughed so hard that she cried into her dinner. Afterwards the girl retired to her cabin, leaving the two men alone.

With the yacht's sails lowered, they kept watch up on deck. Jolyon checked their position every half-hour but their drift was minimal. The conditions were unusually calm, almost as if wind and sea had sought to grant them a temporary reprieve.

'She's an extraordinary young woman,' Jolyon said.

'Yes.'

'You raised her well.'

Edward looked up sharply at that, but he saw no mockery in the other man's expression. Above his head, the halyards rang softly against the mast. They reminded him, vaguely, of church bells.

The next day dragged interminably. They checked and rechecked their gear, forced themselves to eat. None of them knew how long they would be in the RIB, or on the island itself, so they packed a rucksack and two large duffel bags with supplies. Edward took Piper aside and showed her how to use the Glock, but he stopped short of letting her fire it; sound could travel long distances over open water.

As the light began to fade, they checked their equipment one last time, testing their portable GPS and back-up batteries. Jolyon and Edward disappeared below decks, and with grim determination they smashed the sea cocks and drilled through the hull.

The swell had heightened, making their transfer to the RIB more hazardous than they would have liked. Already the *Saoradair* was beginning to wallow. Jolyon insisted on being the last to abandon her. They cast off from the stricken vessel and motored a safe distance away. Huddled in their survival gear, they watched her sink. It was a curiously mournful experience. The yacht filled with seawater, gradually listing to port. Her bow submerged first, lifting the stern. She lingered on the surface for another twenty minutes before finally disappearing beneath the waves.

Edward glanced around the RIB. 'Point of no return,' he said, immediately regretting his choice of words.

As dusk surrendered to night, Pastor Benjamin D. Pope perched on a rock and watched the ocean roll breakers towards the beach. A gold chain hung from his fingers, its locket swinging like a pendulum. Benjamin knew that the keepsake was important, that it signified something from his past, but however hard he tried to remember, his memory failed him.

He thought back to his conversation with Terri Freedman inside the cook tent. '*Just a dumb accident, Pastor,*' she'd told him, referring to her bruised eye. '*Nothin' serious.*' When she cut another slice of bread, the knife stuttered across the crust, knocking against the knuckles of her left hand. Billy Gosselin had appeared, then. And suddenly there were a thousand things to do: catching up with Urchardan, taking a tour of the island, installing himself and his belongings into one of the sleeping tents.

Benjamin heard a scrape of stone and looked up to see Wendy Devereaux. She clutched a Gore-Tex windbreaker around her torso. Her bare legs looked wind-chapped and raw.

Wendy sat down next to him, leaned in close. 'Eric's done a good job,' she said. 'You might wanna think about giving him something permanent once this is over.'

He grunted. 'Once this is over, I'm not sure there'll be a need.'

'What do you mean by that?'

'Wendy, why are we here?'

She glanced up, raised a quizzical eyebrow at him. 'You mean humanity?'

Benjamin shook his head. 'I mean us. Now. Why we're here on this island.'

'You know why.'

'All I know,' he replied, 'is that we're meant to defend this place, against some promised evil that so far hasn't materialised. I know Eric's got teams patrolling the beaches. And I know that he's been ordered to cut down anyone who tries to get ashore. But I don't know *why*.'

Wendy gave him a lopsided smile. 'When God told Noah to build the Arc, did He tell him what was coming?'

'Well, yes,' Benjamin replied. 'Actually, He did.'

She laughed throatily. 'OK, bad example. And zero points to team Devereaux for bible study. What about Job, then? Did he ever know why he was tested like he was? I never thought I'd say this to you, Ben, but I think you gotta have a little more faith. Besides, your man Urchardan promised we'd get final instructions tonight.'

'He did?'

'Right after you went out for some air.'

'What do you think of him? Urchardan?'

'Kind of cool, I guess. Kind of creepy, too, if I'm honest. He's certainly devout.' Wendy filled her lungs, exhaled. She put a hand on his knee. 'I think you need to lighten up.'

Benjamin stared. The tangerine lacquer on her fingernails was beginning to chip. 'Have you seen Deana?' he asked. 'Ladell?'

'Sure.'

'I must find some time to speak to them.'

'I'll bet they'd appreciate that.'

'How'd they seem to you?'

Wendy smirked, squeezed his knee. 'I can't answer for Ladell,' she told him, eyes glinting. 'But Deana seemed like she was *rockin'* it.'

CHAPTER 62

Open Sea

According to the coordinates Piper had given them, the *Saoradair* had gone down twelve miles east of their destination. Jolyon turned the RIB westward, maintaining a speed of ten knots.

Earlier, the girl had explained that a small buffer existed around the island. Any ship that sailed into it would be diverted by the *balla-dìon* without the knowledge of its crew.

'What about us?' Edward asked.

'That's why Mórríghan's here. She can get us through undetected. As long as nothing sees us from the shore we'll be OK. But it doesn't make us safe. Crossing it isn't going to be pleasant. And we'll have to react fast to whatever we find on the other side. That map only showed obstacles to the south and west but I've no idea how accurate it is.'

When they were five miles out, Jolyon halved their speed and the RIB settled lower in the waves. Edward glanced at his watch. They'd been heading west for thirty minutes, now. At ten knots it would take them just under half an hour to reach dry land.

A few minutes later the conditions changed. So far the swell had been moderate, but now it grew more severe. Huge black waves, marbled with white water, began to rise up all around them. Jolyon worked constantly at throttle and wheel, trying to anticipate the most dangerous adversaries and keeping the RIB properly aligned. If a wave tipped them, they stood no chance of righting their tiny vessel; and even with their survival gear, they wouldn't survive long in such hostile waters. Salt spray soaked them thoroughly; within minutes they were all shivering.

Edward began to wonder whether the conditions were entirely natural. If this were another of the *balla-dìon's* defences, they could only expect things to get worse. When the opportunity allowed, he snatched glances through his binoculars at the view directly ahead, but he never saw anything other than dark, angry sea. Worrisome thoughts began to fester in him: What if Piper's information was wrong? What if her coordinates were simply incorrect? What if the *balla-dìon* had already intervened, steering them off course without their knowledge? They were alone in the North Atlantic aboard a rigid inflatable dinghy with no means of communication and no hope of rescue.

He clenched his teeth, refused to let such concerns consume him. But when he glanced at Piper, he read similar fears on her face. *That* troubled him more deeply than anything.

Even though they had known to expect it, when it happened it took them all by surprise. One moment Jolyon was powering them up a wave's steep face and the next, as the RIB crested it, they spotted a huge black fin of rock obliterating the clouds in front of them.

Edward felt a flash of pain behind his eyes. He flung his head back as if he had been stung, almost toppling out of the boat. Fireflies of light jittered and danced inside his head. His hearing seemed to elongate. The crash of sea became a hollow pounding. A moment later his stomach clenched and he vomited, leaning over the gunwales just in time. Blinking away tears, groaning as his vision returned, he saw the others had been similarly afflicted. Blood streamed from Piper's nose. Jolyon, unable to take his hands from the wheel, had vomited all over his clothes. The man powered down the RIB's engine, but he did not kill it entirely. Although they were only a mile from that silhouetted peak, the wind was blowing from the south-west; it would carry the sound of their outboard out to sea.

Edward swabbed the ocean with his binoculars. He could see no rocks knifing up through the water, which relieved him greatly. Ahead, that dark fin of rock was extraordinary, climbing hundreds of feet from the island's landmass. When he panned the binoculars left and right he saw that a central strip of the eastern coast, where the vegetation grew thickest, offered the best chance of hiding their boat.

Landing would not be an easy task. The shoreline was formed of steep headlands opening into narrow bays. Some of the beaches were shingle or sand but most were strewn with jagged rocks. Huge waves rolled towards them in steady sets. While he couldn't see the height at which they were breaking, he didn't imagine it would be less than eight feet.

Then he noticed something else, and his stomach shrank away to nothing. '*Lights!*' he shouted. 'Look to the south!'

Piper scrambled forwards, and when she saw them her mouth dropped open in horror. 'That can't be,' she moaned. 'It's not possible.'

Grim-faced, Edward turned to Jolyon. 'Take us north,' he said. 'We'll have to take our chances on those rocks.'

CHAPTER 63

Dìdean, North Atlantic

They cut their engine a few hundred yards from shore, hoping that the wind and surf would have masked the sound of their approach. Edward and Jolyon threaded the oars, determined to keep their bow properly aligned. They aimed the RIB at a narrow bay of shingle. Two jagged peninsulas flanked it, offering them a good chance of remaining unobserved. Waves rolled them in, growing in power and height.

It's inhabited. We never planned for that.

Edward tried to keep the thought from overwhelming him. The ocean lifted their boat, flung it shorewards. He dug his oar into the sea, took a faceful of freezing water. The next wave would carry them all the way to the beach, but if it broke at the wrong moment . . .

'*Row!*' Jolyon hissed. Feverishly, the man began to work at his oar.

Edward gritted his teeth and joined him. He sensed the wave building behind them, felt the dinghy drop into the preceding trough. He bit down on his panic and rowed. The stern began to lift. Higher and higher.

'Here we go,' Jolyon said. 'Unclip your tethers.'

Edward dropped his oar and unhooked his safety line. He held tight to the nearest grab rail, ready to leap out of the dinghy and pull it clear of the surf. They began to accelerate, racing down the wave's face.

Then, white water. Choking and cold.

It filled his mouth. Pushed into his throat. He couldn't hear, couldn't see. The dinghy spun like a waltzer at a fairground. They were going to capsize – he knew it. The ocean would dash them apart on the rocks. He coughed, spat, managed half a breath before seawater clogged his throat once more. Something punched his face with brutal force. One hand tore loose from the grab rail. Gambling, he let go with the other, kicked free of the boat. Felt himself slammed by a wave even more ferocious than the last.

Suddenly he was waist-deep in raging surf, shouting his daughter's name. He twisted about, panicked, half-blind, until a powerful hand seized his shoulder.

'Keep *quiet*, damn you. I've got her,' Jolyon growled. 'Snag the boat before we lose it.'

He saw Piper, then, and his heart dissolved in gratitude. The waterlogged RIB was drifting a few yards to his left, the rucksack and one of the duffel bags floating around inside. Grabbing a loose line, he towed the vessel towards him. Piper and Jolyon waded to his side. Together they dragged the dinghy to shore, pausing when its hull ground against shingle. Edward took out his dive knife and slashed the tubes. Water poured from the RIB in a torrent, allowing them to inch it up the beach.

It was still a task that almost defeated them. In the end they disconnected the outboard motor from the transom, carried it across the rocks and dropped it into a blowhole they had seen spouting. They hauled the hull into the mouth of a steep-sided chine and hid it beneath a layer of scrub. If someone made a close search of the area it wouldn't remain undiscovered for long, but they'd have to take that chance.

One of their duffel bags had been lost. Edward could only hope that it lay at the bottom of the sea. He slipped his arms into the straps of the rucksack they had rescued. Piper and Jolyon took a handle each of the surviving duffel bag. Silent, the three of them struggled up the chine, pausing every now and then to listen. If the island was defended, as Edward suspected, sentries would doubtless have been posted along the eastern shore. Jolyon's last-minute diversion north might just have saved them from a lethal welcoming party.

In the meantime, they needed to put as much distance as possible between themselves and their landing point. So far, Edward's rush of adrenalin had kept the cold at bay. But now, as he recovered from the pounding the sea had given him, he felt his limbs beginning to stiffen. He shivered ceaselessly. While the chine protected them from the worst of the wind, every time a gust hit him he felt it strip away a little more of his body heat. When he looked at the others, he saw they were suffering just as badly. 'Got to get dry,' he stammered. 'Got to get out of these clothes.'

But first they had to find somewhere safe. They located a spot five minutes later: a bowl-like depression near the top of the chine, roofed by a fallen tree. It offered them just enough space to squeeze inside with their equipment.

By now, Edward suspected that he was in the early stages of hypothermia. His movements were clumsy, his thinking slow. It took him six attempts before he managed to unfasten the duffel bag's clips. He prayed that the PVC skin had not been punctured. Inside, packed tightly, he found the clothing they had worn during their escape from Crafter's Keep. They stripped off their wet things, dressing as quickly as they could. Edward stuffed their discarded clothes into the duffel bag and shoved it under a bush.

He opened the rucksack, dug around inside it. Pulling out a tiny propane survival stove, he began to set it up. 'We lost all the food,' he told them. 'The flares and launcher, too. But we've got water. I can boil a kettle. We're pretty sheltered here. It won't make much light.'

'I stuffed some teabags in the side pocket, wrapped up,' Piper said. 'Sugar lumps, too.'

Jolyon grunted. 'I could kiss you.'

Edward lit the stove. They warmed their hands while they waited for the water to boil. He brewed the tea in the kettle itself, passing it around among them.

'What now?' Jolyon asked.

Edward turned to Piper. 'How are there people here?'

'I don't have an answer, but I can guess.' She hugged herself. 'It's been trying to find me all this time, hoping to get rid of me before I got too close. But it also knew that this was the end-game if it didn't succeed. Tomorrow it'll be vulnerable for the first time in its history. Seems like it organised some back-up. What I *can't* tell you is who those people are. The *balla-dìon* wouldn't have any trouble subverting them, but at four twenty-five tomorrow afternoon they'll be free to do as they like. Clearly it thinks they'll defend it against attack, even without its influence. But I have no idea what it's made them believe.'

'I'm not sure it matters,' Edward said. 'Point is, they're here, and we've got to figure out a way to deal with them.'

'There might not *be* a way.'

He inhaled sharply, troubled by the girl's fatalism. Never before had he heard her sound so defeated. 'The *balla-dìon*,' he said. 'Where will we find it?'

'You remember that huge spine of rock we saw on the way in?'

He nodded.

'Buried under there.'

'How do we get to it?'

'There's an entrance on the eastern flank.'

'We'd better hope it still exists.'

'It will.' She paused. 'But you can bet it'll be guarded.'

'Then we need to scout it out tonight, see what we're dealing with. Get as close as we can before dawn.'

Piper hung her head.

CHAPTER 64

Dìdean, North Atlantic

Pastor Benjamin walked up the beach from the ocean, locket chain wound around his fingers, listening to the music blasting from the marquee. Terrance LaDouceur appeared to have shipped a full-sized Hammond organ to Dìdean, along with guitars, bass and drums. The man had even rigged up microphones. Benjamin heard voices and recognised the song: 'The Lord Is Blessing Me'.

As he reached the top of the beach, he saw the big marquee shining like a Vegas casino. A couple of diesel generators chugged busily outside. When Benjamin ducked his head beneath the marquee's flap he saw that it was nearly full. A few of his flock turned to face him, and then everyone did. When they began to applaud, whistling and crying out their welcome, the pastor could not help but be swept up. He passed among them, allowed himself to be squeezed, hugged, kissed.

At the organ, LaDouceur hammered out the chords of a new refrain: 'So God Can Use Me'. It was one of Benjamin's favourites, and the musician knew it. The band struck up with their instruments and the congregation added its voice.

Benjamin felt his feet twitching, felt his hands begin to clap. Everywhere he looked he saw joyful faces, love-filled eyes. Earlier he had experienced a crisis of faith and now, and now . . .

He gazed around. Here he was, on a tiny uninhabited island

in the middle of the North Atlantic, standing in a marquee that blazed with light and rang with gospel music. Was that, in itself, not a miracle? And yet how strange that every one of the gathered faithful had a military carbine slung over one shoulder and a knife or a pistol strapped to one leg.

Blessed be the Lord, my Rock, who trains my hands for war, my fingers for battle.

As Benjamin mouthed the Psalm's opening lines he felt himself renewed. He reached the front of the throng and stepped onto the makeshift stage hammered together from old packing crates. Emily Coelto and Brian Ray opened up a space for him. He saw Wendy Devereaux in the front row, lips spread wide; and, coming up the aisle, wearing his wide-brimmed missionary hat, sleek grey hair hanging like a silver snake beneath it, Aiden Urchardan.

The man paused regularly as he made his way to the front, focus of the same affection. It irked Benjamin to see that, even though he knew it should not.

Urchardan joined him on the stage and put his hands on the pastor's shoulders. His green eyes pulsed with intensity.

In the corner, LaDouceur's band rolled towards its climax. So much *energy* inside this tent. Benjamin would not have been surprised to see flames rush up the canvas walls and explode above his head. Just as he thought the atmosphere had reached its peak, the Bliss entered him.

He arched his back, screamed out his acceptance. Immediately, his doubts and his troubles vaporised. Around him, the marquee seemed to shatter into millions of golden sparks. They rained down on his skin, electrifying him with their brilliance. He cried out with wonder and delight, heard his voice boomerang away and return as a formless chittering.

Those firefly sparks continued to wink and dance. Through them he began to glimpse the members of his congregation. Everyone writhed with the same ecstasy. Some crouched on all fours, panting and shuddering; some thrashed on the floor.

MY LOVE OUTLASTS ALL.

'*Yes! Ohhh yes!*' Pastor Benjamin screamed. '*Oh Lord, I'm a witness! I'm a witness!*'

I AM YOUR PROTECTOR.

'*We give you praise! We give you praise! We give you praise!*' All around him he heard his words echoed back. He saw hands, reaching up. Tears shining on cheeks.

YOU ARE MY SOLDIERS. MY FIRST CHURCH.

'*We're ready for the good fight!*'

THEN FIGHT THIS. IN MY NAME.

Abruptly, in Benjamin's mind, came an image of such monstrous evil, such transforming darkness, that he collapsed to the floor and wrapped his hands over his head. 'No,' he moaned. 'Oh please, *no.*'

He clenched his eyes shut but the images flickered regardless, terrifying in their clarity. Benjamin rolled onto his back, bared his teeth. The cycling of those nightmare images accelerated; he saw cities burning, children in flames, and the girl, the girl, always the girl. '*Deceiver!*' he shouted. '*Betrayer!*'

The pastor gasped for breath, unable to fill his lungs. He made fists of his hands. And then, just as he thought he could bear it no more – and that further exposure to such horrors would shatter his sanity – the nature of the images changed.

The Bliss showed him something new, something fragile but attainable: a solution.

Able to breathe at last, Benjamin unfolded from his foetal curl. '*Yes,*' he whispered, grateful beyond belief for what he was seeing. '*Yes, that's what we'll do. That's what we* must *do.*' His terror ebbed from him like poison sucked from a wound, and into the vacuum rushed a righteous rage.

STAND.

Obedient, he got up from the floor, saw the rest of his congregation join him. In their eyes he saw the same conviction. They stared at each other, jaws fixed, nostrils flaring.

The pain hit without warning, a searing heat that ignited

deep inside Benjamin's head and rolled like liquid fire through his limbs. He felt a tightening in his eyes so agonising that he wanted to tear them out; felt glass shards slice into his muscles; felt his heart swell, his arteries dilate. A thousand needles pierced his skin. His sinews stretched; his bones cracked and lengthened. He lifted back his head and howled, and heard others howl around him, no longer a congregation but an agonised pack of wolves.

When at last the pain, fractionally, began to recede, he felt himself changed . . . *improved*. He blinked, lizard-quick, saw the faces of his flock in startling sharpness. His lungs, when he took a breath, inflated like a blacksmith's bellows. He felt a new tension in his muscles that would be glorious to unleash, sensed his blood fizzing in his arteries like champagne. When he saw Wendy across the stage, and saw how the Bliss had changed her too, he felt, he felt . . . oh *my*.

Within moments she was at his side and they were ducking through the crowd towards the exit. All around him rose shrieks of excitement, animalistic snarls and sighs. He saw Emily Coelto and Brian Ray topple to the floor, tearing at each other's clothes. Emily's teeth snapped at Brian's shoulder, slicing through his shirt and opening his skin. He grabbed her by the throat and pinned her to the ground but she shook him free and rolled on top. Licking her teeth, she snatched at his belt. Benjamin tightened his grip on Wendy's hand and dragged her through the marquee's flaps.

Outside, Billy Gosselin stood on the grass. The janitor's eyes were wild. When he saw the pastor he lifted his M4 and unleashed a volley of gunfire into the clouds.

To Benjamin's vastly improved hearing the sound was torture. He grunted with pain, staggering away from the marquee towards the line of tents. He yanked Wendy inside the first one he saw. When he let go of her hand she knocked him to the ground, hitched up her skirt and straddled him.

They were not alone in here. In the shadows, Benjamin saw

the silhouette of a couple engaged in a similar dance. He tried to see who it was that he shared—

Wendy slapped him hard across the mouth. Shocked, he stared up at her. 'That's better,' she hissed, grinding against him. She grabbed his wrists and trapped them above his head.

Blessed be the Lord, my Rock, who trains my hands for war, my fingers for battle.

Outside, a jubilant chorus of gunfire began to stitch holes in the night.

CHAPTER 65

Dìdean, North Atlantic

It took Edward, Piper and Jolyon twenty minutes, creeping from one shallow patch of cover to the next, before they found a vantage point from which they could observe their target. They had ditched the duffel bag back at the chine, and now all they carried between them was a knife, a single rucksack and the Glock pistol that had suffered two separate submersions in Atlantic seawater.

Edward went first, sometimes sliding on his belly, sometimes creeping on all fours. He had tied a strip of wet cloth around his bad knee, but the cushioning it offered him was minimal. So acute was the pain that at times he feared he might pass out.

He pushed on regardless, pressing himself into hollows, crouching behind scrags of gorse. Each time he determined that the way ahead was clear he beckoned to Piper and Jolyon, and they emerged from cover to join him. In such fashion they inched their way inland, heading for the spine of rock that swelled like a dorsal fin from the island's heart.

The moon hung motionless above them, pregnant with light. Edward could not shake the feeling that he was watched from somewhere up there tonight, as if a celestial audience had gathered to monitor the unfolding events.

In front grew a sprawling expanse of juniper, a few feet in height. Edward crawled into it, cursing as its thorns gouged him. The others followed. For a hundred yards they wormed their way through. When they found a gap in its western boundary, they eased out their heads for a look.

Rising up before them, blotting out the stars like a vast black canvas stretched against the night, they saw the huge granite peak of Dìdean. To Edward it looked less like a natural geological structure than the fossilised remains of some gargantuan sea creature. Its slopes were gentler here than on the concave face to the south, but they still looked formidable. At its base, perhaps one hundred yards from where they now sheltered, he saw something that made every hair on his body stand erect.

Edward heard Piper's intake of breath and he shared her awe, knowing that for the first time in his life he gazed upon an excavation created by intelligence that was not human in origin. Watching it, he found his heart stirred not with fear, as he might have imagined, but with an almost unassailable joy. He found himself thinking of Laura. How she would have burned to see this. How he would have loved to share it with her.

'It's true,' he whispered. 'It's all true.'

Piper took his hand, squeezed. 'Thanks, Dad.'

He did not know why she thanked him, but right now it felt unimportant. Inevitably he found his gaze returning to that door into the mountain.

It was triangular in shape, three times the height of a man, comprised of a smooth black alloy that sat flush with the surrounding rock. He assumed that a tunnel lay behind it. How deeply it burrowed into Dìdean's spine was impossible to judge, but Edward guessed it would lead right to its heart. A series of circular impressions, pulsing with hard amber light, studded the door's perimeter. They looked like drilled boreholes filled with a substance of luminous viscosity. Flanking the door's apex Edward saw two smaller triangles, both of them inverted. These, by contrast, appeared hollow.

Beneath the sealed entrance, lit by the moon and by the strange amber light pulsing from the boreholes, stood five men.

Edward lifted his binoculars and studied them. The illumination was insufficient to reveal their faces but he saw the silhouette shapes of the assault weapons they carried. He turned to Piper. 'Who are they, do you think?'

'I've no idea. But we've got to figure out a way to get past them.' She paused, tilted her head. 'Do you hear that?'

Edward frowned, realised that he did hear something: music. It swelled out of the south, a harmony of voices. 'Is that *gospel*?'

Far off to his left, he saw the flicker of a torch beam as it bounced off the mountainside. Moments later he saw another, then five more. He could hear shouts of excitement amidst the singing now, catcalls and whoops. The torch beams jostled, grew brighter. Then, over a lip to the south, a crowd appeared.

Edward watched their approach, incredulous. There must be at least forty of them, possibly more: men and women alike. As they picked their way over the rocks, most of them sang the same hymn. Other shrieked wordless encouragement, yipped or laughed. When they arrived at the triangular door in the rock they swarmed around it like worshippers among standing stones.

Edward panned the binoculars left and right, and what he saw dismayed him. Every single one of the newcomers was armed. He saw military carbines, holstered pistols. Bizarrely, though, the atmosphere seemed carnivalesque. While a team to the left of the sealed door began to erect what appeared to be a sandbagged entrenchment, a team on the right started assembling something from metal poles and racks.

'Is that a *barbecue*?' Jolyon whispered. 'Who the devil *are* these people, the Salvation Army?'

Edward kept his binoculars fixed on the group as it worked. Every so often an errant torch beam revealed a face. In each one he saw a righteous fervour burning. 'You might not be too far wrong,' he said.

He lowered the eyeglasses, rolled onto his side and faced the others. His wonder at seeing that alien artefact was dissipating fast. Piper looked overwrought.

'Well, we can't go through them,' Jolyon said. 'So what the blazes *are* we going to do?'

Edward looked at his watch: three-thirty a.m.

Thirteen hours until their window of opportunity opened.

Thirteen and a half hours until it closed.

CHAPTER 66

Dìdean, North Atlantic

The crowd outside the tunnel entrance maintained the same fierce energy throughout the night. At times they seemed more like hedonistic revellers than a defending force. Smoke rolled from their barbecue fires, heavy with the aroma of grilled steaks, glazed ribs and corn. For Edward, Piper and Jolyon, who had not eaten since scuttling the *Saoradair*, it was a silent torture.

The guardians laughed, clapped, sang fragments of gospel. Every so often a tumultuous volley of gunfire lit up the night. At one point a trio of faithful sneaked into the juniper bushes twenty yards away and engaged in brief but enthusiastic coitus.

'I guess they're not Baptists,' Jolyon muttered, watching them lope back to the main group.

As the eastern sky began to blush, the island's defenders formed a circle of interlinked arms and sang 'The Battle Hymn of the Republic'. As he listened to the words, Edward's skin itched. He wondered if this was the beginning of his last day. Eyes gritty from lack of sleep, he lay on his back and watched the coming sun paint the sky with fire. Piper's hand found his own and he knew that all three of them witnessed something important, even if he failed to understand it.

He checked his watch again, saw that it was half past seven. As quietly as he could, he unzipped the rucksack and passed around a water bottle. His stomach felt hollow. To distract himself he raised his binoculars to the tunnel guardians. Now that the sun had risen he could see them more clearly. They were an eclectic group, mixed in age, sex and race. Some conducted themselves in ways that suggested a military background; others more like former desk jockeys. All wore combat fatigues devoid of insignia. Their weaponry looked formidable. Slung beneath a few of their carbines he glimpsed what might be grenade-launchers.

Edward shook his head, wearied at the sight. How could he possibly neutralise such a dedicated defence? He thought about retracing his steps and trying to locate their camp. If he found it, perhaps he could cause a diversion and drag some of them away. But he knew they would never leave in sufficient numbers to offer Piper safe passage across the one-hundred-yard killing ground between the juniper grove and the tunnel door.

Even as he considered his dilemma he heard commotion, and turned in time to see another armed group appear from the south. This one boasted similar numbers to the first. A conversation ensued. Presently the members of the first party began to disperse.

'How many more *are* there?' Piper whispered. Her face, as she watched them, was ashen.

Pastor Benjamin patrolled Dìdean's eastern shore, trying to think with a mind that was no longer his own. He existed, now, in a heightened stupor, too drunk on sensation to concentrate or care about anything for long. His muscles sizzled with electricity. Each time he moved, his heart gunned in his chest like a blipped throttle. He felt the pressure of his blood in his ears, saw it jumping in the pulse points at his wrists. Every minute or so The Bliss annexed his senses and monitored the coastline from north to south, looking always for the girl, the girl, the girl.

He had woken an hour earlier, finding himself naked inside a scrambled nest of blankets and sleeping bags. His chest was a bloody mess of scratches. Wendy lay face down beside him. For a moment he wondered if she were dead, wondered if he had somehow killed her during the night, but then he saw her shoulders rise and fall.

Stumbling to his feet, Benjamin pulled on his clothes. Around him he saw further members of his church, deep in slumber. A memory fragment came to him of last night's excess, but he struggled to make sense of the details. Outside – obeying a voice he seemed not to hear – he tramped over boulders towards the beach.

There he found himself now, walking the eastern shore with the other searchers and examining every rock, every clump of marram grass, every narrow strip of sand or shingle. Fronds of seaweed lay strewn across the rocks like the bedraggled victims of shipwrecks. And, nudging up and down in the surf, he spotted a long PVC duffel bag, of the sort used by sailors.

Benjamin stared at it for a full five seconds before his trance lifted. Then he charged into the sea. The water was freezing; it shocked him fully awake. He snagged the bag by a grab handle and dragged it clear of the waves. Dropping to his knees, heedless of the seawater that soaked through his clothes, he unclipped its straps and opened it. Inside he found bright foil packets of freeze-dried food, boxes of raisins, chocolate. Beneath the food lay signal flares and what appeared to be a launcher.

The bag itself looked new. Inside, it even *smelled* new. Its colours, black and orange along its length, with end-panels in reflective silver, looked crisp and sharp. He saw no sign of fading from seawater or UV. His stomach flopped like an eel. 'I found something!' he screamed. 'I *found* something!'

The Bliss leaped into him, so violently that he clenched his teeth and cracked a molar into sharp pieces. The pain lasted a fraction of a second before it vanished.

THE GIRL!

'*Yes,*' he stammered. 'What should I—'

THE GIRL!

THE GIRL! THE GIRL! THE GIRL!

Up and down the shore, the heads of his fellow searchers lifted towards him. Then, a few hundred yards away, Ricky Delafonte began to yell. '*We got an outboard! We got a freakin' boat engine hidden in this hole!*'

Edward's first indication that something was wrong was when a bell began to toll near the island's southern tip. He had been dozing for the last hour, perhaps longer, but the sound snapped him awake as effectively as a slapped cheek. Deciding to risk it, he peered out through a gap between the juniper bushes.

The crowd around the tunnel door stood with their heads cocked, as if receiving silent instructions.

'What's happening?' Jolyon whispered.

'Don't know. Doesn't look good.'

Suddenly, a mass of defenders shouldered their weapons and formed a protective perimeter around the entrance. Others took cover behind the barricade they'd constructed. A third contingent began to spread out in a fan formation, directly towards the juniper grove where Edward, Piper and Jolyon sheltered. They walked purposefully, their weapons cocked, their heads moving from side to side.

'Time to back up,' Edward said. 'Keep low and take it steady. We can't afford to be seen.'

A man on the extreme left flank raised his carbine and aimed it into a section of the juniper grove. Without breaking stride, he unleashed a controlled burst.

The guardian beside him opened up next.

Closer this time.

Bullets shredded branches, ploughed into the soil.

A third guardian raised his weapon.

'Go!' Edward hissed. '*Now!*'

CHAPTER 67

Dìdean, North Atlantic

Aiden Urchardan stared at the outboard motor Ricky Delafonte had pulled from the blowhole and shook his head, incensed. In his heart he had known that Mórríghan would one day return to the island, that a battle would be fought on Dìdean's soil, but he had expected her to arrive at the head of an army, leading a valiant but ultimately doomed assault. Not like this, in furtiveness and cunning. The sheer *dishonesty* of her approach outraged him, and he was not the only one affronted.

He felt the *balla-dìon* flit in and out of his head like a moth, moving so fast that it dragged with it images from other minds it had co-opted, producing a montage of colour and movement so disjointed and confusing it made Urchardan feel sick.

From the mouth of a steep-sided chine further up the beach he saw commotion, heard raised voices. Five churchmen emerged from its mouth, shouting in excitement. The *balla-dìon* flickered among them, appropriating eyes and memories, and Urchardan perceived what the group had uncovered: the hull of a rigid inflatable boat, its PVC tubes slashed and deflated.

'It was up there!' someone shouted. 'Hidden in the scrub!'

Damn her, Urchardan thought. *Now all our futures are at stake.*

Edward bellied through the soil, tearing his skin on juniper thorns, following Piper's feet as they scraped and kicked inches from his face. Behind him he heard the excited shouts of the tunnel guardians as they spread out from the entrance. Every few moments, gunfire lacerated the air. He crawled with his shoulders raised and his teeth clenched, convinced that soon he would feel bullets smash into him, or watch them rip through his daughter. In the face of such powerful weaponry he could not even use himself as a shield to protect her – his body would do little to slow the velocity of those rounds.

The girl snaked right and Edward crawled after her, praying that she remembered the way they had come. If they could make it back to the chine where they had hidden the boat, they could retreat to the beach and rethink their strategy. Right now, that felt like a huge *if*.

Another burst of gunfire strafed the bushes beside him. Branches snapped and popped. Bullets zinged off stones.

'Mother of God,' Jolyon muttered.

Ahead, Piper's boots stilled. For a horrifying moment Edward feared she must have been shot, that he'd witnessed his daughter killed in front of him. But then he saw her inch forwards.

Looking about him, he recognised the patch of scrub in which they sheltered and realised that they had, at last, reached the top of the chine.

Piper rolled onto her side. 'Back,' she hissed.

Edward frowned, glanced behind him. Saw Jolyon, furiously shaking his head. 'We can't.'

'We've no choice.' Her eyes were terrified globes. 'They're coming.'

Wendy Devereaux stepped out of the tent wearing nothing but combat boots and a down-filled mountaineering jacket. She had slept for perhaps an hour, certainly no longer, but she had never in her life felt better. Her heart raced in her chest like a finely tuned NASCAR engine. Her blood-engorged muscles trembled with tension, ready to snap into service the moment they were called. Her vision had grown so sharp that she could see every rock, pebble and blade of grass in stunning clarity. She could taste blood in her mouth and it excited her, made her think, briefly, of Pastor Benjamin and the intimacy they had shared the previous night. But however pleasurable that memory, she had no time for such distractions now. She knew her task, and was anxious to perform it.

Every minute or so she felt her senses annexed by the presence she'd come here to serve. She acquiesced willingly, hungrily, thrilled that it would choose to use her as its instrument. Whether that presence was the Christian God Benjamin professed it to be, Wendy did not know. Neither did she care. To her, the tunnel entrance at the island's heart looked engineered rather than something created by supernatural means, but whatever the nature of the being that had put it there, she offered it her allegiance with no shred of misgiving.

Wendy strode down to the beach, her carbine bouncing against her shoulder. She had managed to commandeer one of the few M203 attachments the group had brought along, and she itched to see the carnage it could wreak. In the pockets of her jacket she carried five of the stubby forty-millimetre shells the weapon fired; their potential for destruction electrified her even more than her memories of intimacy with the pastor.

Hearing gunfire from further inland, Wendy quickened her pace. She bounded over rocks and boulders, as silent as a hunting cat. If the Deceiver had been uncovered, she wanted to be there for the slaying.

She came around a jag and the beach opened out. Ahead she saw a line of Dìdean's guardians methodically sweeping the gorse-choked slope. From beyond the ridgeline she heard a second chatter of automatic fire, followed by a jubilant shout.

Her heart leaped. Was she too late? Had the girl already been killed?

So intent was she on scrambling across the rocks and racing up the slope that she almost missed the sight for which she should have been attuned. It so surprised her that she skidded to a stop and simply stared.

A moment later she un-shouldered her gun and flicked off the safety.

Wendy grinned, elated that she would be the one to sound the alarm. 'Here!' she shouted. 'Over here!'

Edward peered left and right. The juniper grew so densely on either side that he could see no possible way through. Even if he used his body as a battering ram to force a path through the thorns, the commotion would attract a deluge of gunfire that would doubtless rip them to pieces.

Piper's eyes had grown large with panic. Edward felt his heart begin to slow in his chest, as a fatalistic acceptance descended on him. He focused his attention on Jolyon. 'Can you look after her?' he asked. 'Can you help her finish this?'

Piper grabbed his arm, held on. 'Dad, no.'

Edward kept his eyes on Jolyon. The artist stared, his usually ruddy cheeks draining of colour. He swallowed, nodded.

'No,' Piper insisted. 'Not this, Dad. *Please*, not this.'

Edward pulled the Glock from his holster. He handed it to Jolyon. 'I don't know if it still works. If it does you've got sixteen rounds, no more.' Then he turned to face his daughter.

He opened his mouth, tried to think of something to say, and was still thinking when he heard movement in the undergrowth a few yards away.

'*Here!*' a woman shouted, her excitement palpable. '*Over here! Look!*'

Edward put his hand over Piper's fingers, peeled them off his arm.

He took a last, steadying breath. Raised himself into a crouch. Tensed.

CHAPTER 68

Dìdean, North Atlantic

Pastor Benjamin was still crouching beside the duffel bag he had rescued from the sea when Wendy Devereux cried out her warning. He raised his head, saw the line of searchers on the beach turn and stare up the slope.

Benjamin could see her now, a vivid shape against the sky: bare legs, bright mountaineering jacket. She shrugged her weapon from her shoulder. *'There!'* she cried. *'Over there!'*

For a moment he thought that she pointed at him, and then he realised that she gestured *behind* him. He saw the searchers pivot in unison, saw them tense at what their eyes showed them. They raised their arms, hollered and whooped.

The Bliss flitted into Benjamin's head, flooded his body with adrenalin.

BOATS.

He too pivoted, feet no longer his own, and saw, there on the horizon, a procession of tall white shapes. The boats were far too distant to be viable targets, but that did not dissuade some of the more highly strung members of his church. He heard a few erratic discharges of gunfire before a sharp word of command from the Bliss stopped them.

Benjamin counted the vessels, dumbfounded: five, seven, fifteen. A second flotilla now shimmered into view behind the first. All were sailing yachts; he could see the taut curves of mainsails and jibs. No crew were visible at this distance, but if he assumed five crew members for each boat, that made seventy-five raiders in the first wave alone. The second wave might deliver a similar number.

Numerically superior the invading force might be, but the Church of the Holy Sacrament controlled Dìdean's beaches, and it had something else on its side, too, something far more powerful than favourable ground.

ME.

Hearing that, Benjamin shuddered.

Jenna Black stood on the prow of the *Nicolisa* beside Therron Vaux and watched Dìdean's coastline loom large in her binoculars. What she saw was extraordinary: a huge fin-shaped mountain rising from grass-covered flats protected by rocky headlands and narrow bays. Orla had spoken of the place before she died, identifying it as the location Cathasach and Mórríghan had chosen to site the *balla-dìon*. The woman had explained, too, that the eastern shore offered the only navigable approach, and Jenna saw that her words had been accurate

The landing would be all but suicidal, even so. Spread out along the rocky coastline she glimpsed tiny figures standing in wait. 'It'll be a slaughter,' she muttered.

Therron lowered his binoculars. 'How do we know if Piper made it ashore?'

Jenna shrugged. 'We need to have faith.'

The boy nodded. 'That's about the only thing I've got.'

The *Nicolisa* maintained her position on the northern flank of the fleet. To port Jenna saw the bows of nearby yachts knifing through the waves. There was the *Dún Aengus*, the *Béal Inse*, the *Eamon Maria* and the *An Faoiléan*; others whose names she could not remember. Half of the boats had departed from Dunstaffnage Marina in Scotland, half from Ireland's Lough Swilly, converging at a prearranged rendezvous point in the North Atlantic a few days earlier. The yachts' skippers had been in training for years, the existence of the boats a secret that even Jenna had not known until her conversation in Orla's bower with the dying *Triallaiche*. On board the thirty vessels stood every surviving follower of Ériu and Orla. Between them they brandished weaponry both modern and ancient, all of it sourced from the armoury at Crafter's Keep.

Every person she saw on deck wore the same grim yet determined expression. All of them knew the consequences of the next few hours, the personal cost of both failure and success.

Orla had been unambiguous that night in Cornwall. Jenna, of course, had long understood the consequences for humanity should the *balla-dìon* fall: the secrets of the stars would be revealed to those who chose to see, and the chatter of the earth would become audible to those who cared to listen. She knew, too, that with such revelations, humanity's concept of what it *meant* to be human would irrevocably change. Old certainties would disappear; perhaps even old rivalries.

But until Orla spoke to her, she had not known that the seemingly limitless lifespans enjoyed by the four *Triallaichean* depended entirely on the energies produced by the *balla-dìon* – as did the lives of those earth-born followers, including herself, who had endured far longer than they might otherwise have expected.

Aside from Therron, every single member of the fleet's one hundred and sixty volunteers sailed towards Dìdean for a confrontation that would end either in victory or defeat, but certainly in death. '*Ériu protects*,' Jenna whispered, and permitted herself a small smile. To Therron, standing at her side, she asked: 'What time is it?'

He glanced at his watch. 'Three fifty-seven.'

Half an hour, give or take, until the Ookater Cloud forced the *balla-dìon* offline. Another half an hour before its defences returned.

One hour to change a planet.

Sixty minutes to save a race.

★ ★ ★

Aiden Urchardan charged down the hill towards the beach, his vision kaleidoscopic, his legs moving faster than they had in years. A steady flicker of images streamed before his eyes, views generated from each of the guardians on the beach. He was only half-aware of the commands the *balla-dìon* snapped out, but the decisiveness with which it acted relieved him greatly.

A defensive line of thirty individuals had already deployed along the eastern shore. A further twenty lay concealed in the low-lying scrub behind it. Fast-running scouts were moving north, west and south, reinforcing the parties that patrolled there and monitoring the island's alternative approaches. The remaining guardians – the fiercest and most highly trained – manned the final defence around the *balla-dìon*'s tunnel entrance.

'Come closer,' Urchardan growled, staring at the yachts. His fingers flexed, tightened into fists. 'See what we do to you.'

He itched to watch the *balla-dìon* destroy them, but it could not act while they remained so far away; he felt it scouring the sea for suitable hosts but its investigations yielded no fruit.

Urchardan saw two volunteers on the beach, Ambrose Howard and Debbie Guttuso, begin to strip off their clothes.

He watched them for a moment, perplexed. Then he nodded.

Good idea.

Jenna peered through her binoculars as the two figures on the shore began to undress. They lay down their weapons, pulled off their boots, discarded trousers and jackets. A moment later they plunged into the sea. For a while the rolling surf hid them from view, but soon she saw two tiny heads pop up on the seaward side of the break.

'What the hell are they doing?' Therron asked. 'Five minutes in this water will kill them.'

Jenna frowned. And then a monstrous thought hit her. She shouted to the *Nicolisa*'s skipper, cupping her hands to her lips.

'Turn us away! Get word to the others! We're too close! We're too *close*!'

Already the male swimmer was in trouble, fighting the waves with increasing desperation, but his female counterpart powered through the sea undeterred.

The *Nicolisa* was turning now, its boom swinging around. Jenna saw the skipper shouting into a radio receiver. She waved to the other boats, screamed at them to turn north.

Less than a minute had passed since the swimmers had entered the water, but already the woman was far closer. Now, instead of powering through the waves she slowed, began to tread water, and lifted up a hand to the fleet.

'Ah, shit,' Therron said.

Jenna had seen the gesture at Stallockmore Farm nine years earlier. She gripped the prow with both hands, unable to speak.

On their port side the *Eamon Maria*, a fifty-foot schooner, crumpled like matchwood. Her hull imploded first, producing a fusillade of sharp debris. Then her deck folded and her masts snapped. Portholes burst, metal rails collapsed, fibreglass ruptured into jagged white pieces. Jenna did not see what happened to the crew, but she saw a spray of blood across the mainsail when the cloth fell into the water. A few seconds later the entire wreckage disappeared into the depths, as if dragged beneath the waves by unseen hands.

All along the line, the remaining boats began to react, but they sailed so close to the wind that their manoeuvres were desperately slow.

The female swimmer trod water in a rising swell. Jenna saw her raise her hand once more.

South of the *Nicolisa*, amidst screams that cut short almost as soon as they began, the *Béal Inse* folded beneath the waves like a crushed origami sculpture, leaving nothing but white water in her wake.

CHAPTER 69

Dìdean, North Atlantic

Edward had been about to break from the juniper bushes and charge towards the woman who had spotted them when he heard the timbre of her voice change. 'There!' she cried. 'Out on the water! *Look!*'

At once, a frenzied scrabbling issued from the chine, as if the guardians who had been climbing up now descended at speed.

Careful to remain hidden, Piper peered into its depths. 'They're leaving,' she whispered.

Edward stared at her, numb. He had been a breath away from giving up his life. The realisation that he had been saved was, for a moment, too overwhelming to grasp. Behind him, the guardians who had raked the juniper grove with gunfire began to shout.

He lifted his head from cover. A few men and women, wide-eyed with excitement, were searching frantically for a quick path down to the water. The rest of them sprinted back to the triangular tunnel entrance.

'Something's got them spooked,' he said. 'What the hell could it be?'

'She was shouting about something on the water,' Piper said.

'Do we go down to the beach?' Jolyon asked. 'Or work our way back to where we were?'

'No point going back to the beach,' Piper said. She gestured inland. 'That's the place we need to be.'

Edward grimaced. 'I know you need to get through that door, but we haven't got a chance while it's so heavily guarded. Somehow, we have to draw them off.' He glanced at his watch. 'It's twenty-two minutes past four. Less than four minutes until this thing goes offline.'

'So we split up,' Jolyon replied. 'It's the only way.' He rolled his head, scrunched up his eyes. To Edward, he said: 'Your place is with Piper, that much is clear. Which means if anyone's going to draw off those brutes, it's got to be me.'

They had no time to debate it. Edward nodded. Then he stuck out his hand. 'I don't know what to say to you.'

'How about: "Do not go gentle into that good night"?' the artist shot back. He clasped Edward's hand, squeezed.

Edward had not realised that Jolyon quoted from a poem until he heard his daughter complete the verse.

'"Rage, rage, against the dying of the light",' Piper said. She grinned, eyes glassy with unshed tears. Crawling forwards on her elbows, she embraced the artist as best she could.

Jolyon clutched the girl fiercely before easing her away from him. 'They'd better name a street after me,' he growled. 'Or at the very least a damned fine pub.' Then he crawled away through the juniper bushes, heading south.

The *Dún Aengus* imploded next, disintegrating like a matchstick model. The wreckage disappeared beneath the waves in a splintering cacophony, so violently and so completely that it left nothing, not even a slick of oil, to mark its passing. Seconds later the *Béal Inse* and all her crew followed. Jenna watched, powerless. Four of the fleet's thirty yachts gone in less than a minute. In vain, she searched the water for survivors.

At last, the female swimmer who had channelled the destruction succumbed to the cold. She sank beneath the waves, resurfacing for a few desperate moments. Then a wave swamped her, and she did not reappear.

Jenna trained her binoculars on the shore, saw four more

figures stripping off their clothes. She peered at her watch: one minute left until the *balla-dìon* went offline.

And then what would happen? Would the beach defenders come to their senses? Would they fight on?

Naked, the four volunteers splashed into the surf. Jenna saw them dive beneath the first breakers. They resurfaced, swimming towards the fleet with powerful overhand strokes.

All the boats had now turned north-east. The wind blew fiercely from the west, filling their sails and propelling them through the swell. Undeterred, the swimmers gave chase.

Jenna heard the ripped-linen crack of a high-powered rifle and twisted around. On the deck of the *An Faoiléan*, Mike O'Shea lay prone. The man ratcheted the bolt of his weapon, squinted, fired again. A burst of white water erupted a few feet from the nearest swimmer.

A boat's horn blasted.

Moments later a second horn joined it, then a third. Soon, every yacht in the fleet had added its voice to the chorus. The sound swelled in Jenna's ears, bounced off the ocean waves.

She glanced down at her watch.

Four twenty-five p.m.

Time.

CHAPTER 70

Dìdean, North Atlantic

There were no pyrotechnics. No blazing meteorites or halos. No coronas or glories or shimmering Brocken spectres. The skies did not darken as if from a solar eclipse; the air temperature did not drop. None of the scant wildlife that made its home on Dìdean's slopes fell silent. In the wider world, no televisions broadcast static, no motor vehicles lost power, no dogs barked and no church wind vanes began to spin.

The earth sailed through the Ookater Cloud as it had every eight years since its creation, and except for the three hundred or so souls arrayed along Dìdean's coast nobody noticed a thing.

Aiden Urchardan felt it, at first, as a shrivelling inside his head. He stood on the beach, staring out to sea at the yachts the swimmers had scattered, as the *balla-dìon* issued its last instructions.

IN YOUR HANDS, NOW.

'Yes,' Urchardan said. For the first time in all the years he had served, he could see – however slim the prospect might be – a real possibility of failure.

IF THERE IS TO BE A FUTURE, THERE CAN BE NO FAILURE. THE GIRL MUST BE STOPPED.

'At all costs.'

USE THE POWER WISELY.

'Power?' he asked. 'What—'

And then he was clenching his teeth, arching his back and

throwing out his arms as the energy poured into him. The tendons of his neck tightened like the cables of a suspension bridge. He felt the arteries in his head swelling beyond their natural limits. He wanted to scream, but so much pressure had built up inside him he feared that should he open his mouth his innards would burst up through his throat. Convinced that the same thing could happen to his eyes, he clenched them shut, but the lids sprang open like doors kicked from their hinges. In his ears was a roaring, a thunder, a conflagration of pounding blood.

THE PASTOR IS WEAK. USE THE WOMAN INSTEAD. USE EVERYONE YOU NEED. NO SACRIFICE TOO GREAT. NO ACT TOO ABHORRENT. WE MUST PREVAIL. AT ALL COSTS, AIDEN URCHARDAN. AT ALL CO—

And, just like that, it was gone.

Urchardan stood there shivering, his body pulsing with the power the Bliss had invested in him. He felt as if he observed the world from a place deep inside his head, and yet his vision seemed to encompass everything. He took a step forwards, half expecting to see blue crackles of electricity snake from his boots. He clutched his fists, heard his knuckles crack like pistol shots.

From one of the yachts out to sea a horn sounded, a grating blast that bounced off Dìdean's spine with the vigour of a summoned demon. Others joined it, until an unbroken wall of sound rolled shorewards from north to south. Urchardan saw frantic activity on the decks of those boats. The *balla-dìon*'s swimmers had scared them off, but now their prows arced back towards the landing beach. He saw figures crowding around pushpits and guardrails, readying themselves for the assault.

Urchardan's eyes swept the eastern coast. Along it, volunteers from the Church of the Holy Sacrament maintained a loose defensive line as wide as the oncoming fleet. They stood with chins jutted and shoulders squared, weapons aimed and ready. 'Pick your targets!' he shouted.

From the decks of the yachts came sudden flashes of light. The air filled with the whip-crack of high-powered rifle rounds. They drilled through the surf, burrowed into the sand, exploded off the rocks. One of the guardians toppled over, a red hole in his back.

The retaliation was savage and unrelenting. All along the line, carbines jumped into life, pouring a storm of fire into the approaching boats. The sea turned white. Some rounds struck their targets but not many. Hundreds passed harmlessly through sailcloth, or met no resistance at all.

He heard furious shouts from those with military training, but their demands went unheeded. The most experienced volunteers had been tasked with tunnel defence, leaving the shore in the hands of the hunters, the firemen, the engineers and chefs.

Urchardan saw a man empty an entire magazine into the sea, eject it and snap another into his weapon. 'No!' he shouted, furious. 'Discipline! *Discipline, you dog!*'

Another volley of sniper fire hit. This time two more defenders fell. One went down screaming, clutching his stomach. Another spun as he dropped, bone fragments and teeth erupting from his jaw.

From the gorse-choked slopes raced reinforcements, snatching up the weapons of their fallen comrades. On the southern flank, Urchardan heard the pop of an M203 and saw a burst of smoke. A second later a tall plume of water climbed from the sea.

Urchardan heard another pop. This time the placement was perfect, the ordnance detonating on the deck of a closing yacht. When the vessel emerged from the smoke, he saw that its mast had been destroyed. Two figures lay inert on the shattered foredeck, their clothing blackened and shredded.

From Dìdean's guardians rose an animalistic howl. More percussive pops sounded from the beach. Most of the high-explosive M203 rounds detonated in the sea, but a few struck targets, one blowing apart a yacht's bow, another exploding in a crowded cockpit, raining limbs into the water.

The fleet's first wave was closer now, sinking into the troughs behind the breakers. For a moment they disappeared from view. Then they rose up in the swell like swans. Urchardan could see the crews clearly, could see the fear in their eyes, and a fatalistic resolve. Such a cruel chain of events Ériu had unleashed. Such an unnecessary waste of life. The landings would be bloody and futile. Those boats were never designed to be beached, let alone in such treacherous conditions. An incoming wave rolled beneath their hulls. The next one would take the closest yachts right onto the shore.

The carbines lit up again, and this time the range was far more favourable. He saw the *Triallaichean*'s recruits fall dying into the sea. Bodies bobbed like wine barrels leaking claret.

The sun had set; along the horizon, the sky was indistinguishable from the ocean. Behind the guardrails of the incoming boats, the followers of Ériu and Orla tensed themselves for the wave that would carry them to the shore. Men and women in combat fatigues clutched assault weapons and knives. They shouted encouragement to each other, bared their teeth. The line of defenders opened up again, mercilessly thinning their ranks.

The yachts sank into a trough, began to rise. Urchardan lifted his head and screamed at the clouds. So much dark energy coiled inside him; his torso felt like a pressure chamber ready to blow. The boats were so close that he could hear the clanging of lines against masts, the taut snap of sailcloth.

The wave broke in an explosion of white water, and through it, like galloping chargers, came the first nine yachts. So powerful was the torrent that their rudders and sails could not keep them on course. Their sterns swung around. Booms scythed across decks. Men and women dived into the frothing surf.

The first boat hit the beach and immediately capsized, the

undertow dragging it back into deeper water where it was swamped. Another vessel slammed into its hull. He heard cries, screams. From the cover of the gorse bushes the M240s opened up. The sea turned white and then pink as the machine guns stitched murderous seams through the water. Smoke billowed and rolled along the beach. Grenades ripped open the hulls of floundering boats. The sea filled with wreckage. Perhaps half the recruits in the attacking first wave were already dead, but out of the surf came the survivors. Those who still held weapons began to return fire, sheltering behind whatever cover they could find.

The second line of yachts was closing now. Their momentum would take them straight into the flotsam of those already wrecked. *Good*, Urchardan thought: more chaos, more confusion, less chance of a breakthrough. He scanned the decks in hope, but he could neither see, nor sense, Mórríghan's host. For a while he had begun to believe that the dinghy hidden in the chine had been a trick, a sly diversion, and that the girl would arrive in the midst of this invading flotilla. Now he realised he had been mistaken.

Everywhere he looked he saw attackers cut down by volunteers from the Church of the Holy Sacrament. And while Dìdean's guardians took casualties of their own, they manned a far superior defence.

The beach, he knew, would be held.

Which meant Urchardan was needed elsewhere. Turning from the carnage, he strode inland.

Billy Gosselin, standing in a sandbag dugout beside the God structure he'd been tasked to protect, listened to the sounds of warfare rolling in from the eastern beaches and kicked at the scrub in rage. Forty of the church's most experienced fighters hung around outside that huge triangular slab.

'We should be down *there*, fighting!' he yelled, directing his anger at Marcus Dyke. A few hours earlier, Eric Bocanegra had deputised Marcus, a decision that had made Billy seethe with indignation. 'Our brothers and sisters are down on that beach, and right now it sounds to me like they're *dyin'*! Meantime, we're sat up here with all these *guns* an' shit, just twiddlin' our dicks.'

As if to make his point, a huge explosion echoed off Dìdean's slopes. Moments later came the industrious hammering of the M240s. Billy faced his co-defenders, incredulous. 'Am I the only motherfucker who can *hear* that? Am I the only motherfucker who wants to *do* somethin' about it?'

'Shut up, Billy,' Marcus growled.

'Oh, I'm the enemy now, huh? You're asking *me* to shut up?'

The man's face hardened. 'No, Billy, I'm telling you. We got our orders, they got theirs. We start doing our own thing, there'll be chaos.'

'Newsflash!' Billy screamed. 'That ain't the sound of a bible study meet! They're gettin' creamed down there!'

'Told you to shut up.'

'An' while we're lyin' around up here like dogs in the sun, they—'

Before he could finish his sentence Marcus Dyke punched him, a sailing right cross that burst Billy's nose and put him on his back. He lay there, spluttering with outrage. Then his eyes widened and he snarled. His hands flew to the M4 hanging around his neck just as Eric Bocanegra stepped forwards and used his boot to pin the weapon against Billy's chest.

'Bad idea, Billy,' Eric said. The man held a pistol at his side in a way that suggested he would have few qualms about using it.

Billy's eyes grew wider still. A pulse beat in his neck. Then he sagged, lifting his hands from the gun and raising them above his head. 'I warn't gonna shoot him, Eric.'

'Looked that way.'

'I was just lettin' off steam.'

Eric Bocanegra shook his head. 'You're losing it. And I can't have that on my watch. Hand it over.'

Billy's mouth dropped open. 'You can't—'

'Give me the gun, Billy.'

Shocked, outraged, but cowed by the lack of emotion in Eric's eyes, Billy unslung the M4 and handed it over.

'Pistol.'

'For f—'

'You heard me.'

He unholstered his Browning and passed it to Eric, who in turn handed it to Marcus Dyke. That pissed Billy off even more.

'Knife,' Eric said.

'What, you're gonna make me defend this place with my bare hands?'

'You're not *fit* to defend this place. Look around you. You see anyone else playing up? Anyone else stepping out of line? If you can't figure out the importance of what we're doing here, I don't need you on my team. Knife.'

Billy glanced around at the other guardians, looking for support. They stared at him, impassive. He spat in the soil, unsheathed his knife, tossed it at Eric's feet. 'Fine.'

'Now get up.'

Sullenly, he complied. 'Something stinks about this whole damned thing, Eric.'

'Get the hell back to camp. And if you see anything worth reporting on the way down there, you come running back here and tell us.'

Somehow, as the *Nicolisa* surged towards the shore, powered not just by sail but by a titan wave that lifted and catapulted her, her skipper managed to steer her north of the peninsula framing the main landing beach.

The peninsula itself was a narrow spine of spray-blasted rock a few yards in height. And while it would shield Jenna, Therron and the other crew from the fury of those heavy guns to the south, their new landing site would be far more treacherous than the bay in which the other boats were breaking up.

Ahead, the surf crashed not onto a shingle beach but a series of natural steps in the rock: sharp, hard and unforgiving. Jenna could not take her eyes off them. If she and Therron remained aboard when the *Nicolisa* struck, they would doubtless be consumed by the wreckage. Yet if they took their chances in the sea, they risked being pulverised against those stone steps.

The boy shot her a hollow-eyed look. When he tried to grin through his fear she wanted to weep for his bravery.

Wind battered them. Spray flew from the white-tops like driven steam.

'You jump before we hit,' Jenna shouted.

Therron nodded. He turned his face to the looming steps.

'Get into cover as soon as you can,' she urged. 'Keep your head down. Listen for their reloads.' She gestured at the handgun strapped to his leg. 'You remember how to use it?'

Before Therron could answer, the *Nicolisa* dropped into a deep trough. When the wave lifted them, Jenna saw a man in khaki fatigues perching on the peninsula's spine. He stared at her, his face contorted with hate, and raised an assault rifle. Feet planted, he unleashed its magazine at the yacht. Bullets ploughed furrows across the coach deck. They smashed portholes, punched through fibreglass, ricocheted off winches, eye plates and cleats.

Jenna saw two of the rounds strike her skipper in the chest, knocking him flat. As she struggled to loosen her pistol from its holster she heard the steady crack of Therron's gun. The boy held his weapon with both hands, one leg straddling the forward pushpit. Nearly all of his shots missed, but one of his last hit the man with the rifle in the throat, toppling him from his perch.

A moment later, the wave carrying the now skipper-less *Nicolisa* broke around them. Therron, his balance already precarious, plunged off the bow and disappeared into the surf.

Jenna screamed. Seawater filled her throat. Through a white-water mist she glimpsed the steps rushing up. The yacht shuddered as her keel ripped loose. The stern swung around, offering the rocks a broadside target. Jenna slung her legs over the pushpit, gripped the rail.

The *Nicolisa* began to tip.

Now or never. Those steps terrified her, but if she stayed on board a moment longer—

She jumped.

The cold was shocking, so overpowering that she felt her diaphragm contract. Jenna gulped salt water, kicked her legs, felt herself turned by the surf. She put out her hands, tried to protect her head from the impact she knew was coming. Prisms of blue-green light danced in her eyes. She heard thunder, the roaring of wild sea. Something struck her across the back, an impact so brutal that she thought her spine must have shattered.

Jenna tumbled again, lost all control of her arms and legs. Something sharp pierced her thigh, burrowing deep. The pain was a firework inside her flesh. She gritted her teeth, kept her mouth closed against the breath that threatened to burst from her lungs.

Yet again she felt herself turned. A solid edge of stone slammed her cheekbone and now, at last, the breath bubbled out of her. Drowning, she scrabbled with her fingertips, felt flat rock, tried to get a handhold on something, anything, felt another wave lift her and batter her against a shelf. Nothing but a soulless ringing in her ears now; and pain, astonishing pain.

Abruptly, those prisms of blue-green light turned white. Her face was above the waves and she was drawing breath. Her right arm wouldn't work. She dragged herself forwards with the left. A darkness in one eye. All around her the surf foamed pink. 'Therron!' she screamed. 'Therron!'

Somehow, Jenna managed to turn herself around. A fresh wave slammed her, carrying her back ten feet. As the surf receded, she saw a body half-submerged, dressed in the same black jacket the boy had worn. Blood streaming from her injuries, she staggered into the waves.

The sea rolled in. It punched her against the rocks, slamming her spine once more. She moaned with pain, allowing the undertow to suck her out.

This time she floated sufficiently close to hook Therron with her good hand, but when she pulled him towards her she found that while she clutched his jacket, the boy himself was gone. 'No!' she cried. '*Therron!*'

Frantic, she peered along the beach. Ten yards to her left, the *Nicolisa* lay half submerged, torn open from bow to stern. Seawater rushed in and out of the breech, weighing the vessel further and hastening her destruction. Jenna could see her skipper floating face-down in the surf. But not the boy.

Another breaker struck, rolling her over. She cracked the back of her skull against rock. White sparks spiralled behind her eyes. Her thoughts loosened. Much more of this and she'd be dead.

Sobbing, apologising, guilt dragging at her far more insistently than the undertow or her waterlogged clothes, she crawled hand-over-hand out of the water's fury.

Every muscle, every inch of her flesh, felt as if it had been pounded by steak hammers. Her left ear rang. Her right ear felt curiously hollow. When she glanced up, trying to gauge her location, she saw one of the island's guardians standing five yards in front of her.

The woman wore laced combat boots, and a thick mountaineering jacket zipped to her throat. In her hands she carried a military carbine, the barrel of which she aimed at Jenna's head. Her eyes were hard and bright, empty of all mercy.

CHAPTER 71

Dìdean, North Atlantic

Marcus Dyke watched Billy Gosselin shuffle down the hill towards camp and shook his head, deeply troubled.

How had it come to this? They had arrived at the island in faith, in solidarity, utterly convinced by their cause. And yet some of their behaviour during their stay defied explanation. He had witnessed acts of depravity, had partaken in depravity. His had been the actions not of a devout follower of God, but of a savage, an apostate.

When Billy disappeared over the ridge, Marcus sought out Eric Bocanegra. 'You know,' he said, once they'd walked some distance from the others, 'I hate to say it, but Billy's got a point.'

Eric grimaced, turning his head east towards the strip of coast where battle still raged. 'And we've got our orders.'

'Yeah, but from whom? That Urchardan guy?' Marcus shook his head. 'Dude creeps me out, if I'm honest. It's like my mind was foggy back there for a while, and now it's starting to clear.' He gestured over his shoulder at the triangular black slab framed by amber-filled boreholes, now dark. 'What the hell *is* that thing, anyway?'

He saw Eric open his mouth to answer, and interrupted. 'Sure, I know what it's *meant* to be, what that creep Urchardan *says* it is. But have a damned look, Eric. Does it seem like any kind of thing the Bible might have mentioned? Man, I'm no priest, but that looks to me like some kind of weird engineering project. And while Urchardan's got us kicking around up here protecting it, down on the beach the rest of our guys are getting –' he shrugged – 'well, who knows what's happening down there.'

Eric Bocanegra scowled, spat on the ground. 'Something about this ain't right, I'll grant you. But we can't just abandon the place.'

'And we can't turn our backs on the guys down at the beach, either. Especially while there's so many of us up here doing nothing.'

Eric stared at him. 'Can I trust you to keep things locked down?'

'Yeah. Course.'

'Then pick some guys,' the man said. 'You stay here, lead them. You *defend* this *thing*, whatever it is. I'll take the others down to the beach, reinforce it.'

Marcus nodded, relieved. 'I'm beginning to think we were sold a turkey.'

'I'm beginning to think you're right.'

'If we're not out here serving God, like we thought . . .'

'Best not dwell on that,' Eric told him.

Jolyon Percival crept over a fold in Dìdean's southern heathland and saw, below him, the guardians' camp. Beside a neat line of tents, white marquees stood with their canvas walls rippling. The sides of some had been rolled up, offering him glimpses of trestle tables and cooking equipment. On the northern fringe he saw a latrine trench, freshly dug. Nearby a fire smouldered, fed by timber scavenged from packing crates.

Jolyon could see no signs of life down in the camp, not a single guardian defending it. Those he had seen at the tunnel entrance had been well armed. Perhaps, here, he could locate their arsenal. Glancing at his watch, he discovered that only twenty minutes remained before the *balla-dìon* came back online.

Alert for movement, ready to throw himself into the heather at a moment's notice, Jolyon picked his way down the slope. He reached the cooking tents first. On a gas-fired griddle, now cold, he saw stiffening strips of bacon and blackened sausages. His stomach muttered but he ignored it, moving towards the nearest marquee. A row of silent generators stood outside. Inside, he found a crude wooden stage and musical instruments plugged into amps of various sizes.

The second marquee looked like it had served as an ops centre. Spread across two trestle tables lay a huge hand-scribed map of Dìdean. He saw a small black triangle symbolising the tunnel entrance, and routes marked around the island's perimeter for what he supposed were sentry patrols.

Deciding to search the smaller tents, Jolyon slipped back outside. He crossed a patch of grass trampled to mud by the camp's inhabitants, and as he was about to duck into the first shelter he heard something, over the sighing of the wind.

It was a miserable sound, like that of a wounded animal, except there was something inescapably human to it. When he heard it again a few seconds later, he pinpointed its source to a tent set a little apart from the others, near a stand of sickly looking trees.

Jolyon crept closer. No mistaking that sound now; it was a thoroughly human lament. He eased open the flap and peered inside. What he discovered horrified him.

The tent's primary use had been a weapons dump. Lining the canvas walls on each side he saw black plastic crates. Their foam interiors had spaces cut for assault rifles and handguns. Most of them were empty, but weapons glimmered in a few. Nearby lay ammunition boxes, holsters, a satchel of shotgun cartridges.

Jolyon saw all that in an instant, but it did not hold his interest. Because at the far end of the tent, atop a pile of filthy sleeping bags and towels, cowered four women, their wrists secured to a wooden support by lengths of thick rope.

Their faces were bruised, their mouths bloody. Their bare shoulders bore what looked like bite marks. In their eyes Jolyon saw humiliation, outrage; and, as they considered him, a mounting terror.

'I'm not here to hurt you,' he said, gently lifting his hands. 'I'm going to get you out of here, as quickly as I can.' He retreated to the packing crates, this time conducting a closer search. He ignored the firearms, hunting instead for a knife. He found two.

Moving to the nearest of the captive women, he dropped to his knees. 'What's your name?'

'*Dee . . . Dee . . . Deana*,' she whispered. '*They . . . they . . .*'

Jolyon nodded, began to saw through her bonds. 'I know what they did. It's over, I promise.' The moment he severed her rope she scrambled away from him. 'Here,' he said, tossing her the second knife. 'Give me a hand with the others.'

Deana snatched the weapon up, and for a moment he thought she was going to attack him. Instead, she bounded across the makeshift bed and began to hack at her neighbour's bonds.

Jolyon went to the woman third along the line. Silent, eyes wide, she offered him her wrists. He cut her loose, turned to the last of the captives.

'I know you're scared,' he told them. 'What happened in here is . . . is so damned barbaric that I have no words. But like it or not, what's happening outside is even more important than your pain. You were brought here under false pretences. You, and everyone who came with you. If we don't intervene, if we don't—'

Jolyon hesitated, stilled.

Outside, he heard the thud of footsteps in the mud. Behind him, the tent flap flicked open.

A reedy voice said: 'I'm givin' you fair warning, girls. Billy ain't in the mood for no . . . man, who the *fuck* are you?'

Jolyon turned on his haunches. He saw, standing between

the packing crates, a wiry, gap-toothed stranger with a spiky ginger goatee. The man wore an angry, petulant look; fingers twitching, eyes hardening, he stepped further into the tent.

It was, unquestionably, the worst decision he could have made. The woman Jolyon had just freed snatched the knife from his hand. She loosed a grating scream, charging across the tent towards Billy.

Alarmed, the man raised a hand to ward her off. She slashed with the knife, lopping off three of his fingers. Before he could react to that, Deana dived towards him, brandishing the second blade.

All three fell to the ground. Within moments, the remaining two women had piled in. Caught beneath stabbing blades, slashing nails, falling fists, Billy Gosselin began to scream. Quickly, those screams devolved into gurgles, and, soon enough, into sighs. Soon all Jolyon could hear were the snarls of the women he had rescued, and the wet ripping of their steel.

CHAPTER 72

Dìdean, North Atlantic

Edward watched from the cover of the juniper bushes as a large contingent of guardians broke from the dugout and headed down the slope towards the eastern shore. Minutes earlier, he had witnessed an angry confrontation between one member of the group and two of its commanders. Now this.

He tracked the departing force until it disappeared beneath the lip of the slope, and then he shifted his attention to the tunnel entrance. Only four guardians now remained. But as much as their depleted ranks helped his cause, he still saw no way through. One hundred yards of rock-strewn ground stood between the juniper grove and the triangular door in the mountainside. No way he could take on four armed men defending a fortified position.

Edward delved into his rucksack. He found the water bottle and drank, careful not to take too much. Handing it to Piper, he glanced at his watch. Sixteen minutes and thirty-five seconds until the *balla-dìon* came back online. If Jolyon didn't figure out a way to draw off those remaining defenders soon . . .

'He will,' Piper said. 'I'm sure of it.'

'You've a lot of faith in him.'

'I've a lot of faith in you both.' She took a sip from the water bottle, swallowed. 'Dad, there's something I have to tell you.'

Edward looked up sharply. Something in her tone had scratched him. 'What is it?'

'That door.' Piper faltered when she saw him watching her. She took a breath, expelled it. Hunched her shoulders. 'I have to go in there alone.'

He blinked. Felt his stomach begin to grow cold.

'When I do,' the girl continued, 'I want you to get as far away from here as possible.'

With some concentration, she stood the water bottle upright in the soil. Afterwards she laced her hands over her knees and waited.

'Why would you say that?' Edward asked. 'Why wouldn't you want me in there with you? Unless . . .'

He stopped as an insight struck him, so bleak that he heard the rush of blood in his ears, a sound like the ocean captured in a seashell.

Beò-Ìobairt.

Living Sacrifice.

Piper hugged her knees to her chest. 'I *can't* come out. What I have to do in there . . . when I destroy the *balla-dìon* . . .'

She dropped her head and Edward felt his world begin to disintegrate.

All the walls he had built these last sixteen years, all the patchwork repairs and defences; he felt the whole ramshackle construction come crashing down. He tried to lift himself above the debris, but found himself pummelled by a hopelessness so unbearable that he could hardly draw his breath.

His voice cracked when he spoke. 'You'll die in there.'

'Yes.'

Edward stared, too shocked to do anything else.

It was the worst news he could have expected. And yet, bizarrely, as he began to roll it over in his mind and make it his crushing new reality, he discovered that, in a way, he *had* expected it. Not just expected it, either; he had *known*. He had known since holding her in his arms on the night of her birth.

'There must be another way,' he said, even though he knew that no other way existed. 'Some alternative.'

Patiently, compassionately, Piper shook her head.

'Let me speak to Mórríghan. Perhaps—'

'Dad, this is why I'm here. It's what I was born to do. Nothing can change that.'

When Edward saw how determined she was, how brave and how scared, his eyes swam. 'This is your *life* we're talking about.'

'I know that.'

'Your life for an idea.'

'Not just an idea. A future.'

'What if you're wrong? What if all this . . .'

Edward gestured towards the tunnel entrance, but he had no words to finish his question. How could he deny what he had seen, not just here but at Crafter's Keep, at Joyau Caché, at Stallockmore Farm?

And then, through that suffocating weight of sadness, Piper's earlier words penetrated.

When I do, I want you to get as far away from here as possible.

Edward crawled to his daughter's side, wrapped his arms around her. 'All my life,' he said, pressing his cheek against her hair. 'All my life I've told people I love that I wouldn't abandon them. And later, when it mattered, that's exactly what I did. I did it to Laura. I did it to my unborn child. I did it to Therron.' He scowled at those memories, set his jaw. 'I won't abandon you, Pie. I won't.'

She put her hand over his. 'But you have to.'

He shook his head. 'I can't.'

'Dad, I've always known this was my fate. Sometimes I've denied it, I'll admit that. But it's always been there, always been a part of me. It's who I am. Who I've been for as long as you've known me.'

She looked away from him, towards the triangular black slab in the mountainside. 'The thought of what I've got to do in there, it scares the hell out of me. But do you know what's keeping me going? The fact that you'll get to live through what happens next.'

Again, Edward shook his head. 'I don't *want* to live through it. Not without you.'

'You will,' she told him. 'Humanity won't be the same after this thing comes down. We'll change, all of us, I know it. It'll be a different world. You can finally say goodbye to the old one, make a life in the one that's coming.'

He pulled away and stared at her, saw how honestly she implored him, and knew, without doubt, what he must do.

'We go in there together, Pie,' he said. 'You and me. Father and daughter. There *is* no other way.'

Marcus Dyke stood behind the dugout he had helped to construct and stared east. He could not see the beaches from here, could not see the battle he knew was taking place, but he could see the ocean, and there was some comfort in that.

He no longer trusted himself to look at the triangular black slab at his back. Every minute that passed, his disquiet at what might lie behind it magnified. He tried not to think of the depravities in which he had engaged down at the camp, but they kept surfacing in his mind like night-spawned horrors.

Nor was he the only one affected. Brian Ray, Dexter Myers and Andy Bartholomew – the three men he'd picked to remain behind with him – appeared similarly troubled. Brian Ray fiddled constantly with the safety switch on his carbine. Dexter used the heel of his boot to carve patterns in the dirt. Andy Bartholomew sat on a sandbag, lips engaged in constant yet inaudible commentary.

'It's not letting up,' Marcus said, keeping his eyes on the sea.

'Armageddon,' Brian replied. He snapped back the charging

handle of his M4, chambering a round. 'That's what this is. And I reckon we picked the wrong team.'

'Not too late to make amends.'

'You think?'

Marcus shrugged. 'I don't know what to think. You wanna sing something? Maybe say a prayer?'

'I could sing,' Dexter Myers said, looking up. 'Don't feel like it much, but I reckon we oughta.'

'Me too,' said Andy, breaking from his monologue.

'Anyone have a suggestion?'

'How about "Onward Christian Soldiers"?'

Brian Ray snorted. 'Anything but that. How about "Abide with Me"? That was my momma's favourite. Always kinda liked it.'

Marcus smiled, nodded. 'You start us off.'

Crouched before that triangular black slab, with voices that faltered and hitched, the three men began to sing.

> Abide with me; fast falls the eventide;
> The darkness deepens; Lord with me abide.
> When other helpers fail and comforts flee,
> Help of the helpless, O abide with me.

As they launched into the second verse and their voices began to lift, Marcus noticed movement to the south and spotted five heavily armed figures running towards the dugout. Four of them he recognised as women from camp. Deana Taylor was one; Ladell Williams another. He could not recall the names of the others. What he *could* recall made him cringe with shame.

Among the women ran a red-bearded stranger wearing a wild-eyed look.

Brian, Dexter and Andy were still singing, so engrossed in the hymn that they didn't notice the newcomers until Marcus shouted a warning. That same moment, as he threw himself to the ground, Deana Taylor emptied her gun at them.

Andy Bartholomew and Dexter Myers died instantly, falling like pins in an alley. Brian Ray reacted faster, hurling himself down beside Marcus. Lifting his M4 over the sandbag parapet he returned fire, sweeping the weapon left and right.

'No!' Marcus yelled at him. 'They're our own! Our *own*!' He dived forwards, tried to knock Brian's weapon away. 'Goddamn it,' he screamed, 'I said they're our own!'

Either Brian did not hear the plea, or – panicked by the slaughter of his friends – he no longer cared. He shoved Marcus away from him, pushed to his feet and brought down his weapon into firing position. When he saw the identity of his assailants his expression changed to one of disbelief. An instant later, a bullet struck him in the chest.

He flew backwards, crumpling against the dugout's far wall and sliding down it. His head lolled and he stared, dumbfounded, at the blood pulsing from his sternum. 'I didn't . . .' he said. 'I wasn't . . .'

He coughed. Choked.

Marcus watched him die. On the other side of the dugout, the guns fell silent.

He did not know what to do. He could not bring himself to use force against the women who had killed his friends. Not so many days distant, he'd called them friends too.

He could sense them growing closer, knew that when they arrived they would show him as much mercy as he deserved.

But the first face he saw appeared from the south, and it belonged not to Deana Taylor, as he had expected, but to a lean, dark-haired stranger with red-rimmed eyes and a grey-streaked beard. Beside him stood a teenage girl. Marcus recognised her.

His gun was in his lap. All he had to do was lift it and pull the trigger.

But he couldn't do that.

Wouldn't.

The stranger with the grey-streaked beard raised a semi-automatic pistol.

Marcus stared into the black circle at the centre of its barrel and sighed. Instead of terror, he felt enormous relief.

CHAPTER 73

Dìdean, North Atlantic

With the light fading all around them, Edward stared at the man cowering in the dugout and lowered his pistol.

His adversary had been smiling, as if he welcomed the oblivion a bullet would bring. When he saw Edward's finger lift from the trigger he began to weep. 'Do it,' he pleaded. 'Why wait?'

Edward cast his eyes over the barricade's sandbag lip. Walking towards him, accompanied by Jolyon, were the four women who had attacked the dugout. He glanced back down.

'Please,' the man whispered. 'Do it quick. I don't want to look at them. I don't want them to see what I've become.' Abruptly, his expression changed. 'Oh dear Jesus, what is *that*?'

Edward turned to look. A few yards away stood the sheer rock wall that formed the base of Dìdean's spine. In it he saw the triangular black stratum, flanked by two similarly shaped boreholes at its upper vertex.

Whereas before it had appeared solid, as if the surrounding rock enclosed a seam of coal or obsidian, it now appeared liquid, although of a kind that seemed strangely resistant to gravity. When the wind gusted, ripples rolled across its surface.

He became aware of Piper at his side. The girl studied the undulating mass, her lips parted in fascination. A bead of blood, black in the fading light, trickled from one nostril.

Edward heard movement behind him – the four women

arriving inside the bunker. The man on the floor drew up his knees and sobbed, but the women ignored him, staring instead at that swirling black mystery imprisoned in the rock.

'It's not what Urchardan told us,' one of them said. 'But it's something almost as strange. Isn't it?'

Edward nodded.

'Dad,' Piper said.

He looked at his daughter and saw, at once, how hard she fought to control her emotions.

'It's time,' she told him.

Edward swallowed, glanced around. His eyes met Jolyon's.

'These blasted goodbyes,' the man said. He gripped Edward's shoulder, squeezed. 'You're going in with her.'

'She's my daughter,' he replied. 'She's everything I have.'

They embraced.

Now, Jolyon turned to Piper. 'Looks like this is it.'

The girl nodded. 'Will you do me a favour?'

'Name it.'

'Find Therron for me. Keep him safe.'

'I'll do my best.'

She smiled, winked. Then she reached out for her father.

Edward grasped her hand in his own, and when she advanced a step he matched her. They stood mere inches from that shifting black surface.

He looked over his shoulder; at the windswept juniper grove that retreated towards the island's eastern shore; at the indigo waters of the Atlantic. Overhead, the last of the day's light had faded. As well as the Pole Star, he could see the first constellations beginning to shine. The moon hung among them, a bright white bulb, shedding its light generously on Dìdean's slopes.

Edward thought about all that had gone before. He found himself wondering what would come after.

As if Gráinne stood beside him with her lips pressed to his ear, he heard the words she had spoken to him sixteen years earlier.

It's a beautiful world, isn't it, Eddie?

'Ready?' he asked, turning to his daughter.

The girl steadied herself, offered him a defiant grin. 'Yeah.'

Gripping her hand tightly, holding his breath, Edward Schwinn plunged forwards, out of the world he had known and into one whose boundaries he could not begin to fathom.

CHAPTER 74

Dìdean, North Atlantic

Benjamin D. Pope – he could no longer call himself *Pastor*, even if, for a while, he had regained his appreciation of that title – stumbled along Dìdean's eastern coast, heedless of the bullets that flew around him.

A second flotilla of yachts, this one as large as the first, was now sliding into the troughs behind the furthest breakers. Those waves would lift and transport the vessels shorewards, smashing their hulls into the wreckage of other boats languishing in the surf. Already small figures lined their decks, waiting to leap into the water and fight their way onto dry land. Benjamin viewed their preparations with mounting dismay. The pulverised wrecks provided scant cover for any who might survive the landing.

Bodies tumbled and dragged in the surf. Yet as distressing as it was to see them, those casualties from the Church of the Holy Sacrament affected him more. He had brought these people here, had convinced them that this was a battle they should wage.

And all of it had been a lie.

Benjamin did not know what power his congregation on the beaches now served, but he knew that it was not God. None of the behaviour he had witnessed on Dìdean spoke of holiness, of divinity. If anything, he had watched his people regress. For a while he had joined them.

Now, for whatever reason, that invading influence seemed to have fled, and in its absence he saw the deception it had spun. That he could have become an accessory to such falsehood sickened him.

All those years since the accident, he had preached the Word with a heart empty of belief. And now, despite the monumental lie he had been sold, and had propagated – bizarrely, perhaps even *because* of it – he felt his faith return to him, renewed.

Benjamin frowned.

The accident?

With that single question, it felt as if a partition inside his head had collapsed. Dark memories rushed through. His hand closed around the locket he carried and he understood, immediately, whose it was.

Linda's.

'*Dear God,*' he moaned. '*Oh dear Lord Jesus, please don't forsake me, please don't.*' He recalled standing at his wife's bedside. He saw himself switch off her ventilator alarms, followed by the ventilator itself.

Her fingers had twitched in his, as if she tried to communicate a desperate last message.

Holding his hands to his mouth, Benjamin staggered, nearly fell. The enormity of what he had done was too much to grasp. He wanted to vomit, but no physical purge could rid him of his horror. As he tripped across the rocks to a stepped cove he glanced up to see a woman kneeling in the water.

She appeared forlorn, lost. Blood sheeted down her face. One arm bore a filthy cast; the other hung loosely at her side. Around her knees the surf foamed pink.

The woman did not look at him, did not register his presence. Because a few yards further down the cove's stone steps, out of the sea's reach, stood Wendy Devereux, wearing an expression of such bestial savagery that Benjamin hardly recognised her.

Wendy dug the stock of her M4 carbine into her shoulder, and the woman in the sea bowed her head.

Around them, breakers boomed against rocks, ocean-borne devils demanding a sacrifice.

CHAPTER 75

Dìdean, North Atlantic

To Edward, it felt like walking through a liquid metal that radiated no heat. The fluid exerted a thickening pressure against his eyelids and throat, a sensation that filled him with such revulsion he almost turned back; but within moments of entering that lightless prism he lost all sense of direction. He dared not open his eyes or mouth, and he tried in vain to suppress his panic. The pressure in his ears equalised with a roar. After that he heard nothing but the laboured pounding of his heart. Piper led him onwards, and he submitted himself reluctantly to her care.

All his life he had hated confinement. He had chosen to dwell far from cities and crowds, fleeing to the mountain spaces where he could breathe without restriction. Wherever possible, he had avoided the horrors of tunnels, cellars, packed train carriages. Even the feel of tight clothing could set his heart racing. During his Alpine years the prospect of a crevasse plunge had been his only fear. He had never willingly set foot in a cave or ravine; and this was far, *far* worse.

With each step he held Piper's hand tighter. She flexed her fingers, as if he caused her pain, but he could not loosen his grip – if anything, the thought of her slipping away heightened his panic.

The pressure against his eyelids was awful; not constant but undulating, like the probing of wet tongues against his face. His lungs grew tight. He ached to take a breath. Surely this must end soon. Surely.

But it didn't.

They walked on. He felt that dense liquid pressing at his lips, seeking an opening. Above him he sensed the weight of millions of tons of rock, worse than any nightmare he had ever experienced.

Edward's chest began to burn. His diaphragm twitched involuntarily, trying to empty his lungs and inflate them with fresh air. He felt Piper's other hand on his chest. Her fingers walked up to his face. She tapped his mouth and he shook her away. Undeterred, she took his fingers and put them to her own face. The girl's mouth was open.

Realising that, he panicked, thrashed loose.

And then, even worse, he was cut off from her, all alone and drowning inside that liquid-filled prison, and now he was on his knees, shaking, clutching at his throat, squeezing his eyes shut even tighter and wanting to scream out his horror, and knowing that he must take a breath, and that he couldn't, he couldn't—

He breathed.

The air bubbled out of him and the black liquid flooded his lungs, and there was no pain, no pain at all, just cold. He felt weightless, dizzy. The tightness in his chest fled. It took him a moment to realise what was happening, and then the reality dawned: he was not dying; he was breathing.

His horror did not diminish. He was still captive in here, robbed of his senses, deaf and blind to his environment. But his panic, by degrees, began to ebb.

He had to find Piper, he knew that, but in which direction should he go?

Remembering his rucksack, he shrugged it from his shoulders. Supported by the buoyant medium, it floated slowly to the tunnel floor. Kneeling beside it, he unzipped a pocket and withdrew his torch. The chance of it working was minimal, he was sure, but he had to give it a try. He flicked it on.

However hard he tried to summon the courage to open his eyes, he failed. Instead, he pressed the torch's lens against one of them.

He was rewarded with a weak orange glow, as the beam illuminated the blood vessels in his eyelid. Even better, a few moments later Piper's hand touched his shoulder. He tried to speak, but the metallic liquid absorbed all sound.

She tugged at him and he stood. Then, her hand clutching his once more, she led him on.

For how long they walked, Edward could not have guessed; he lost all concept of time. He knew they journeyed deep into Didean's spine, that the mass of rock above their heads increased with each step, but it felt meaningless now, horror piled upon horror.

His emergence, when it came, felt almost as shocking as his initial immersion. One moment his body was supported on all sides and the next it was free. That vile black liquid sucked clear of his ears with an abruptness that made him shudder. He found himself coughing, retching. The next time he breathed he drew in dank air that tasted of ancient stone, lichen and damp.

His eyes were still clamped shut. When he heard Piper's voice, he nearly wept with relief.

'Dad?'

'I'm OK,' he said. 'You?'

'Yeah. You can open your eyes.'

Slowly, Edward did. Darkness, everywhere, except the torch beam angled at his feet. A moment later he raised it to Piper's face.

Her skin was pale. She smiled. 'That was intense.'

He nodded, shone his beam around. They stood in a small airspace at the end of the tunnel, perfectly pyramidal in shape. Three of the four tapered walls were smooth stone; the one from which they'd emerged undulated gently. Beneath their feet, the floor was a carpet of glittering black sand.

'What now?' he asked.

Piper surveyed the walls. 'Can you give me your torch?'

Edward passed it to her. He put his rucksack on the floor and unpacked it. At the bottom he found two headlamps. He donned one, tossed the other to Piper. Then he took out his water bottle and offered it. She declined, playing the torch beam over the walls with increasingly erratic movements.

'What's wrong?' he asked.

It was a while before she answered. 'I don't know where we go from here.'

Edward climbed to his feet. 'What does Mórríghan say?'

'She doesn't know.'

'She doesn't *know*?'

'She never came this far.' Piper glanced down at her watch. 'And we've only got six minutes before the *balla-dìon* comes back online.' She turned towards him. Began to tremble. 'Dad, I don't know what to do.'

CHAPTER 76

Dìdean, North Atlantic

Jolyon watched Edward and Piper disappear through the black triangle in the rock and knew he would not see them again. For a moment he could do nothing but stare at the rippling entrance gate. Like a skin forming on cooling candle wax, its sheen began to dull. Moments later he touched his hand to its surface: hard, cold.

However emotional he might feel at the loss of his friends, he could not afford to dwell on his sorrow. There was still so much to do.

Jolyon glanced around at the members of his group: the women he had rescued from the tent, the single male survivor of the dugout. All five stared at the triangular black slab into which Piper and Edward had disappeared. Slowly, their eyes rolled towards him.

'My name,' he said, and for a moment he could not continue. Swallowing his uncertainty, he squared his shoulders. 'My name is Drustan. I don't know what lies you were told, what reason you have for being here. But you have a different task now, should you choose it.'

'What . . .' began one of the women, pointing to the hardened black triangle in the rock. 'What *was* that? Where did they go?'

'They went to save you,' he said, and felt his chest heave

with the knowledge of their sacrifice. 'Now it's time for you to save yourselves.'

Another of the women spoke. He recalled her name: Deana. 'What do you want us to do?'

'Come with me,' he said. 'Down to the beach. We have to stop the killing. There's not much time.'

'Drustan,' Deana muttered. '*Drustan*.' Eyes shining, she reached out her hand to the man cowering on the ground. Shakily, with the moon's light glimmering in his widening eyes, he took it.

'Drustan,' he whispered. Fat tears began to slide down his face.

'Follow me,' Drustan told them, and as one they offered him piety. When he heard their affirmations, his spine tingled. He groped for a memory that had not yet surfaced.

Turning from the prism in the rock, bidding his friends a silent farewell, Drustan led his new followers east.

Therron Vaux – scratched, bleeding, battered from his contest with the waves – lifted his head over the peninsula behind which he sheltered and looked left and right.

So cold, he felt. Seawater dripped from his clothes and hair. When the wind gusted, it sucked away his body heat. He shivered uncontrollably, found it difficult to draw full breath.

To the south he could hear the rattle of gunfire and the screams of those cut down. The sounds pulled at him, and he knew he should try to make his way there and offer his support. But he had lost his gun during his plunge from the *Nicolisa*'s bow. Somehow, as the yacht broke up on the rocks, he had fought his way clear of the surf. He appeared to be the only one to have survived.

While his conscience told him to head south and join the main landing party, his heart told him to find Piper, and it was to his heart he listened. He knew that the girl would have headed west on arrival, knew without being told that the extraordinary spire rising from Dìdean's heart must be her destination.

From where he crouched, behind this spray-slicked prom-ontory of rock, he could see no movement, no visible threat. Ahead, leading up from the beach, stood a steep-sided chine a little like the one he had spied during the *Nicolisa*'s approach. That chine had been choked with gorse. This one was rocky, devoid of life.

Behind him, the surf boomed. Further along the shelf he could hear the rasp of the *Nicolisa*'s hull as she sawed herself apart.

Therron bounded from cover, dashing across a shingle bed and into the chine's wide mouth. He was protected here, both from the wind and from the attentions of anyone who might come along the beach. Night may have fallen, but the moon offered plentiful light.

Therron scrabbled over the rocks littering the chine's entrance. Quickly the gradient grew more intense. He hauled himself up, trainers squelching. He slipped on a loose stone, bashed his elbow, grimaced and forced himself on. Higher he climbed. Split rocks and shingle surrendered to car-sized boulders. He could see the top, now, an indigo V framed by the chine's silhouette. Overhead, stars glittered with a platinum intensity.

As Therron neared the summit, he felt eyes on him from below. When he glanced back down the slope towards the beach, he saw a figure from an old nightmare watching him.

It was too dark to see the man's features. Perhaps – just like in his dreams – there *were* no features. Perhaps the man's face, beneath that wide-brimmed missionary hat, was smooth skin uncluttered by eyes or nose or lips.

Moaning his fear, Therron continued to climb. He scrabbled onwards as fast as he could, leaping over boulders, hauling himself up. But the top of the chine was too far away, and the figure at the bottom too close. Each moment that passed, he felt his skin tighten around his flesh in anticipation. He didn't need to turn his head to know what was happening behind him.

Therron panted with exertion, murmured wordless sounds. The nightmare on the beach raised its hand heavenward. If it possessed a mouth, it would doubtless be showing teeth.

CHAPTER 77

Dìdean, North Atlantic

Piper peered around the confines of their prison walls with burgeoning panic. 'What are we going to *do*, Dad?' she wailed.

She slammed her fists against the side of the pyramid, kicked it with her boot, her eyes wild. 'All those people outside – all those at Crafter's Keep, Joyau Caché. And it's all *meaningless* if I can't find a way through.' She looked at her watch, pressed her palms to her temples. 'We've got four minutes. Four *minutes*.'

Edward went to her side, took her firmly by the shoulders. 'There's a way,' he said. 'We've just got to find it.'

'Yes, but what?'

He couldn't answer that, of course, could offer her no counsel. And then, suddenly, he could. He glanced around him, so surprised that his hands dropped from his daughter's shoulders. 'I . . . I *recognise* this place.'

Piper stared, incredulous. 'How could you?'

'I don't know,' he said. 'But I do. I'm sure I do.'

And then it struck him.

He recalled the night that Jolyon Percival had arrived at Joyau Caché, seeking accommodation. The man had owned no tent and towed no caravan, so Edward had installed him in one of the static vans at the top of the site. He had felt uncomfortable that evening, especially when Jolyon asked him, directly, about his family. So great had his disquiet grown that later he paid the artist's lodgings a visit on the pretext of delivering fresh laundry. Finding the place unoccupied, he let himself in and discovered Jolyon's cache of artworks.

Nearly all the canvases had been of Piper, but one of the works – hidden behind the sofa, wrapped in brown paper and far larger than the others – had been different. Edward had lifted the package up and ripped away the paper, revealing a life-sized oil that depicted not just Piper but himself.

At the time he had been appalled. The image showed him crouching over his daughter in near-darkness, holding a knife to her throat. On either side of them, smooth black walls tapered to a point above their heads.

The inherent violence of the image had long since ceased to bother him. He knew that Jolyon had painted it as a result of dreams twisted by the *balla-dìon*'s influence. But the chamber the artist had depicted was clearly the one in which they stood, with the exception of a detail that Edward, until now, had dismissed.

While a fine black sand covered the floor beneath his feet, the floor in Jolyon's painting had been of smooth stone, delicately engraved with swirling geometric patterns. At the time it had reminded him of Celtic knotwork, although far more complex in design.

Dropping to a crouch, Edward scooped away handfuls of the glittering black sand. Only a two-inch depth covered the floor, a portion of which he quickly revealed. Just like the walls surrounding him, it was perfectly flat. Just like Jolyon's representation, its surface was finely inscribed.

On hands and knees, Edward swept away more sand, pushing it to the far corners of the pyramid.

'What is it?' Piper asked, shining her torch on the subject of his excavations.

'I don't know,' he said. 'But I think it's important.'

He worked faster, revealing more of the geometric pattern. He could see no focus to it – no gradually revealed secret, no symbolism that he could grasp or code he could unlock.

Piper stood as far back as possible, her torch angled high to assist him. Edward could feel her urgency like a flame against his skin.

Already he had revealed the entire floor on his side of the pyramid, but still he could see no purpose in the whorls and coils his efforts had exposed.

Wiping sweat from his forehead, he paused for breath and noticed something odd. The terminations of those inscribed lines, where they disappeared beneath the sand closest to Piper's feet, seemed to glow with a faint bluish light, like the bioluminescence of phytoplankton stirred by ocean waves.

Excited, he crawled towards her, uncovering more of that meandering pattern as he went. The closer the revealed lines grew to Piper's position, the more radiance they cast off.

'It seems to recognise you,' he said. He worked even faster, using his forearms as brushes. The girl now stood at the edge of what looked like a glowing Celtic tattoo, comprised of lines as sharply defined as the light inside fibre-optic cables. 'Come towards me,' he said. 'Stand in the centre.'

Piper obliged, and with each step the brightness intensified. The lines at the centre of the motif shone white, fading to turquoise at the edges. Then, without warning, the floor plummeted.

Edward grunted, momentarily weightless, heard Piper cry out in shock. They accelerated, falling like stones dropped down a shaft.

So disorienting was the effect, so heart-stopping, that it took him a moment to realise that he still knelt on the floor. The light pulsed under Piper's feet. She swayed but kept her balance. The walls hurtled past so quickly that their surfaces seemed to shimmer, liquefy. With some difficulty Edward pulled himself upright.

He thought of how far beneath the earth they must already have dropped, and of the tons of rock massed above their heads.

They were lower than the ocean now, had to be. He sensed it lending its own unbearable weight.

His ears popped. His breath grew tight. He wondered if this was to be their end, that the last thing they would experience was the stone floor crashing to such an abrupt stop that their bones would shatter to dust. Once the thought had surfaced he could not dispel it, and it ran amok inside his head, delivering him a hundred graphic deaths, each more visceral than the last.

Piper held out her hands and he gripped her tightly, resolved that he would not let her see the nature of his thoughts. He clamped his mouth shut, tried to stop his breathing from dissolving into unrecoverable gasps.

The walls now blurred past so quickly that they must be travelling at *hundreds* of miles an hour, far faster than their terminal velocity should have allowed. He experienced no turbulence around him, no whistling of parting air; it felt as if they fell in a hermetically sealed bubble. And yet he could hear *something*: a faint humming sound, steadily increasing in pitch.

Piper stared at him, and he thought he detected a slight vibration in her pupils. 'What if we don't—' she began, and stopped when he shook his head, warning her from contemplating such horrors.

Faith, he mouthed, even though he had little of it himself.

Abruptly, in a brutal reversal, the platform began to decelerate. Edward's weight increased exponentially and he crashed to the floor, felt himself squeezed to its surface with monstrous force. His vision began to darken as the deceleration intensified, but he kept hold of Piper's hands, even though he lacked the strength to do anything else. When he tried to take a breath, it seemed as if a hundredweight of bricks had been piled upon his chest. His vision failed completely, followed by his hearing. The floor pressed at him so ruthlessly he worried that his skin would burst from the pressure.

At last, he felt the ferocity of their deceleration begin to ease. A trickle of air reached his lungs. A smear of vision returned.

They slowed more gradually now, although the walls still passed in a blur.

Finally, without a whisper of friction, the platform halted.

Edward gasped, felt his brain boomerang in his skull. He filled his chest with breath. Slowly, he blinked away the darkness. 'Are you all right?'

Piper nodded. She pushed herself upright. Together, they craned their necks and peered into the black void above them. 'How far down do you think we've come?'

'Couple of miles, at least.' He looked around. 'What happens now?'

As if in answer, the wall to his right grew slick, disappearing into its surrounds like crude oil sucked from a well. Behind it they saw a triangular tunnel lit by angry scarlet light.

Edward had seen that light too many times before. On every occasion it had augured death. He knew this time would be no different.

Piper looked at her watch. 'Three minutes,' she said, her voice hoarse.

CHAPTER 78

Dìdean, North Atlantic

Side by side, they stepped into the tunnel's furnace glow. Immediately Edward noticed the pungent scent of ozone. It reminded him of the air after a thunderstorm, but sharper, richer, far more concentrated.

Waist-height along the tunnel walls ran a smooth seam of copper the thickness of a finger. He sensed that touching it would be unwise. Every five seconds or so the air around them pulsed, as if carried by a peristaltic wave. It delivered a cloying warmth.

When Edward turned to Piper he saw that blood had begun to leak from her nostrils in a steady flow. She wiped it away with the back of her hand. Within moments, more had dribbled over her mouth.

Grimacing, she licked her lips and spat. 'Don't think there's any way to stop it,' she said. She peered into the tunnel's depths. 'We'd better hurry.'

Within twenty yards, the stench of ozone had increased tenfold, so sharp that Edward nearly gagged with each new breath. Beside him, Piper stumbled. He grabbed her just in time to save her from a fall.

She clung to him, and when her face pressed against his clothes it left a bloody print. 'The air,' she muttered. 'I think it's poisonous.'

He nodded, felt the beginnings of a migraine-like pain behind his eyes. 'Want me to carry you?'

She shook her head. 'Not yet.'

They limped along the passage, Piper's arm around his waist. After fifty yards they came to a crossroads, where a second triangular tunnel bisected theirs. Peristaltic pressure waves pulsed down it.

Edward's heart laboured in his chest. Each new breath filled his lungs with needles. 'Which way?'

'Straight.'

Another fifty yards and they passed a diamond-shaped incision in the walls on either side. Edward glanced through and saw, plummeting away from him, a void of such immense depth that it could have swallowed any of the mountains he had climbed in his youth. The air inside it throbbed as if alive. He saw dark things flickering, drifting lights. Turning his face away, he struggled onwards.

They managed another ten yards before Piper collapsed.

Edward dropped to his knees, pulled the girl into a sitting position. 'Pie,' he said. 'Love.'

Her eyelids flickered. 'Water.'

He shrugged off his rucksack and found the bottle. She drank greedily, and when the last drop trickled from the neck she croaked an apology.

'It's OK,' he told her. 'You need it more than me.'

'Can't last long in here.'

Edward nodded, cast the bottle away. 'I'll carry you.'

Piper smiled at him. Tears gathered in her eyes.

Sliding his arms beneath her, he braced his spine and pushed himself up. His knee screamed in protest but it seemed, in context, such a trifling thing that he barely gave it thought.

Ahead, the passage opened into a pyramidal chamber the size of a cathedral. Knowing that they had reached the end of their journey, Edward carried his daughter inside.

CHAPTER 79

Dìdean, North Atlantic

Benjamin D. Pope stood on Dìdean's beach as events unfolded around him, wondering how his life had taken such a savage turn.

Ten years ago he had been a middling preacher in a failing church, thanking God every day for the riches with which he had been blessed. Linda's accident did not rob him of his faith but it bruised it, and his many wrangles with her claims adjusters stripped away a little more. Six months later, the bank's foreclosure on his church spun him like a weathervane, but he borrowed an abandoned commercial space in Montopolis and continued to preach.

His performances in the pulpit, though he tried to control them, grew angry, steadily more vitriolic. Then, a funny thing happened. His congregation, after years of stagnating, began to grow. The people came, at first, to watch his temper fly, but they stayed in the hope that he would deliver them a revelation, an answer to the world's ills.

Benjamin could not pinpoint the moment that the last of his faith drained away, but with its loss he became aware that all he had left *was* his congregation, and in many cases all they had left was him.

He worked on his narrative, refined it. God was still here, he told them (even though he no longer believed it) but He simply wasn't listening. And why should He? The world had filled up with so much evil that He had shunned his creation. It was up to the members of Benjamin's church to turn that situation around. It was salvageable, he told them, but not without faith, and certainly not without money. Bags of it.

The dollars rolled in. Soon, his pauper's ministry outgrew the dismal retail space in which it operated. Within six months he moved into a much larger building. Within two years he was laying the first brick of what would become the Church of the Holy Sacrament. Suddenly he could afford twenty-four-hour care for Linda. He built her a house with purpose-built facilities. A few weeks later, he performed his first televised ministry. From there, his career went stratospheric.

For almost all of that journey, Wendy Devereux had been at his side. Back in Montopolis, she had started out as his unpaid assistant, organising transport for those who needed it and ensuring that the church's bills were paid on time. As the demands of the job grew, so did Wendy's capacity to meet them. He placed his trust in her and she rewarded him with probity. Now, on this lonely stretch of coast, beneath a cold sky dusted with stars, he was about to watch her execute a fellow human being.

And all because of him.

Not only had he allowed whatever demon Aiden Urchardan served to deceive him, but he had also made himself its accomplice, calling on the members of his church to come to this island and defend it. The corruption it had sowed among his flock had been absolute. Since his arrival at Dìdean he had seen – and participated in – acts of licentiousness he could never previously have imagined. Worse, on the heels of that depravity his faith had *returned*, no longer a cause for joy but a trigger for deep, immutable terror. The only thing more frightening than a *loss* of faith, Benjamin had learned, was the discovery that one was damned. But damned or not, his responsibility to those he had led astray was clear.

The woman with the filthy cast knelt in the surf, head

bowed in anticipation of the bullet that would take her life. A few yards further up the stone shelf, Wendy Devereaux raised her carbine and sighted along it.

Benjamin charged down the shingle, but he would never reach her in time. Already the weapon's stock was tight against her shoulder. Her index finger curled inside the trigger guard.

'No!' he screamed. '*Wendy, NO!*'

The gun barked out its shot. Benjamin barrelled into her a moment later. He clasped her to him as they fell, and she hit the wet stone hard, breath gushing from her lungs.

Wendy rolled, hissing like a wildcat, but he used her momentum against her, rolling her a second time and ending up on top. Her eyes flooded with hate. She tore her arm free and scratched at his face, tearing deep furrows. The pain was agonising, but no more than he deserved. In response he hugged her tightly. She thrashed, snarled, kicked. She tried to bite his shoulder, his throat. Benjamin pressed his cheek against her own, forced her head against the rock.

A few yards away he saw the woman with the cast, still kneeling in the surf. He sobbed, overcome with relief, heard himself praising God. While he had failed to stop Wendy from taking the shot, he had distracted her enough to spoil her aim.

'Let it go,' he whispered, lips close to her ear. 'Wendy, this is not you. Think about what you're doing. This is *not you.*'

Teeth bared, she wrenched her face towards him and savaged his cheek. Blood flowed over her lips. Benjamin gasped in agony. One hand pinning her jaw, he straddled her. Then, as hard as he dared, he struck her across the mouth.

The blow knocked her head to the side, rolled her eyes in their sockets. '*Please*, Wendy,' he moaned. 'Please come back to me.'

Her fingers had loosened on the gun. He took the opportunity to wrest it from her, tossing it into the sea. 'It was a lie,' he said. 'All of it.' But his words weren't getting through.

Wendy's eyes hardened. '*You* lie!' she spat.

'No. I promise you.'

She glowered at the woman climbing from the surf. '*Bitch! Kill the bitch!*'

Benjamin closed his eyes. Finally, he did what he should have done from the start. Using his weight to keep her pinned, he put his lips back to her ear and began to tell her a story.

He told her *their* story: of how wretched he had been at the outset, of how she had helped him, of all the good things that between them they had achieved. He told her, too, of the lies he had told and his faithlessness even as he preached faith. He explained how sorry he was for the way he had duped her. He admitted what he had done to Linda and how, even in the midst of all this horror, he had regained what he had thought forever lost. Above all, he begged for her forgiveness.

As he talked, Wendy's struggles began to lessen, until at last she grew still. When he dared to look at her again he saw that the hatred in her eyes had dulled. What remained he did not understand. Not empathy nor forgiveness, exactly, but *something*: a spark of humanity he might somehow coax into flame.

'We have to stop this,' he whispered. 'It's not too late. Those boats are still coming in. I think, if we're quick enough – *courageous* enough – we can intervene. It might cost us our lives but I don't care too much about that. What I care about is making things right.'

With no words left, he released his grip. Wendy stared. Then her eyes slid away from him.

Benjamin saw that the woman with the cast had limped to his side. She watched him intently, blood and seawater dripping from her face. 'If you meant all that,' she said, 'if you're as sincere as you seem, then you'd better hurry. Both of you.'

After a moment's pause, she held out her good hand. Benjamin took it, and the woman hauled him up. Next, she offered her hand to Wendy.

CHAPTER 80

Dìdean, North Atlantic

Edward saw no source for that blood-dark light and yet it was all around him, a scarlet haze that hung inside the excavated cathedral like a fog. Strange currents stirred the air, a soup of conflicting temperatures and pressures. One moment he felt weightless and warm, the next his shoulders sagged with the press of cold air pushing down on him.

The pyramidal ceiling climbed many hundreds of feet. How such an ancient and deeply buried space had survived the earth's tectonic shifts eluded him. Directly beneath its apex, he saw a bowl-like depression in the floor. A gossamer-like membrane rose over it in a dome.

Head bowed, Edward carried his daughter towards it. Every step drained him of what energy he still retained. The stink of ozone was overpowering. He could hardly draw breath for the pain it caused him. His eyes watered. His throat burned.

As he came closer to the gossamer dome and the shallow-sided depression it protected, Piper raised her head. Her face paled when she saw what awaited her but she did not turn away. 'Let me stand,' she croaked.

'Are you sure?'

She nodded, and Edward lowered her as gently as he could. His daughter limped up to within a few feet of the membrane. It curved away from her, the height of a double-decker bus at its tallest point.

Piper took a final step and the membrane collapsed, dissolving into glittering silver threads that fell like confetti into the bowl-like depression – which was, Edward now saw, filled with a pale greenish liquid that emitted its own soft luminescence.

Piper sank to her knees beside it. 'Help me in.'

He sat down beside her, dipping his fingers into the liquid to test it. It felt neither hot nor cold, but where it touched his skin it made his nerves tingle as if with electricity. He feared, as he tried to judge its depth, that Piper would lack the strength to hold herself above the surface.

'Quickly,' the girl urged him. 'We don't have much time.'

Fighting his instincts, determined to trust her until the end, he eased Piper down the bowl's gentle gradient. The green liquid accepted her, covering her boots, then her knees, then her waist. Gripping the girl beneath her armpits, he lowered her until only her head floated above the surface.

'Now, let go of me,' she told him.

Edward stared at his daughter, his arms locked in place.

'Dad . . .'

He let go of her, and Piper slipped away.

CHAPTER 81

Dìdean, North Atlantic

Drustan led his followers past the juniper grove in which he had hidden the previous day. As he reached the lip where the land fell steeply to the sea he saw the eastern beaches lit by moon and stars. It was a sight shocking to behold.

Smashed to pieces on the rocks, rolled back and forth by raging surf, lolled a score of wrecked boats. Waterlogged corpses bobbed among them. He saw a second flotilla of yachts sailing in. Dark figures clung to guardrails, preparing themselves for death. Every few seconds a machine gun on the shore chattered, lighting up the night with its muzzle flash. He could hear the crack of handguns, the screams of the wounded.

'We've got to get down there!' he shouted. 'Save as many as we can!'

Deana pointed past his shoulder. 'That way.'

When he followed the line of her finger, he saw the top of a rock-filled chine. He strode over to it, peered into its depths. The first thing he spotted, scrambling up the boulders towards him, was Therron Vaux. Below the boy, on a shingle bed in the chine's mouth, stood the faceless man in the missionary hat who had terrorised Drustan's dreams back at Joyau Caché.

He was faceless no longer, and possessed, now, of a dark energy that seemed to crackle like static electricity around him. When he saw Therron, his mouth split into a leer more chilling than any conjured by a mere dream.

'Hide!' Drustan shouted to Therron. 'Don't run. Hide!'

The boy glanced up, his eyes widening. Then he looked over his shoulder at the figure on the beach. He slipped on a rock, scrabbled upwards.

'*No!*' Drustan roared. '*Lie flat! LIE FLAT!*'

The man on the beach lifted his hand, made a pincer of his fingers.

Therron lurched to a halt. His spine arched. His eyes bulged and his mouth burst open.

Crying out his fury, Drustan launched himself into the chine. He skidded down patches of shingle, ricocheted off boulders. Careening past Therron, his momentum building, he shoved the boy between two rocks. He wheeled his arms, caught, now, in an avalanche of tumbling stones impossible to resist.

Below, the man in the missionary hat made a pincer of his other hand, too. But before he could act, Drustan rugby-tackled him. They tumbled together across the beach, a cracking, snapping cartwheel of arms and legs.

On a wet strip of sand they came to a rest. When the next breaker hit, the surf washed over them. Drustan blinked seawater. His face lay inches from Urchardan's.

Of course. That's who this is. Cathasach's scribe.

'It's over,' he said.

Aiden Urchardan shook his head. His eyes looked stricken.

'Yes,' Drustan told him. 'Piper's inside the mountain. Mórríghan, too. What happens now is up to them alone.'

CHAPTER 82

Dìdean, North Atlantic

Edward knelt at the edge of the liquid-filled pool and searched in vain for signs of his daughter. Since the girl's disappearance a minute earlier its surface had stilled, but still it cast off that soft green luminescence.

The smell of ozone was all around. Edward's head felt light from lack of oxygen. His eyelids fluttered like moth wings. All he wanted was to lie down and wait for death, but he wouldn't do that – not until he had determined, without doubt, that Piper had really gone.

Spying his rucksack, he crawled towards it. He took out his water bottle, before remembering that he had tipped the last of its contents into the girl's mouth. His throat raged with fire, the pain so fierce that he dared not even swallow. He dragged himself back to the lip of the pool and dipped his hand beneath the surface. He felt the same strange sensation as before.

Edward hesitated only a second. Scooping up a handful of liquid, he slurped it from his palm and swallowed. The relief was immediate. At once, the pain in his throat subsided. The needling sensation in his lungs disappeared, too. Lowering his head, he drank like a lost traveller emerging from a desert. He was gulping down his third huge mouthful when the surface began to churn and froth. Out of its depths exploded Piper, and he saw that in her arms she clutched someone else.

A man.

'Help me,' the girl cried. She sank out of sight, resurfacing a few moments later. This time she kicked her way to the side of the pool and Edward managed to grab her. Together they dragged out her prize.

The man was tall, lithe and naked – so shockingly pale that his skin seemed to radiate a light all of its own. His eyes were closed but his lids were translucent; beneath, his pupils were like dark embryos glimpsed through sacs of amniotic fluid.

He was hairless, lipless. His ears were little more than narrow boreholes in his skull, absent of surrounding cartilage or fat. They leaked the same greenish liquid that filled the pool. His fingers were glutinous strands. Absent of nails, they tapered to worm-like points.

His chest rose and fell, its movements slow.

'Cathasach,' Piper said, recovering her breath.

Edward stared. When he considered the trauma caused by the creature lying unconscious beside him – when he considered Piper's lost years of childhood, the poverty she had endured, the sheer hopelessness and misery – he was surprised to find his anger was not greater than it was. Exhausted, he raised his eyes to his daughter. 'What now?'

'We end it.'

'How?'

Piper nodded towards the pool. 'I need to get back in there.'

'Then what?'

Her expression gave him his answer. It broke his heart to acknowledge it. Piper slipped her legs over the side, and this time he joined her. Together, they lowered themselves in.

The liquid was far denser than he had expected. It kept him afloat with little effort on his behalf. After a few moments he grew accustomed to the mild currents of electricity it transmitted through his skin.

Edward moved behind his daughter so that he could cradle her in his arms. Piper rested her head against his chest and he squeezed her to him, kissed her hair.

'Dad, I'm so glad you're here,' she whispered.

'There's nowhere else I could be.' He found himself recalling the first time he had held her, that night in Snowdonia all those years ago. 'You know,' he said. 'Tomorrow is your birthday. Sixteen years old.'

'Birthdays are overrated.'

Edward laughed. 'It's been a long road.'

'Yeah.'

'I'm sorry it's been so hard.'

'You've no need to apologise,' Piper said. 'Not to me. Not to anyone at all.' She took a shuddering breath. 'It's the right thing, what we're doing. It really is. We'll give back what should never have been taken away.'

'Are you scared?'

'A little.'

He swallowed. 'Did Mórríghan ever . . . did she ever give you any indication of what comes after?'

'Hints,' the girl said. 'Nothing concrete.' She twined her fingers around his. 'It's time, now. Are you ready?'

Edward's stomach felt lighter than air. His heart fluttered like a butterfly against the bars of a cage. He took a breath, held it in his lungs; nodded.

'I love you, Dad.'

'I love you, too.'

Piper closed her eyes.

Edward closed his own. He fixed an image of Laura inside his head. Pulled his daughter into an even tighter embrace. Allowed the breath to trickle from his lungs.

From out of the girl came a light.

Until light was all there was.

CHAPTER 83

Dìdean, North Atlantic

Benjamin Pope ran along the shore towards the fighting, flanked by Wendy Devereaux and Jenna Black.

He did not know whether any of his congregation would listen to him. If they refused to yield, he would stand in front of their guns and use his body to make his point. He could think of no better option.

When he rounded the headland and came upon the landing beach, he met a scene of devastation that would remain with him for the rest of his days.

In the moon's pale light, the Atlantic was a black expanse flecked with silver. Waves pounded Dìdean's shore, crashing into the wreckage scattered across it. He saw bodies rolling in the surf, others lying face-down on the rocks. On a ridge above the beach lay the surviving members of his church, their weapons trained on the second flotilla of yachts racing in. They wore expressions of pure savagery, ready to unleash a killing storm upon those who made it ashore.

'Stop!' Benjamin cried, waving his arms. Immediately, their gun barrels swung towards him. A thrill of terror chased up his spine but he ignored it, breaking into a sprint. He waved his arms more frantically. '*Stop!*'

A wide strip of shingle separated them. Benjamin scrambled across it. Soon he was crouching among his flock. 'It's a trick,' he said, touching their faces, their hands, hoping to break the spell. 'A deception, a lie. Those people, they're not your enemies. They're our brothers and sisters. Our friends.'

Daniel Mierke frowned over the sight of his M4. 'Pastor? What're you tellin' us?'

'I'm telling you to throw down your weapons. I'm telling you to get down there and help those people ashore. We need to stop this. Right now. We were deceived, but it's not too late to make amends.'

Daniel stared at him, bewildered.

'He's right.'

Wendy's voice, that one. She pulled her pistol from its side holster, threw it to the ground. 'We go through with this, we damn ourselves. We listen to our pastor, we might just be OK.'

'They're coming!' someone shouted.

Benjamin turned towards the sea. A huge wave was building, lifting six white yachts towards the shore. Along their decks stood men and women ready to hurl themselves clear. The wave broke, a booming explosion of white water. One of the yachts capsized immediately, its crew disappearing into the spray. Another smashed into an upturned hull and tore itself apart.

'Throw down your weapons!' Benjamin cried. 'Help them!'

Without waiting to see if his plea was heeded, he leaped to his feet and charged down the beach. Another yacht slammed into the rocks, its rigging tangling with the mast of one already wrecked.

Benjamin saw someone flailing in the surf. He waded into the water and caught a fistful of clothes. When he hauled the man towards him he took a punch to the jaw for his efforts. He surrendered his grip and saw the stranger fall back into the surf. 'Friend!' he shouted. '*Friend!*'

This time, when he reached out his hand, the man grabbed it.

All around him, the members of his congregation sprinted into the waves. They worked quickly, efficiently, plucking the injured from the sea and dragging them up the beach.

Benjamin staggered out of the water, his arm around the man who had punched him. Together, they picked their way across the rocks towards safety.

And then he felt it.

A tremor so violent that it dropped him to his knees. It seemed as if a tectonic plate had shifted, or the Earth's mantle had ruptured, deep beneath his feet.

The ground rumbled like thunder. Benjamin saw someone pointing. He followed the line of their finger to the spine of the rock at the island's heart.

'Oh Lord,' he whispered. 'Oh Lord.'

CHAPTER 84

Dìdean, North Atlantic

Lying on the beach at the bottom of the chine, Drustan felt the earth groan beneath him and knew at once what it meant. He looked over at Urchardan, saw defeat in the man's eyes; unassailable grief. Wincing, he pushed himself upright. Deana came close and helped him stand. The ground lurched again.

'What's happening?' she asked.

'*Beò-Ìobairt*,' Drustan muttered, and hung his head. While the knowledge that his friends had succeeded was a cause for joy, he felt their loss like a sack of stones piled on his heart. It was wonderful, what they had done. Truly. And yet he could think only of their sacrifice.

Another shockwave rolled across the island, this one far more powerful than the one preceding it. Rocks and small boulders clattered down the chine, dragging with them an avalanche of soil and grit. Drustan raised his head, struggling to stay upright as Dìdean trembled beneath him. Further inland he heard cracks like cannon fire, the splitting of eons-old rock.

Moonlight daubed the island's slopes. Drustan saw that the central peak was a unified mass no longer. Deep fissures had raced up its flanks. As he watched, the steep southern face collapsed entirely, billions of tons of rock sliding into the sea. The noise was terrific.

Out of the mountain's shattered summit shot a column of

white light. When it hit the thermosphere fifty miles above the earth it triggered a mass ionisation, filling the sky with auroras the likes of which Drustan had never seen.

He stared, agape. Above him, all around him, vast threads of green and pink twined like celestial creatures released from their purgatory. At the heart of their dance, the column of white fire burned like a ribbon of magnesium, so intensely that Drustan felt his cheeks beginning to redden, even though he sensed no heat. He raised an arm to shield his face, and in doing so noticed Therron at his side.

The boy watched the light display, his Adam's apple bobbing, his eyes large and filled with tears. 'They've gone,' he said. 'Both of them.'

Drustan did not know what to say to that, so he draped his arm across Therron's shoulders and pulled him close.

'It's what she wanted,' the boy said. 'It's all she ever wanted.'

'*Beò-Ìobairt*,' Drustan replied, and wondered if any phrase could capture the magnitude of Piper's deed.

'I loved her.'

'That was plain to see.'

Drustan became aware of others, up and down the beach. He saw those who had defended Dìdean's coast uniting with those who had stormed it. Every face pointed heavenward, witness to that cleansing white light.

'What will happen?' Therron asked.

Drustan shrugged. 'There are no absolutes.'

'But this is good.'

'It's a turning point.'

The strength went from Drustan's legs.

Mouthing a curse, he collapsed to his knees, letting go of Therron in case he dragged the boy down, too. He tried to maintain a kneeling position, but he felt the energy pour out of him like water from a sink. He toppled forwards and his head struck the ground. Sparks danced before his eyes.

Therron crouched beside him, put a hand on his shoulder.

'Jolyon?' he asked. 'What is it? What's wrong?'

Drustan tried to speak, tried to find some words of reassurance – in the last few minutes the boy had lost both his lover and his adoptive father – but he lacked the energy to speak. Never had he imagined that it would happen this fast. A slow decline, perhaps. Not this. Already he felt his body shutting down: his heart slowing; his organs, one by one, beginning to fail.

The feeling was strangely dissociative, as if he were an observer rather than a participant. He experienced no fear, no sorrow; nothing, in fact, except the vague acknowledgement that this was both inevitable and long overdue.

Inches from his face he saw a single blade of grass, a vivid shade of green in that purifying white light. It was not a bad sight to make his last. All those lives he had lived, all those years of experience, reduced to a single, simple image.

It would have been wonderful to linger long enough to find out what came next. But he knew it was not his story. That one belonged to humanity alone. Would those who lived it make good choices, he wondered, or bad? Would they prosper? Would they flounder?

Drustan died with a smile on his lips, fingers clutching great sods of the earth.

Jenna Black held herself upright for as long as she could. Above, the sky was a coruscating canvas, a mirror to the earth's beauty and a promise of what waited beyond.

How long she had prayed for this moment. How dearly she wished she could witness what would follow.

It was not to be. Too weak to maintain her balance, she collapsed to the sand and rolled, fortuitously, onto her back. It meant she could bind her eyes to the beauty overhead for as long as her vision endured.

She had only a little time left. With the *balla-dìon*'s destruction, the energy that kept her whole – and kept whole every earth-born follower of the *Triallaichean* who had lived longer than they might have expected – began to dissipate like threads of invisible smoke.

Wendy Devereaux knelt at her side. 'What can I do?' the woman asked.

'Stay with me,' Jenna whispered. 'Please.' *And how remarkable,* she thought, *that even in death our fear of solitude defines us.*

The last thing she saw was Piper's white light.

Benjamin Pope eased to the ground the stranger he had rescued from the sea, awed and frightened by the events unfolding around him. The sky shone with the most wondrous colours he had seen, and yet everywhere he looked, the survivors plucked from the surf lay dying.

He knelt beside the man he had helped ashore. 'I'm here,' he said. 'I'm with you.'

The stranger clutched Benjamin's fingers. 'That's good.'

'What's happening?' he asked. 'What *is* this?'

'The first day,' the man croaked. His face relaxed and his chest grew still.

Therron Vaux leaned over Jolyon, smoothed away the man's unruly red hair and kissed his forehead. All along the beach he saw small groups gathering around the fallen, those who had defended Dìdean's beaches maintaining a vigil over those they had fought. It was a sight that made his throat ache.

The two people he had loved most in the world had left it, and that knowledge brought with it a numbing of the spirit, a smothering of feeling or thought. He would not meet Piper again in this life; nor would he hear her voice or her laugh, or feel her touch. Never again would he see Edward Schwinn.

And yet when he raised his face skyward and saw the mystery it contained, the sharpest edges of his grief were blunted by wonder. On the way to Dìdean, Jenna had explained to him, as gently as she could, the consequences should Piper and Edward succeed. He knew that what he saw above him was only the beginning.

The column of light still blazed from the island's ruptured summit, but its intensity was starting to fade. It sputtered, leaped, sputtered again, a planetary Roman candle in the last throes of its passion.

Therron watched it die, his hand clutching Jolyon's shoulder. Those startling auroras continued to swirl – bright inks shimmering in a limitless vat of oil. Slowly they, too, began to recede.

What they revealed was a sky changed from the one he had known.

Therron climbed to his feet. He lifted his head. Filled his lungs with breath.

EPILOGUE

Atlantic Ocean, Three Hundred Miles West of the Irish Coast

On the British Airways 747's flight deck, Captain Paul Sawyer sat with a dinner tray balanced on his knees and thought about the coming days. If they didn't have to sit in the hold too long before landing at Heathrow, he should be back in Windsor by nine p.m. This was his one weekend in three with William, and he wanted to be ready for his son's arrival. He would pick up some groceries on the way home, although no chocolate this time; Marcie had admonished him endlessly for that.

Sawyer was just debating the option of Legoland or the National Maritime Museum when a harsh, automatic voice from the overhead speaker shattered the quiet.

'*Traffic! Traffic!*'

He lurched upright in his seat, spilling chicken korma across his lap. Beside him, First Officer David Ninnavan ducked his head and peered out of the window. 'What the fuck?'

Sawyer glanced down at his navigation display, but he found no amber circles or red squares that would indicate a possible conflict. Leaning forward, he searched the sky to the north.

The TCAS warning system barked again, this time more urgently.

'*Climb! Climb!*'

'Jesus.' Dumping his dinner tray on the jump seat behind him, Sawyer disabled the autopilot and pulled back sharply on the control column. As the Boeing's nose lifted, he felt his stomach plummet away. The warnings made no sense, corroborating nothing he could see on his display.

Beside him, Ninnavan keyed his radio. 'Shannon Control, Speedbird one seven six, TCAS RA.'

'*Descend! Descend now!*' the TCAS demanded. '*Descend! Descend now!*'

'Descend?' Sawyer shouted. Grimacing, he pushed forwards on the controls, reversing the climb he'd just initiated. Through the cockpit door, he heard a crash of falling crockery, panicked screams.

'*Increase climb! Increase climb!*'

Ninnavan scanned the sky. 'I don't see . . . what is *that*?'

The cockpit flushed pink, then green. For a moment Sawyer thought a bomb had detonated behind him, but he heard no sound, felt no loss of pressure. The Master Warning and Master Caution lights winked on. A cacophony of different alarms erupted from the overhead speakers. Reams of messages in red and yellow text began to scroll down the Crew Alerting System screen.

Relying on instinct alone, Sawyer levelled out the Boeing and wiped sweat from his eyes. He switched off the audio alarms. Then he keyed his own radio. 'Shannon Control, Speedbird one seven six, please respond. We are experiencing a major navigation malfunction. I am resetting our TCAS. Repeat, I am resetting our TCAS.' To Ninnavan, he said. 'Shut it down.'

The cabin phone lit up. An air steward started hammering on the door.

Once Ninnavan switched off the anti-collision system, some of the warning lights winked out. All around the aircraft, the sky glowed green and pink.

'Have you ever seen anything like this?' the First Officer asked.

Sawyer shook his head.

'Some kind of sun spot activity, you think?'

'I have no idea.'

'*Speedbird one seven six, Shannon Control, sit tight. We are . . . uh . . . we are experiencing issues across the board.*'

Sawyer blinked. In thirty years of flying he had never heard a transmission like that. 'Shannon Control,' he said. 'Speedbird one seven six. We are holding steady at flight level three zero zero, awaiting your instructions.'

He flexed his shoulders and watched that prismatic display of colours in quiet awe. When, at last, it began to fade, it revealed a sky unlike any he had seen.

'My Lord,' he whispered. Suddenly, more than anything, he wanted to be at home, in Windsor, with his son.

Jodrell Bank Observatory, Cheshire

Lena Rawlings was sitting at a monitoring terminal in the Lovell Observing Room, a football pitch's distance from the base of the huge Lovell Radio Telescope, when she noticed something unusual on the display.

'Hey, Matty,' she said. 'Come and have a look at this.'

Dr Matthew Humphries wheeled over to her console. 'That doesn't look right.'

'No shit.'

'What's the sampler reading?'

'No idea. I've only just noticed it.'

'Did they change the array?'

'According to the log, not since five.'

He frowned, reached past her and punched up a different screen. 'That's odd.'

On the desk, her phone started trilling. Behind her, she heard Matty's phone start to ring, too.

'We're popular.'

Now, the observing room's main phone began to shrill. A moment later the door burst open and Charlie White ran in.

Lena looked up at him. 'We're seeing something very weird on these read-outs.'

White-faced, sweat running down his cheeks, Charlie pointed at the windows behind her. 'Forget the read-outs,' he said, and in his voice she heard a wild excitement. 'Look out there.'

Lena turned, and felt the blood drain from her head. She slid to her feet. 'Matty? What *is* that?'

The astrophysicist was still focused on the computer display. 'This just isn't possible,' he muttered. Reaching out a hand to the trilling landline, he picked up the receiver. 'Matty. What's up?' He paused. 'From Greenbank? What do *they* want?'

The Lovell dish – jewel in the crown of the Jodrell Bank Observatory – was the third largest of its kind in the world. The biggest, in West Virginia, was the Green Bank Telescope.

'What signal?' Matty asked. 'What frequency? You know it's not the first of April, right?'

Keeping her eyes on what she could see through the window, Lena retreated to the monitoring terminal. Gently, she took Matty's head in her hands and turned it until it faced in the same direction as everyone else's.

Matty stood up too fast, and when he stumbled, she supported him. Together, they looked up at a night sky unveiled – one that was as alluring as it was strange. Lena found herself weeping, shaking. Filled with hope.

ACKNOWLEDGEMENTS

Huge thanks (and beers on me) to the following people, without whom this book would not have happened: Greg MacThòmais, for answering numerous Scottish Gaelic language queries with patience and enthusiasm; Charlie Boscoe, for ensuring that the chapters set on Mont Blanc were technically accurate (his book, Chamonix, (*Rockfax*, 2016) is a must-read for anyone intending to climb in the region); David Kennard, for educating me – with legendary humour and kindness – on the finer points of lambing and hill farming; Stuart Adey, for generously explaining commercial jet parlance and donating far more of his time than I could have reasonably expected. All mistakes are, of course, my own.

Extra special thanks to Emily Griffin, my brilliant editor at Headline, who spent many long hours wrestling the story into shape. Finally, to my wife – and three boys (to whom the beer offer does not apply) – my humble thanks for super-human levels of patience, love and understanding.

The String Diaries

Stephen Lloyd Jones

He has a face you love. A voice you trust. To survive you must kill him.

The rules of survival are handed from mother to daughter. Inherited, like the curse that has stalked Hannah and her family across centuries.

He changes his appearance at will, speaks with a stolen voice and hides behind the face of a beloved, waiting to strike.

Generation after generation, he has destroyed them. And all they could do was to run.

Until now.

Now, it is time for Hannah to turn and fight.

'So gripping, you'll want to read late into the night; so terrifying you shouldn't' Simon Mayo, the Radio 2 Book Club

978 1 4722 0468 4

headline

Written in the Blood

Stephen Lloyd Jones

High in the mountains of the Swiss Alps Leah Wilde is about to gamble her life to bring a powerful man an offer. A promise.

Leah has heard the dark stories about him and knows she is walking into the lion's den. But her options are running out. Her rare lineage, kept secret for years, is under terrible threat. That is, unless Leah and her mother Hannah are prepared to join up with their once deadly enemies.

Should the prey trust the predator?

Is hope for future generations ever enough to wash away the sins of the past?

With a new and chilling danger stalking them all, and the survival of their society at stake, they may have little choice . . .

978 1 4722 0472 1

headline

THRILLINGLY GOOD BOOKS
FROM CRIMINALLY
GOOD WRITERS

CRIME FILES BRINGS YOU THE LATEST RELEASES FROM
TOP CRIME AND THRILLER AUTHORS.

SIGN UP ONLINE FOR OUR MONTHLY NEWSLETTER AND BE THE FIRST
TO KNOW ABOUT OUR COMPETITIONS, NEW BOOKS AND MORE.